ANOTHER WORLD

Samuel Best

PROLOGUE

It was a wet, dirty morning, like all the rest of them.

The ticket man didn't care.

He whistled as he walked down a pedestrian lane, drumming his fingers against the large folded cardboard advertisement under his arm. Puddled sludgewater seeped into his tattered boots with every step. The intermittent oil-slick rain drizzle soaked his dark green jacket as water trickled down his back from a hole just under the collar.

Despite the dreariness, the ticket man's taut face twisted in a grin, revealing yellow teeth.

Above him, beyond the crumbling towers of downtown Houston, a pale, forgotten sun gleamed through a dense haze.

Ramshackle booths crowded each side of the narrow lane, some no more than a skeleton of pressed laminate planks connected by twine.

They advertised to the ticket man in faded, misspelled words, offering discounts on booze, smokes, and lottery tickets. Only a few were staffed. Their stalwart occupants were, without fail, toothless and weathered, clearly unable to afford even the most basic dermetic rejuvenatives. They grunted and turned away when they recognized the ticket man, waving him off dismissively.

Still, he didn't care. In less than a month, he would buy his Suncruiser yacht and sail away from the filth, into the Gulf and toward the golden horizon.

One month, he told himself.

The countdown had become his mantra, his lifeline. He'd made a promise to himself: no more scraping by. No more begging. He would escape, once and for all.

He would write his own destiny.

Naturally, escape required money. Where better to find it than with those who were also searching for a way out — or at least for a temporary escape from their sad reality?

The ticket man stopped in front of an empty booth. A few rain-soaked brochures lay in puddles, disintegrating on the pressed laminate counter, left behind by someone who had probably once held the same dream of escape clutched to their own malnourished heart.

He glanced up and down the lane. Seeing that no one was watching, he swept away the remnants of someone else's dream. With a flourish, he unfolded his cardboard advertisement and propped it on the counter. Gaudy colors exploded in fireworks behind plastic holding racks. Reaching into the inner pockets of his long jacket, he produced several thin stacks of glossy brochures and set them in the plastic holders.

He stepped back to admire the display.

See the World from Your Bed! promised one of the brochures, offering a near-impossible discount on the latest altered-reality body system.

Tickets to Sunrise Station — CHEAP! exclaimed another. Sled rides to the orbital station went for a premium price, but there were still a few bulk crates lying around in warehouses waiting to be discovered by those without black market qualms.

His best seller, though, showcased the simple silhouettes of a couple at sunset, overlooking a red canyon.

Find Love, read the brochure cover. Inside was a coupon for a one-night singles cruise over the city of Houston, booze included. The ticket man wasn't sure how the red canyon factored into it, but no one ever asked.

He wiped off a flimsy crate that had been kicked aside and sat on it.

There was no hurry. He only needed a few sales each week for the next month to buy his yacht. Through scrupulous planning and devious opportunism, he had tucked away enough money for retirement. To truly last in the business of sales, one constantly needed to unearth new ways of increasing one's profit margin — and the ticket man had been in the business a *very* long time.

Admittedly, it was getting harder and harder to dodge the authorities. A chronic indifference had plagued the local police until recently — an indifference which had allowed him and his ilk to thrive. Some recently-elected council member had undoubtedly lit a fire beneath them in order to stir up more votes for their next campaign, making the ticket man's job all the more difficult.

Perhaps that explains all the empty booths, he mused.

Back when he'd started hawking his wares in every avenue of greater Houston, this particular lane was bursting with activity. Tourists — such as they were in those days — could find anything the legal shops were unable to sell. This included not only items one would be ashamed to carry around in public, but harmless trinkets and everyday novelties that were banned for obscure reasons.

The ticket man listened to the gentle patter of rain on the ripped canvas roof of his temporary storefront.

The booth directly across the lane had been removed so a new billboard could be installed on the smeared wall behind. In a cartoonish, purposefully unrealistic style, it depicted a man in a robber's mask reaching for a young boy. The protective mother held on to her child with white-knuckled hands, recoiling in horror and screaming for the police. Bold lettering on the billboard proclaimed, *Stop Snatchers Before They Strike! It's YOUR Responsibility!*

The ticket man rarely reflected on his past, yet he never regretted not having children. Billboards like the one across from his booth only served as a reminder that he'd made the right choice. The minuscule amount of pity he occasionally conjured for his fellow humans was generally reserved for the adults who managed to bring offspring into the world.

He intended to ponder the subject in greater detail, but his reverie was interrupted when he heard a deep voice down the lane.

The ticket man leaned forward on his rickety crate to look. The lane was empty except for one man near the far end. He wore a loose plastic poncho and an oversized, misshapen backpack.

The booth occupant he spoke to pointed down the lane, toward the ticket man.

As the stranger approached, the ticket man leaned back in his booth well out of view. His eyes darted back and forth as he thought of every possible outcome, every possible escape route from the lane should the stranger turn out to be a policeman. By all the rules of law, the ticket man owned every ticket in his pocket, yet he hadn't come to own them in the traditional manner. A policeman surely wouldn't appreciate not being able to trace their origins.

The man in the poncho appeared before his booth, dripping wet from the rain. He looked up and down the lane, hesitating. He had the bearing of a strong man made weak by the vat-grown soy diet inflicted on the populace since Earth's soil had turned.

One month, thought the ticket man.

His jack-o-lantern grin split his face, and he asked, "A good, fine morning, innit?"

The ticket man laid out his offerings, conspicuously sliding the singles cruise brochure to the forefront.

"What are you searching for, friend?" he asked. "Eager to travel from your couch? Need to find a partner? No one should be alone."

The man in the poncho picked up the brochure offering a discounted ride to Sunrise Station.

"Ah," the ticket man said, nodding sagely as his potential customer flipped through the brochure. "Looking to leave all of it behind. You know, I hear Sunrise has entire rooms dedicated to one type of food." The ticket man had heard no such thing. "Stuff you can't get here anymore. Fruits, vegetables, even meat proteins. They grow it up there, in space."

The man in the poncho tossed the brochure onto the counter.

"I need to go a little farther," he said in a low voice.

The ticket man studied him more closely. Square face, dark beard stubble, weary eyes full of suspicion, and clothes so shabby they made the ticket man's look as if he'd just plucked them off a store rack. The potential customer adjusted the straps of his over-sized backpack, hoisting the load higher on his shoulders. If the ticket man didn't know any better, he would have thought something inside had moved.

"No offense, friend," he said, "but you can't afford a ticket to the lunar colony. Everyone who can is already there, and the rest are at the end of that infamous hundred-year waiting list."

"I need to go farther than that."

The ticket man laughed. "But the only thing farther is—" He stopped laughing and sobered up in a snap. His eyes narrowed. "So you *do* have money. How'd you get it, I wonder?"

The man in the poncho offered no explanation. He stood still as a statue, dripping in the rain.

The ticket man shrugged nonchalantly. "What if I don't have the tickets?"

"Then I don't need you."

He started to walk away.

"Ho there, wait a minute!" said the ticket man, nearly falling off his crate. "Let's not jump to the end just yet. How many tickets do you need?"

The man turned back. "Just one."

"Why don't you buy it from the shuttle company?"

"I'm...traveling with someone."

"Ahhhh," said the ticket man as it all clicked together in his mind. "And you don't want them turning up on the official registry." He made a big show of scooping up the brochures on the counter and tucking them away in his jacket. "Well, look. I'd love to help you, but my operation is one-hundred-percent legal. I can't afford to be associated with black market sales."

He pretended to look for other customers, indicating the conversation was over.

"I can pay double," said the man in the poncho.

He showed his credit card-sized hellocard, squeezing its worn metal grip reluctantly. The other half was a translucent screen, its orange glow flickering as rain spattered its surface.

The ticket man chewed on the proposition a moment. He reached into an inner jacket pocket and produced a card-reader cube, several inches to each side, worn and cracked. The screen on one side emitted a flickering orange glow, the same shade as the hellocard. He quickly tapped a long series of numbers on the screen and set the card-reader on the counter.

"Make it triple."

Enough to buy my yacht today, he thought.

The man in the poncho looked down at the glowing sequence of numbers on the small cube: 300,000. He stared at it for a long time. Just when the ticket man was going to pick it back up, the man in the poncho stepped forward and pressed the flat side of his hellocard to the screen.

The cube beeped, and the ticket man snatched it up greedily.

"My ticket," said the man in the poncho, leaning closer.

In no great hurry, the ticket man pulled out a black wallet from a zippered pocket in his jacket. He kept the contents hidden as he thumbed through the various rectangles of hard plastic. He found a stiff, transparent ticket with vibrant blue etchings, then read the name of the passenger as he held it out.

"Have a safe journey, Mr. Boone."

The man in the poncho took the ticket and walked away without looking back.

After he had turned the corner at the end of the narrow lane, the ticket man sprang to his feet. He whistled a cheerful song as he folded up his brochure-filled cardboard advertisement and tossed it behind the booth, then dramatically wiped his hands and kissed the whole mess goodbye.

As he strolled down the lane with his hands in his jacket pockets, rubbing one thumb over the screen of the card-reader, he made it a point to greet all of the other booth occupants—the bottom feeders who would still be there, soaking in the rain, fighting for scraps, while he lounged on the deck of his yacht that very evening.

He looked up at the tepid sky, grinning, and took a deep breath of polluted air.

What a sucker, he thought.

PART ONE

LEAVING EARTH

CHAPTER ONE

MERRITT

To enter Houston Spaceport, one first had to show proof of passage at the security gate. The gate was a series of stalls, each occupied by an employee whose sole responsibility was sifting wheat from chaff so that only verified passengers got past.

Merritt Alder stood in a light rain under a gloomy midday sky, watching those employees from under the dripping hood of his poncho. Between him and the gate, three security guards wearing full body-armor patrolled the entrance to the port, strolling slowly from one end of the stalls to the other. Each cradled a large rifle in their muscular arms. Black face shields under fitted helmets hid their faces.

Behind him, dilapidated skyscrapers shrugged in the rain, their broken windows sagging like sad eyes.

Merritt shouldered his heavy, awkward backpack higher and tightened the straps. His arms had gone numb an hour ago, but he knew it wouldn't be long until he could remove the load.

A wide tickerboard above the security stalls displayed a scrolling list of departure times for the bus and hyperrail depots — hundreds of them throughout the day — and a time for the next sled launch to Sunrise Station. If Merritt missed it, he wouldn't catch his connecting flight.

He swiped a finger over the cracked screen of his watch.

There was still time.

The concrete exterior of the spaceport vaulted up at an angle behind the tickerboard and disappeared into a thick haze. An orange glow bloomed deep within the mist: the burning engine of a sled as it launched into the sky, heading for Sunrise Station.

As the glow faded, a lone taxi rolled to a stop in front of the gate. A businesswoman in an expensive suit got out and hurried for the nearest security stall, waving her plastic, rectangular ticket at the employee.

The employee, an older gentleman with a face like stone, was unmoved by her demands for special treatment.

Merritt turned his attention toward the other stall employees.

He'd been watching them interact with passengers after they emerged from old, beat-up taxis. He'd been studying their mannerisms and their behavior patterns as they scanned ticket after ticket and answered the same questions again and again.

An older person would be ideal. Pensions were a thing of the past. Those beyond mandatory retirement age were always looking for a way to earn extra income. A small bribe could be enough to get Merritt through the gate without being interrogated. He had his hopes set on old stone-face in stall five, but after the back-and-forth with the business-woman, he decided against it.

Eight of the ten other stalls were staffed by employees a decade younger than Merritt. He instinctively wanted to avoid bright-eyed over-achievers — too much risk of them blowing their whistle for a chance at a commendation.

He needed someone halfway between hungry and indifferent — and if he couldn't get either of those, he'd have to settle for oblivious.

An elderly woman stood in the tenth stall, a permanent smile on her serene face. She waited for the next passenger with her bony fingers laced over her stomach. Most passengers went straight for the middle stalls, causing lines to form, but stalls one and ten were usually wide open. Either of those would allow for a modicum of privacy during the unavoidable conversation Merritt expected to endure.

He slowly walked toward stall number ten, pretending to be more interested in the empty street ahead of him than in the older woman.

There was a sharp *bwoop-BWOOP!* from behind. Merritt spun around to find the source, his heart thudding. An unmanned police cruiser rolled past, its blue-and-red lights flicking against the buildings on either side of the street.

"*Keep a hand on your wallets*," said a robotic, monotonous voice from a loudspeaker on the roof of the cruiser. Bullet holes pocked the car's scratched and dented exterior. *"Mind your child. Don't let the snatchers get another one. Curfew is 10 PM. Be smart. Stay safe."*

It disappeared into a heavy mist down the lonely street, its looped, endless warnings fading to eventual silence.

Merritt shook off the temporary fear and approached stall number ten. He presented two translucent rectangular tickets, each one etched with glowing blue lettering, but the old woman held up a finger for him to wait. A moment later, a young man entered the booth. He exchanged a few quick words with the older woman, then she left.

Merritt took a step back.

The young man's name tag read EDWARD. A black caterpillar mustache clung valiantly to his upper lip. He pulled on his headset and adjusted his seat, muttered something unflattering about the older woman, then crisply gestured for Merritt to approach the stall.

"Where you headed, poncho man?" he asked.

Merritt looked around, stunned with indecision.

"Yo!" said Edward. "What's the hold-up?"

One of the heavily-armed security guards strolled past, glancing in his direction. His hand moved noticeably closer to the grip of his rifle.

Merritt stepped toward the stall and slid his two tickets through the small slot at the bottom of the thick plexi window.

"Sunrise Station," he said.

Edward slid the tickets over a scanner built into the surface of his desktop. He typed rapidly on his keyboard. "Is that your final destination?"

He stopped typing and whistled as he read the screen, his eyebrows rising slowly. For the first time, he made eye contact with Merritt.

"You're going through the Rip? Well, lemme just get the red carpet ready for Mr. High Roller!" He chuckled, shaking his head. "Gonna leave Earth behind, is that it?" He smirked and typed on his keyboard. "I'm seeing one stop at Mars on your way out."

"That's fine."

"Is it? Great."

He stopped typing abruptly, then swiveled his chair around toward Merritt, a look of concern on his face.

"Two tickets," he said, holding them up. Then he pointed at Merritt. "Only one *you*."

Another security guard walked past the booth. Merritt waited until the guard was out of sight, then he carefully took off his unwieldy backpack and unzipped the top.

He held the opening toward Edward, who leaned forward uncertainly to look inside.

It was the second time he was surprised since Merritt approached his booth. He plopped back in his seat, rubbing his open mouth thoughtfully.

"You got guts," he said finally.

Merritt closed the backpack and pulled the straps up over his shoulders, grunting against the lopsided weight.

"May I pass?" he asked.

Edward sucked on his teeth while he mulled it over, tapping the plastic ticket against the palm of his hand.

"You know what?" he said, shaking the tickets at Merritt. "I'm gonna guess your real name isn't on either one of these. Do you know what that means?"

He held up a hand to call over one of the security guards.

Merritt stepped closer to the stall. "I can pay you fifty thousand."

Edward lowered his hand, the ghost of a victorious smile tugging at the edges of his mouth.

"Guy like you that can afford a trip through the Rip?" he said. "I think two-hundred K."

He set a card-reader cube against the plexi window with its glowing orange screen facing out.

"That's too much," Merritt said through clenched teeth. "That money is for housing and food."

Edward shrugged. "Suit yourself."

He beckoned one of the guards over.

"Two-hundred K," Merritt hissed.

Edward tapped the screen of the card-reader until the numbers read 200,000, then held it against the plexi, smiling smugly. Merritt glanced behind him at the approaching security guard. He hastily pressed the flat side of his hellocard against the plexi opposite the card-reader, swallowing the urge to vomit as the glowing numbers plunged lower on the screen of his hellocard and surged upward on the reader.

The security guard walked to the side of the booth. Edward stood and opened a narrow door, then spoke to the guard in hushed tones. They shared a laugh, then Edward nodded toward Merritt and rolled his eyes. The guard squeezed his rifle grip.

Merritt clenched his hellocard until it dug painfully into the flesh of his palm. He slowly turned away from the booth, preparing to run.

Edward slammed the door on the side of the stall and dropped back into his seat with a sigh.

"Okay, Mr..." he said, consulting the tickets. "Mr. *Boone*. Enzo here is the best guard in the force. The absolute *best*." Enzo made a rude gesture at Edward, who grinned without humor. "He's gonna escort you through security. Have a safe journey, blah blah blah."

He waved Merritt away from the booth indifferently.

Enzo flicked on his rifle safety and slung the weapon over his back. He walked through the security gate.

Merritt looked up at the sky, trying to see Sunrise Station through the haze. On a semi-clear day, which was the only good kind Houston experienced, it appeared as a small, gleaming metal asterisk arcing rapidly across the sky, its six tapered arms glinting as they rotated around a central core.

Part of him was happy he couldn't see it, for catching a glimpse of the station was one of the few truly beautiful reasons for remaining on Earth. As he followed the security guard through the gate, he hoped he would never see it from the surface again.

TULLIVER

The darkest moods find the darkest corners.

Tulliver Pruitt sat on an overturned suitcase in the shadows of a dusty room in a poorly-lit section of the Houston Spaceport, nursing one such mood. His thoughts were thunderous and grim, as they often were those days. The room had no door, and Tulliver sat in the dark, watching passengers scurry past without noticing him as they rushed to catch their rides.

He rubbed his thumb over a golden locket which lay open in his meaty palm. The slender gold chain dangled between his fingers. He stared down at the pictures of his wife and daughter, and he tried to cry.

Tulliver had never been able to conjure tears, not even when it concerned his family.

He snapped the locket shut and clenched it to his chest, taking a deep, cleansing breath, then rubbed his hand slowly over his bald head, wiping away the sweat.

Baggy clothes covered his loose skin. Tulliver was a powerfully-built man, over two meters tall, but he carried a lot of unnecessary weight. His shapeless clothes concealed everything but his sagging, jowly cheeks and the vague outline of a pear-shaped torso.

He wheezed.

Tulliver couldn't help it. He'd tried medication, tried losing weight. None were effective. His wife slept like a log, bless her, and never complained about his snoring. The problem was his nose. It was broad and squat, and difficult to breathe through, so Tulliver had to wheeze through his mouth.

On the floor next to him was a pile of forged tickets. One of them had enough travel credit left to get him through the first security checkpoint and no farther, but all of the others had been rejected by the self-scanners outside the sled terminal. Bright red lights flashed overhead whenever an invalid ticket was scanned, so Tulliver had decided to wait an hour between each attempt.

He tried the last ticket yesterday, so now he was stuck in limbo, unable to leave the terminal after passing through the first set of gates, and unable to pass through the next set without a ticket containing more travel credit.

Sleds launched to Sunrise Station several times a week, but only one more departure would get him there in time to catch his next ride. He needed to board that sled in less than two hours, but all he had was a pile of worthless tickets.

The silhouette of a man with shaggy hair stepped into view just outside the room.

"We got one, Tull," he said.

The gravelly voice belonged to Roland Day — a wiry, skeletal man half Tulliver's width and two heads shorter. Roland let his hair run shaggy to compensate for his inability to grow a beard — a sore point that one quickly learned to never bring up in casual conversation.

Tulliver carefully secured the locket in a zippered pocket of his ill-fitting, sand-colored jacket. He wheezed as he stood from the overturned suitcase, then left the pile of forged tickets behind as he followed Roland into the dim light of the starport.

Upon emerging from the muffled, cave-like room, Tulliver was immediately assaulted by sound and movement.

Tin music blared from unseen speakers. Video billboards covered every square inch of wall, shouting at him, selling to him, appealing to him.

One such billboard played a looping publicity reel for one of the two remaining pharmaceutical conglomerates. It showed a happy young couple cradling a newborn. The background was blown out, overexposed to imitate a brilliantly sunny day that no one believed in anymore.

"Find out what the good doctors at PharmaGen are doing to fight Low Birthrate," proclaimed the billboard. *"Sign up for a local study today."*

Tulliver followed Roland across a broad, open white concourse with a peaked ceiling reminiscent of a circus tent. Smeared, opaque windows shaped like teardrops let in a small amount of outside light.

Roland walked quickly, his shoes clacking loudly on the hard, polished floor. It didn't take Tulliver long to pick out his mark in the crowd.

A man in a tailored suit walked hurriedly across the room, heading for the sled terminal. One of his hands held a cup of coffee and pulled a small suitcase on wheels. With the other hand holding his phone to his ear, he struggled to keep the strap of his messenger bag from slipping down his shoulder.

A rectangular plastic ticket with glowing blue lettering bounced in his back pocket as he walked.

Roland glanced behind him, and Tulliver nodded. Roland sped up to a jog, passed the man in the tailored suit, then abruptly turned around and bumped into him. The man's coffee cup crumpled between them, spitting hot liquid everywhere.

While the man yelled his face red at Roland, Tulliver lightly lifted the ticket from his back pocket and whisked it into his jacket in the blink of an eye. Roland apologized a dozen more times before managing to extricate himself from the encounter, then met up with Tulliver around a corner.

"One more ticket to go," said Tulliver, holding up the hard piece of plastic. "After that, no more running."

Roland grinned and reached for it, but Tulliver snapped it away and wagged a finger at him.

"Uh-uh. You owe me for Dallas, remember?"

"That was six years ago!" said Roland, throwing up his hands.

"And I'm just about ready to forget about it."

He squeezed the back of Roland's neck and guided him toward the concourse to find a new mark.

"Oh, great," Roland growled as he looked across the room.

The man in the tailored suit was speaking to a group of armed security guards, excitedly pantomiming his encounter with Roland and the subsequent loss of his ticket.

The guards looked across the room in unison, and saw Roland.

"Time to go," said Tulliver.

He spun and bolted, his heavy boots and his heavy feet within them pounding the hard floor. Roland easily overtook him, running at full speed toward the last remaining automated ticket terminal.

He glanced back with wide eyes, his shaggy hair bouncing side to side. He slowed enough so he could reach out and grab for the ticket.

"Give it to me!" he shouted.

Tulliver shoved him away and looked back, wheezing hard. The guards were gaining fast. Just a few more seconds to the gate, but he wouldn't make it in time.

Roland could, if he had a ticket.

"Here!" shouted Tulliver.

Reluctantly, Roland slowed down as Tulliver held out his hand. Tulliver slowed down even more, hearing the boots of the guards right behind them.

"Come on, come on!" yelled Roland.

Tulliver grabbed something from his inside jacket pocket and shoved it into Roland's grasping hand, then stumbled into him, knocking them both to the floor. Tulliver landed on his shoulder and rolled away, screaming in pain.

"He has a blade! He has a blade!" he cried.

Roland sat on the floor, staring without understanding at the knife in his hand. Then he figured it out, and the confusion on his face turned to rage. He lunged for Tulliver, slashing with the knife, but the guards fell on him, slamming him to the floor.

As he screamed and fought, Tulliver shuffled away, holding his gut, pretending to be wounded. He fell against the automated terminal for support and swiped his stolen ticket across the screen. The plexi door slid open and he stumbled through, into a brighter section of the spaceport.

As the door closed behind him, one of the guards brought the butt of his rifle down to crack against Roland's head, silencing his squeals.

Tulliver straightened up and cracked his back. Giving one last look at the limp form of Roland as the guards dragged him away, he turned to find the boarding terminal for Sunrise Station.

LEERA

Leera bit nervously at one of her fingernails as she rode in the black limo on the way to the spaceport. Rain streaked the tinted back window, through which the blurred outline of her military escort SUV was barely visible.

Few drivers and even fewer pedestrians were willing to brave the storm. The empty streets and oppressive haze swirling overhead made Houston feel like a ghost town.

In direct contrast to the sterile uniform she endured at the lab, Leera now wore a short, black cotton jacket over a white T-shirt, with dark green pants and hiking boots. Somehow it felt more adventurous — more like she was going on safari instead of into the cold vacuum of space.

At fifty-five years old, she hadn't expected to do either.

The route to Galena opened when she was just a girl in Birmingham. Every child dreamed of going, but the earliest pioneers were unmanned probes. Humans wouldn't be allowed through the Rip until Leera was forty-seven. She figured by that time the opportunity to visit Galena would be awarded to any one of the dozen talented, fresh young graduates in her department.

That's why she was so surprised to get the contract.

Across from Leera, in the back of the limo, Paul leaned forward, smiling, and gently pulled her hand down into her lap. Her own smile was tinged with sadness as she squeezed his fingers tightly.

Ten years her junior, Paul hardly looked older than when she'd met him in his thirties. His short hair was putting up more of a fight than many of his peers, thinning slowly, but not receding. Like so many others, he'd received corrective eye surgery after it was lumped into the universal coverage initiative. Leera thought he looked even younger without his glasses.

Next to her, Micah sat leaning into her side, his hands on his thighs in proper fashion, staring out the back window. Leera's son rarely stopped running around long enough to show her any kind of affection, but he'd been a barnacle as of late. She wondered if he sensed she was leaving.

The boy had a keen sense of foreshadowing, picking up on signals to which Leera and Paul never gave a second thought: her empty travel bag pulled from a closet; a small container of toiletries; her adventurous attire, so different from her lab uniform.

Leera couldn't help but wonder if his prescience was a result of his condition — a heightened sense compensating for his losses.

Spinal meningitis had found him as an infant, permanently dulling his hearing, delaying his speech as a toddler, and causing recurring kidney problems. The last round of treatments he endured resulted in a promising improvement, but he would soon need another to maintain his health. Leera planned to spend every last credit of her upcoming contract fee on a kidney transplant.

Her family had ridden in silence after the limo picked them up from their one-bedroom condo on the north side of the city. The entire morning had been silent.

Leera had known for almost a year she would be making the journey to Galena. Paul had known. They didn't have to talk about it for the first few months after her team had been approved for passage on the next tour. It hung quietly in the background, this enormous *thing*, pushed into the distance and safely ignored.

Micah was three. He would be five when Leera returned. So, yes, there were things to discuss. Many, many things.

Paul was handling the situation with his patented stoicism, attacking it from a practical angle. He broke her absence down into year-long chunks — 'bite-sized pieces', he called them. Two slender journals sat on his bedstand, each filled with scribbles of his plans with Micah while she was away.

He looked at his son, his brow knit with uncertainty. Leera was certain Paul felt more concern for Micah than he felt for her. Yet instead of bitterness, warm comfort washed over her, and she second-guessed her decision to leave for the nth time.

The limo stopped in front of the spaceport's

employee entrance. Leera picked her travel bag off the floor and set it in her lap. She gripped the handle nervously.

"Are you coming in?" she asked.

"In this weather?" Paul replied, craning his neck to look up at the sky. "Of course."

She couldn't help but smile. "I told you to stop being so charming, or I'll never leave."

"That's not really motivation for me to stop, is it?"

The driver came around and opened their door.

"Ready, bud?" Paul asked loudly as he picked up Micah. "It's wet and cold."

He ducked out into the rain and hurried for the spaceport. The port was a towering concrete monstrosity, the shape and size of which one had to stand ten blocks away to fully grasp.

Leera ran after them, her hiking boots splashing in puddles, until they stood under an awning out of the rain. Micah leaned his head on Paul's shoulder and grinned.

"Was that fun?" asked Leera.

He nodded.

Four armed soldiers got out of the escort SUV and walked unhurriedly through the rain.

"Dr. James," said one of them in a booming voice, "if you and your family will follow me, we'll get you through security."

He spoke quietly to the other three soldiers. They fanned out behind Leera and her family as they entered the building.

The lead soldier swiped his badge on a keypad by the employee entrance, and the heavy metal door slid open.

Leera clutched her bag to her side with one hand and held Paul's hand with the other. Micah clung to his father's neck as they walked through the spaceport.

People stared, but Leera couldn't be sure if it was because of the military escort, or because of Micah.

"I saw another news story about a missing child at the port," said Paul as they walked. "He was taken *after* his parents got him through the security gates. Those snatchers are getting bolder."

"Fewer children to go around," Leera replied. "More people willing to pay for them." She squeezed Paul's hand. "I spoke to the Board of Directors. You'll keep the military escort until I get back."

"It's been nice taking him to the park," he replied, nodding toward Micah.

Leera brushed a strand of brown hair away from her son's face. He had her hair, straight and thick, though his was not yet lined with silver. He had his father's pug nose. She tapped it and he smiled.

They reached an automated ticket terminal and stopped. The soldiers stood a respectful distance away, and Leera realized this was it — this was where she left her family.

Paul set Micah gently on the ground and took his wife's hands. Leera found she couldn't meet his eyes.

"It's two years," she said quietly.

"Two *short* years."

He wrapped his arms around her and held her close. When she tilted her head up to kiss him, there were tear-marks on his shirt.

She knelt and put her hand to Micah's cheek. He looked down at the floor.

"I love you very much," she whispered, unable to speak louder. "Mommy will be back before you know it."

She hugged him fiercely, choking back a sob, then kissed his forehead and stood.

"I love you," she said to Paul, then she swiped her blue ticket at the terminal and went through the gate.

"Don't look back, don't look back," she muttered as she walked away.

She turned around. Paul and Micah were already being guided back through the spaceport by the soldiers. She watched until they disappeared from sight, then reluctantly shouldered her bag and continued on.

The main sled terminal was a large, circular room with a low ceiling and a thick, concrete central pillar. Sedate food stands and coffee trolleys hugged the pillar. Four boarding gates lined the outer circumference of the terminal, each crowded by twenty or so ratty, upholstered chairs. Most waiting passengers leaned against a wall or sat on the floor.

Leera stood at the entrance to the circular terminal, unsure which gate was hers. She checked her ticket, but could find no gate number.

"Dr. James?" a man said behind her.

She turned and saw bright red hair. It belonged to a short man in a dark blue suit. He had a small mustache the same coppery red as his cropped hair, freckled cheeks, green eyes, and pale skin.

They shook hands. He spoke very quickly, in a thick, Scottish accent, and said, "Glad to finally meet ya. I'm your liaison for the tour. If you'll come this way, the other team members are already here."

Leera followed him to an unmarked door between two gates. He held it open and gestured inside, raising his bushy red eyebrows apologetically.

"I know it's not so fancy," he said. "Better than outside, though, eh?"

Leera walked into a small meeting room with dirty walls. A dim, buzzing fluorescent overhead light illuminated a warped card table, around which sat the other two members of her team and a young man with a shaved head in a Marine Corps field uniform.

She sat in the last empty folding chair next to Walter Lyden, the team's physician. In proper Walter fashion, he wore the same attire as he did at the lab: one of his several blue puffer vests over a long-sleeved, gray thermal shirt, and thick cargo pants. Most of the course hair atop his head had migrated south and settled in his red beard. He was one of the few who hadn't gone in for corrective eye surgery. He adjusted his thin spectacles and spun a Styrofoam coffee cup in his hand, looking at Leera as if to say, *What have you gotten us into?*

She shrugged, then arched an eyebrow at Walter's cup, intrigued by the prospect of coffee. Walter made a disgusted face and quickly shook his head, warning her off.

Next to him sat Niku Tedani, the team's microbiologist. His straight black hair was pulled back in a ponytail. He sat with his arms crossed over a light blue, collared shirt. A slight smile graced his broad, smooth face, as if he was privately amused by the current situation.

"Right," said the liaison, shutting the door behind him. He stood at the head of the table and clapped his hands once, then spoke in a clipped, rapid manner. "You three brainiacs are familiar with each other. We've got a medical man, a microbiologist, and a systems biologist," he said, pointing at Walter, Niku, then Leera. "This is Corporal Miles Turner." He motioned toward the marine. Turner nodded at each of the others. "I'm Kellan McEwan, your government liaison. Some of you know a little, some of you know even less. We've got a lot to go over and only twenty-five minutes to get through it before you board the sled for Sunrise Station. Now that we're all best friends, let's get started."

He withdrew a palm-sized, shiny black disc from his pocket and set it on the rickety table.

"Galena," he said.

A thin blue beam of light extended from the center of the black disc, then expanded into a flickering, glowing blue-green sphere two feet above the table.

"Only habitable world we can find that side of the Rip," Kellan continued. "Perfect ratio of land mass to oceans, as you can see. It was named for the abundant mineral lead sulfide deposits on the surface, which are visible from orbit. You can see a patch there," he said, pointing at a small gray smudge of dirty silver hiding in the green.

Leera found herself mesmerized by the hologram. She had never seen a rendition of Galena in such great detail. The planet spun slowly. It was covered in a maze of narrow, green land formations that seemed to crawl like snakes through bright blue oceans. Two large continents on opposing sides of the planet formed misshapen blobs, each roughly the size of Australia.

"Gravity is a comfortable ninety-nine percent of Earth's," Kellan went on. "You can't tell the difference."

He tapped the middle of the black disc and the hologram vanished.

Leera and the other three around the table leaned back in their squeaky chairs, blinking off their collective trance.

"Look," said Kellan. "I know that none of you wanted to get in bed with the government. I can't blame you. It's not like we have the best track record lately. I wouldn't be here if your grants hadn't fallen through. But they did. So here we are. Right then. Moving on."

He stuck his hands in his pockets and paced the room as he spoke.

"Cygnus Corporation is a third-party company which owns and operates the starliner that will carry you through the Rip and on to Galena. They are contracted by the government for that purpose. We can't afford to build our own, so we have to use theirs. It allows us to run scans on the surface, measure the weather, all the technical stuff we can get out of the way without actually going to the surface. The company makes extra cash by taking tourists through the Rip. It's good for everyone. Each trip, they've been sending down colony supplies, things like house kits and crop silos. If we weren't forced to delay the initiative so long, the colony would already be thriving. But no one has been allowed on the surface of Galena. Until now. You'll be traveling with the first wave of settlers. It won't be many, I'm sad to say. Most canceled their contracts when Cygnus started charging an arm and a leg for the journey. Those who are still going are farmers and pioneers who will lay the groundwork of our first extrasolar colony. While *you* are only contracted for a two-year tour, many of those you're with will make Galena their permanent home. They'll be stockpiling food while trying to adapt Earth crops to the foreign soil so we won't have to choke down that spliced-soy garbage we grow in plastic tubes. But the food will be too heavy to send back to Earth. That's not a practical choice, which is why we need to move there."

The room was achingly silent for a long moment, then Kellan continued.

"Now, you're probably wondering why we're having this meeting in the first place after all the hoops you had to jump through to get your contract approved. Well, you've been given clearance to wander the countryside, so to speak. You'll run your tests, collect your samples, do your research. Who knows? Maybe you'll even get to name something after a loved one. It's a new world, after all. Corporal Turner will make sure you go about your business undisturbed."

"We weren't told there would be a military escort," said Leera.

"Surprise," Kellan replied with a wry smile. "The truth is we don't know everything that's down there. But I can tell you that our scans have shown no significant lifeforms."

"*'Significant'*?" said Niku.

"Nothing larger than a teddy bear." He held up a warning finger. "Except in the oceans. We've detected *massive* movement below the surface, but our scans can't make out any details. Could be organic, could be land mass. Either way, best not go for a swim."

Leera, Niku, and Walter shared a hesitant glance.

"Everybody good with what we've covered so far?" Kellan asked, his arms spread as if he welcomed comments or questions. "Yes? Good. Okay. Now we come to the heart of it. Running this kind of operation isn't cheap. The contract with Cygnus Corporation expires after your return, and they're asking far too much money for a renewal. The people I beg for funding are going to say no. That means you might be the first and last scientific expedition to Galena. It *also* means the colony will die before it has a chance to take root."

He paused dramatically so his audience could absorb the information.

Leera chewed her lip nervously. She had no idea the fate of future travel to Galena was balanced on a knife's edge.

"Look at our planet," Kellan said gravely. "No livestock. No crops. Birthrate is dropping faster than we can reproduce. Earth is done with us. We've tried to fix it, but nothing is working. Galena is our chance at a fresh start, but the people in charge need a reason to keep going back, something they can use to justify the expense. Simply starting another colony is not it. I'm not alone in my belief that this is the right course of action, but my allies bear the heavy weight of bureaucracy. Those people don't deal in hopes and dreams. They need more tangible currency. A native plant that boosts fertility. A sapling that will spawn entire forests so we can have trees again. You're all here because you're the best in your respective fields. Whatever the reason to keep going back through the Rip, you have to find it. Otherwise we lose Galena. Because this is how we leave Earth. This is how humanity survives."

"What if we don't find anything?" asked Walter.

"I really hope you do," Kellan replied. "Your fee for this tour depends on it."

They stared at him, dumbfounded.

"You didn't read your contracts?" he asked incredulously, looking at each of them in turn.

"Why put it in the contract at all?" asked Niku.

"Retrieving such a sample is absolutely *vital* to our future," Kellan answered, jabbing the tabletop with his finger for emphasis. "We need to make sure the people we send have a reason to succeed beyond their innate curiosity."

Leera shifted in her uncomfortable chair. Without that extra money, there would be no more treatments for Micah, no more medicine.

"So, run your tests," said Kellan. "Learn what you can about the planet. But, I beg you, bring something back that will change their minds."

Kellan stood up straight and took a deep breath.

"Okay," he said. "Speech is over. Sorry. I get a bit carried away sometimes."

"You convinced *me*," said Walter.

"Well, that's a start." Kellan pulled three translucent tickets with glowing red lettering out of his pocket and set them on the table. "Here are your red tickets. Swap them out for your blues before you leave. Trust me, you'll appreciate it on the ship." He looked each of them in the eye. "Good luck out there."

Kellan walked out of the room quickly, leaving silence in his wake. Corporal Turner stood, saluted the scientists sharply, then followed after him.

Leera picked up a red ticket and thoughtfully turned it over in her hand.

"What do you think?" asked Niku.

Leera sighed. "I think we have our work cut out for us."

CHAPTER TWO

MERRITT

The straps of Merritt's lopsided backpack cut into his shoulders as he walked around the circular terminal carrying his dripping poncho.

The outer walls of the north side of the terminal were mostly glass, showcasing an expansive view over a cracked field of asphalt, shrouded in fog.

Spaceport employees walked the asphalt below the terminal, their yellow safety vests glowing in the haze. Several towering J-shaped ramps loomed behind them, their tops disappearing into the fog. As Merritt walked around the terminal's wide, central pillar, there was a loud, metallic *CLINK* from outside—the telltale sound of a sled being released from its mooring.

A moment later, one of the dart-shaped launch vehicles dropped down the long side of the nearest J-ramp like a cart on a rollercoaster. The single engine burped flame before dipping into the curve of the J, then roared to full power as the sled shot up the short side of the ramp and launched into the air, angled toward the sky. With a sharp *TING*, the sled-rails popped off the bottom of the craft and tumbled back down to Earth. They landed and rolled to a stop on a wide, padded square patch of ground a hundred meters from the ramp.

Inside the terminal, Merritt's gate was on the opposite side of the central pillar, which he preferred, as it offered a barrier between him and the entrance hallway.

It wasn't his view of the exit he was concerned about. He was worried that too many others would see what was inside his backpack.

Twenty ragged chairs faced the exit gate. Only a handful were occupied, all by passengers traveling alone. On either side of the grouping of chairs, smaller support pillars hugged the wall. Merritt stood in the wedged corner that was created where the pillar touched the wall.

He slowly took off his backpack and set it gently on the floor. Kneeling down, he unfastened the knotted cord at the top of the pack and unzipped it, pulling the sides down past the head of his frightened son.

Merritt put his hand to Gavin's cheek and rubbed the corner of his eye, where dried tears had crusted against his pale skin.

"Are you okay?" Merritt asked quietly.

Gavin looked around the terminal slowly, taking it all in. He nodded.

The boy was eight years old, thin, and sickly. He had been ill nearly his whole life. It was the food. Some people could process the heavy soy diet, others couldn't. Gavin had struggled to keep his meals down since he was born. Emily, his mother, hadn't been able to nurse him, instead relying on powdered formula created in a lab.

"You remember what we talked about?" asked Merritt. "Don't wander off. You stay close. We're not safe yet."

Gavin nodded that he understood, then Merritt lowered the sides of the open backpack so his son could step out.

The boy was short for his age, coming up no higher than Merritt's waist — a negative side effect of his intolerable diet. Merritt and his wife, Emily, had struggled to find protein alternatives, burning through their limited expendable income by trying new products. None of them allowed Gavin to put on any weight.

He was bright, Merritt knew, but it pained him to think he was putting his son at any kind of disadvantage simply because the diet of the masses didn't agree with his stomach.

Gavin stood on his tip-toes to look out through the window at the launch field, his eyes filled with rare wonder. Another sled shot down a J-ramp in the foggy distance, zipped through the curve at the bottom, and rocketed skyward.

Merritt ruffled his son's hair while they stood watching the launches.

"It's really something, isn't it?" said a tired voice from behind.

Merritt's hand dropped instinctively from Gavin's head to his shoulder. He pulled his son close and pressed him against his leg before glancing back at the old man who had spoken.

He wore the uniform of a spaceport janitor: gray

coveralls and blue waterproof boots. Two thin, reflective strips of bright yellow material ran down his uniform, starting at his shoulders and ending at his knees. Merritt allowed himself to relax, but only slightly.

The old man shuffled forward to stand next to Merritt at the window, deliberately putting distance between himself and the boy. He peeked around Merritt and wiggled his white, bushy eyebrows at Gavin. The boy smiled and buried his face into the side of his father's leg.

"He doesn't get out much, I take it," said the old man. "Given the current state of things, I can't say I blame you." He clasped his hands behind his back and sighed as he watched an employee loading suitcases into a J-ramp cargo elevator outside. "Smaller craft benefit more from the J-ramp, did you know that? The launch system caused quite a stir when it was first introduced. Vertical runways! The future had arrived." He shook his head fondly, then bent at the waist to address Gavin. "Listen for the loud clang, my boy, then count to ten. That's how long it takes for a sled to drop and launch." He straightened up and spoke to Merritt. "Took them a while to figure out the formula. There's a warehouse out there full of rusted J-ramps, even some U-ramps, that they couldn't get to work. Once they realized they could fill the sled-rails with fuel, it all came together. No more clunky booster rockets." The old man chuckled. "But it's a good thing they tested it without passengers. You can still see some of the crash trails near the older ramps."

"How long have you worked here?" Merritt asked.

"Thirty-seven years."

"Then you're very lucky."

"I know it." He glanced at the plastic ticket jutting from Merritt's jacket pocket. "And now you're leaving to find your own luck."

Merritt pushed the ticket deeper into his pocket and stood taller.

"Don't worry," said the old man, his grin creasing the weathered skin at his temples. "I won't scold you about the dangers of your particular journey. I'm sure you've heard it already." He looked down at Gavin with a twinkle in his eye. "I hope you find what you're searching for."

He turned and walked away, humming a soft tune.

Gavin looked up at his father.

Who was that? he signed, his hands moving rapidly.

"Just a nice person," Merritt replied, squeezing his son's shoulder. *For once,* he thought.

He reached into the inner pocket of his jacket and withdrew a faded brochure, creased and flimsy. Merritt had opened and closed it so many times the folds threatened to pull apart with every touch.

In bold, square letters, the front page of the brochure invited one to *SEE ANOTHER WORLD!* A smaller subtitle below that read *Your Pioneer Adventure Starts Today!*

Merritt didn't need to open it to know its contents. He had memorized the text long ago, when he first found the brochure at the bottom of a stack of clothes in his wife's dresser drawer.

The brochure painted a picture of frontier life on Galena in broad strokes, highlighting the benefits of working the soil of a new planet. It was an advertisement for the Galena Farming Initiative — a program instituted by the government to send workers through the Rip to grow food on a distant world.

The first page showed a happy family of four walking through a sunlit field, healthy crops growing in the background next to their company-purchased house.

The opposite page showed two options for build-it-yourself homes. The first was the Wilderness Cabin, a modest two-bedroom abode "perfect for singles or new families", said the brochure. Merritt's wife had drawn a faint circle around this choice long ago.

The second option was the Pioneer Lodge, a sprawling, ostentatious mini-mansion with more of everything than one truly needed. Emily had drawn a face rolling its eyes next to that picture.

In the early days, if one's application to the program was accepted, they were put on a waiting list, and their eventual journey to Galena was expected to be free. One would receive a plot of land upon arrival — their *own* land — and enough supplies to grow fresh crops with the stipulation that seventy percent of what they grew went into communal silos until the engineers could figure out how to get it back to Earth.

Once the government scrapped their only star-liner that could transport colonists to Galena, they further delayed the Farming Initiative, and Cygnus Corporation was awarded the flight contract. They were the only corporation with a Rip-capable vessel, and passage was no longer free. The cost of a ticket was more money than most people saw in a lifetime.

Applications to join The Farming Initiative on Galena were still available — one just had to buy their own way.

An artificial voice spoke over the terminal intercom.

"Flight six-four-three to Sunrise Station is now departing. Please present your tickets at the gate and exit in an orderly fashion."

"Here we go," said Merritt.

He picked up Gavin and carried him with one arm. The boy hugged his father's neck and rested his head on his shoulder. Merritt left his poncho and empty backpack in a pile on the floor.

A dozen passengers lined up at the automated ticket station near the gate, shuffling through like cattle, silent and resigned. Merritt stood behind a large, bald man with sweat stains around the collar of his heavy jacket.

Gavin scrunched his face at the man's offensive odor, but Merritt squeezed his leg sharply, scolding him to be polite.

After swiping their tickets at the gate, Merritt carried his son down a long flight of stairs and out a door that opened onto the launch field. Their clothes flapped in the cold, misty air wooshing across the ground.

A spaceport employee in a bright yellow vest guided them to a passenger elevator at the base of the nearest J-ramp. The passengers crowded in, looking everywhere but at each other. Merritt stood in a corner as the elevator rapidly ascended, angling Gavin away from the crowd.

He wondered if his instinctive protectiveness would fade the farther he got from Earth.

At the top of the J-ramp tower, a short jetway led to the open door of a sled. The small, slender craft was reminiscent of a private jet, but with stubbier wings and a bell-shaped housing at its narrow tail that covered its ten-core engine. After passengers were secured on board, the docking clamps would pop free and the sled would coast a few meters on an angled track. Then it would tip over the precipice and drop a hundred meters before the track curved upward at a forty-five degree angle.

Merritt chose two seats near the back of the small cabin. He set Gavin down near the foggy window and strapped the boy in before securing his own harness.

A woman wearing a black jacket and dark green pants sat across the aisle. She tucked her silver-shot brown hair behind her ears and took a deep breath as she wiped away a tear.

Merritt looked away before she saw him looking at her.

Gavin craned his neck to look out the window.

"Scared?" asked Merritt.

The boy shook his head quickly, but Merritt could see that his hands were trembling.

There were no spaceport employees aboard the sled. The pilot was a computer. Shortly after the last passenger had taken their seat, the hatch closed and the jetway retracted.

"Passenger in seat J-5, please secure your harness," said the same artificial voice from the terminal.

Merritt looked up the aisle, toward the front of the sled. The large, bald man cursed under his breath and struggled to get the straps of his harness over his broad shoulders. There was an audible *click* from his seat, then a small red light at the front of the cabin flicked to green.

"Prepare for launch," said the voice.

Gavin grabbed his father's hand and squeezed it with the intensity of one hanging off the side of a cliff.

The sled jerked forward as the gate clamps popped free. Merritt leaned over Gavin to look out the window. The track wasn't visible, and the ground below was lost in fog.

After coasting down the track a few long moments, the nose of the sled dipped slowly. The vessel seemed to waver at the precipice of the ramp, as if it might not drop after all.

Then it rolled over the edge and plummeted down the ramp.

A few passengers screamed.

A short burst from the engine slammed Merritt back into his seat. His stomach fluttered as the sled dropped into the curve of the ramp and shot back up.

The engine roared to life, pushing the passengers deeper into their seats. A bone-rattling tremor shook the hull.

There was a terrifying downward lurch as the sled dropped off the track and a jarring shove from behind as it lifted again under the awesome power of its engine. The sled-rails, now empty of fuel, popped off with a loud *TING*, and the vibration in the cabin subsided.

The sled rose higher into the atmosphere, heading for Sunrise Station, leaving Earth behind.

Merritt did not look back.

TULLIVER

Tulliver hated flying.

He hated everything about it, from the sinking feeling in his gut to the sweat that constantly dripped from his pores no matter how hard he tried to convince himself he wasn't scared. It was a shame there was no other way to get to Sunrise Station.

Yet the station was in space, and Tulliver hated space even more. The very *idea* of it made his skin crawl. Cold, silent, and never-ending; indifferent to his existence. There was no power to be exerted over it. There was no way to bend it to his will. A few moments of raw exposure to its simple existence would be the end of him.

Up until a short time ago, Tulliver couldn't imagine why anyone would willingly leave the cozy embrace of Mother Earth. Space was the frontier of trillionaires and madmen, as far as he was concerned — if there was even a difference between the two.

He tightened his straps for the tenth time, then gripped the flimsy arm-rests of his seat with damp, white hands. Apparently, the pilot had figured out a way to make a three-hour journey feel like eternity.

Tulliver's bulk spilled over into the neighboring seat, forcing the small, aging man beside him to lean away.

"First time off-world?" said the aging passenger in a friendly manner. "The first time is always the hardest."

Tulliver growled low in his throat, and the man minded his own business.

The sled cabin had gone deathly still since the main engine cut off several minutes ago. Outside the window, the brown-tinged blue of Earth's atmosphere thinned to twilight, then gradated to black.

Tulliver's feet drifted up from the floor. He obstinately stamped them back down.

Despite the fact that achieving weightlessness shed its collective awe-inspiring novelty long ago, passengers still gasped in amusement when loose possessions floated into the air.

A slowly-tumbling stylus bumped gently against Tulliver's temple. He swatted it away, cursing its owner.

Outside, there was only void.

He gulped and closed his eyes, praying as only the godless can do for salvation.

"*Prepare for arrival,*" said the disembodied, artificial voice over the intercom.

Tulliver risked a peek out the window through his clenched eyelids.

The sled maneuvered in a wide arc around Sunrise Station, coming around toward a dock at the tip of one of eight tapered arms that jutted like spikes from a central core. The station resembled a white and gray star-like Christmas ornament.

A centrifuge ring spun slowly around the central core of the station.

Tulliver's dirty fingernails dug into the fabric of his chair's armrests as the sled drifted alongside one of the station's arms, then bumped to a stop as docking clamps latched on to the hull.

More sleds were docked on nearby arms, and Tulliver was genuinely surprised at the sheer enormity of the station. The other sleds looked like cars parked near skyscrapers. He couldn't imagine why the station would need to be so large. From what little information he'd picked up in passing, once a passenger rode the elevator down to the central core, they spent all of their time in the centrifuge.

It struck him as a failed dream, once being a hopeful venture that had since soured. The groundwork for vast future expansion had been laid, the infrastructure installed, yet the dream limped along, unfulfilled.

Tulliver sighed with no small amount of relief when the artificial voice announced it was safe to leave the sled. He squirmed out of his harness and floated up into the air, his stomach doing somersaults as he struggled to right himself. Using the top of the seats to propel himself, he floated down the aisle toward the exit, bumping other passengers out of the way without apology.

Popping out of the shuttle's airlock hatch and into the arrival hallway, he took his first deep breath of space station air, then nearly lost a lung hacking it back out.

A nearby worker wearing suction boots and coiling a length of cable around his arm grinned. "The trick is to try not to breathe," he offered. "Only two more months until the next shipment of oxygen filters."

Tulliver scowled at him as he drifted past.

He had been expecting the air in Sunrise Station to be filtered and pure, a far cry from the polluted smog he was forced to choke down on Earth. Instead, it was thin metallic, and burned the back of his throat with a sharpness that triggered an instant gag reflex.

The arrival hallway was windowless and without decoration, the four walls an identical off-white, smooth but for the occasional electrical junction box. Tulliver reflected that there was no distinguishable floor nor ceiling. One didn't need either of those when one's feet never touched a flat surface.

He grabbed a hand-hold on the wall at the end of the arrival hallway and mashed the elevator button. When the doors opened, he and several other sled passengers drifted in. They bumped into each other, mumbling apologies, until everyone was able to grab one of the dozen silver poles evenly spaced within.

The elevator slowly ascended. Tulliver and the other passengers slid down the poles until their feet hit the 'floor', feeling an increase in pressure as the elevator accelerated. For a moment, it felt as if they could have been riding an elevator on Earth.

To give them time to adjust, the elevator slowed down gradually. They lifted off the floor, floating in zero gravity, as the doors opened.

A sign up ahead read CENTRIFUGE ENTRANCE in big, orange letters. Tulliver pushed away from his pole and drifted past the sign, entering a dimly-lit hallway that gently curved upward. Bright light faded behind him and was replaced by a dull red. The red hallway led him to a spherical room, also lit by the same dull red. Several exits, which were no more than holes in the outer edge of the sphere, were each labeled with a destination.

Promenade, *Food Stations*, *Hotel*, and *Conference Hall* were Tulliver's options.

He chose the exit for *Promenade*, and maneuvered himself into the passageway leading away from the spherical room.

After a few moments, he found himself being pulled to one side of the hallway. A ladder was bolted to that particular wall, and soon Tulliver grabbed onto it as gravity slowly increased.

He realized he was climbing through one spoke of the centrifuge, moving from the central core of the station toward the rotating ring surrounding it.

Tulliver let out a sharp yelp as a section of the ladder he was clinging to spun like the needle of a compass, rotating him around until his head was aimed back at the way he'd come. Hesitantly, he stepped off the ladder to the small platform below, and bent his knees several times, testing the gravity.

A door whooshed open in front of him, and he walked into the station proper.

What had been pitched in the advertisements on Earth as a thriving hub of commerce was, in actuality, the shadow of a shadow of that vision.

The promenade followed the gradual curve of the centrifuge, rising up into the distance at either horizon. Couches, lounge chairs, and neglected vendor stalls populated a wide walkway. Streaks of dark mildew crept across the furniture. Empty pots sat near the couches, the plants that occupied them a distant memory to even the most seasoned station employee. Plastic sheets covered most of the vendor stalls. The rare few that were occupied offered traveler's insurance, sightseeing tours of the lunar colony, or discount dental work — performed on demand, inside the station.

Tulliver's shoe soles peeled off the sticky floor with each step. He wheezed, breathing the thin, stale air as he walked the promenade, grateful for the slight decrease in gravity compared to Earth's.

Dejected employees wandered at random, picking up the occasional piece of garbage.

How is this still here? thought Tulliver. *Why haven't they melted it for scrap?*

He had seen a place like that, as a child, before he lost his parents. It was a shopping mall, rundown and forgotten. The shop owners had slowly migrated away to find cheaper rent, or had closed permanently, shuttering their doors from a public unable to contend with rising inflation. Online retailers, having already dominated the shopping market for decades by that time, had swung the killing stroke to physical stores across the nation by locking prices on many of their household goods, protecting them from future price-hiking. Some of the more adaptable brick-and-mortar stores had attempted to match this tactic. Without being able to shift their gains to a myriad other product lines like their online counterparts, they were unable to eat the profit loss, and eventually went under.

A large kiosk dominated the center of the walkway up ahead. It was three-sided, with a large diagram of the space station printed on each side, and a smaller information screen above each diagram.

After finding the first two screens broken, Tulliver successfully activated the third.

A three-dimensional model of the station spun toward him, growing from a single pixel to fill the screen. Small text labels faded into view over various parts of the station. A small red dot told him *You are here.*

The left side of the screen listed a dozen options for more information. Tulliver tapped *Arrivals & Departures.*

Destination: *Avalon, Sunrise Earth Cruise, Mars Mining, Galena, Other Spaceport?*

He tapped *Galena.*

The 3D model of the space station faded away and was replaced with three buttons: *Book Tickets, Flight Details, Cancel Reservation.*

Tulliver pressed *Flight Details.*

A soft, feminine voice spoke to him from the kiosk.

"Starliner Halcyon. Current voyage: Champagne Cruise over Avalon. Recently departed from Tensu Station. Expected arrival at Sunrise Station: three... hours... twenty-three... minutes."

Tulliver navigated to the screen detailing the voyage to Galena and tapped *More Information*.

The screen faded to white, then black. Stars glowed to brilliance in the void. From the left side of the screen, the nose of a large ship drifted into view.

"Starliner Halcyon," said the computerized voice. *"Your chariot to the stars. On board, you'll find every amenity you can imagine, from a warm bath once a week to fresh fruit in your stateroom upon arrival. Red ticket holders will enjoy private staterooms and an upgraded dining experience. Want to catch up on your sleep? Passengers with red tickets can take advantage of the ship's hypergel stasis system, which offers increased radiation protection and the opportunity to arrive at your destination with that fresh, just-woken-up feeling. Speak to your travel agent to upgrade your ticket."*

Frowning, Tulliver ran a thick thumb over the plastic surface of his etched, blue-lettered ticket.

More of the ship came into view on the small screen.

A blunted pyramidal nose, like the head of a pit viper, pulled an elongated, rectangular body. Its hull was the color of sand. Three massive, bell-shaped engine wash shields protruded from the back, aligned side-by-side.

"*Traveling through the Rip can be dangerous*," the voice continued, "*but we at Cygnus Corporation have worked diligently to ensure your safety from every possible form of radiation. The hull of the starliner Halcyon houses a series of—*"

Tulliver thumped the screen with the bottom of his clenched fist. The voice stopped with a burst of static and the display flicked to black. He clenched his blue ticket in his other hand, eyes scanning the promenade.

Besides a few employees, he was alone.

Continuing along the promenade, he eventually entered the food station. It was a wide-open space filled with mostly-empty tables and chairs, with a few food stalls lining the walls.

Tulliver plopped down onto a bench heavily. He covered his belly with the flaps of his open jacket and crossed his arms, studying the few people eating meals.

A group of four passengers, three men and a woman, sat at a circular table near a food stall that claimed to specialize in old-world Chinese fare. A haphazard pile of hard-shell travel suitcases rested on the floor nearby, each plastered with expressive FRAGILE stickers.

Three of the passengers seemed to know each other somewhat intimately, but one man sat conspicuously apart, chewing his food with deliberateness while the other three conversed. Tulliver took special note of the man's military uniform, then disregarded the lot of them.

A middle-aged man sat alone, methodically cutting his soy ham and eggs. He wore a tailored suit, and his briefcase was manufactured by one of the few companies that specialized in custom accessories.

Was he going to Mars, perhaps? Tulliver mused. *Or was he a corporate supervisor along for the ride to Galena?*

It was possible he wasn't heading that way at all. Maybe he was waiting for the next sled departure to Earth.

At another table, a man in a long, baggy jacket offered tiny bites of food to a small boy, who was equally as disheveled. Tulliver's eyes narrowed as he studied them. They carried no baggage, no possessions of any kind.

Did they live on the station? Were they stuck there? It wasn't unheard of for passengers to spend their last credit just to travel to Sunrise Station, enamored by glitzy brochures proclaiming it to be a wealth of affordable luxury the likes of which no longer existed on Earth: hydroponic fresh fruit farms, cheap hotel rooms, purified air, and ample employment opportunities.

Once they arrived, they quickly realized there was no way to earn enough money to buy a ticket home. They became ghosts, haunting the station, surviving off garbage-can scraps left behind by passengers who could afford a meal. Occasionally, a few of the more disruptive unintended inhabitants were shipped back down to Earth, but the space station administrators rarely bothered.

Tulliver wondered where they were all hiding.

He turned his attention back to the lone businessman, who had finished his meal and stood from his chair.

Tulliver stood as well, smoothing down the sides of his jacket as the businessman headed for the bathrooms. After he turned a corner, out of sight, Tulliver walked quickly in that direction, his jowly cheeks bouncing with each hard step.

Sterile fluorescent lights beamed down from above as he entered the bathroom. Everything was surfaced with tile, and every surface reflected the harsh lighting, causing Tulliver to squint.

He stood at one of the two sinks and washed his hands, glancing in the mirror at the shiny shoes of the businessman behind a stall door. A moment later, the businessman emerged and washed his hands in the other sink.

The corner of a passenger ticket with glowing red lettering peeked out from his jacket pocket. Tulliver shook water off his hands over the sink as he looked back at the entrance to make sure no one else had entered, and he turned to face the businessman.

"Hey there, friend," he said with a smile. "Traveling to Galena?"

CHAPTER THREE

MERRITT

Each bite of food was poison to his small body, yet Gavin dutifully chewed another forkful of soy eggs.

Merritt was convinced the boy's skin grew paler with each bite, yet he had to eat. Reluctantly, he offered another cold triangle of the rubbery egg. Gavin ate it, closing his eyes in disgust as he chewed.

Sorry, Merritt signed when Gavin opened his eyes.

The egg was all he could afford after the fleecing he'd received getting to the station. Between the exorbitant cost of the ticket itself and the inflated bribe to get through security, Merritt was left with an empty hellocard, and no way to buy shelter once he got to Galena.

Gavin choked down the last bite of egg. Merritt ignored his own rumbling stomach, telling himself there would be something to eat aboard the ship.

He and his son left the food station behind and followed signs for the departure gates. Some small amount of relief was to be gained from the fact he could allow Gavin to walk around without fear of Snatchers. Stealing a child on a space station had to be far more complicated than doing so on the streets of one of Earth's major cities.

Gavin appreciated it, as well. He walked close to his father, looking around at the station with wide, absorbing eyes.

The food station and promenade had been nearly devoid of other people, but more appeared as they approached the departure gates. They didn't strike Merritt as itinerant passengers, but rather as permanent inhabitants of the station.

Makeshift shelters had been tucked into dark corners of the shop-lined walls: flimsy plasterboard roofs with thin blankets draped from their corners, creating a modicum of privacy.

In the distance ahead, the departure gates became visible at the top of the rise in the centrifuge floor. A few filthy station inhabitants dressed in rags sat against both walls, knees tucked to their chins or sprawled on the floor indifferently, as Merritt and several other passengers walked past.

Some held out dirty hands and dim hellocards, pleading for food scraps and bank transfers.

The sparse pockets of beggars became a throng. Merritt picked up his son as they waded through the mass of grabbing hands and prostrate individuals mumbling pleas. It seemed that, with the imminent arrival of a starliner, everyone on the station had congregated around the departure gates with the hope of gleaning a handout.

The crowd thinned abruptly at the gates, which were guarded by two men in thick riot armor. They wielded thick batons and heavy rifles. Those coupled with their grim frowns was enough to ward off even the boldest of beggars.

Merritt held up his tickets and the guards nodded him through. He set Gavin down once they cleared the gate and walked toward the boarding platform. The starliner wouldn't arrive for another couple of hours, but he preferred to spend that time in the station's smaller waiting area.

The din of the crowd lessened to a background susurration as Merritt left the departure gates behind and walked toward a security booth. He presented his blue tickets to a thin man standing behind a window of bullet-proof plexi. The man wore a faded maroon uniform and white gloves. A pointed goatee further narrowed his thin face.

The man stared at Merritt as he took the tickets and rubbed the first one over a scanner. A soft green light blinked on from the scanner, illuminating his face from below. He rubbed the second ticket over the scanner, and a red light filled the booth.

"Theese teeckit, okay for Galena," the man said in a heavy accent, holding up the first piece of plastic. He then held up the second ticket — the one Merritt had purchased from the man in the alley on Earth. "Theese teeckit, only good for half-deestints. They drop you, *shweesh*, in space." He made a swooping gesture with one white-gloved hand.

Merritt clenched his jaw, realizing the man on Earth sold him a ticket with only enough distance credit to get him to the Rip, and not beyond.

The thin man in the booth shrugged. "I see it every day, theese same teeckit. Is a big problem, yes

yes."

"How much for the full distance?" Merritt asked, his voice thick with anger.

"One-feefty K. But is no return teeckit. Just one way."

He set the tickets down, and Merritt slowly slid them off the metal counter and put them into his jacket pocket.

In a daze, he walked back through the crowd of beggars outside the departure gate entrance. He found a quieter section a short distance away and sat on a bench against the opposite wall. Gavin climbed up onto the bench and sat next to him, watching the throng near the gates. Seen from the outside, it appeared as a single organism, swelling, calming, shifting to one side and back again. The dark, shabby clothes blended together, as did the dirty skin and unwashed hair.

Where is the ship? Gavin signed.

"It will be here soon," said Merritt. "It stopped at another space station on the other side of Earth."

The night side?

"That's right. But it will be day there soon."

Because the Earth spins, Gavin signed, smiling.

Merritt ruffled his son's hair.

The crowd moved closer to the departure gates as a large group of passengers approached, revealing a second gate against the far wall. No guards stood before this gate. There was a conveyor belt in the wall for luggage, and a subtle walk-through security scanner that led to a simple door.

A man wearing a starliner foreman's uniform — identical to a workman's blue coveralls except for the addition of three black bands around his left bicep — stood at a desk next to the security scanner. He was short and swarthy, with hardly a neck, and a face lined like a stack of pancakes, out of which he forever squinted at the world. He chewed a wet, unlit cigar.

As Merritt watched, the door was kicked open from the other side. The foreman turned as two armed men dragged a third man wearing a workman's blue hat and uniform, kicking and screaming. They dropped him unceremoniously to the floor.

The armed men exchanged a few words with the foreman, then went back through the door. Springing to his feet, the workman jabbed a finger at the foreman, who was a head shorter. The workman's face reddened as he hurled vehement curses at the foreman, his family, and anyone who had the misfortune to meet him. The foreman looked up at the other man, regarding him with the countenance of stone, his cigar slowly trailing from one corner of his mouth to the other.

The workman threw his own hat on the floor and kicked it away, then stomped off, leaving the foreman shaking his head in his wake.

Merritt left the bench and approached this smaller, secondary gate. Gavin stayed close by his side, gripping the fabric of his father's baggy pants with a small, tight fist.

The foreman ignored him as he approached, ostensibly absorbed in the touchscreen built into his desk surface. The screen painted his face a sickly yellow.

"Employees only," he croaked in a low voice without looking up from his screen. "Can't you read?"

Merritt looked above the door behind the foreman. A small plaque with faded, near-unintelligible lettering above it read *Flight Crew Entrance*.

"I'll take that man's place," said Merritt, gesturing in the direction of the irate workman's exit route. "Trade my salary for passage to Galena."

The foreman turned off his screen and slowly looked up. He thoughtfully chewed the end of his cigar as he scrutinized Merritt's face.

"My ticket has enough credit for half-distance," Merritt continued. "I would work off the rest."

"Waiting list for his job is forty years long," said the foreman.

"I'll work harder than any of them. Besides, how many of his replacements are on the station right now?"

The foreman grunted. "Last job?"

"I was in the Labor Union operating and repairing cargo lifters for the Port Authority."

"You were laid off?"

"Two months ago when they busted the union."

"I heard the stories. What other skills you have?"

"I'm a journeyman."

"So's he," replied the foreman, jabbing a thumb

at a passing janitor. He took the cigar out of his mouth and squinted harder at Merritt, his eyes nearly lost beneath a drooping brow. "You can weld?"

"Yes."

"You can patch a hull?"

"Yes."

"You can repair GravGens?"

Merritt hesitated a moment too long, then said, "Yes."

The foreman noticed the pause, but the hint of a smile passed his lips.

"I wouldn't bother replacing him so close to launch," he said, making a rude direction toward the absent workman, "but I already fired nine others." He held up seven fingers and wiggled two knuckle-stumps. The ring and pinky fingers on his left hand were missing. "You work in the ship's belly most of the time. No gravity down there."

"No problem."

The foreman grunted doubtfully. "That means no hypergel sleep for you, either, in case you thinking 'bout sneaking into a tank with your employee badge. You stay awake with the other workers. If you work in the belly, you exercise all the time, or your bones snap like twigs."

"That's no problem."

The foreman leaned to the side and looked down at Gavin. "And who's this? A stowaway?"

Gavin burrowed his face into Merritt's leg.

"My son. He has a full ticket."

The foreman smiled at the boy, his face temporarily graced by an unexpected warmth. "Hard life for a boy, here," he said. "And down there." He pointed at the floor, through the station, at Earth. "Will be hard on Galena, too."

"Only at first," said Merritt.

The foreman snatched the two tickets and set them flat against his desk screen. He swiped a screen to the side and tapped on the screen, then handed the tickets back to Merritt.

"Talk to Stoney on board. He set you up. I will go, too, calling the shots." He slapped his belly importantly. "And if you change your mind about Galena, my brother works on Mars. You tell him Willef sent you, he get you fast work."

Merritt looked at the tickets, his response sticking in his throat. Gavin pinched his leg.

"Thank you, Willef," said Merritt at last.

The foreman stuck the wet, unlit cigar back in his mouth and nodded as well as a man with hardly any neck could. "See you on board."

Merritt put his hand behind Gavin's back and guided the boy through the security door before the foreman could change his mind, leaving the chaotic departure gate behind and entering a modest waiting room with rows of chairs facing a small viewing window. A few starliner employees slouched in their chairs or tried to doze while awaiting the ship's arrival.

Merritt sat at the end of the front row, closest to the window. Gavin climbed up in the seat next to him. He was short enough that his knees didn't reach the end of the chair. He tapped the toes of his threadbare sneakers together as he looked out at the stars.

"Do you see it?" asked Merritt.

Gavin shook his head. Merritt pointed at the center of the window.

"Just there. It's small, like this."

He held his thumb and forefinger close together, almost touching.

The ship approached slowly, heading right for the space station. At such a distance, coming at the station head-on, it appeared as a sand-colored rectangle with rounded corners. A smaller, black rectangle — the cockpit window — nested within the larger.

Gavin hopped down from his seat and ran to the window. He pressed his palms and nose against it, his breath fogging the glass.

It's going to work, thought Merritt as he watched his son. *We'll make it to Galena, I'll get my farm. We'll start over.*

Unbidden, the image of his wife on her deathbed flashed in his mind. He shut his eyes against it, but it didn't fade.

Pale as the white sheets that covered her cancer-ravaged body, she held out her hellocard and the brochure for Galena — the brochure she stared at longingly during the quiet moments of her day, starting before she met Merritt.

It would not be the first time she offered, and it

would not be the last.

Merritt took the brochure and the hellocard and set them aside, lying, as he always did when Emily insisted so earnestly, that they would both take Gavin someday. Yet, as he knew, and as she had no doubt forgotten, their two hellocards combined had perhaps enough for a trip no farther than the lunar colony, and that didn't include a visit to the surface. They could splurge for an overnight sight-seeing cruise instead, yet doing so would render them utterly destitute.

Later, Emily told him a secret.

She pulled him close and whispered in his ear that her hellocard would soon be, suddenly and in-explicably, brimming with credits.

He pulled away with a tight, practiced smile, not in the mood to entertain another one of her fre-quent delusions.

It would be several weeks before he realized she'd been telling the truth.

As he awaited the arrival of the ship that would carry him and his son to Galena, he rubbed his thumb over the hard plastic screen of her hellocard. Besides the brochure and a small leather pouch he wore on a thong around his neck, it was his last physical reminder of her. All of their possessions had been sold off soon after her diagnosis to pay the mounting medical costs.

Emily had never said where she got the money to buy tickets to Galena.

Merritt spent many sleepless nights trying to

figure it out, but — as Emily often teased — she was smarter than him. If she didn't want him knowing where it came from, he would never know.

Gavin turned away from the window to grin up at Merritt as the starliner performed a banking maneuver, turning at an angle to the space station and showcasing its entire profile.

Merritt rose from his seat without thinking, suddenly lost in the spectacle of the ship's very existence.

The centrifuge of Sunrise Station boasted a three-hundred meter diameter. Its docking arms extended from the core an additional two-hundred meters. The starliner was easily twice again as long as the total distance between the tips of two opposing docking arms, and at least as wide as the centrifuge.

That's a big ship, Gavin signed excitedly.

Sunlight hit the plated hull of the starliner as it continued its wide, slow turn, glinting off forty-meter letters etched into its hull: Halcyon.

Merritt stood next to Gavin at the window, resting a hand on the back of his head.

"That's *our* ship, son. It's going to take us home."

LEERA

Leera floated down the departure hallway, heading for the gate at the tip of the docking arm. Two starliner employees, vaguely reminiscent of airline stewards, sat strapped into chairs bolted against the wall. They greeted Leera at the open gate with tired eyes and fake smiles. One of them scanned her ticket with a hand-held reader and directed her onward.

She drifted into an open airlock, the massive hatch hinged open to one side, taking up half the spherical room. Warning labels plastered the walls. As Leera floated past the open airlock door, she read: *ATTENTION! In case of sudden loss of atmospheric integrity, safety doors close automatically. DO NOT LINGER!*

Up ahead, the entrance foyer was divided into two paths, identified by two signs: *Red Tickets* and *Blue Tickets*. She followed the path for passengers holding red tickets, using the silver hand-holds attached to the walls at frequent intervals to propel herself forward.

The other members of her team were already on board. She had remained behind until the last possible moment, citing a desire to explore more of the station.

In truth, she spent those remaining minutes staring down at Earth, perfect as could be when viewed from the indifferent void surrounding it. Out there, in the black, one couldn't see the dirty streets of London, where she'd been born, nor the seemingly ever-burning landscape of Birmingham, where she'd been raised before the fires started.

Gray cloud cover hid most of Earth's scars, allowing the imagination to paint the planet with a forgiving brush.

She turned away when the United States rotated into view. The clouds had momentarily parted to reveal a portion of central California, wherein lay Pasadena, where she'd worked — and lived with Paul and raised Micah — for the past nine years.

The entrance hallway of the starliner *Halcyon* led to a small refreshment room, where stewards standing upright on the floor offered warm face towels, lemon-scented handwipes, packaged biscuits, and sachets of red wine, which, as the stewards continually pointed out, was produced by the last remaining vineyard on Earth.

Immediately after floating into the room, gravity increased, and Leera wind-milled her arms as she tried to aim her feet at the floor. Instead, she gently alighted on her hands and feet, crouching like a frog, before standing and tugging down the hem of her shirt.

One of the stewards, a man with brilliant white teeth and yellow cat-eyes, grinned at her. "Better than most," he said.

Leera took a sachet of water and a warm towel before continuing on.

The hallway beyond the refreshment room ran perpendicular to the hull, cutting deeper into the ship, toward its core. Soft, diffuse lights glowed from ornate settings in the wall, illuminating the rich, red carpet and brown pin-stripe walls. Thick anti-radiation doors hung suspended in the ceiling every ten meters, ready to slam down in the event of a hull breach.

After fifteen minutes of walking, Leera came to her first hallway junction. Consulting her ticket, she followed a series of guide signs around corners and down identical passageways, hunting for her stateroom.

She passed several starliner employees as she walked, each one greeting her with a broad smile and a quick nod — yet she saw no other passengers. Perhaps they were all in the observation lounge, awaiting the starliner's departure. She wouldn't mind seeing Sunrise Station once more at close distance. Even from far away, it was a sight to behold.

Stateroom 843 had a genuine wooden door and a polished brass handle. Leera stared at the door as if she'd never seen one before in her life, her mind stalled on the thought of where the wood had come from. Stockpiles were discovered on a fairly regular basis — perhaps Cygnus Corporation had purchased a cache for the starliner.

Her stateroom was dim, damp, and slightly

cold, but quiet save for the gentle hum of the Grav-Gen unit under the floor. She rested a hand on her pack, which awaited her on the pristine, one-person bed, relieved to see something familiar.

Besides the bed, there was a faux-wood dresser, a sink sticking out from one wall, and, tucked inside a broom closet, a toilet and cramped shower. A slim spacesuit hung from a hanger on the wall, and beside it, from a small hook, dangled the accompanying helmet. *EMERGENCY USE ONLY* read the inscription on a small plaque above the suit.

Leera sat on the bed carefully, as if not to disturb the room as it was in that moment.

Atop the dresser was a welcome card and an info tablet. She picked up the tablet and activated the ship's directory.

"Welcome aboard the starliner Halcyon," said the narrator in a deep baritone. *"Don't be fooled by the practical exterior. As a red ticket holder, you'll find every amenity you could wish for...and more."*

Leera skipped past the opening spiel and navigated to the technical specifications.

On the screen, a profile view of the *Halcyon* split apart into its component pieces, showing a detailed view of its layered interior.

"Over eighty percent of the starliner is radiation shielding," said the calm narrator, *"designed that way for your protection."*

The three-dimensional exploded image of the *Halcyon* rotated and enlarged on the tablet screen, spinning closer to show the nested-doll construction of its various hulls. A long, cylindrical section at the heart of the ship was highlighted in bright yellow.

"The central core of this great vessel will be your home for the duration of your voyage. Let's take a closer look at the luxuries you will enjoy as you—"

Leera turned off the screen and tossed the tablet onto her bed.

"Still nervous about the radiation?" Walter asked.

She jumped, then put a relieved hand over her chest when she noticed him standing in the open doorway.

"Guess I forgot to close that," she said.

"I should have knocked." He leaned against the doorway with his hands in the pockets of his puffer vest, watching her carefully.

Leera sighed. "It's enough concentrated radiation to cook all of us alive. You bet I'm nervous. It would be like floating exposed in space—"

"—a hundred miles from the sun," he finished. "I remember the briefing. This ship's already been through the Rip eight times, twice with each voyage to Galena. The fact we're not glowing already is proof we'll be fine."

"Until we get there, at least."

"When did you become the pessimist?"

"Someone has to pick up your slack. You've been uncharacteristically cheery so far."

He shrugged. "It's exciting. Don't worry, I'll switch back to normal soon."

"No rush."

"Niku already found the bar. I was about to go through the equipment one last time, make sure everything's still there. Wanna come?"

"Thank you, Walter, but I need some rest. It's been a long day."

His brow furrowed with concern.

"I may explore the ship for a while, then get some sleep," she added.

He hesitated, then nodded reluctantly and turned to leave. "I'll see you later?" he asked.

"Nowhere else to go," she replied, offering a weak smile.

As soon as he left, she closed and locked the door behind him, dimmed the lights, and curled up on the bed, facing the wall.

She hoped the ache of leaving her family would fade the farther she got from Earth, the pain stretching like taffy until there was no more material to sustain a connection. It was the only way she could imagine being able to do her job.

Leera clenched her eyes shut, scolding herself for not being stronger. She had tried to prepare herself for this, tried to train her mind to delay any negative emotions until she had the strength, or the distance, to cope with them.

She was failing.

She was failing because she loved her family, she missed them, and, in that moment, she feared she was never going home again.

TULLIVER

The center of Tulliver's bed sagged as he sat down, surveying his stateroom with the cautious gaze of one who expects his newfound gains to be taken from him at any moment.

It was small, but clean, much like the emergency-use spacesuit hanging from the wall. Tulliver didn't have to try it on to know it wouldn't fit. The chances of a hull breach making it through all the blast doors, deep into the passenger levels of the ship was so minuscule as to be unmentionable in all the brochures. Yet that didn't stop Tulliver from being slightly disturbed by its presence, as if it was a reminder that he was hurtling through space in what, as far as the universe was concerned, was little more than a flimsy tin can.

Yes, thought Tulliver, *a person could be happy in this room.*

Yet he wouldn't allow himself to be impressed; wouldn't allow himself to *like* it. Maintaining that distance was the only way to protect himself when they came to take it all away. So, he would make use of it, but he wouldn't grow complacent with its presence.

Tulliver noticed a small blood smear on the corner of his ticket. It quickly vanished with a rub from his thick thumb.

He nodded, pleased with the way things were going — mainly because they were going his way.

Time to rest on your laurels, Tull? said a voice in his head. Tulliver looked up sharply. It was the gravelly tenor of Roland Day, his partner-in-crime at the spaceport.

Time to relax? asked another voice, higher-pitched. It belonged to the man from the spaceport bathroom.

Tulliver closed his eyes and wiped his sweaty face, shaking his head to clear away the voices. He hoisted his bulk from the bed and shuffled for the door, working the creaks and cramps from his thick legs.

The air pumping through the starliner's circulation systems was a notch above Sunrise Station's in breathability. Tulliver qualified this on the basis of not hacking out a lung with every step.

A diagram on the wall of the hallway near his stateroom displayed a layout of the passenger areas of the starliner. Red-highlighted sections indicated areas of the ship only accessible by passengers carrying red tickets. Blue indicated the cramped compartment stuffed near the aft of the vessel that housed the sleeping quarters for passengers holding blue tickets. A yellow section in the middle of the ship was open to everyone.

Tulliver ran his finger over the various rooms until he found one that suited his needs, then tapped it with satisfaction.

He was a large man, and powerful. Still, as he walked the long hallways, he found himself wishing for a moving walkway. After five minutes, he would have settled even for a return to zero gravity.

The hallways were empty. As he navigated the maze of corridors, heading for, what he hoped, was the center of the ship, he began to suspect that only a small fraction of the staterooms were occupied. Clearly, Cygnus Corporation would not cancel a voyage if they didn't meet capacity, which left Tulliver wondering if they were getting funding from somewhere else.

Finally, breathing hard, he emerged in a dome-shaped atrium, with towering palm trees curving up to dangle vibrant green fronds above a glimmering pool of water. Gripping a handrail, Tulliver walked onto a small bridge over the water. He looked down into the pool, curious how the engineers had managed to make it stay in place. A slight vibration tickled the water's surface, and he had his answer: they must have lined the base of the installation with a blanket of GravGen units, keeping the water pooled in its shallow bowl instead of floating around the atrium in globules.

The ceiling of the domed room was glass, supported by a grid of chrome crossbeams. Behind the glass was a massive projection of the ship's surroundings, as realistic as if the glass were a true window to space.

Sunrise Station drifted away, a spiked ornament gleaming in the foreground. Earth lay in the background, glowing blue, green, and brown.

Tulliver frowned. He had expected to feel the engines kick on as the ship departed from the station, yet there had been no noticeable movement. For a reason he couldn't articulate, that lack of tactile proof deeply disturbed him.

The bridge led to a large opening in the wall of the dome. Soft lights dance under the floor and above the ceiling as Tulliver passed through the opening and entered a promenade as well-tended as the space station's was neglected.

The pathway stretching before him was five meters across, decorated with verdant planters and faux wood benches. Chandeliers on rigid poles hung from the vaulted ceiling, their light sparkling off the black tile floor.

A procession of shops lined both walls. Most of them were closed, only being in use for the shorter cruises to the lunar colony or sunset dinners over Earth.

Light spilled from a shop entrance farther down the promenade, and soft music played within. Tulliver followed the stimuli like a moth to flame, arriving at The Velvet Speakeasy, a bar seemingly ripped straight from the back streets of every rundown city in the United States.

The air was a different kind of stale, more textured. Tulliver took a deep breath of it as he crossed the bar's threshold. Warm, multicolored light from open bulbs in the ceiling welcomed him. Inoffensive ambient music pulsed quietly from hidden speakers.

The Velvet Speakeasy was deeper than it was wide, an elongated box containing several distinct sections. The first was a small, currently empty live music stage next to the entrance. A long faux dark-wood bar lined the wall beyond that. After the bar, several dining tables stood before a large, padded booth that filled the entire back wall.

Three men sat in the booth, which hugged the curved wall in a half-circle, their drinks resting on the circular table before them. They were dressed as if they had come from a business meeting, the tails of their fitted collared shirts untucked, the top buttons undone. Administrators of some kind, perhaps, thought Tulliver. Mars inspection team? He remembered hearing something about a corporate disruption at the headquarters on Earth.

Only one other patron sat at the bar. It was one of the group of four Tulliver had watched in the food section of Sunrise Station — the man with straight black hair pulled back in a ponytail. He wore a blue collared shirt and immaculately-pressed tan slacks, a drunken smile plastered on his face. The small glass of amber liquid he spun slowly between his fingers on the bar was only half-full. Six empty glasses stood in a line near his elbow.

Tulliver lowered himself onto a bar stool and signaled to the robotic barman, which had been polishing an already-clean glass with a white rag. It was a delicate construction of thin metal rods, gears, and wires, having the general shape of a humanoid down to its waist. A thick metal piston connected it to a metal track in the floor behind the bar. Two glowing white discs in place of eyes blinked occasionally.

"Gin and tonic," said Tulliver as the robot barman whisked over on its track.

The robot tapped a small screen in the surface of the bar: a hellocard reader. Tulliver showed it his red ticket, hoping it would be enough to get him a drink in lieu of actual money. The robot shrugged.

Scowling, Tulliver shoved the ticket back into his pocket and turned away.

The other man at the bar mumbled something to himself, his eyebrows rising over closed eyes as he proceeded to reply.

Tulliver turned his attention to the men in the padded booth at the back of the bar. One of them burst out laughing, the sound carrying easily across the room. He slapped his friend on the back and approached the bar.

"One more please, my good man," he said to the robot. His boyish face was flush from the alcohol. A shock of red hair tumbled over his eyes. He swept it back, then grabbed the bar for support and pinched the bridge of his nose with his other hand, swaying in place.

"You okay?" asked Tulliver.

The young man blinked hard and sniffed.

"Forgot my sleeping pills on the station," he said, chuckling and shaking his head. "Can't sleep without them anymore. 'Non-habit forming', it says on the bottle." He shook his head again.

Tulliver looked into his eyes. They were so bloodshot he could hardly see any white.

"Your friends don't have any?" Tulliver asked.

"Nah. And the ship doesn't sell 'em. All the shops are closed!"

The robot barman set a fresh drink in front of the young man. He swiped his hellocard over the reader in the bartop and drained half the drink in one gulp.

Tulliver watched every move carefully.

"I could get you some," he said.

"Some what?" asked the young man. "Oh, pills." He regarded Tulliver doubtfully. "Really?"

"Sure. I can get anything."

A few minutes later, Tulliver strolled from the bar in search of a bottle of sleeping pills and an empty hellocard. On a ship that large, he surmised, they had to be *some*where.

If he were a whistler, he would have whistled. Instead, he passed the time daydreaming of his future. It was getting brighter every day.

CHAPTER FOUR

MERRITT

Until he received a schedule for his first farming session, Merritt had thought there were no rooms on the *Halcyon* larger than the atrium, which itself appeared larger than its actual size due to its domed ceiling and strategic placement of towering palms.

He stood in the gymnasium on Deck 4, forward, with a dozen other farmers, awaiting their instructor. Gavin stood next to him, shifting on his feet impatiently.

The farmers stood around a large rectangle of fresh soil that took up most of the floor, roughly ten meters by twenty, covering up and extending beyond what Merritt assumed used to be a basketball court. Two sawed-off poles rose from the soil, approximately the same distance apart as two goal support posts.

The walls of the room were a deep cream color, and its ceiling had been painted black. Halogen lamps hung from long cords in the ceiling, warming the soil.

The rest of the converted gymnasium was empty save for a collection of ancient farming equipment along one wall. The pieces looked like they were on loan from a centuries-old agriculture museum, built of faux wood and metal, all of them hand-powered. Merritt recognized one of them as a plough, but, even with his multiple readings of the government-supplied farming primer in the ship's archives, he couldn't name the other equipment.

None of the other farmers had children, Merritt noticed, or they had come alone. There were two couples standing near each other opposite Merritt and Gavin, and eight men spaced out at the soil's edge in between.

"Thank you for waiting," said a woman as she strode briskly into the gym. She carried a dirty pint jar filled with dark seeds.

Her curly brown hair was pulled back in a haphazard bun, several strands spilling out to bounce on her shoulders as she marched to the middle of the patch of soil. Tanned skin spoke of a life spent in sunny locales. She was in her mid-forties, lean, and wore a green collared shirt, unbuttoned, over a dark maroon T-shirt, khaki shorts, and faded brown hiking boots.

She set her jar on the soil by her boots, then put her callused hands on her hips as she addressed the group.

"I'm Uda Jansen, your instructor," she said with a hint of Northern European accent. She made eye contact with everyone in the room, her eyes a deep blue that gleamed in the glare of the overhead halogen lamps. Her gaze lingered on Gavin before moving on. "And you are farmers." She smiled, her sun-worn skin crinkling at her temples as she flashed bright white teeth. "Or at least, you will be when

I'm through with you. There will be time for introductions later. Who knows what this is?"

She stamped one boot on the dark soil.

"Galena soil?" said a tall man standing at one corner of the rectangular patch. He was older, with a thick white mustache.

"It's our best guess," said Uda. "Which means the real thing will be different. Which *also* means your crop won't grow the same on the surface as it will in here. It isn't all bad. There are freshwater springs for irrigation, and the sun is in the sky for twenty hours a day. But you are not here to learn the exact steps you must take on Galena to produce a decent crop. You are here to learn the *theory* behind those methods, and how to improvise in a foreign environment. This knowledge will be crucial if you hope to survive. Each one of you owes your government seventy percent of your harvest. Failure to pay attention in here will lead to a loss of crop down there, and that is something none of you can afford."

Gavin tugged at Merritt's pant leg.

Do I have *to be here for this, Dad?* he signed.

Merritt grabbed Gavin's two small hands in one of his own and squeezed them together, shushing him.

Uda had seen the interaction. She smiled and knelt down with one knee in the soil, then looked at Gavin.

Her hands moved slowly, but accurately, as she signed, *This is very important for both of you.*

Gavin's eyes went wide as saucers, and Merritt

couldn't help but grin.

Uda stood up, her knee wet from the soil.

"I've sectioned off this field into equal shares, one for each ticket purchased. I can already tell by a quick count that not everyone enrolled in the farming initiative is here." She shrugged. "Best of luck to them on the surface. They will need it." She picked up the jar by her boots. "Now, can anyone tell me what *this* is?"

"Soyflower seeds," said one of the women. She was short and sturdy, with a pleasant face and flushed red cheeks. The man standing at her side smiled at her proudly.

"That's right," said Uda, turning in place to show the jar to the group. "So far, it's the only Earth crop we can grow in this soil. We have tried thousands of variations, even produced a hectare of corn, but two bites off the cob would kill you. The soil on Galena is more acidic than what we're used to back home, and soyflower is resistant to this difference. It has been engineered to produce its first flower within a month of planting."

She dug in her pocket and pulled out a fleshy white petal, more similar to a mushroom cap than a flower.

"It's edible right off the stalk, though the texture leaves much to be desired, in my opinion. Most of you are already familiar with its processed form, which I'm sure you won't miss once we arrive at Galena. However, you *will* need to find ways to process your harvest, as that extends shelf life. Galena's winter lasts two months. You get two harvests a year before the cold arrives. If you seed too late, your crop will die. We spliced acid tolerance into the seeds along with the necessary vitamins and minerals. We even managed to up its radiation tolerance, but we still can't keep the plants alive during a freeze. Keep that in mind."

Merritt felt the leather pouch of seeds Emily had given him pressing against the center of his chest. There might be enough in it to spare a few for the journey, but there would be no way to hide the abnormal plant if he managed to nurse a bud out of the soil.

"Everyone take a handful of seeds and choose a section," said Uda. "We'll get started with the basics."

As the farmers lined up to take their seeds, with Merritt and Gavin at the rear, she added, "Some of you have probably noticed there is no powered machinery in this room. Remember that there will be minimal electricity on Galena. We'll be sending down several solar and wind turbine kits along with the materials to construct two hydroelectric dams. It won't be nearly enough to power traditional farming equipment. Your hands will be your power source."

A few farmers expressed shock at this revelation.

"Don't worry," Uda said with a sly grin. "Humans were tilling fields long before machines came along. If half of you can grow a full stalk of soyflower by the time we reach Galena in six months, I'll show you how to build a plough and harrow from scratch."

It came time for Gavin to collect his seeds.

Uda knelt down and offered him the jar. Blushing, Gavin reached inside and scooped out a small handful. Uda winked at him and stood. Her face hardened as Merritt approached, last in line, while the other farmers wandered around the soil, laying claim to their own square patch.

"Brave of you to bring him all this way," she said.

Merritt dug into the jar and grabbed a fistful of seeds.

"Braver still to remain on Earth," she continued, "where he wouldn't be alone."

Merritt's hand froze halfway out of the jar. "There are other children on board."

"Administrator's children," she said. "They will not go down to the surface."

She pulled the jar from around his hand and walked away. Merritt stared at his closed fist, unsure about what just transpired.

Gavin tapped his leg and pointed to an unclaimed patch of nearby soil.

I saved you one, he signed. As they walked across the soil, he added, *Bet I can grow mine faster.*

I bet you can. I think she gave me a fistful of duds.

What's a dud?

Something that doesn't work. He stopped when Gavin did. *Is this our patch?*

This one's yours, Gavin signed. He pointed at the

one next to it. *That's mine. It's not a dud.*

"Okay then, Mr. Expert," said Merritt. "Show me how it's done."

CHAPTER FIVE

MERRITT

TWO MONTHS LATER

At full capacity, the *Halcyon* carried six-hundred crew and nearly ten-thousand passengers.

This hadn't occurred in years.

The vessel was only the second mega-starliner to be constructed — and the last to remain in active service to the public. Despite its monopoly of the starliner market, a weekend cruise around Earth's moon in recent days saw, at best, a guest roster barely topping one hundred passengers and a crew complement of forty. In truth, ten employees could do the job, but adding another thirty — as well as skillfully restricting passengers to specific areas of the ship — helped distract from the impression that the *Halcyon* was a ghost ship.

Just over a hundred passengers had chartered a ride to the Mars mining colony. On the whole, they were construction workers helping to build a massive holiday resort. How Diamond Aerospace, the corporation funding the construction, could expect a return on their investment given the plummeting expendable income of the average Earth citizen was beyond the imagination of even the most skilled financier.

Yet still the workers kept coming, toiling away

in the red sand of Mars in twenty-two month shifts. They hitched a ride with the *Halcyon* on its way to Galena, then again on its way back to Earth. According to newscasters with little to no knowledge of the subject, Diamond Aerospace intended to build a resort town on Mars that rivaled the glimmering twin cities of Avalon and Haven on Earth's moon.

Fifty passengers had purchased tickets to Galena at staggering expense. Thirty-two were enrolled in the Farming Initiative, and eighteen were tourists — adventure-seekers, Rip enthusiasts, and all-around bored richfolk.

A handful of passengers were flying on their government's dime. These researchers, administrators, and safety engineers would travel back to Earth when the *Halcyon* departed Galena after its one-year radiation-shedding cycle.

At launch, this voyage of the starliner boasted one-hundred and fifty passengers, and fifty members of the crew. After dropping the workers off at Mars a month ago, the total number of souls on the *Halcyon* came to just over a hundred.

For those so inclined, it was certainly easy to avoid company. Yet, for those who didn't like the feeling of being alone in a ship nearly a mile long, it was sometimes difficult to convince oneself there was anyone else on board.

For members of the crew who slept in the cramped quarters below Deck 6, it wasn't difficult at all.

Merritt awoke with his back against the ceiling,

elbow-to-elbow with other members of the crew, who were still dozing in their cocoon-like sleeping bags. The floor was a meter below him. A bright blue ladder bolted to the floor disappeared in both directions, running the entire length of the crew quarters.

A low-grade vibration coursed through Merritt's body. A layer of GravGen units had been installed under the floor of every passenger deck, keeping travelers rooted to the floor instead of adrift in zero gravity. Since GravGen units were unidirectional, pointing them up toward the passenger section of the vessel did nothing for the crew on the decks below except jostle them gently in their sleep.

Merritt stopped the vibration alarm on his watch and unzipped his sleeping bag. His face and hands felt puffy from the zero gravity as he pulled on his work boots. Reaching out, he grabbed a rung of the floor ladder and pulled himself against it.

As he made his way to the nearest junction, he passed beneath other members of the crew. Some were awake and scrolling through the screens of personal tablets, perhaps checking their messages from home.

Communications from Earth were disseminated to the crew's message server once a week, so the days following an upload were especially quiet. Instances of person-to-person collisions spiked as crew members walked around with their noses buried in their tablet screens.

Merritt never checked his messages. Even if he did, he would find the inbox empty.

Something bumped against his head and he looked up. An apple spun away slowly. Above it, Willef grinned down from his sleeping bag.

"Oops," he said, his voice more raspy than usual after just waking up.

Merritt plucked the apple from its tumble and stuck it in a pocket of his coveralls.

"My last one!" Willef protested.

"Better hold on tight next time, then," said Merritt as he continued along the ladder.

"You fix that GravGen in section five?"

"Ask me in an hour."

"Like I said yesterday," Willef called after him, "it's a waste of time. Thing's as old as this ship."

"So are you," Merritt shouted back, "and you're still kicking!"

Willef grunted and nestled deeper into his sleeping bag amidst a chorus of annoyed groans from sleepy coworkers, mumbling something about ungrateful workmen.

Merritt reached a junction and kicked off the ladder, floating up into a tunnel that ran past the GravGen level, toward the passenger deck. He grabbed the ladder as gravity slowly increased, then stepped onto a small platform which led to a service door. After swiping the cuff of his sleeve over a security panel in the wall, the door whooshed open and he emerged in a lushly-carpeted red hallway between two stateroom suites.

Consulting the screen of his wristpad, he followed a pulsing yellow dot toward the malfunctioning GravGen unit.

The giggles of children drifted down the hallway as Merritt walked. He turned a corner to see a young boy and girl, perhaps five years old, floating in the hallway, laughing with glee as they bumped against the ceiling and sank back down to the floor. The boy rolled out of the pocket of zero gravity, then ran toward it, jumped, and tumbled end over end up to the ceiling, still laughing after hitting his head on a light fixture.

"You found the magic spot," said Merritt as he stood next to them. He held out his hand and felt the weightlessness. The floor under his boots lacked the tell-tale vibration of a GravGen unit.

"Magic spot?" said the girl, giggling as she laid with her back to the ceiling.

Merritt nodded. "It's the only one on the ship. It moves around, though, so it might be gone later."

"Where does it go?" asked the boy. His straight blond hair stuck out in all directions as he floated upside down.

"It's a secret."

"We'll find it!" said the girl.

"I hope so."

"Arthur! Shurri!" snapped a woman's voice from behind.

Merritt glanced back to see a middle-aged woman poking her head out from a stateroom door, eyeing him with distrust. She had a wet bath-towel wrapped around her head and white facial cream smeared on her cheeks in large circles.

"Get in here *now!*" she barked.

"But *Ma*-muhhh!" the children whined in unison.

She held up a warning finger, scowled at Merritt, then slammed the door. Reluctantly, the children drifted out of the zero-g pocket and trudged to their stateroom, shoulders drooping in defeat.

Merritt knelt down and found a panel seam in the floor. With a hard press of his thumb near the corner, a small silver ring popped up from the seam. He pulled up the one-meter-square panel, thick with shielding, and leaned it against the wall, shying away from the blast of heat erupting from the hole. The heat created a shimmering pillar of air in the hallway. Merritt stayed on the edge of it as he lowered himself into the space under the floor, already sweating.

He dropped into zero-g, careful to swing his legs up to avoid banging against the shell of the GravGen unit. It pulsed below him, emitting an electric-blue light from its circular outer edge. The light trailed in sinuous threads over the surface of the broad, grooved disc, disappearing into a black hole in the center.

The unit was in a failsafe stasis mode. Merritt pulled a multi-use spanner from a utility box secured to the floor and hinged open the unit's control panel. A faded blue-and-white logo adorned the inside of the lid. Most of the letters had peeled away, but Merritt was still able to read the words *Diamond Aerospace*. He frowned, trying and failing to recall where he'd seen that name before.

Other children on board, he thought absent-mindedly as he ran through the GravGen unit's self-diagnostics protocols.

In the two months since the *Halcyon* had departed Earth, he had seen none besides his own son. The Galena Farming Initiative encouraged families to make the journey, yet affording a single ticket was already difficult enough.

Something about the mother led Merritt to believe they weren't enrolled in the initiative. She didn't strike him as the farming type. A year ago, he wouldn't have believed it about himself, either.

Yet, a year ago, he still had Emily.

Merritt wiped sweat from his brow, flicking it off his fingers into zero gravity, then shut the control panel. All systems were in the green. He drifted down, dipping beneath the lip of the GravGen unit. Its outer shell was shaped like a covered bowl, with various sensor and equipment bricks clinging to the curved sides like remora.

The bottom of the bowl was a dense column of metal tubes and glowing blue cables. The column turned at a right angle when it hit the floor, trailing away toward the back of the ship.

The info screen atop the junction box at the column's right angle was blank. Merritt checked the link with his wristpad. He was picking up signals for the GravGen units to either side, but not the one right above him.

A floating drop of sweat hit his eye. He wiped it away with his shoulder as he typed a request for parts into his wristpad. It was a futile gesture, he knew. Never once had the equipment foreman delivered a replacement. The man had a habit of making himself difficult to find, lurking in the bowels of the ship with a deactivated transmitter, forcing Merritt and the other workman to play hide-and-seek to keep the ship running smoothly.

Still, he typed up and submitted the request. He'd have time during his second or third shift to swap out the junction box. Until then, let the children play.

If their mother lets them, he thought, grinning as he pulled himself up toward the hole in the hallway floor.

The crew showers on the passenger deck were blissfully unoccupied when Merritt finally peeled out of his blue, grease-smeared coveralls and dropped them into the communal laundry bin. He entered a small booth with no door and stood under a shower head the size of a dinner plate hanging down from the ceiling.

Merritt squeezed two drops of liquid soap from a dispenser and lathered his face and body. He slapped a red button on the wall with his palm and waited. Something groaned behind the tiled wall, then *chug-chug-chugged* like a car engine struggling to start. A short blast of lukewarm water slapped his head and shoulders, barely pulled down by the thrumming GravGen under the floor. He quickly wiped the soap from as much of his body as he could. As always, his towel would have to do the rest.

Pushing his luck, Merritt slapped the red button again, to no effect. He could wait out the ten minute reset timer, but he only had an hour before his next shift, and he needed every minute of it.

After donning a nearly-clean set of workman's coveralls, he made his way up several levels, toward the aft passenger section of the ship — the area designated for blue ticket holders.

Two months was enough time for Merritt to grasp a basic understanding of the layout of the starliner. Many parts of the habitable core of the vessel remained unexplored, but those were areas with limited or no mechanical equipment, places a workman would be sent only to weld a loose panel or swap out a light fixture.

The blue ticket sleeping quarters weren't individual quarters at all, but rather a series of long hallways lined with bunk beds on both sides. The beds were stacked three-high, the lowest being level with the floor. Several of them were occupied by passengers who ignored him, but most were empty.

Merritt walked the long hallways, having memorized his route in the first few days after launch. He passed a rack of emergency spacesuits and helmets — claimed on a first-come, first-served basis for blue ticket holders — only to be used in the event of a catastrophic loss of atmosphere.

He knelt down next to a floor bunk and smiled at Gavin. The boy sat at the head of the bunk, knees tucked up to his chest, tablet expertly balanced upon them as he read a book.

Gavin returned his father's smile.

"Whatcha reading?" whispered Merritt.

Treasure Island, signed Gavin.

Merritt signed back, *Again?*

It's the best one.

At last count, he had read nearly a novel a day since leaving Earth. The ship maintained an extensive entertainment archive.

My favorite, too, Merritt signed. *Have you been studying?*

Gavin wrinkled his nose and reluctantly shook his head.

We need to know how to grow crops, or we won't be able to eat, signed Merritt.

What about food from the ship?

We're only bringing enough for a couple of months, Merritt told him. *After that, we eat what we grow, or we don't eat.*

But why do I *have to know it?* asked Gavin, frustrated. *You'll be doing all the work anyway.*

Oh, is that *what you think?* Merritt signed, smiling. *I'm going to need your help down there. I can't do it by myself, and you're so good at it.*

No I'm not. Gavin sighed. *I'll study after I finish this chapter, okay?*

Deal.

How's work?

Merritt grimaced. *You don't want to know.*

Don't worry, Dad. Only four more months.

He coughed into his hand, then winced and covered his stomach.

Hungry? asked Merritt.

Gavin shook his head weakly. Merritt knew he wasn't telling the truth, but he couldn't press the matter. What could he say? *Here, son, eat more food that will make you feel like you're dying.*

He pulled the apple from his pocket and gave it to Gavin.

A gift from Willef, he signed.

Gavin stared at the apple in disbelief. He pressed it to his nose and sniffed its bright red skin, a slow smile spreading on his lips.

Merritt ruffled Gavin's hair and said, "I'm working in the shuttle bay this afternoon. I'll check back afterward."

The boy gave him a thumb's up and took a loud bite of his apple, then immediately fell back into the world of his story.

Merritt walked away slowly, mind torn with concern.

He had been expecting to get Gavin into one of the hypergel tanks as soon as they got on board. His son could ride out the voyage in stasis, without the need to eat food his body rejected.

Yet, the hypergel tanks were only for red ticket holders, a detail Merritt neglected to notice before boarding.

He hunted and he queried, hoping to find alternative menu items in the ship's official stores, but without luck. Seemingly, the only food to be had on board came fresh from the rapid-grow soy-vats behind the galley.

Merritt had heard of a man on the ship, someone who might be able to help him.

He'd been ignoring that path for a while, because this man didn't work for free. Merritt heard that a fair amount of crew members had gone into serious debt by doing business with him.

Some said he was a man best avoided.

Others said he could get you anything you wanted, day or night, no questions asked...for the right price.

LEERA

The administrative section of the starliner *Halcyon* occupied most of Deck 1, and was comprised of officer's quarters and the bridge. On a minimal-occupancy cruise, the number of active officers had been significantly trimmed from the usual fifty or so to a lean half-dozen.

Each having oversight of a different department, they only saw each other for meals in the officer mess hall or for social events in the late evenings.

The captain never joined them for either.

As Leera strolled the stark white hallway leading to the bridge, she glanced at portraits of past captains on the wall. They began with the daughter of Cygnus Corporation's Chief Financial Officer who commanded the ship's maiden voyage and progressed all the way to the man Leera was on her way to meet for the first time.

Two months aboard the *Halcyon* with not much else to do besides gossip had brought a lot of rumors her way.

Regarding the captain, he didn't fraternize with his subordinates because he worked twenty hours a day in the bridge, taking meals in his chair, watching every data screen for anomalies. He had the best operational safety record of any vessel in the company. Additionally, he wasn't much fun at parties, whenever he did pause long enough to attend them.

Leera had heard the rumors, but she still knew little of the man himself. She paused in front of his portrait in the hallway, and shivered. His piercing, glacier blue eyes stared out from a plain, unremarkable face that was neither hard nor soft, striking nor repulsive. In fact, Leera reflected, there was nothing to make his appearance stick in her memory besides those eyes, which, though she couldn't articulate the reason, unnerved her to her very core.

She checked her watch and realized she was a minute late for the requested meeting. Several empty frames lined the wall as she hurried toward the entrance to the bridge farther down the hallway, awaiting portraits of future captains.

The thick blast door at the end of the hall rose steadily as she approached.

The captain sat in his command chair in the center of a large circular room, facing a wide, curved wall of viewscreens. Warm, subdued lighting glowed from the outer edge of the low, round ceiling. In the light, rich, golden hues bloomed on the various darkwood workstations.

Leera entered the bridge, stepping onto padded carpet which muted her footsteps.

The entire room was nearly silent, she noticed. There was no music; no audio playing from the many security camera feeds displayed within a portion of the viewscreen wall.

Besides the captain, and now herself, only one other person was on the bridge: a young female officer sitting at a console, absorbed in a string of data running up her screen. She wore a pair of thick headphones and typed soundlessly on a small keyboard.

The captain sipped from a small white teacup as Leera crossed the expansive room. As she approached his chair, he set his cup in a matching saucer and stood abruptly, tugging down the hem of his black uniform shirt as he turned to face her.

Even in the modest lighting, his eyes immediately stabbed her consciousness.

A thought leapt into her mind, unbidden: *This man sees everything.*

"Doctor James," he said, extending his hand. "I'm Captain Williams. Thank you for coming."

His palm was pleasantly warm in hers. "My pleasure, Captain. I wasn't sure I'd ever get to see the bridge."

"They wanted to redesign it before this voyage," he said, clasping his hands behind his back. He walked away, following the curvature of the viewscreen wall. It took a moment for Leera to realize he meant for her to join him. "They said it was too outdated. I disagreed. It is efficient." He stared at her. "Clean work spaces are the most efficient, wouldn't you agree?"

"I would."

He nodded and looked forward, seemingly satisfied. Next to them, the towering viewscreens cast flashing various colors on their clothes: green from the text of multitudinous data streams, white from the security feeds, and greenish-purple from the large screen dedicated solely to an image of the Rip.

Leera stopped before it, then took several steps back so she could see it all at once.

The viewscreen was roughly six meters tall, and the Rip took up four of those meters, the screen surrounding it filled with darkness.

From the angle of the *Halcyon*'s approach, the 300-mile-wide Rip appeared as an asymmetric circle with shredded edges, as if the claw of some great animal had torn a hole in the very fabric of space.

"Do you know why it's a circle?" asked the captain.

"Ceres was spherical," Leera answered.

"Correct. If we had detonated a mass of any other shape, the Rip would hold that shape instead. Though I wonder what else would have served."

"Lucky we had Ceres," said Leera.

"Indeed," he replied, looking at her inscrutably.

A dancing ribbon of brilliant purple and green light delineated the outer edges of the Rip from the void surrounding it. Through the ragged outline, the dim light of a distant blue star was barely visible.

"That's Aegea," said the captain, pointing up at the star on the screen. "The first of seven we can see through the Rip. The other six aren't visible to the naked eye, but Aegea burns the brightest."

He stared at the star reverently, his face awash

with purple and green hues.

"The farthest of her two planets, Canis, is an ice world. Scans show evidence of ancient riverbeds in the frozen surface. Yet the nearest planet, Bastia, has oceans. Continents. Mountains and rivers and streams, just like 7."

"But a toxic atmosphere," said Leera, recalling a passage from one of the thick binders detailing every piece of information about the space beyond the Rip. "Not only isn't it breathable, exposure to it would boil our skin."

A small, sad smile touched his lips and vanished just as quickly.

"Alas," he said, walking on. "How is the rest of your team? Are they enjoying the journey?"

"Actually, Walter is already in a hypergel tank, and I believe Niku is going in as we speak."

"What about you?" he asked pointedly. "Are you enjoying yourself? It's a far cry from what you're used to on Earth, I'm sure, but we try our best."

"Have you been there recently, Captain?" asked Leera with a slight grin. "I can assure you, this is much better. But I can only double-check our equipment so many times. To be honest, I'll be joining my colleagues in stasis this evening."

"Truly? Before the Rip?"

"We're interested in a planet *beyond* it, Captain," said Leera. "And I suspect we'll need to be well-rested when we get there. May I ask a question?"

"You want to know why I asked to see you."

"It crossed my mind."

He straightened up as they walked next to each other.

"As you know, the Halcyon will remain in orbit around Galena for one year so the hull can shed all the radiation it absorbs passing through the Rip. At the end of that year, I'll send a shuttle down to collect you and your team."

"That's my understanding, yes," Leera agreed.

"I believe you were instructed to return to Earth with organic material native to Galena."

Leera was momentarily speechless. Unless one of her team members had spoken of their plan to bring something back to Earth through the Rip, there wasn't any way for the captain to know.

She took a slow breath and regained her composure.

"I don't know how you came by that information, Captain," she said coolly, "and I certainly don't know that it's any of your concern how my team chooses to conduct their research, especially while not on this ship."

"It very much *is* my concern, madam," said Williams. "Galena is a unique place. What we see with our own eyes does not always make up the entire picture. I will not be responsible for transporting organic material back to Earth which could potentially harm its citizens."

"Of course we would run any samples through rigid quarantine procedures before bringing them on board."

"Take pictures," he said as they continued their

stroll around the bridge. "Study. Do your research on the surface, but don't bring anything back, or I'll have it destroyed. I wanted to inform you before we arrived to save having this conversation in the future."

Leera took a deep breath and let it out very slowly.

"That's not an option for me, Captain," she said. "If we don't come back with a sample that proves it's worth going back to Galena, this could be the last trip anyone ever takes through the Rip. You'd be out of a job."

"A price I would gladly pay."

They stopped at the door to the bridge.

"Thank you for meeting with me," said the captain. "I apologize for the circumstances."

Leera smothered the urge to scream as the blast door rose into the ceiling, spilling white light from the hallway onto the carpeted floor. She left in silence, trailing a black cloud of rage.

Later, in her stateroom, she took the maximum allotted five-minute hot shower, letting the scalding water hit the knot of tension at the back of her neck. Afterward, she neatly folded her clothes and put them in the faux-wood dresser, then stuffed the rest of her personal belongings into her travel bag and slid that under the bed. She wore only a clinging black-and-white neoprene body suit, specially-designed to accelerate hypergel absorption while in stasis, and a pair of slippers one size too large. Before leaving, she thought better of it and donned a thick robe hanging from a hook on the bathroom door.

She passed no one on her way to the stasis room. It was several decks below hers, on the bottom-most level before the habitable portion of the ship ended and the radiation shielding began.

A blast of icy air hit her when the doors to the stasis room whooshed apart, revealing a long room with metal, rust-colored walls and a grated floor. To Leera, it appeared as more of an industrial warehouse than a hub for sophisticated technology. The ceiling was twenty meters high, the walls were ten meters apart, and the end of the room was not visible from the entrance.

Cylindrical hypergel tanks filled with thick, pinkish fluid lined one side of the room, starting near the doors and disappearing into the distance. They were attached to the floor and connected to the ceiling by long metal tubes as wide as the tanks.

Leera checked the tank assignment code on her ticket as she shuffled over the grated floor in her slippers, grasping her robe shut with a white hand. The first few tanks were unoccupied, but then she passed one with a slender woman suspended in the viscous pink gel, wearing a black-and-white neoprene body suit to match Leera's own. The woman hung like a fly in amber, with a small black oxygen mask covering the lower half of her face. A thin black tube ran from the mask to a cluster of apparatus on the side of the tank. The woman looked peaceful, as if she had simply dozed off for a nap.

Leera had never been inside a stasis chamber before. One could pay good money on Earth to sleep for years at a time, leap-frogging into the future with the dim hope of a better life on the other end, or the dimmer hope that a member of one's now-deceased family struck it rich and left behind a sizable inheritance.

She passed Walter's hypergel tank, and couldn't help but smile when she noticed the surprised look on his face within the mold of pinkish gel, obvious even though he wore an oxygen mask. His slight paunch pushed against the neoprene of his body suit. While the open legs of Leera's suit nearly reached her ankles, Walter's suit stopped just below his knees.

One of the tanks next to his was meant for Niku, but it was empty. Leera frowned inwardly, guessing he was probably still drinking at the bar, yet hoping he wasn't.

She checked the number on her ticket to the one etched on the thick plexi surface of a nearby tank, verifying it was coded for her use. She swiped the ticket over a small control panel and a large exclamation point flashed on the screen. A flurry of warnings scrolled by. Leera tapped all the accept buttons the warnings threw her way.

There was a beep at the end, and a small door popped open on the side of the tank. Leera stepped out of her slippers and took off her robe, the cold air nipping at her wrists and ankles. She placed her items in the nearby storage compartment and shut the door, then stood in front of the tank, waiting for something to happen.

A small red square pulsed on the plexi surface of the tank. She pushed it impatiently. The curved plexi exterior parted down the middle, hinging apart to expose the pink gel within.

Leera had watched the safety videos. She had replayed the stasis orientation a dozen times, yet still she was nervous.

A black oxygen mask rested in a formed pocket on the right side of the tank. Leera slipped it over her head and tightened the strap. A cold blast of oxygen hit her mouth and cheeks. After a few breaths, she felt more calm.

Enter quickly, she remembered from the safety videos. *Push into it and turn.*

She stepped onto a metal lip protruding beneath the tank, then leaned forward with her eyes tightly shut and squished into the tank in one quick motion. The warm pink goop sealed around her back as she pushed forward, and she turned around while she still had a loose pocket of disturbed gel in which to move.

As soon as she went still, the gel formed to her body, seeping between her toes and fingers. Following the instructional video's advice, she relaxed her muscles. Her legs contracted slightly, bending at the knees on their own and rising from the floor of the tank. She risked a quick peek, but the gel stung her eyes.

It could take anywhere from five to fifteen

minutes for the stasis effect to take hold, she remembered reading. The delay depended on the physical makeup of the person in the tank, how many times they'd previously been exposed to the gel, and how resistant they were to stimulants. Leera couldn't help but think it would take Niku half an hour to pass out.

Her skin tingled.

She wanted to scratch her itching scalp but found she was paralyzed. Her body was absorbing the gel that seeped through the pores of her body suit, pulling it into her bloodstream.

Just a quick sleep, she told herself as she drifted off. *Four months for the ship, but mere seconds for me. A year on the ground, then back home to my family. My family...what am I going to do?*

And with that thought, she fell asleep.

TULLIVER

Too many stars, thought Tulliver.

He sat on a bench in the domed atrium, staring up at the ceiling. Beyond the looming palm trees, a field of stars was projected on the ceiling, each one burning with a brilliance Tulliver had never seen.

On Earth, catching a clear glimpse of the night sky was rare, at least in the bigger cities. Blankets of fog seemed to settle in over the populace in late evening, if they hadn't been there all day, glowing with the sickly light cast upon them from below.

Tulliver shivered and looked away from the ceiling. Such a sight unnerved him. It was difficult for a man his size to feel small, but gazing into the endless reaches of space did the trick every time.

He shifted his bulk from the bench and walked across the bridge, glancing down at the reflection of the stars in the pool's surface below.

Tulliver felt a presence walking behind him, a void in the constant background murmur of his surroundings. A hawk-faced man with a sharp widow's peak had appeared from an inconspicuous spot tucked away behind the bridge. He was nearly as tall as Tulliver, but possessed only a quarter of his mass and a fraction of his intellect.

Though he walked with a loping gate — the result of a childhood injury to his left knee, courtesy of his own father, leaving him with a permanent limp — he managed to do so with shocking deftness, and, just once, had managed the difficult feat of sneaking up on Tulliver.

That was how they met, a week after the *Halcyon* left Sunrise Station.

Tulliver was sitting in the galley, pushing cold soy mush around on his plate with a fork, when he felt a faint rustle in his back pocket. With surprising speed, he whipped around and snatched his ticket from the would-be thief. It was a wiry man, eyes wide with fear at being caught red-handed. He had curly black hair, a pencil-thin mustache, and tufts of downy fuzz on his cheeks which were, Tulliver thought, the result of his attempt to grow a beard.

Tulliver grabbed his jacket lapels with both hands, balling the cloth in his tight fists and pulling him closer. The man was terrified, looking around for a chance at escape like a wild, captured animal. He tried to break free, but was held in an iron grip.

Forcing the whimpering man down into the seat next to him, Tulliver stared deep into his eyes with grim seriousness. The man's darting gaze eventually found Tulliver's, and he was unable to look away. The gaze dug deep into his psyche, seeming to unearth the very core of his being.

Later, when he was sure no one else could hear, he admitted that the experience had made him feel like weeping.

"I can get you a red ticket," Tulliver had said in

the galley, shaking the man earnestly. "And I can get you so much more."

Ivan had been his shadow ever since.

He only spoke a few words of English, but he understood it well enough. Fortunately for them both, Russian was one of the four languages of which Tulliver had a passing knowledge — one of the only positive side effects of being raised in one of New York's finest all-boys authoritarian multi-national boarding houses.

Tulliver beckoned. Ivan was suddenly at his shoulder, staring at Tulliver's face like a dog stares at a master's while awaiting an imminent command. He had put on a few pounds since he began working for Tulliver. Though he was still wiry, his sunken, hungry face had filled out and become less pale. His bone-and-sinew limbs had fleshed out and grown some muscle. A full beard, however, eluded him.

"Run ahead to the bar," said Tulliver, squeezing Ivan's shoulder. "Tell them I'm coming."

Ivan looked at him, hesitant to obey.

"It's alright," Tulliver assured him. "I'll be fine. You run along."

Reluctantly, Ivan departed, padding out of the atrium with barely a sound. At first, Tulliver thought he accomplished his stealthy movements with the aide of a special shoe. It was several days before he realized Ivan was barefoot, and his feet were so filthy they were completely black. He had refused Tulliver's attempts to buy him a new pair.

"*REMINDER,*" said an artificial female voice over the ship's intercom. "*Hypergel provides increased radiation protection when traveling through the Rip. Speak to a crew member to upgrade to Red Class.*"

As he left the atrium, Tulliver passed a workman kneeling next to a light fixture in the floor.

"Good day, Mr. Pruitt," the man said with a wide smile.

"Hello, Jack."

"I wanted to thank you again for that...item... you got for me," said the workman as Tulliver walked past. "It's really working great, and I—"

"Don't mention it," Tulliver replied, waving him off.

"If only the other guys could see—"

"Jack," Tulliver said sharply, turning around to face the workman. "Don't *mention* it."

Jack swallowed hard, as if his mouth had suddenly gone dry. "You got it, Mr. Pruitt. No problem, okay? You have a good one."

He turned back to his work with shaking hands.

Tulliver greeted Mick, the doorman, at the entrance to The Velvet Speakeasy after trying to enjoy a leisurely stroll along the promenade.

The bald doorman sat on a metal stool, muscular arms crossed over his barrel chest, face locked in a permanent scowl below a simian brow. Tulliver had hired him after he was put on suspension by his maintenance supervisor for brawling with a passenger.

"Anything new?" Tulliver asked outside the establishment.

"That scientist is drunk again," said Mick, nodding his big head toward the bar. "We got two more orders for parts from the workmen."

"Foreman won't sign the work orders?"

Mick nodded, and Tulliver sighed. The shop foreman was becoming a major source of irritation. He had been just a minor blip on Tulliver's periphery, but he seemed to have noticed he held some amount of control over the distribution of parts within the ship. Lately, he had decided to exercise some of that control by refusing certain work orders until his demands were met.

Tulliver could forgive someone skimming off the top. It was how he himself scraped by, for the most part. What he couldn't forgive was someone with the responsibility of a ship's foreman using his position for financial leverage at the expense of those he was sworn to see safely to Galena.

"I'll handle it," he told Mick.

"You sure?"

"I've been meaning to get down there anyway. What else?"

"Someone's waiting for you by the booth."

Tulliver looked inside. Beyond the bar and the dining tables, a workman stood in the shadows near the large booth at the very back, hands in his pockets, staring down at the floor. Ivan sat at one of the tables, drinking a soda, keeping an eye on the workman.

"What's he want?"

"Wouldn't say."

Tulliver grunted thoughtfully, then patted the doorman on the shoulder.

"Thanks, Mick."

Soft jazz music played as Tulliver passed the bar. The robot barman produced a ready-made gin and tonic and set it on the counter. Tulliver fished out his hellocard and tried to set it on the card reader, but the robot barman waved him off. The robot pointed to the floor, as if to say, *It's on the house.*

Tulliver smiled graciously, pocketing his hellocard and saluting the robot.

"Thanks, Bartee."

Their little charade played out every time he returned to the bar, a little scene he had one of the workman hardwire into the robot's circuitry. The name was his idea, as well.

He slapped Niku Tedani on the back as he walked by. Niku turned slightly on his stool, looking out through drooping eyelids.

"Still no hypergel, doc?" asked Tulliver.

"Jus' one more," said Niku, drunkenly holding up his half-finished cocktail.

"Need help getting there?"

"Pfffft," said Niku, turning back to his drink.

Tulliver barked laughter and took a sip of his gin and tonic. He made a point to savor every sip, knowing there would be no alcohol once they landed on Galena.

He nodded at Ivan but ignored the waiting

workman as he sat in the capacious booth at the back of The Velvet Speakeasy — *his* booth, as he now thought of it.

"Is this him?" he asked Ivan.

Ivan nodded.

Finally, Tulliver deigned to look at the workman. He was no different from the others at first glance: dirty blue coveralls, grease-smeared face, hair cut short for safety reasons, and tired, overworked eyes. Yet Tulliver recognized him as being one of the few passengers with a child on board.

"Come," he said, calling the workman over.

The man stood in front of the booth. He took his hands out of his pockets, clasped them in front of his waist, then put them back in his pockets again.

"Don't be nervous," said Tulliver easily. He took a sip of his drink and settled deeper into the padded booth. After a few moments of silence, he gestured calmly for the workman to proceed.

"I need a red ticket," said the man.

Tulliver enjoyed another sip. "What's your name?"

"Merritt."

"Merritt *what*?"

The man hesitated. "Alder."

The corner of Tulliver's mouth twitched. "You didn't want to tell me." The man opened his mouth to lie, but Tulliver held up his hand to stop him. "It's smart. But, if you're here to do business, we need to know each other. I'm Tulliver Pruitt."

"I know who you are."

"Good. Then we can skip that part."

Merritt eyed a chair near the booth, but was not invited to sit. Behind him, Ivan rhythmically tapped a bottle opener against the top of his dining room table.

"I need a red ticket," said Merritt.

Tulliver regarded him intently for a long moment.

"You know what I do here, Mr. Alder?" he asked quietly.

Merritt shrugged. "You get things for people."

Tulliver shook his head. "I provide a service. That service comes at a cost."

"I can't afford much."

"I don't want your money."

Merritt frowned, confused.

"Surely you've heard about my deals with some of the other farmers," said Tulliver.

"I don't understand."

"Galena. You can pay me on Galena."

"How?"

"You will harvest your crop. Some of it will go to me."

"How much of the crop?"

"Twenty-five percent."

Merritt's confusion was replaced by the seeds of anger. "The government takes seventy. That's not enough left over for me and—"

He fell silent, chewing on his next words instead of letting them slip out.

"How is Gavin doing, by the way?" asked Tulliver. "Still having a problem with the soy diet?"

"How did you know about that?" Merritt said through a clenched jaw.

"It's a small ship, Mr. Alder. I imagine the ticket is for him, correct? How nice it would be to let him soak in one of the hypergel tanks until we arrive at Galena."

Merritt bit back a comment, then visibly forced himself to calm down.

"I'm not a tyrant, Mr. Alder," added Tulliver. "I would take my cut from your remaining thirty percent. That should leave plenty for you and your child. From what I've heard, he isn't a voracious eater."

Ivan chuckled.

Merritt glanced over his shoulder at him, then met Tulliver's dead-eyed stare.

"The ticket," he said. "How would you get one?"

Tulliver shifted in the booth and took a sip of his drink. "You can hear the answer to that question, or you can have the ticket...but you can't have both. Our meeting is over, farmer. What's it going to be?"

CHAPTER SIX

ONE YEAR AGO

Merritt's worst memory was of a visit to his wife's hospital bed — what would, in fact, turn out to be her death bed. Up until that point, he hadn't allowed himself to believe she was dying.

The antiseptic sterility of the hospital washed over him as he stepped through the entrance, Gavin at his side, trailing a humid fog which clung to the city that morning like a thick blanket. The nurses who knew him nodded their greetings as he led his son to see his sick mother.

She had a window room, which was fortunate in every aspect save for the draw on their bank account. Merritt wanted her to have what little sunlight pierced the dense cloud cover.

Gavin walked to her bedside timidly, leaning in to allow himself to be hugged. Emily smiled as she wrapped her thin arms around him, pushing her cheek against the top of his head.

She had lost her hair two months ago, and Merritt was ashamed to discover he could barely remember what she looked like with her long brown curls.

"I got you something," she whispered to Gavin.

He pulled away and looked at her with hesitant expectation. Emily gestured to a wrapped box on the far side of the room.

"Go and see."

He hurried over to the box and knelt before it, looking back for permission before ripping off the wrapping paper to reveal a yellow excavator with swappable treads, doors, and bucket.

While Gavin played happily on the floor, clicking different pieces on and off his new toy, Emily took Merritt's hand and guided him into the seat by her bed.

"Bad health report this morning," she said softly, her voice strained.

Merritt looked away. There had been plenty of bad reports, and plenty of good ones, too. The bad ones didn't seem to affect Emily like they used to, which is more than he could say for himself.

"I'm sorry I left," he said.

"If you don't work, they'll give your job away."

Merritt grunted. They'd been over the subject many times before. He still couldn't find a way to balance his guilt at not being constantly at her side with the satisfaction of having a job in a nearly-jobless economy.

She patted his arm lovingly, then pressed a small leather pouch into the palm of his hand. He looked at it, frowning. The logo of a small leaf with a plus sign in its center was stamped on the front. He rolled it between his fingers, feeling small spheres within, almost like beads.

"Seeds," whispered Emily.

She produced her faded Galena Farming Initiative from under her waist and pressed it into his palm.

"I know you don't want to go," she said. Merritt opened his mouth to protest but she put her finger to his lips, hushing him. "It's alright," she told him. "You would do it for me." She looked at Gavin. "But now you have to do it for *him*."

Emily closed her hand around Merritt's, holding the pouch.

"There are a hundred seeds in here," she whispered. "A hundred drops of hope. Our boy needs better food, my love. He needs better *everything*. You must plant these seeds on Galena."

"Only one crop grows in that soil," said Merritt, "and it's poison to him."

"But these," she whispered, patting his hand covering the pouch, "oh, but these are special. One of them will grow."

"Where'd you get them?"

She looked at her son, watching him with tear-filled eyes. Merritt noticed the hellocard in her other hand.

"Emily, what's going on?"

She looked back at him, and a single tear rolled down her cheek. Holding out the hellocard to him, she said, "There's enough on here to get the two of you to Galena."

He refused to take it, just as he had the last few times she offered, knowing it was a fantasy she had constructed. Yet there was something different in her eyes that time — an honest belief so powerful he was compelled to accept, if only to make her feel better in the moment.

Emily died that evening, while Merritt and Gavin slept in a guest room just down the hall. The doctor came in and gently touched his shoulder, and he knew. He knew before his head left the pillow and before he walked down the hallway in a daze while the doctor droned on about how peaceful it was and how she had a little smile on her face.

The day after, Merritt left Gavin at the nearest police station's daycare program and took the small leather pouch to one of the last print shops in the country. He had already discovered Emily had not been lying about the new funds on her hellocard. There was indeed enough money to get him and Gavin comfortably to Galena.

Gavin showed a bent old man behind the cluttered counter of the print shop the pouch's logo: a single leaf with a small plus sign in the middle.

The man grunted as he held the pouch under the light of a large magnifier.

"Real leather," he said, his voice low and rough. "How much for it?"

"Do you recognize the logo?" Merritt asked in return.

His own queries had revealed no answers. No one at the municipal building downtown, where Emily used to work, remembered her. She hadn't been there in almost two years, and the employee turnover rate in the government offices was so high it was a wonder anyone learned their coworkers' names.

The only useful piece of information Merritt walked away with after his visit was that no company in those offices used the leaf for a logo.

"Mmmmm," said the old man thoughtfully. "I know this logo. I have made business cards."

He flicked off the magnifier light and swiveled it away, pushing the pouch across the counter.

"Five thousand, and I tell you," he said, staring at Merritt unapologetically.

It was the first major draw on Emily's hellocard Merritt had been forced to make, and it would not be the last.

The old printer's information was correct. Merritt soon found himself standing on the street in a heavy rain, looking up at a towering downtown skyscraper.

Halfway up the tower, a large green leaf glowed brightly in the gloom, the outline of a plus symbol in its center. A woman carrying an umbrella hurried past him, scanned a badge at the door, and ducked into the building. Merritt followed her, catching the door a moment before it closed.

She eyed him suspiciously as she shook out her umbrella.

"Delivery for agriculture," he said, showing her the leather pouch.

The woman rolled her eyes as she folded down the collar of her coat. "Agriculture, right. That's Marty. Broom closet on six. I hope he didn't sell you any of his magic beans."

"That's what I'm here to find out."

He waited until after she took the lobby elevator, then went up to level six.

A single hallway led from the elevator, one side covered with glass windows overlooking a clean room. Several people hunched over workstations, wearing white lab coats and hair nets.

A door on Merritt's right showcased the leaf logo and a small, stenciled plaque which read, *Martin Douglas, Ag.*

Inside the room, a rotund man stood with his back to Merritt, bent over a microscope, his legs like the clapper of a bell within his capacious lab coat.

"Marty?" said Merritt.

The man yelped and spun around, knocking a petri dish to the floor.

"Who are you?" he asked after he'd caught his breath, his eyes narrowing.

"Emily Alder's husband."

His face went slack and he swallowed thickly. "Then she's…is she…?"

Merritt showed him the pouch. "What's this?"

He handed it to Marty, who flattened out the logo, then gave the bag a gentle squeeze.

"Seeds," he replied.

"What's special about them?"

"I spliced samples of Earth crops with strains of bacteria I believe will be resistant to the soil on Galena."

"Samples?"

Marty looked past Merritt nervously, assuring himself the door was shut. He lowered his voice and said, "Corn. Wheat. A dozen more. Emily gave me the samples, but she—she wouldn't tell me where she got them."

"Why?"

"So we could grow vegetables again. And so Gavin could be healthy. I deconstructed the soy germs that grow in the sample soil and applied some of the resistant strains to these seeds. Some of them *will* grow, if they make it to Galena."

He gave the pouch back to Merritt.

"Scientists have been trying to get Earth crops to grow in fake Galena soil for years," Merritt said. "How is this different?"

"They never asked *me*," Marty replied.

Outside the building, Merritt turned up the collar of his coat against the rain. In one pocket, he held the leather seed pouch Emily had given him. In the other, he rubbed his thumb over the plastic half of her hellocard.

Wind whipped his jacket and rain pelted his back as he walked through dirty puddles, heading for the police station.

Galena had always been Emily's dream, not his. Losing his job had heaped mass quantities of stress on an already stressful life, but there were always options that didn't involve taking his son through a rip in space to an unexplored planet on the other part of the galaxy.

Inside the police station, Merritt stood dripping water from his clothes as he watched Gavin and two other boys through a wide window. The two boys sat near each other at a long table, chowing down plates of soy mush squirted from a food dispenser in the wall.

Gavin sat alone, half the size of the other boys his age. He poked at the gray, gelatinous mass with a fork. Then he looked up, saw his father, and smiled.

In that moment, Merritt's decision was made for him. He squeezed Emily's hellocard tightly, feeling its sharp edges dig into his palm.

He and Gavin were going to Galena.

CHAPTER SEVEN

MERRITT

He stood before Gavin's hypergel tank, hands in the pockets of his faded blue coveralls. The boy was turned sideways, curled up in a fetal position, the overlarge oxygen mask swallowing his small face. Merritt had needed to make adjustments to the boy's neoprene body suit so it wouldn't slip off his slim frame. The ankle and wrist cuffs were still loose — wrinkled folds of fabric pressed against Gavin's skin by the pink gel.

Every day for the past two months, Merritt had come down to the stasis room on Deck 6 to check on his son. Ostensibly, he went there to perform routine maintenance on the hypergel tanks. He became familiar with the data stream continuously ticking up the info screen on the side of Gavin's tank, learning how to identify the shorthand code for his heart rate, breathing patterns, and REM cycles.

Apparently, one still dreamed while in the tank.

The times in between those dreams were spent in a shallow sleep, artificially induced by the gel that had seeped into the occupant's body.

Merritt rubbed his sternum, remembering when, two months ago, he had forcefully pushed Gavin into the mass of thick pink gel. His son had kicked him square in the chest with surprising strength as he fought to stay out of the tank. When they first approached the looming cylinder of goop, Gavin had taken one look at it and tried to pull away from his father. Merritt had to push the boy into the thick pink gel, kicking and scratching in silence, sinking his own arms into the gel up to his armpits while whispering apology after apology.

After Gavin calmed down within the tank, his arms and legs slowly contracted, tucking close to his body as he drifted to sleep.

Aside from his visits to the stasis room, the rest of Merritt's time on the ship was spent working. He structured his schedule to leave as few quiet moments as possible, knowing they would inevitably fill with dark thoughts of loneliness.

A heavy metal wrench fell onto the grated floor by his feet, the clang echoing loudly down the long stasis room.

"Look out below!" a voice called from above.

Another workman clung to the side of a thick stasis tube, the one right next to Gavin's, ten meters off the floor. He pulled a smokeless cigarette from his thin lips and saluted as Merritt shot him a rude gesture. A safety harness hung loose around the man's thin waist, secured to a track that ran the length of the tube, from the hypergel tank at the bottom, to its terminus at the ceiling twenty meters above.

The workman shut the cover of a large electrical box and climbed down the rust-brown ladder rungs bolted to the side of the tube.

"Loose temperature regulator," he said with the voice of a smoker, his gangling form carried down the tube by bony limbs.

He hopped down to the grated floor next to Merritt, scooped up his wrench, and brushed straight brown hair from his eyes. After relighting his smokeless cigarette, he offered it to Merritt with black-stained fingertips. Merritt refused.

At first glance, Skip's weathered face, salted brown face stubble, and brittle hair made him appear older than Merritt, yet he was ten years younger. Skip acknowledged this, and attributed his "wizened visage" to a youth of hard smoking and drinking, a period of his life he steadfastly refused to regret.

He emerged from this personal epoch as a true man, he claimed, with three sons and three daughters to prove it.

Skip slapped Merritt's shoulder and walked away.

"Your boy's lookin' alright, chief," he said. "Let's go see about them rad-deflectors. Willef'll birth a cow if it don't happen this shift."

Merritt followed him toward the exit of the stasis room, their boots thudding on the metal, grated floor.

Steam hissed from a pipe in the wall opposite the row of hypergel tanks.

"Ho, now!" said Skip.

He hefted his wrench and dodged the steam to get closer to the pipe. With a quick turn of his wrench, he tightened a fist-sized bolt, and the steam vanished.

"One more reason they should give me an extra hectare on Galena," Skip said as he slid his wrench into a fabric loop of his coveralls. He sucked on his cigarette as they continued walking. "I swear, if it weren't for you and me, this whole ship would implode." He made a detonation sound and brought his hands together like he was crumpling a large ball.

"Two hectares is enough," said Merritt.

"Maybe for you, chief. You only got one kid. I got *six* of 'em, *and* the missus." He shook his head. "She ain't gonna be happy with just two No, *sir*."

In their short time working together, Merritt had learned more than he cared to admit about Skip's life on Earth. His family would depart on the next *Halcyon* voyage, arriving at Galena after Skip established a working farm.

The government had come knocking on Skip's door after his wife gave birth to their second child. After the sixth, they were throwing so much money at the family for permission to study her fertility that, according to Skip, it was better than winning the lottery.

Instead of opting for a suite atop one of the twin cities on the moon, he would quit his job and move the family to Galena, where, he boasted, he would quickly build the largest farm that side of the Milky Way. He had already ordered the ready-to-build packages of two Pioneer Lodges to be delivered to his site.

When Merritt asked him why he wasn't participating in the farming classes, Skip looked offended. He shot back, "Would you try teaching Mozart how to play Twinkle Twinkle Little Star?!"

Down the hall from the stasis room, Merritt and Skip passed through a series of restricted blast doors, ending up in a brightly-lit, spherical airlock. Two types of spacesuits hung on the wall: all-purpose, bright orange Constellation Mark VI's, and the workhorse of the *Halcyon*'s EVA teams: the gray, heavy-duty Magellan space suit. Unlike the streamlined Constellation suits, the Magellan suits came equipped with a pair of robotic arms folded into two cubes, one to each side of the occupant's waist, which extended their range of manipulation by three meters.

Merritt shed his coveralls and stuffed them into a wall receptacle. Emily's hellocard dangled from a chain around his neck, a hole drilled through the metal grip. He tucked it into his shirt. The linked bank account was empty, but he didn't trust leaving the card tucked into his sleeping bag, as he was forced to do with his wife's brochure for the Galena Farming Initiative.

He backed into one of the two Magellan suits while Skip did the same. After donning their suits, they helped each other button up, triple-checking seal integrity. Merritt pulled on his bulbous, full-pressure polycarbonate helmet and clicked the sliding seal under his neck into place.

He activated his suit's wristpad, pawing at it with thick, gloved fingers. After syncing it with the ship's mainframe, he called up a diagram of the ship and navigated to the section awaiting him and Skip beyond the airlock door.

"Panel Y-27 is flashing again," he said over the helmet intercom system. He tapped the blinking red light on his wristpad. *ALIGNMENT ERROR* flashed across the small screen.

"It's *always* Y-27," said Skip, shaking his head.

His narrow frame swam in the large spacesuit, triggering Merritt's memory of the time he walked into his bedroom to find four-year-old Gavin wearing his father's shirt and pants.

"Ready?" Skip asked.

Without waiting for a reply, he turned a switch and slapped a yellow button on the wall. The Grav-Gen under the floor cut off, and the two of them lifted gently into the air.

"I hate it when you do that," said Merritt.

"I hear that a lot."

The hatch in front of them rotated in its setting, as if being turned from the other side. It slid toward them a few inches, then slowly opened inward to bump silently against the inner airlock wall.

Skip said, "After you, chief," and cackled with laughter as he fired a burst of nitrogen from his pack, zooming through the open hatch.

Merritt shook his head, half-smiling, as he followed after him.

He emerged into the dark, vast, empty chamber

surrounding the innermost shell of the *Halcyon*.

Worklights flicked on in the darkness — piercing halogen beams that painted the chamber with swaths of bright light.

Behind Merritt, the hull of the habitable portion of the ship disappeared into the distance at his left and right. Above and below, it curved out of sight at a noticeable angle. He felt as if he were floating in mid-air next to a mile-long submarine.

Thick support struts connected the innermost hull with the next one at a distance of roughly twenty meters.

Halfway between the hulls, ten meters from each, was another wall. This one was more akin to a fence, comprised of five-meter-tall rectangular slats which could be turned independently of the whole, all of them suspended by an airy support lattice which encapsulated the innermost hull.

"I know you like to keep to yourself," Skip said as they floated toward the lattice, "but me'n the boys are gettin' together tonight fer the passage. We wanna be blackout drunk in case the ship explodes. Sort of a tradition. I'm callin' it 'Get Ripped in the Rip'. You should come."

Merritt had planned on spending the *Halcyon*'s passage through the Rip tucked up in his sleeping bag, listening to a recorded loop of wind rustling tall grass.

"They're gonna put it up on the big screen in the observation lounge," Skip went on. "I ain't ever been sober enough to see what happens, but it's supposed to be quite the show."

"Maybe," said Merritt. Then he added, "Thanks."

He bumped against one of the monolithic panels and drifted gently to its edge, grabbing hold of the thick lattice which connected the panel to all the others. A white label on the side of the panel identified it as W-15.

"Two down," he said.

He and Skip descended two horizontal rows and moved twelve panels to the right, to Y-27.

Merritt checked the rad-meter on his suit's wristpad. A small red line wavered just above nominal, rising noticeably higher when he moved around to the other side of the panel.

"Surface integrity looks good," he said, running a gloved hand over the ribbed exterior. "No visible damage."

"Gotta be the tracking servos," said Skip. "I'd bet my grammy's wooden teeth."

"What?"

"Grammy's wooden teeth," he repeated. "They don't have that expression where you're from?"

"*No* one has that expression."

Skip huffed. "And you call yourself cultured."

Merritt activated the info screen near one corner of Y-27, waiting as the system ran through its internal diagnostics checks.

Each thick panel contained a complex series of servos which, when activated, adjusted the panel's angle relative to the lattice, keeping the phalanx mostly parallel with the two nearby hulls. As the

Halcyon passed through the Rip — or close to any other celestial body— tracking servos in the panels worked to keep their surfaces facing the object, deflecting the brunt of the radiation that burrowed past the ship's outer hulls.

After a few moments, the screen spit back an error code.

"Looks like your grammy keeps her teeth," said Merritt.

"Really?"

"Yeah. It's the tracking servos."

"I'd be more excited if I didn't know what that meant."

"Me, too."

Y-27 had been hiccuping the entire voyage. At first, it was blinking in and out of active status, even though its servos were fully operational. Then the servos truly *did* begun to fail, and Merritt had been forced to shut down half of them. As a result, the panel could still track a celestial object along with the others, but it lagged behind while doing so.

Now, the error told him the other servos had failed.

"We'll have to aim it manually," he said.

"We can't be *in* here when we pass through the Rip, chief. This whole chamber's gonna be flooded with radiation."

"I know that," said Merritt. "We'll do it now, then toss up some extra shielding inside the habitable section. Adjusting it manually will at least provide some initial protection. The panel won't track with the others, but it's better than nothing. Best we can do."

"Willef won't like it."

"I don't like it, either. This bank of panels deflects most of the radiation that would hit the stasis room."

"Aw, chief, don't worry about *that,*" said Skip. "The goop can absorb more rads than the hull. Your boy's gonna be just fine. I still can't believe the ship has to stay in orbit for a *year* while it sheds all those rads! What a waste of time."

"Otherwise it would go right through to the passenger section."

"At least on Earth they can do them dinner cruises while it sheds. Out here, it's a whole bunch of nothin'."

Merritt checked his wristpad. The radiation indicator was slowly but gradually going up.

"Let's get it done fast," he said. "This place is already starting to cook."

After his shift, Merritt showered and put on the only set of clothes he owned, provided by his employer: a pair of gray slacks and a blue T-shirt with the stylized astrolabe logo of Cygnus Corporation printed on the chest. Having no other option, he pulled on his scuffed work boots over threadbare socks.

The observation lounge was only open to passengers and crew on special occasions, such as arrivals and departures, and, of course, passage through the Rip.

As the doors whooshed open before him, Merritt hesitated, hands clasped behind his back. Pockets of soft light bloomed in the dark lounge, revealing passengers involved in deep conversation, others laughing uproariously over tables full of cocktails, and still others sitting alone, staring at the wall-sized viewscreen opposite the bar.

The room itself curved away from the entrance in a half-moon arc, the long bar on one side, opposite the viewscreen. For now, all that was visible in the vast reaches of space were the pinpoint brilliance of distant stars.

Merritt entered the lounge and the doors whooshed shut behind him. It took him a moment to pick Skip out of the crowd. He sat on a low stool with his back to the door, at a round table with four other workman, some still wearing their coveralls. They raised small glasses filled with blue liquid, shouted something in unison, then downed their drinks and pounded the table three times. They pointed and hooted with laughter at the man who finished last. He grinned sheepishly as he wiped droplets from his chin.

Skip looked around and saw Merritt. With a flailing, drunken wave, he called him over.

"Guys!" he said with half-closed eyelids as Merritt stood next to the table. "Guys, this is Gavnnn... this is Gavvvv...Gavvvon..."

"I'm Merritt," he said, though he knew all of the men sitting at the table.

They brushed off Skip's behavior with laughter

and pulled over an empty stool. Merritt sat, then accepted a glass brimming with clear blue liquid.

"To my health!" Skip shouted.

They drank, they hooted, they pounded the table. For the first time since he left Earth, Merritt was under a very real threat of enjoying himself.

After several rounds of drink-and-thump, there was a collective gasp from the lounge.

Merritt turned on his stool and squinted at the other passengers, drunkenly trying to figure out why they were so excited.

He noticed Tulliver sitting alone at a table, facing the screen. The large man had chosen the only table in the lounge not lit by a dim overhead lamp. He sat in darkness, clasping a thin chain in one fist as he stared at the projection of space. Behind him, tucked into the shadows, Ivan leaned against the wall near the bar, his eyes glinting as they found Merritt's. He looked away quickly.

A table of four elderly women, dressed in their finest clothes and wearing jewelry worth more than the cost of ten tickets to Galena, played Tah-Go, setting down shimmering tiles with loud clicks. One of them pointed at the wall screen.

The Rip had come into view.

It gradually increased in size, its electric green and purple torn edge rippling against the void. Its center was deep gray, the color of heavy smog, and through it, a single blue star was barely visible.

Someone shouted, "Aegea!" and all the passengers cheered.

Merritt stood up, swaying in place, attempting to regain his sense of balance. He stumbled forward and slumped into a chair at an empty table, closer to the wall screen.

The Rip now filled the screen from floor to ceiling, its mouth ever-widening like the maw of some great space creature.

A shudder coursed through the floor, shaking Merritt's bones. The four elderly tourists giggled with delight as glasses rattled and clinked on tabletops.

As the *Halcyon* approached the Rip, its top and bottom edges disappeared from the screen, filling the wall with a gray haze.

Merritt was mesmerized by the sight, unable to blink.

The lamps in the lounge dimmed. Merritt stood slowly, reverently, his face dancing with purple-green light, as the *Halcyon* entered the Rip.

The universe slipped away.

On the screen in the lounge, all of the stars moved slowly into the distance, pulled toward a single point in the void. They converged on that spot and amassed into a spinning white sphere the apparent size of a golf ball.

Streaks of light shot past the screen, heading for the sphere, which sucked in the light, and grew.

It filled the screen from ceiling to floor, gorged on light, then seemed to implode upon itself in a microsecond, plunging the lounge into darkness.

A spinning dot, like a distant quasar, flickered

where the sphere had vanished.

Something emerged.

It appeared as an expanding circle of light, shaped like the rings of Saturn, growing from the tiny dot to all points on the horizon.

The passengers in the lounge gasped as the ring slammed into the side of the ship, causing the wall screen to blind them with a flash of solid white.

Merritt's stomach lurched sideways. He looked down at his feet, but he wasn't moving. Amidst exclamations of shock and excitement, his feet lifted off the floor as the lounge lost gravity.

He drifted several inches to the side, then gently landed on the floor.

The image on the screen exploded in a panoply of electric colors, shooting out in lightning-edged bands from a central point, around which they danced furiously. The central point on the screen, the point where the bands of light converged, expanded until it appeared as if the *Halcyon* were zooming through the inside of an infinite rectangular box, its walls aglow with thick lanes of varying color, vanishing toward the blinding horizon.

The screen went dark as if it suddenly lost power, and Merritt stood there, blinking in the darkness, his eyes filled with tears.

STARLINER HALCYON

When scientists on Earth first detected a quantum anomaly in the Perseus spiral arm of humanity's own galaxy, ten-thousand light years seemed like an awfully big distance to cover.

There was no small amount of waffling in the academic community about the nature of the anomaly from the start, causing more university lunch-room brawls than any subject since The Big Bang.

Yet, over time, one thing became clear: the anomaly emitted a unique quantum signature which, when recreated in a vacuum at the University of Massachusetts, flooded the laboratory with enough radiation that the entire science wing was deemed uninhabitable for the next thousand years.

The chemical makeup of that radiation matched expectations for the area surrounding the Perseus Anomaly.

In the brief moments before the laboratory vacuum was purged, the two distant points in space were linked.

This had been achieved by bombardment of a small mass — in this case, a tennis ball — with supercharged particles emitting the same quantum signature as the Perseus Anomaly.

Clearly, the next step was to recreate the experiment in space...but where to find the mass? Hoisting the vast islands of garbage from Earth's oceans into space was improbable and impractical. The moon was too close to home, and housed nearly a million souls besides.

What were the eager scientists to do?

Along came Ceres.

The largest asteroid in the belt boasted a diameter of just under six-hundred miles and orbited the sun between Mars and Jupiter. It would also, the scientists excitedly pointed out, be in the perfect position for quantum bombardment in four years—the estimated time it would take for them to build a machine capable of delivering the supercharged particles.

The rest is history.

The scientists built their machine. Ceres was obliterated, leaving behind the Rip —a static tear in the fabric of our solar system which burrows through space to a point in the Perseus spiral arm ten-thousand light years away.

The journey to Galena from Earth takes six months, provided you have a ship that can handle the Rip's intense gauntlet of radiation.

The *Halcyon* had seen a lot in its ninety years of service.

Eight journeys through the Rip, countless dinner cruises around Earth in between, not to mention the punishing early years hauling construction materials to the twin cities on the moon as well as to the mining colony on Mars.

If any ship had earned the right to be decommissioned before it imploded from overuse, it was the *Halcyon*.

Yet still it held together; still it suffered the impossible pressures of the Rip and the concentrated bombardment of radiation.

The tip of its nose entered the Rip, and vanished.

The first of two expected pulses rippled across the *Halcyon*'s exterior hull, warping the conjoined plates of its outermost shell in a wave that traveled down its length to the stern before being absorbed by the three modified bell housings of the hybrid antimatter engines.

More of the ship vanished into the flat surface that was the mouth of the Rip. Though massive in its own right, the *Halcyon* looked like a sewing needle disappearing into a 300-mile-tall shimmering disc.

When most of the ship had passed beyond the threshold, its nose emerged from the gray fog on the other side, half a mile away.

The second pulse traveled down the length of its hull, briefly separating the sleeve of outer plates from the rest of the shell.

Deep inside the vessel, the lattice network of deflector panels thrummed furiously as they tilted in unison to face the Rip's edge, repulsing radiation that hadn't been absorbed by the ship's outer layers.

Panel Y-27 vibrated like a struck tuning fork.

It rattled in its setting, banging against its connecting joints and disrupting its neighbors like a child shaking a chain-link fence.

One corner exploded, jetting particulate into zero gravity and ripping the panel free of the lattice. It spun in place amidst a cloud of its own material, then caught the magnetic field generated by the network of panels and rode it like a surfboard, gaining speed as it zoomed over the lattice, heading for the back of the vast chamber.

The lattice curved to follow the innermost shell of the passenger section. Panel Y-27 broke free of the magnetic field and blasted through the next hull like a torpedo.

WILLIAMS

On the bridge, the captain stared at a small blinking light on one of the many screens encircling the room. The light indicated a radiation leak in the hull surrounding the passenger section.

He tapped a series of commands into the control screen on the arm of his chair, forcing the system to verify the anomaly.

The screen beeped, and the warning light blinked off.

Williams sighed and settled back into his cushioned chair. He was growing weary of false alarms. The ship's computer seemed to be riddled with them recently, forcing him to send the crew on wild goose chases for problems which turned out to be nothing.

He watched the viewscreen as the tail-end of the *Halcyon* emerged from the far side of the Rip. The engines were out, but that always happened during a passage. A welcoming vibration gently shook his chair, then gradually dissipated, as they kicked back on.

It did not escape notice that, as the *Halcyon* passed through the Rip, there were a few moments when a good portion of the vessel was unaccounted for. The ship also reemerged half a mile from where it entered, which made for quite the puzzle — one no scientist on Earth had been able to solve.

Every year or so a new research paper would emerge from the world of academia, professing to have cracked it, yet was inevitably proved untrue by jealous peers.

Some said the ship passed through another dimension to arrive in the neighborhood of Galena. Others said it was torn apart at the molecular level, transported to another spiral arm of the galaxy, then reassembled along with everyone inside.

The captain shrugged off the disturbing thought and resumed his vigilant watch, happier to remain firmly rooted in reality than to ponder such mysteries.

Leave that to the scientists, he thought, *and leave this ship to me.*

PART TWO

BEYOND THE RIP

CHAPTER EIGHT

MERRITT

Soyflower grew in tall stalks, like corn. Each stalk produced multiple flowers each harvest — white blooms with thick, fleshy petals radiating from a sticky, bright red pistil. A rigid, brown tassel hung limp from the top of the thick stalk, growing longer as the season progressed. Broad green leaves with the texture of sandpaper hugged the stalk, browning and peeling as the plant aged to be replaced by fresh growth.

Merritt leaned in close to one of the white blooms and sniffed gently.

Dirt and mushrooms, he thought, sniffing again. *Maybe manure?*

The experience was less than pleasant. He frowned at the thought of an entire field of blooming soyflower. The scent would be overpowering.

A single, dim safety lamp glowed in the dark recesses of the converted gymnasium's high ceiling. It cast the long shadows of soyflower stalks across black soil.

Merritt stood in his designated square patch of soil, admiring the dozen or so chest-high stalks he had managed to coax from their seed pods. All the farmers had managed to grow at least half a dozen stalks of their own, though some were noticeably healthier than others.

Uda required each of them to formulate their own seeding and irrigation patterns. The bulbs in the halogen lamps hanging from the ceiling had been switched out for ones that approximated the light of Phobis, Galena's star.

Merritt walked to Gavin's patch of soil and had to push aside a broad, scratchy leaf as he entered a dense stand of soyflower stalks. Even though the boy was in a hypergel tank, his crop still thrived. Gavin's soyflower stalks a head taller than the rest, with thicker stalks that produced nearly twice as many blooms.

Uda had revealed the reason for this was two-fold. One reason was because the irrigation trenches Gavin had dug with one of his small fingers channeled just the right amount of water to the seeds. The rest of the farmers were sending too much water to the base of the stalks, sogging the roots and stunting their growth. They would still produce under similar circumstances on Galena, said Uda, but the harvest yield would be considerably less.

Gavin had also packed the soil atop his seeds much more loosely than the other farmers. Soyflower rooted quickly, but the roots were initially weak. If they couldn't push through Galena's thick soil, they wouldn't form the root ball necessary for efficient growth.

Merritt smiled to himself as he rubbed a finger over the scratchy surface of a stalk leaf. He had been licked by a cat once, as a child, and he vividly remembered the shudder its sandpaper tongue had sent through his small body.

The door to the gymnasium banged open, startling him. The halogen lamps flicked on, and someone walked briskly across the room, their boots loud on the hard floor.

Merritt pushed his way out of the dense stand of soyflower stalks to find Uda with her back to him, kneeling down beside one of the harrows she had built for the farmers.

This improvised version was little more than a square piece of chain-link fencing attached to a narrow beam. Sharp tines protruded from one side of the fence, used to break up soil clods and cover seeds after planting. Two chains were attached to the beam so the contraption could be pulled by a farmer.

"I *thought* someone else was in here," said Uda. "The air smelled different."

Merritt sniffed the arm of his coveralls. He thought he didn't smell particularly worse than usual.

Uda smiled as she stood up. "That's not what I meant. I was just checking on some things before heading to stasis."

She wore a white T-shirt and faded jeans, along with her perennial hiking boots. Her curly brown hair was down for once, spilling over her shoulders.

"What about the class?" asked Merritt.

"I've taught you what I know. The rest is up to you and the other colonists."

"Don't you want to see Galena?"

She hesitated, then said, "I would prefer to sleep now and wake up back home, in Earth orbit."

"It's okay that I'm in here?"

"As long as you're not poisoning the other farmers' crops." She walked over and stood next to him, at the edge of the small field. "It's remarkable that they're still standing, isn't it?" she asked, nodding toward the stalks.

"Why wouldn't they be?" asked Merritt.

She regarded the plants dreamily.

"When a ship passes through the Rip...plants feel it. At the heart of this vessel, past all the protective shielding, they feel the radiation. That's why all the ones in the atrium are dead. Except for the palms. Those are fake."

"I haven't had the chance to ask how you know sign language," he said.

"I haven't exactly given you the opportunity," she replied. "Two hours a week for classes is about twenty hours too little." She flashed a brief, melancholy smile. "Leaves no room for chit-chat. But to answer your question, I teach sign language to parents all over the world."

"How do you know so much about farming?"

"That would be courtesy of my *other* job. I evaluate genetically modified crops in other nations and offer what help I can to sustain their food supply."

"How's it looking out there, in the wide world?"

Uda hesitated a long time, then said, "Grim."

She rubbed a thick soyflower petal between her thumb and forefinger, then turned toward Merritt. "I was rude to you when we first met, and I never apologized."

"No time for chit-chat, like you said."

"That's not it," she admitted. "When I first saw your boy, it forced me to really think about where you're taking him. It's no place for families. Not yet. What we really know about Galena could fit on a single sheet of paper, yet there are *volumes* to be written."

"Why are you doing this if you don't think we should go?"

"Because you'd go anyway. And if not you, then someone else. I do what I can to prepare you for what lies ahead, but Galena is not what people think." She peeled a dying leaf from a soyflower stalk and held it up to the light, casting a shadow over her face. "It is as powerful and dangerous as the ocean on our own planet, yet taken for granted just as much. A forty foot wave off the coast of South America looks beautiful from a distance, but for the fisherman in a wooden boat at its peak, that wave means death." She dropped the leaf and pushed it into the soil with her boot. "To think you could swim the tide after your boat shatters beneath you is hubris of a mythical kind...yet many still try. It's much the same with colonists. Take childbirth, for example. They think suddenly their reproductive systems will work differently on Galena than they do on Earth. They think it's the *planet's* fault the birthrate is so low. So they pack their bags with false hope and buy a ticket for another world. I've seen it before."

"Where?"

Uda opened her mouth to speak, then quickly shut it with an embarrassed smile. "I'm sorry," she said. "Sometimes I talk too much."

She began slowly walking the perimeter of the small field, inspecting the stalks.

"When did your son lose his speech?" she asked.

"When he was two," Merritt answered, walking at her side. "He was just figuring it out and it was taken away."

"Meningitis?"

He nodded.

"Tell me about him."

Merritt looked at her, surprised.

"If you'd like," she added.

Uda stopped to prune two wilting flowers from a stalk before they walked on.

"Gavin started babbling like crazy at twelve months," said Merritt, a faint smile touching his lips as he remembered. "I thought he'd speak nonsense forever, but at twenty months he started blurting out full sentences." He chuckled, caught up in the memory. "My wife and I used to joke that—"

He cut off suddenly as if he'd been struck, his excitement vanishing in a flash. Merritt swallowed hard and looked down at his trembling hands. He balled them into fists and stuffed them into the pockets of his coveralls.

"Sometimes I wish I never would have heard his sweet little voice," he admitted quietly. "Maybe that would have been better. I know that sounds horrible."

"Actually," said Uda, "you'd be surprised how often parents say that."

Merritt shook his head slowly. "It was just so... *perfect*," he whispered.

"So now you go to Galena to give him a better life. Merritt, look at me." He looked into her eyes, and she said, "I hope you find it."

His wristpad beeped under the left sleeve of his coveralls.

"Alder, it's Willef," said a muffled, gravelly voice. "Meet me up topside. Time to have words with the captain."

"What does he mean by topside?" asked Uda.

"It's what he calls the officer's quarters." Merritt looked at Gavin's crop of soyflower stalks. "Do I need to do anything to those since Gavin's done with the class?" he asked.

Uda shook her head. "Just let them grow."

CHAPTER NINE

MERRITT

The small leather pouch bounced against Merritt's chest under his shirt as he and Willef walked down the long, white hallway leading to the bridge. He unconsciously gave it a squeeze, and tugged on it to feel the cord dig comfortingly into the back of his neck.

"Worst part of my job," Willef grumbled next to him.

He scowled up at the bright lights in the ceiling, squinting and blinking like a hibernating animal seeing the sun for the first time all season.

"A man's a fool if he deals with fools," he spouted.

"What does that make me?" asked Merritt.

"Har!" Willef barked.

He rubbed his eyes with his knuckles. His squat head shook from side to side as he cursed the situation.

They reached the door to the bridge and Willef stopped Merritt by throwing his arm across his path.

"Let me do the talking," he said.

"I don't know why you want me here in the first place," Merritt admitted.

Willef grinned. His broad, lined face curled up

at the edges, like someone lifting the sides of a stack of pancakes.

"Misery loves company," he said.

He took another step and the doors whooshed open.

Merritt felt as if he'd just entered a museum. The equipment within the room was old, but in good repair. Every polished surface shone in moody pockets of light, the space between each station pleasantly dark.

The far wall of the circular room was a single long screen, segmented by various windows filled with data streams and security camera feeds.

The captain's chair swiveled around and the man occupying it stood up briskly.

"Foreman," he called out stiffly.

"Evenin', Cap," said Willef.

He and Merritt crossed the quiet room and stood before the captain, who regarded Merritt with an arched eyebrow.

"New this tour?" he asked.

"Yes," Merritt replied.

Willef elbowed him.

"Yes, sir."

The captain turned his attention back to Willef. "What can I help you with, Foreman?"

"Well, Cap'n Williams, I know you're busy, so I'll get right down to it. I think we should add all those spare escape modules to the hypergel tanks. They're already set in the launch tubes, after all."

"That goes against regulations when carrying

so few passengers, as you well know," said Captain Williams.

"Yes, sir. I also know that most of the passengers don't have red tickets. The internal hull breach that occurred passing through the Rip is flooding the pod chamber at the back of Deck 2. Those are all blue ticket escape pods, sir."

"I know the layout of my ship, Foreman," Williams said haughtily. "The system didn't register a hull breach. Did you visually confirm it?"

"The lattice chamber is flooded with radiation, sir," Willef said, grinding his teeth.

"I thought the Magellan suits were designed for such environments."

"Normally, yes. But as I said, the breach is letting extra rads into the chamber." He glanced sideways at Merritt, as if to say, *Can you believe this guy?* "Passengers can't access any other escape pod without a red ticket. It would be prudent to add escape pod capability to the hypergel tanks. It is my firm belief that there is something wrong with this ship. *Sir.*"

"Foreman," said Williams, straightening his back, "under no circumstances will you disobey regulations. Is that clear? I have personally investigated the infrequent shudders afflicting this ship, as per your request. The survey teams found nothing out of the ordinary. Engine diagnostics report no errors. If the system isn't registering any problems, and you can't confirm their existence, then there are none. Bring me evidence and I'll review the facts at that time."

"I could bring you the facts," Willef said through clenched teeth, "if you let me do my job."

"Is that so? If you find yourself unable to handle the stress of your duties, Foreman, I will happily find someone to replace you. Life is too short to spend it in a constant state of dismay, wouldn't you agree? Dismissed."

He turned around and sat in his chair. Pushing a button on his armrest, he called for a cup of black tea, no sugar.

Willef stomped out of the room, indifferent to the general air of quietude, Merritt following close behind.

When they were out in the hallway and the doors had closed behind him, Willef pounded the wall with his fist.

"We're doing it anyway," he said, fuming. Then he jabbed a finger toward the bridge. "How that boy scout ever got command of a ship like this boggles my mind."

"Won't the captain know?" asked Merritt.

"What do I care?!" Willef shouted, throwing up his hands. "Can't kick us off the ship. Let's go."

A swipe of Willef's foreman's badge got them into a crew elevator at the end of the hall. They floated up into the air as they entered, grabbing chromed hand-holds to pull themselves all the way in.

The elevator jerked sideways after Willef punched in the code for the stasis room. It ran parallel to the hallway, then stopped abruptly and began its descent to the bottom of the ship's habitable section.

"The problem with these bureaucratic types," Willef mused as the pair of them floated in zero gravity, "is that they can't think outside the box. Everything is regulation *this* and regulation *that*. That imbecile wouldn't know a hull breach if one split the wall screen in front of him."

Merritt rode in silence, firmly gripping two hand-holds to keep from bumping into the walls.

"Take these elevators, for example," Willef continued. "All of 'em shut down if there's an emergency. But what if it ain't a fire, or a *total* hull breach? What if it's just a rad leak in a passenger's stateroom? What if some guy has a heart attack and his wife punches the alarm? Wouldn't you want to use the elevators?"

He stared at Merritt, seemingly intent on getting a response.

"Sure," said Merritt when he realized he should say something.

"Absolutely!" Willef shouted triumphantly. "But try to tell it to the guy in the big chair and he threatens to take your job away." He looked at Merritt sharply. "Did you test the black boxes like I asked you?"

Merritt nodded. "All of them are recording. I couldn't test the nav beacons, though."

"They're on a closed system, linked to the colony beacon. Was there a blinking red light?"

"No."

"Then it's picking up the colony's signal. That's good enough."

The elevator gradually slowed to a stop. When the door opened, Merritt dropped out of zero-g onto the floor of the hallway, his stomach dropping a moment later, sending a wave of nausea rolling up his throat. He swallowed hard.

"Gets me every time, too," said Willef. He slapped Merritt on the shoulder and headed for the stasis room. "Come on, let's get this over with."

Just off the entrance to the stasis room was another door that led to a room filled with boxes, each as tall as Merritt. They were stacked vertically, three-high, and filled the room almost to the door.

"I always wondered what these were for," he said.

Willef grunted as he grabbed a hand truck and tipped a box onto it.

"Mystery solved," he said. "Best thing about using the hypergel tanks for escape pods is they don't have ticket restrictions if everything goes south. I never understood why they labeled them in the first place."

"Need a reason to sell more red tickets," said Merritt, straining as he tilted a box onto a hand truck.

"Probably. Just wish the equipment foreman could locate the nav beacons for the gel tanks. He can't *find* 'em, or so he says. Guy couldn't find his own face if he had ten hands, if you ask me."

"I've been down to the storage warehouse," said Merritt. "It's a disaster."

Willef chuckled. "Ain't *that* the truth. Well, I guess there's a bright side. At least we don't have to install impact foam canisters on the gel tanks like we do with the escape pods. Those weigh a ton."

"Is the foam stronger than hypergel?"

"It's solid once it expands inside the pod. Fills up like *that*," he said, snapping his fingers, "right before the pod hits the surface. Heaven help you if the hatch don't open, 'cause the only way you're gettin' through that foam is with an industrial roto-saw." He wheeled his cart around and pushed it out the door. "We'll start with your boy's tank first, then install them in the other tanks."

"Do you really think things are that bad?" asked Merritt.

Willef paused in his struggle to lift another box onto the hand truck.

"It almost never goes bad," he said seriously. Then he held up the index finger of his left hand — the hand with missing ring and pinky fingers. "But sometimes, *just* sometimes, it does."

TULLIVER

TWO MONTHS LATER

The promenade on Deck 5 was emptier than usual.

Between the passengers who opted for a tank full of gel to the ones who kept to themselves, the place was all but deserted.

Tulliver didn't mind.

His bar still saw enough action, and the lack of prying eyes made it easier to do business. He and Ivan were in a dark corner of the promenade, convincing a reluctant passenger that doing business was in his best interest.

Ivan held the man up by his neck, feet kicking against Ivan's shins as he struggled for a breath. Tulliver was impressed by Ivan's strength, but what he appreciated more was the fact he didn't see it coming.

At a quick glance, Ivan was skin and bones. Clothes meant for someone his height were invariably baggy on his wiry frame, yet he possessed an animalistic power that was on full display in that moment. His eyes bulged with anger. The tendons in his neck stood out in thick cords. A vein bulged in his forehead.

All because he was told this passenger wanted

to hurt Tulliver.

The man gagged and spat as he tried to speak, clawing impotently at Ivan's hands.

Tulliver rested his hand on Ivan's shoulder, guiding him to lower the man's feet to the floor.

"What's that you say, friend?" asked Tulliver, cupping a hand to his own ear.

The man sucked in a breath, then coughed it back out. A thick sheen of sweat covered his ghost-white face. Wet curls of dark hair plastered his brow.

"I—I told you I don't have it," he croaked, wincing as he rubbed his red throat.

"I heard you the first time. I just didn't believe it." Tulliver's eyes gleamed as if he were looking into the pit of the other man's soul. "But now?" he added thoughtfully. "*Now* I believe you. Ivan, make sure he never forgets that there are consequences for his actions. He made two promises he couldn't keep, so take two fingers as payment."

"*Nnnno!*" the man yelled, launching himself from the wall.

Ivan caught him by the throat and slammed him back. Tulliver handed him a pair of wire cutters, and Ivan stared at then dumbly.

"Snip, snip," said Tulliver, making cutting motions with his fingers.

Ivan swallowed hard and looked from the cutters to the passenger, who had gone still, eyeing the cutters with dread.

"Go ahead," urged Tulliver.

Ivan's hand began to shake. His mouth worked as he tried to speak, but all that came out was a whimper. He looked at Tulliver helplessly.

"That's alright, that's alright," Tulliver said soothingly. He gently took the wire cutters and rubbed the back of Ivan's neck. "I know it's the first time I asked you to do something like that. We'll try again next time, okay? We need to be ready for Galena, and life down there will be a lot harder than it is here."

Ivan sighed with relief as Tulliver grabbed the man's neck. He covered most of it with his large palm, whereas Ivan needed both hands to maintain a strong grasp.

"Look away now, Ivan," said Tulliver, as if speaking to a child.

Later, in the bar, Ivan looked surprised when Tulliver tossed a red ticket onto the table in front of him.

"Took longer than I'd hoped," Tulliver admitted. He wiped his hands with a white napkin. "Now we'll *both* live like kings."

Ivan gingerly picked up the ticket with etched red lettering, smiling dreamily, his wide eyes absorbing every detail of the translucent plastic rectangle.

Tulliver patted his shoulder as he walked away, leaving him to his reverie.

A sense of foreboding had settled on Tulliver's shoulders in recent days. He attempted to slough it off as he slid into his booth at the back of the bar, intent on enjoying a tender soy steak and a glass of wine, yet the feeling would not be dismissed.

It was the disquiet of knowing his current situation would not last forever.

Tulliver was pleased with what he'd built for himself in such a short time. To anyone that asked, he could proudly say he was sitting in *his* bar, a hellocard full to bursting, debts and favors owed to him from all corners of the ship.

It was a small empire, he admitted, but an empire nonetheless. Yet when the ship arrived at Galena, he would have to rebuild some of it from scratch. The debts and favors would carry down to the surface, providing the foundation for his *new* empire, yet he would still need to find a way to operate outside the warden's jurisdiction.

He picked up his tablet and scanned through the articles in the ship's archives pertaining to the colony. He'd read each one twice already, and others more than that. Tulliver paid particularly close attention to the information regarding colony administration. Two wardens were to go down with the colonists as government representatives. They were to manage crop payment and storage, colony safety, and regulations.

Tulliver was browsing an article about irrigation when Ivan brought his steak and wine.

"Why you always read that stuff, boss?" asked Ivan.

Tulliver picked up his knife and fork and sawed off a large chunk of steak.

"Because knowledge is power."

Ivan shook his head. "Strength is power." Then he grinned, showing crooked teeth. "Why you think I work for you?"

"I'd hoped it was because I was your friend."

"But if I had these strength, I don't need friends!" He curled his arms in a bodybuilder's pose, then bent over laughing and slapped his knee.

Tulliver popped the chunk of steak into his mouth and chewed thoughtfully.

"Your English is improving," he said. "I'm not sure I like that."

Ivan walked away, tapping his new red ticket against the palm of his hand, whistling happily.

As Tulliver cut off massive pieces of the fake meat and chewed with his mouth open, smacking his lips with each bite, he puzzled over the conundrum plaguing him lately.

How will I get down to the surface?

So far, his attempts to acquire a genuine authorized pass had been for naught. The farmers could go, and so could the administrators and that group of scientists. Yet tourists weren't allowed to visit the planet. The red ticket he had stolen from the businessman on Sunrise Station was meant for Mars. It would be immediately flagged if he tried to use it to board the shuttle for Galena.

He chuckled to himself as he remembered when two of the ship's stewards had come knocking on his stateroom door after the *Halcyon* departed the space station orbiting Mars.

They were tired, bored, and, best of all, indifferent.

Instead of showing them his ticket as requested, Tulliver managed to twist the situation to his advantage. By the time the stewards left, they each had promised to pay him ten thousand in exchange for more favorable work shifts — a deal he knew he could secure based on his relationship with the shift operator, who still owed him thirty thousand.

Tulliver loved vice. It made his world go 'round.

Drop me in a tank, he thought as he took another bite of soy steak, *and watch me grow.*

Shifting focus to something a bit more positive, he amused himself by daydreaming about the grand new life that awaited him once he successfully arrived on the surface. Perhaps he could find a hill to build his house upon, a hill that overlooked the other farms.

Next he ought to see about a house, he presumed. One of the workman had showed him where the build-it-yourself kits were stored on board. They would be tucked into the surface shuttle's cargo hold to join the other kits that were remote-delivered to the colony site on past visits.

Tulliver had to hand it to the government for managing to squeeze extra money from the hopeful colonists. Not only did Cygnus Corporation drain their bank accounts with the cost of a ticket to Galena, the government scraped the accounts clean by selling clapboard homes it should be providing for free.

Everyone's gotta eat, thought Tulliver as he bit a chunk of meat from his fork. *The trick is to get in good with the people offering the food.*

Up there, on the ship, Tulliver did it by *being* the person offering the food. He filled in the blanks, got the people what they needed, or what they *thought* they needed. Down on the surface? The crop debt some of the farmers had racked up with him would carry him through the first harvest. After that, he would need to find a new way to thrive.

Who knows? he thought with a wet grin. *Maybe I could be mayor.*

The thought cheered him up.

"Bartee!" he called. "Loud music."

The robot bartender paused while dusting a row of liquor bottles behind the bar. It cocked its head and the lights of its eyes blinked rapidly. A moment later, bass-driven, thumping dance music blared from the ceiling. The room dimmed and multicolored spotlights painted the walls.

"Louder!" shouted Tulliver.

He raised his wine glass to his lips as the music swelled, and he grinned in the shadows of his booth.

CHAPTER TEN

MERRITT

The grated floor of the stasis room shuddered under Merritt's work boots, rattling in its setting.

Tremors had coursed through the bones of the ship with disturbing regularity, the first one occurring a month ago. Now that the *Halcyon* was performing its braking maneuvers to enter the orbit of Galena, they happened once an hour.

Merritt slid the sole of his boot over the floor uncertainly as the tremor subsided. The lattice chamber remained sealed to investigation due to unusually high levels of radiation, though Willef was certain panel Y-27 had caused a serious problem.

The proof was in the shaking, he said.

The only time one ought to feel the floor of a starliner shudder in such a way was under abnormal engine duress. One of the hybrid antimatter drives was working too hard, he claimed.

Gavin floated in his hypergel tank, curled up in a fetal position. The gel had formed a thin crust over his skin, encasing him in a thin cocoon. Tiny cracks ran throughout the mass of gel, like a network of synapses — indications that its texture had changed. Merritt had learned that, while the gel was a thick, viscous fluid on its own, it hardened when it came into contact with human skin, forming a protective shell around the person in stasis. It took on the density of hard rubber — still pliable, but only just.

The countdown timer on the info screen next to Gavin's tank hit zero. Merritt checked his own watch: less than an hour until the ship was officially in orbit around Galena.

The tank beeped, and the curved plexi doors swung open. A loud hiss escaped from the back of the pod, and the mass of pinkish gel within sagged noticeably. Gavin sank a few inches as the gel oozed down to the floor, dripping through the metal grate.

Merritt caught him as he rolled out of the tank, smearing his grease-stained coveralls with the pink gel. He wrapped his son in a thick green towel and held him upright as he pulled off the oxygen mask and wiped gel from his face.

Gavin's eyes fluttered open slowly, rolling in their sockets.

Merritt rubbed his upper arms with the towel to get the blood flowing. Gavin eventually emerged from his fog and saw his father.

"Welcome back," said Merritt. "Do you feel sick?"

The boy sniffed and wiped his nose with his forearm. He shook his head and looked down the row of tanks.

You woke me early, he signed with shaking hands.

I missed you, Merritt signed back. *And I wanted you to see something.*

What about them?

They'll be out in a few hours.

Gavin looked at the woman floating in the tank next to his. Ear-length brown hair, shot through with silver, occluded her face.

I had a dream, Gavin signed.

A nightmare?

Gavin shook his head. He seemed content not to share more.

"Let's get you cleaned up, get some food in you," said Merritt.

After his shower, the two of them went to the galley. As each step took them closer, Gavin's eyes sank lower, until he stared at his plodding feet, limply holding his father's hand while mentally preparing himself for a meal that would make his stomach cramp with sharp pains.

They found themselves alone in the galley. All of the other passengers were gathered in the observation lounge or, like the crew, preparing for the upcoming exodus.

Merritt sat Gavin at one of the long metal tables, looking slightly refreshed in a clean white shirt and dark blue slacks. The boy watched him cross the room with dismay, but, instead of dispensing a bowl full of soy mush from a wall nozzle, his father opened a cabinet beneath the nozzle and pulled out five crinkling, colorful packages.

Gavin sat upright when he heard the noise, stretching his neck to see what his father carried.

Merritt dumped the noisy bags on the table in

front of his son: potato chips, flavored popcorn, sunflower seeds, and bite-sized chocolate chip cookies — all of them without a trace of soy.

Gavin picked up the cookies first, gently pulling open the bag and peering inside, as if he expected the contents to evaporate at any moment.

Merritt sat opposite him, a small smile on his face, watching him eat. It had taken him nearly the entire time his son was in stasis to procure those five bags. Some were obtained more easily than others. He still owed two other farmers a reasonable portion of his second and third harvests on Galena in exchange for the popcorn and sunflower seeds, foods which could typically only be purchased by traveling to one of Earth's few orbital hydroponic farms.

After the third cookie, the boy's face twisted, and he started to cry.

Merritt came around to the other side of the table and rubbed his back.

"I know," he whispered. "I know."

After a few heavy sobs, Gavin sniffled and ate another cookie. His eyes were red and swollen, his cheeks wet with tears. Merritt squeezed his shoulder, and Gavin nodded that he was alright.

It took him twenty minutes to empty each bag, then turn them inside-out, hunting for crumbs.

They walked to the observation lounge, passing several other workmen on the way who were hurrying to their next job. Merritt's list of tasks grew daily the closer the ship came to Galena. It was the same for all the workmen. In the days before arrival, he was pulling ten-hour shifts with four-hour breaks in between.

Merritt hadn't seen many starliner stewards walking the halls in the past month. They maintained a help desk where passengers could go for information about the voyage, but their interactions with quests were few and far between. Perhaps, thought Merritt, they were close enough to the end of their duties regarding the passengers that they had given up all pretenses of professionalism.

The observation lounge was lit by the glow of Galena on the wall screen, a bright orb reflecting the light of its yellow star, Phobis.

Brilliant white clouds swirled in the atmosphere over vivid blue oceans and green continents — reminiscent of Earth decades ago.

Merritt navigated through the standing passengers, who stood watching the rotating planet in awe. He dropped to one knee on the carpeted floor at the front of the group and set Gavin on his leg.

"*Welcome to Galena,*" said an artificial female voice over the ship's intercom system. "*Shuttle departure begins in ONE... HOUR... FIFTEEN... MINUTES. Please have your tickets ready.*"

"Look there," said Merritt, pointing at the screen. Five long fingers of land descended from a massive continent, curling upward in gentle arcs next to each other, like nested half-moons. "And there," said Merritt, pointing elsewhere. Mountains topped by muddy brown peaks formed a vast range that divided one continent.

"The Tolbard Range," said a man standing nearby. "Named after the explorer who correctly stated they were *mountains*, and not craters, as previously thought. He won an award for it, I believe."

Gavin hopped down from his father's knee. The man who spoke was the same height as Merritt, eyes such a deep brown they were nearly black, and a stained white beard. A band of off-white hair encircled the back of his head, having successfully retreated from the top, leaving behind a pate of sun-worn skin. He held a wide-brimmed hat in one hand, casually tapping it against his thigh.

"How does an explorer get that close?" asked Merritt.

"He bribes members of the crew for surface scans," the man replied. His dark eyes gleamed with amusement as he looked down at Gavin.

"I'm Henry Tolbard," he said, holding out his hand.

Gavin took it and shook, smiling broadly. Henry laughed with delight and wiped the corner of his eye.

"It should be such a simple thing, to see a child," he said softly.

"You built Haven," said Merritt, shocked to realize he was talking to the person most responsible for the existence of the moon's second luxury city.

"Shhhh," said Henry, waving him down. "In another life, yes. Most of that was my wife's doing, to be honest, but she couldn't stand the press. In this life, I'm just an explorer, going where the winds take me. So far, they've brought me to Galena every time humans have been allowed through the Rip."

"You don't use stasis?"

"Of course I do! I pop out for the Rip passage, then go right back in as soon as the gel is out of my system. Too fast and the kidneys shut down. I've seen that happen." He shook his head sadly, then sighed. "My body is purging more slowly with increased use, it would seem, so I have to wait two weeks now outside the tank instead of just one. But, extending my life a few months each voyage is an added benefit of traveling to Galena."

"I thought that wasn't true."

Henry smiled. "It's working so far." He turned his attention back to the screen. "A whole new world to explore. Just imagine."

"So now you're turning farmer?" asked Merritt.

"Heavens, no. My back would never allow it."

"But tourists aren't allowed on the surface."

Henry frowned.

"Neither are explorers," Merritt quickly added.

"Well..." Henry said thoughtfully, "rules change." He sighed wistfully as he gazed upon the wall screen. "I always come out of the tank early to see it. I take it you're enrolled in the farming initiative."

"That's right."

"We can't see the colony site in a prograde orbit," said Henry. "The shuttle will carry you east, over that horizon. The government chose a small continent sandwiched between two larger ones for the colony. Oceans border the north and south sides, and there are narrow seas to east and west. Lots of water," he said, shaking his head and smiling. "More than Earth, if you can believe it."

A shudder rocked the lounge, eliciting surprised gasps from the passengers.

"They're getting worse," said Henry, looking up at the ceiling.

The floor shook, sending a few passengers stumbling sideways.

The screen went black, plunging the room into darkness, and a woman said, "Oh!" in surprise.

Red lights in the ceiling flicked on, casting their sickening glow upon the passengers. Merritt bent down and picked up Gavin, an uneasy feeling swelling in his gut.

"*ATTENTION,*" said the ship's artificial female voice. "*This is an emergency. Please move to the nearest escape pod. Red tickets, Deck 3 forward, Deck 4 forward, Deck 6 forward. Blue tickets, Deck 2 aft. REPEAT, this is an emergency.*"

Nobody moved. The passengers stood in the lounge, staring at each other while their brains struggled to process the message.

The floor began to shake, and it didn't stop.

Someone screamed, and suddenly there was a mass of bodies rushing out the door. Merritt hugged Gavin close and stood against the wall, breathing hard.

"*This is an emergency,*" repeated the ship's announcer. “*Please move to the nearest escape pod.*”

“Where’s your ticket?” Merritt said loudly over the rattle of glass in the lounge.

Gavin pulled his red ticket out of his back pocket.

Merritt kissed the side of his head and said, “Smart boy. Hold on tight.”

Then, with the walls of the ship shaking around him, he ran.

TULLIVER

Tulliver paused with his fork halfway to his lips, a wet chunk of soy steak dripping from its tines.

A second person had just run past the The Velvet Speakeasy.

The first — a short man with long hair — barreled past at breakneck speed, a look of wild terror on his face. Tulliver paid him no mind. He was used to chasing people himself, and for that to happen, one needed someone to chase.

Yet the second runner came far too late to be chasing after the first.

Tulliver lowered his fork and got out of the booth. Thumping dance music blared from the ceiling, synchronized with the frenetic, colorful spotlights zooming over every surface. He wiped the corners of his mouth with his stained napkin and threw the napkin on his plate.

He shouted at Ivan, the bar's only other occupant, but Ivan didn't hear. Tulliver banged his fist on the bar and pointed up at the ceiling speakers. Bartee cocked its head and the music cut off instantly, leaving behind a lingering echo that quickly faded.

"*—an emergency,*" said a computerized female voice. "*Please move to the nearest escape pod.*"

"What's that about?" Tulliver asked, glaring at Bartee.

The robot shrugged.

Tulliver walked to the entrance, growing increasingly wary with each step. He entered the promenade. Red lights glowed in the high ceiling.

Someone ran past him. Tulliver's hand shot out and grabbed the runner's collar. The man gagged as his feet left the ground and slammed back down, his momentum suddenly neutralized.

"What's happening?" Tulliver growled, pulling the man's face close to his.

"Emergency!" the man squealed, pushing at Tulliver's sweaty hands. "Gotta get to the escape pods!"

"*Why?!*"

The man shoved away and slipped from Tulliver's grasp. He hit the floor hard, then scrambled to his feet and kept running.

Too fast, thought Tulliver. *Happening too fast. I need more time.*

He patted the many pockets of his overlarge jacket.

He didn't have a ticket. One needed a ticket to enter an escape pod.

In his mind, he saw the corner of it sticking out from the dresser drawer in his stateroom, where it had resided now for weeks, useless to him for the remainder of the voyage.

Until now.

The promenade occupied much of Deck 5, he remembered. The Velvet Speakeasy was located halfway from midship to the nose, which meant Tulliver had quite a jog ahead of him to retrieve his ticket from his aft stateroom on Deck 2. Then it was another hike back to the red ticket pods at the front of the ship.

Yet again he was grateful for the steady stream of information that flowed through the bar. Mere days ago, he had learned from a drunken workman that the chamber containing the blue pods was flooded with radiation. One could brave the exposure to reach a pod, but the heavy dose of rads would most certainly kill them. The crew had been working on a way to flush the chamber, said the workman, but dismissed all of the current options as impossible when Tulliver pressed him for details.

Ivan stood at the bar's entrance. Tulliver beckoned him to follow as he walked briskly down the promenade.

Within The Velvet Speakeasy, Bartee raised a lonely, mechanical hand, and waved.

Tulliver put his hand on the back of Ivan's neck and gave it a gentle squeeze.

"I'm gonna need your ticket, my friend," he said, massaging Ivan's neck.

Ivan looked up at him, at first confused, then frightened, then defiant in rapid succession. He shook his head, no.

"Now don't be like that," said Tulliver soothingly. "There's another one in my room. You can get there faster than me, can't you? Sure you can. You're a runner. I'd just trip over myself the whole way.

You'll be just fine. But you should hurry."

He reached for Ivan's pocket.

Ivan pushed against Tulliver's broad chest, but Tulliver's grip tightened like a vice around the back of his neck. He drove his fist into Ivan's stomach and pushed him down.

"It doesn't have to go this way," said Tulliver through clenched teeth.

A distant cousin to regret teased the edge of his emotion, then vanished when Ivan tried to twist away. Tulliver kicked his legs out from under him and cracked his head against the hard floor. Ivan rolled onto his back, eyes glazed over, looking up without seeing. A thin trickle of blood ran from his head, threading across the floor like a tiny river.

Tulliver knelt down and dug through his pockets. After finding the red ticket, he pushed against Ivan's chest to stand up, eliciting a weak groan.

"*ATTENTION*," said the ship's announcer. "*Situation critical. Evacuate. Evacuate.*"

To drive the point home, the *Halcyon* lurched sideways. Tulliver stumbled, putting out his hands for support as he smacked face-first onto the floor.

Ivan was suddenly upon him, clawing at his back like a crazed animal. Tulliver got his hands beneath himself and shoved off the floor...and kept rising, up and up, as the GravGen units in the promenade failed. Ivan had been thrown off Tulliver's back, but he never hit the floor. He let out a terrified yelp and tumbled end over end in slow motion, rising toward the high, arched ceiling.

Tulliver's arms pinwheeled as he tried to stabilize himself in midair, to no effect. He drifted a meter above the floor...heading in the opposite direction of the red escape pods.

His jacket billowed around him like a balloon, blocking his vision. His knees gently knocked against a decorative pillar near one of the promenade's many seating areas. Tulliver grabbed it and gave it a bear hug, pressing his quivering cheek against its cold surface.

Looking farther down the promenade, in the direction of the escape pods, the pathway was cluttered with floating debris. Empty planters, benches, and garbage cans bumped into each other in zero gravity, creating a shifting obstacle course.

Tulliver looked up.

The ceiling of the promenade was arched glass, supported by a grid of metal beams.

He drifted up to the top of the pillar and held on to the sharp edges of its square capital at the top, then pushed off and floated toward the ceiling.

Tulliver reached for a metal crossbeam, and missed, instead hitting the center of one of the tinted-blue glass panes. He started to drift away, but managed to grasp a metal beam and pull himself flat against the ceiling.

After stabilizing, he used the beam to pull himself forward. Tulliver's back was to the floor, his stomach a few inches from the ceiling. His reflection in the glass before him wavered as if he were looking at himself underwater.

He craned his neck to look at the floor, and the thought of gravity returning to the ship seized his mind, and he began to shake. There were no handholds in the ceiling. The metal beams supporting the glass arch were perfectly smooth. If the GravGens suddenly reactivated, he would fall four stories to the hard floor.

He pushed off the next beam, gaining speed, tapping each beam as he floated past. He was soon flying faster than he could have run.

The promenade ceiling tapered down to form a large hallway which led to the forward decks. Tulliver kicked off the next beam, angled toward the hallway. He soared through the opening and hit the floor, growling in anger as he tumbled past an elevator.

Grabbing hold of a light fixture as he bounced against the wall, he pulled himself back to the elevator door. Small words backlit in red glowed next to the control panel: OUT OF SERVICE.

Tulliver's curses would have blushed the cheeks of the *Halcyon*'s most hardened sailor.

Glass shattered behind him.

Tulliver maneuvered to the hallway opening and looked back at the promenade. The arched glass ceiling was cracked. Spears of broken glass tumbled and glittered in the air.

Flame belched through the cracks and Tulliver instinctively jerked back. The light fixture he clung to vibrated in his grasp.

Amidst an eruption of glass shrapnel, fire exploded down from the ceiling, licking the air of the promenade before vanishing almost instantly. A section of wall between two shops cracked apart. The lightning-bolt crack ran up the wall, crawling toward the ceiling.

Tulliver turned around and left the promenade behind, refusing to look back as more explosions rent the air.

Sweat poured down his face in streams. His eyes were frozen open, wide with fear.

Decks 3, 4, 6, he kept repeating in his mind.

The promenade was on Deck 5.

He found the nearest stairwell and drifted upward, holding the handrail for support.

Emerging on Deck 4, he was greeted by a blast of hot air which flapped his jacket and cheeks. Tulliver blinked away the sting and stared into a wall of liquid flame.

He retreated, moving quickly up the stairwell to pull open the door to Deck 3.

There was no fire here...yet.

He kicked off the door frame and drifted down the red, carpeted hallway. A black door on his left opened onto an unexpectedly industrial hallway that seemed more like a utility room than something meant for passengers to see.

As Tulliver entered the long, dark hallway, he reflected that, in the event passengers *would* see this section, their situation would be so bad the aesthetics wouldn't matter.

Steam hissed from pipes near the ceiling of the long, dark hallway. Rust covered much of the grated metal floor. Thick metal hatches, like small bank vault doors, lined one wall. Tulliver drifted to the first metal door, but could find no way to open it. Then he saw two thin rectangles embedded in the wall above a control screen. The red rectangle glowed brightly, but the green was dim.

Tulliver tried the next door, but found another red rectangle.

He soared down the hallway, gaze flicking to the side at each hatch, finding only red lights.

The walls shook around him, blurring as he watched, before gradually smoothing out again.

He burst through a wall of swirling steam and collided with another passenger. The impact spun him sideways, into the wall, where his head cracked against a metal pipe and everything went dark.

MERRITT

Merritt drifted into the industrial escape pod section on Deck 3, Gavin clinging painfully to his neck.

Gravity had given out as Merritt followed the mass of passengers flooding out of the observation lounge. Screaming and flailing, their momentum carried them out of a short hallway and into the atrium, where they bumped into planters and tumbled upward. Some managed to grab hold of palm fronds, which wavered in zero gravity as if floating underwater. Most bumped into the domed ceiling, collecting in a clump, like debris on a storm drain.

Merritt stayed low, grasping the leg of a secured bench, then working his way across the floor of the atrium with one hand, holding Gavin with the other.

Making it to the aft section of Deck 3 hadn't been too difficult, but the explosions that seemed to follow them through the ship had Gavin shaking like a leaf in a storm. The boy trembled as he clung to Merritt, teary eyes buried in his father's neck.

There were fifty escape pods on Deck 3, Merritt knew. He drifted down the long hallway, steam hissing at him from cracked pipes, searching for a pod with a green light.

He reached the fourth pod from the end, the first one to show green. With a quick glance, he saw that only two of the remaining pods beyond it hadn't been claimed.

Merritt dug Gavin's red ticket out of his own pocket and swiped it across the pod's control screen. The green light blinked off and the metal hatch swung open. Merritt waited anxiously, glancing back down the hallway as a distant explosion shook the walls and rattled the grated floor.

Gavin whimpered and Merritt kissed the top of his head.

The pod's black, curved hatch slid up with agonizing slowness. Merritt stared at the small space within, stricken dumb by the minuscule size of the padded compartment.

He pried Gavin's arms from his neck as he drifted into the pod, turning so his back was against the padding. The compartment was barely large enough to contain a single adult, so he turned slightly on his side to wedge Gavin next to him.

Merritt slapped the rectangular yellow button by the hatch and a shrill beep chirped above him. He looked up at a flashing yellow screen which read ONE PASSENGER ONLY.

Merritt pounded the yellow button with his fist, but the hatch wouldn't close.

Another explosion shook the walls of the ship.

Merritt's lower lip trembled as he drifted out of the pod. He turned to push Gavin back inside. The boy had grabbed a fistful of his father's coveralls and followed after him.

No no no, the boy signed rapidly with a shaking hand.

Merritt yanked the small leather pouch he wore around his neck, snapping the cord. He pressed the seed pouch into Gavin's small hands as the boy tried to sign *Daddy, no, I'm scared—*

He held Gavin against the back wall of the escape pod and said, "I love you."

He pushed the yellow button and the pod's hatch slid shut.

The metal outer hatch swung into place. There was a loud clunk from within the wall, and a fast *whoosh* as the pod launched.

For Merritt, floating in the hallway, time froze.

The rest of the ship seemed to disappear around him as he stared at the center of the metal hatch as if in a trance, eyes wide in disbelief.

An alarm klaxon blared, like an air raid siren, swelling to a shrill peak before clipping off.

Merritt snapped back to reality. He grabbed a hand-hold in the wall and pulled himself to one of the other available pods, swiping his blue card over the control screen. A warning screen flashed, alerting him he was unauthorized to enter.

He got the same result at the other pod.

It would be the same story on Decks 4 and 6, he knew. All of those pods were coded for red ticket passengers.

As he hurried back down the hallway, pulling himself along a pipe on the ceiling, a sudden burst of steam exploded ahead, forcing him to push off toward the center of the hall. He shot through the wall of steam and crashed head-first into someone else.

The other passenger rolled away and smacked his head against a pipe. Merritt held on to the wall and rubbed his own forehead, wincing in pain.

It was Tulliver.

The first thing Merritt noticed about him — after the bloody scratch on top of his bald head — was the corner of his red ticket sticking out of a jacket pocket.

Tulliver was unconscious. Steam roiled around his body, licking at his skin like gray flames. He twitched, then blinked hard. His eyes swiveled in their sockets as he tried to regain his bearings.

Merritt drifted closer, hand reaching out for the ticket. When he was inches away, a small locket attached to a thin gold chain around Tulliver's neck floated in front of the ticket. The open locket showed a picture of a young girl on one side and a young woman with long blonde hair on the other.

Merritt's reaching hand closed into a fist. He kicked off the wall, leaving Tulliver behind.

When he reached the exit door, he turned to look back. Tulliver disappeared into one of the pods at the very end of the hall.

The alarm klaxon persisted, flooding the corridors of the *Halcyon* with its ear-splitting shrill as Merritt made his way toward the middle of the ship.

Two decks down from there and a short ways down the hall, and he'd be at the stasis room.

He descended a stairwell to Deck 6 and hurried down the carpeted hallway leading toward the middle of the ship. The soft up-lighting that usually filled the hallway with a warm glow had been replaced with the harsh red pulsing of swiveling emergency lamps.

Merritt paused at the door to the stasis room, hearing someone calling from down the hall.

Willef drifted into view, leading a group of nearly a dozen passengers and crew members. Several of them wore the streamlined emergency suits stowed in small numbers around the ship.

Like Merritt, the foreman still wore his grease-covered blue coveralls.

A sustained rumble shook the ceiling. With a sudden crack, it split open above Willef's group... and continued to split wider. The crack reached the walls and ripped down them like lightning to the ground.

"We're going to the officers' pods!" Willef shouted over the noise.

Merritt turned to look toward the front of the ship. The hallway in that direction was dark. A single, dim lamp flickered in the distance.

Willef reached the door to the stasis room. He grabbed a hand-hold in the wall and bumped to a hard stop.

"Use the hypergel tanks!" Merritt shouted.

Flames exploded down from the widening crack in the ceiling. Several passengers screamed. Merritt noticed Ivan at the back of the crowd, looking behind in terror.

"They never gave us nav beacons for the gel tanks!" Willef cried. His eyes, usually squinting and observant, were wide and bloodshot. "I'm not landing in some ocean!"

"You won't make it past the security doors!"

Willef jabbed a thumb behind him, at one member of his group. "Jenkins is an officer." Jenkins held up his officer's badge — a master key to unlock any door on the ship. "Once we're past the gates," said Willef, "the pods don't have any restrictions."

"Neither do the hypergel tanks in an emergency! You told me that yourself!"

As another explosion of flame burst from the ceiling, Willef shook his head firmly and pushed off the wall. Merritt grabbed his forearm, forcing him to spin around.

"You don't have time!" said Merritt. "It will take you ten minutes to reach those pods."

"Less if we stop yappin'. Come with us!"

Merritt looked at the frightened group of people behind the foreman.

"We can use the hypergel tanks to reach the surface!" he shouted at them.

Willef peeled Merritt's fingers off his arm and pushed away. "I am the foreman of this ship, and I'm going to the colony!" he yelled, moving down the hallway.

Every member of the group but one followed after him. Some glanced at Merritt as they drifted past, too afraid to speak.

Ivan floated against the wall, holding a light fixture. A large purple bruise covered half his forehead. Dried blood had crusted under his nose.

Merritt opened the stasis room door and drifted inside. He frowned at the grated floor in confusion as he tried to figure out what was causing the orange light playing across its surface.

Ivan looked up at the ceiling as he entered the room, and whispered something in Russian.

Merritt followed his gaze. The ceiling crawled with flame. The blanket of fire surrounded the hypergel tubes ascending to the ceiling, causing them to glow like red-hot irons.

"We don't have much time," said Merritt.

He gripped the grated floor and propelled himself down the long room, down the row of hypergel tanks. Passengers floated within them, blissfully unaware of the chaos engulfing the ship.

Why haven't they launched yet? he wondered.

Looking farther down the row of tanks, Merritt saw the main control console sticking up from the grated floor like a black podium, several screens and buttons adorning the square top.

Someone needed to activate the launch sequence manually.

He paused in front of the first empty tank and tapped the control panel nearby.

"This one's yours," Merritt told Ivan.

As the tank doors hinged open, he maneuvered to a rack of emergency suits on the opposite wall. He peeled one off its snaps and gave it to Ivan, who tossed it away. He spoke vehemently in Russian, pounding his fist against his palm, then kept repeating, "*Nyet! Nyet!*"

The orange glow from the ceiling seemed to brighten. Merritt looked up to see a dome of liquid flame bulging from the center, extending down, swelling lower into the room.

"Get inside, then!" Merritt shouted.

Ivan stepped up on the lip of the hypergel tank and put on his oxygen mask. Merritt grabbed a support rung bolted to the side of the tank with one hand and shoved Ivan into the thick pink liquid with the other, cutting off a flood of velvet expletives.

As the doors of Ivan's tank closed, Merritt grabbed a helmet and emergency suit, then made his way to the main control console halfway down the row of tanks.

He floated before it, twirling in slow motion as he struggled into his emergency suit. Unlike the Constellation and Magellan suits, it had no limb joints; no articulated waist panels. It was simply an insulated one-piece suit with a two-hour air supply, minor radiation protection, and a gold-tinted polycarbonate helmet.

"Emily would hate it," he said out loud, feeling insane for doing so.

She had always disliked yellow gold, saying white gold was classier. At the beginning of their relationship, Merritt joked that silver looked the same and would save him a few bucks at the jewelry store.

As he worked the controls of the main console, he wondered if he would be seeing her soon.

He navigated to the emergency launch screen for the hypergel tanks, then set the countdown for one minute. After putting on his helmet and clicking the slide-lock under his chin into place, he hit the console's *ACTIVATE* button.

A countdown timer flashed on the screen, counting backward from sixty.

The bubble of flame in the ceiling exploded, spraying globes of molten metal in all directions. Before the blanket of fire could close in on itself to seal the gap left by the explosion, the ceiling cracked like a snapped bone. A shockwave of energy shot down from the opening and slammed Merritt to the grated floor. A sphere of molten metal the size of a basketball passed through the grate right in front of his helmet's face shield, melting through the metal without slowing.

Don't just lay there, he scolded himself.

Merritt pushed himself off the grated floor, moving toward the nearest empty pod.

WILLIAMS

The captain frowned at a small blinking light on the arm of his command chair. He tapped the light, but it persisted.

"Korinne?" he asked over his shoulder.

"Yes, sir?" said a woman sitting at a workstation near the door. She pulled down her headphones and swiveled in her chair, brushing back her long, brown hair.

"The system is reading a pressure anomaly in Engine 3. Could you pull that information up on screen for me, please?"

"Yes, sir."

She swiveled back around, fingers flying over her console.

Williams had always been happy with his choice of Korinne as his first officer. She was intelligent, courteous, and quick to action. The only reason she wasn't already a captain herself was because of her age. At twenty-three, she was still two years shy of taking her captain's exam. Williams had no doubt she would pass on her first attempt. It had taken him three tries in four years to earn his stripes.

He would have to remember to start drafting her recommendation letter, as she would, no doubt, be asking for it before the exam.

New information scrolled up the center wall screen— lines of dense numbers and corresponding descriptions. A large section of it was surrounded by a thick red line.

"There," he said, pointing. "Enlarge that section."

The rest of the text vanished, and the highlighted portion grew to a legible size.

Williams scanned the text as slow, horrific realization dawned on his face.

The mood lighting in the bridge faded to black. Red emergency lights clicked on in the ceiling.

"*ATTENTION,*" said the ship's announcer, an artificial female voice Williams had chosen because it sounded the most authentic. "*This is an emergency. Please move to the nearest escape pod. Red tickets, Deck 3 forward, Deck 4 forward, Deck 6 forward. Blue tickets, Deck 2 aft. REPEAT, this is an emergency.*"

"Sir?" Korinne asked, worry pitching her voice.

He stood and tugged down the hem of his uniform jacket.

"Pull it up on your console," he said, walking over to her quickly.

Information flooded her screens. A wireframe diagram of the three massive hybrid antimatter drives showed a jagged patch of red on the side of Engine 3, port side. The patch of red was shaped like a radiation deflector panel.

Williams crossed his arms. "Seal the breach," he said calmly.

Korinne entered the correct command sequence. Three small rectangles in the wireframe diagram blinked green.

"Only three blast shields responding, sir." She reverse-pinched the diagram screen, enlarging a section of the engine chamber.

"What's that black spot?" asked the captain.

"The fourth shield is gone, sir." She zoomed out, then back in on Engine 3. "Something's lodged in the wall of the antimatter chamber," she said.

"Why didn't the system register the damage?"

"It's an old ship, sir."

"That's no excuse," he said to himself as he studied the screen. "Shut down Engine 3."

A violent shudder rocked the bridge. Korrine's chair swiveled and knocked the captain to the floor. She grabbed her console with both hands to keep from falling out of her seat.

"Shut it down!" Williams shouted.

Korinne nodded and tapped her console. "It's not responding, sir!"

He pulled himself up to his knees and held the edge of the console as the bridge continued to shake.

"The kill signal's passing through the system," she said loudly, "but the antimatter isn't cooling. Sir, it's heating up."

Williams considered sending out a patch team, but if that chamber was leaking antimatter, they wouldn't get within twenty meters of the breach before being ripped apart in their space suits.

The shudder subsided, leaving a soft warning beep from elsewhere on the bridge.

"This is an emergency," repeated the ship's announcer. *"Please move to the nearest escape pod."*

Captain Williams stood and smoothed down his uniform.

"It's time for you to leave, Korinne. Grab an emergency suit on your way to a pod."

She shook her head, frowning. "I'm not leaving."

He sighed. "Go find a comm tech, then. There's something I'd like to try. Something that could save us."

She looked up at him, the barest hint of suspicion in her eyes.

"Go," urged Williams. "I don't trust the system to send the message."

"But..." she said, hesitating, "the elevators will be out, sir."

"You'll have to run. I'll be fine until you get back."

Korinne pulled her headphones from around her neck and set them on her console. Williams picked them up and prepared to put them over his ears.

"Go!" he repeated.

After a last, hesitant look, Korinne ran from the bridge.

Williams tossed the headphones on the console and went to the door. He tapped his personal command override sequence into the door's control panel, locking himself in the bridge.

Someone pounded from the other side of the door.

Williams sat at Korinne's station and swiped her headphones to the floor. Tapping quickly, he pulled up information about every escape pod on the ship. So far, only two percent of them had launched, half from the red ticket section of pods, half from the officer's.

On a full cruise, Williams knew, there wouldn't be enough pods for everyone. It was an unspoken fact he prayed never made it to the public's ear. The operational record of the starliner series of ships was exemplary, justifying the savings during construction.

Another red pod launched.

The captain pulled up a schematic for the blue pod section — Deck 2, aft. The entire chamber was flooded with radiation. Its doors were sealed.

Williams leaned back slowly. He looked up at the ceiling, for the first time seeing the ship as an adversary instead of an ally. He had put his faith in the *Halcyon*, and it had betrayed him, the crew, and the passengers. It wasn't that the warning signs had escaped his vigilant watch, it was that they had never been reported by the ship's systems in the first place.

He wheeled his chair close to the console and bypassed the crew interface. He checked the time, then performed a quick calculation in his head. The security code to activate the commanding officer's console interface required the input of a morphing password based on the current time and that officer's personal identification number.

After the screen popped up, he immediately navigated to the emergency display screen and fired off a distress call. No signals pierced the Rip, but perhaps it would be picked up by the nav beacon near Aegea and relayed to the next passing vessel.

Williams confirmed the ship's multiple distress beacons were active, then navigated to the interface for escape pod control. Tapping each screen that popped up in rapid succession, he removed the red ticket requirement from all pods. They were now available to all passengers, no matter their class.

He tapped the button to transmit a ship-wide message.

"This is the captain. All restrictions for escape pod use have been removed. All passengers and crew report to Decks 3, 4, and 6 forward."

Williams walked to his command chair. He took a long look around the bridge, bathed in deep red light, searing the sight into his memory. Then he sat and tapped a command into his armrest console.

The wall screen went black, and the glowing orb of Galena faded into view, its brilliance dulling the red warning lights.

Aside from a gentle beeping off to the captain's left, the bridge was silent, just the way he liked it.

Williams settled into his chair, staring at the screen.

Galena stared back, a single, giant eye, wide

open against a black sheet that extended to infinity.

The ship lurched, as if something had struck one of the outer hulls. Gravity failed. The captain slowly rose from his chair, drifting up in the sudden zero gravity. He grabbed an armrest and pulled himself back down, then secured himself to the chair with its built-in safety harness.

After tightening the straps almost to the point of cutting off circulation to his limbs, he stared once more at Galena, and he waited.

MERRITT

Movement near the entrance of the stasis room caught his eye.

Two crew members hovered just inside the door, looking up at the ceiling in horror.

Merritt glanced at the countdown timer: 45 seconds left.

"Hurry!" he yelled, his voice painfully loud within his helmet.

The two men noticed him for the first time, waving at them like a madman. They pushed off the wall, heading down the row of tanks.

A voice spoke over the ship's intercom, coming through a small speaker inside Merritt's helmet.

"This is the captain. All restrictions for escape pod use have been removed. All passengers and crew report to Decks 3, 4, and 6 forward."

Merritt froze in place, his train of thought leaping a gorge and missing the track on the far side.

All he could think of was Gavin's face, twisted in fear, as the escape pod door slid down.

A pipe burst from the wall behind him in a cloud of steam and smacked his back, pushing him against the main control console.

Merritt snapped out of his momentary shock and went to the nearest empty tank. He entered the command to open it, but nothing happened. A red error screen flashed on the console.

"Come on come on," he said as he drifted to the previous tank right next to Ivan's.

This one opened up, the process seeming to take a hundred times longer than usual.

Merritt stepped onto the lip of the hypergel tank and stuck one arm in.

The orange glow in the ceiling blinked out, and Merritt looked up to see the last tendrils of flame being sucked into a network of deep cracks.

He jumped into the tank and spun around in the pink gel as the ceiling of the stasis room ripped away in broken pieces, sucked upward in a sudden vacuum.

The two crew members were sucked up along with all the loose debris in the room, vanishing into the jagged-edged mouth that had opened at the top of the room.

The surface of the hypergel rippled like a lake in a strong breeze as the vacuum tried to pull it from the tank. As the plexi doors hinged shut, the gel sealed around Merritt's suit, cementing in place.

His fast breaths were loud inside his helmet. He turned his head to look down the row of tanks, but could only see Ivan's right next to his.

It disappeared, sucked up its tube.

Merritt braced himself for launch, but there was no need. Cushioned within the gel, he felt nothing as his pod shot up its tube. The stasis room blinked out of sight, and all was dark. Strobes of light pulsed like a heartbeat and he shot from the outermost hull, into space.

He squinted against a piercing glare of light. At first, he thought it was Phobis, the nearest star, but it was one of the ship's engines.

Engine 3 emitted the concentrated light of a hybrid antimatter drive caught in a feedback loop, generating so much of its own internal energy that it could no longer be shut down.

Small explosions bloomed from the hull of the *Halcyon*, like sand falling through water. A massive scar, like a black lightning bolt, crawled across the hull from the back of the ship to a point near its center, half a mile away.

As Merritt's escape pod turned, Galena came into view, dull in comparison to the burning effulgence of the *Halcyon*'s overloading engine.

Through a gauze of pink gel, he could still see the details on its surface. Many of its small continents were connected by narrow land bridges, surrounded by vast oceans. He assumed a broad patch of white to be one of the planet's poles.

The pod shifted direction, turning him toward a view of endless space as it sent him on an undeniable impact course with Galena.

There were a few silent moments where Merritt had time enough to worry about his son.

He searched the distant stars for familiar constellations, knowing he would find none. They formed alien patterns in the black, sparkling brilliantly even through the pink hypergel.

Dancing fingers of flame extended along the surface of the pod, starting above Merritt's head. Soon his entire field of view was bright orange, and he knew he was falling through Galena's atmosphere.

For the first time since entering the hypergel, he began to worry about his landing.

There was no way to manually control the tank from the inside. Even if there *was*, the occupant was usually under the effects of stasis. Merritt wiggled his fingers within the gloves of his emergency space suit, but couldn't move them deeper into the gel, which had hardened to a barely-pliable state.

The orange light vanished, and Merritt burst into blue sky.

A field of white mammatus cloud-cover extended toward the horizon, its surface fluffed up like a blanket made of cotton balls.

Bile rose in his throat as the pod leveled out, rotating until Merritt faced the sky.

An impact rocked the pod and debris flew past the doors, but the pod kept flying. Tall cylindrical poles, like naked tree trunks, zipped past his field of view.

The pod hit something else and turned sideways, spinning like a top. It slammed into the ground and bounced back into the air, pieces of its metal shell flying in every direction. It hit again, cracked like an egg, and bounced up, sending the remains of the outer shell spinning away in ragged strips.

All that remained was the formed mass of gel

as it tumbled end-over-end through the air, Merritt suspended within.

It splatted against a large lead-colored boulder half-buried in the ground, and stuck there.

Merritt's back was to the boulder. He hadn't felt a thing.

The gel slowly lost its firmness, sagging against the rock. Merritt slipped down from the mass and hit the hard ground on his side. He rolled away from the dripping goop and got to his knees, breathing hard.

He pulled off his helmet and took his first lungful of Galena air as salty wind blasted his face.

There was a noise behind him and he quickly scrambled to his feet.

Ivan stumbled out from behind a large boulder the color of dull silver and fell on his hands and knees, coughing pink gel from his mouth. The viscous fluid streamed in thick strands from his clothes. He crawled past Merritt, toward the ocean.

Merritt turned and noticed it for the first time.

The boulder against which he'd come to a crashing halt was on the shore of a long beach of glimmering black sand. Lead deposits, some as large as houses, dotted the shore in both directions.

Towering waves rose from the gray surface of the water as far as he could see, their twenty-meter faces slashed with white in the strong wind. They seemed suspended in time, like permanent fixtures in Galena's landscape.

Merritt walked across the black sand, sinking in

up to his ankles, drawn toward them as if by magnetism. The fine sand felt warm, even through his emergency suit.

Ivan reached the water's edge and splashed his hand in the surf, testing. He looked at his palm, then at the back of his hand. Merritt stood next to him as he rolled into the shallow water, sputtering in the wind as he washed pink gel from the arms of his jacket.

The sound of a distant explosion reached down from the sky.

Through a break in the clouds, Merritt saw the *Halcyon* in orbit — a ship in miniature, roughly two inches long.

A flower of fire erupted from its hull to join the several already growing, and the ship's nose dipped, angling down toward the planet.

Merritt started in fright when another person silently appeared next to him on the beach, his broad, smooth face turned skyward.

He stood barefoot in the sand, wearing one of the black-and-white neoprene body suits. His long black hair was slicked back with gel.

The constant rumble from the ocean grew louder as the wind changed directions to blow offshore.

The water's edge rapidly retreated from the shore, sucked back as it rushed over sand and rocks to leave Ivan sprawled out on the wet shore, exclaiming his confusion in agitated Russian.

A wall of water rose from the ocean, a stone's

throw from shore, reaching up to block the sky.

"*Run!*" Merritt yelled.

He turned away from the water, moving painfully slow in the black sand. The barefoot man ran past him, sand flinging up from his feet.

Merritt looked back as the wall of water rose higher. Its top curled forward as the wall leaned toward the shore. Ivan swiped water from his face and scrambled up the shore.

The world darkened before Merritt's eyes as the wall of water pitched forward, reaching out over the shore.

"*Here!*" shouted the other passenger.

Merritt whipped around, searching for him. He crouched with his back to a large boulder, chest heaving. Merritt ran to the boulder and jumped behind it just as the massive wave crashed down. Water rushed around the boulder as if it were poised on the edge of a waterfall, battering his shoulders and legs and knocking his head back against the rock.

In its wake, he heard only the howl of the wind. After he wiped water from his eyes, he saw Ivan pinned against another rock several meters away. He was looking up toward the sky in horror.

Merritt leaned around the side of his boulder to see that another wave had already formed.

"Get to the other side!" he shouted at Ivan.

Too late.

The next wave hit, stronger than the first, pushing Merritt and the other passenger away from their feeble shelter in a torrent of water that carried them away from shore.

Merritt's stomach hit something hard and his body buckled around it as water beat against his back.

As the flow of water subsided, he slumped back down to the ground on his back, looking up at a towering tree trunk without bark. Three fat, leafless branches protruded from the top. He groaned as he turned his throbbing head to look inland.

An entire forest of the bare trunks bordered the shore, blanketing the land toward the horizon. Merritt pictured Gavin alone, out there in that strange wilderness.

"I think the swell is over," said the other passenger. He walked over to Merritt on unsteady legs and helped him up from the sand. "I'm Niku."

Merritt unwrapped a snaking length of purple seaweed from around his leg and threw it aside. He winced in pain as he straightened his back. "I'm Merritt," he said.

Ivan walked past them, half of his face covered in blood from a gash on his scalp, muttering in Russian as he stared up at the sky.

Merritt and Niku turned around to look up.

The *Halcyon* was headed for Galena. It approached head-on, a small, growing, sand-colored rectangle spitting fire against a cloudy blue sky.

"Here she comes," said Niku.

Ivan shaded his eyes with a bloody hand. His stream of Russian mumbles trailed off, but his jaw kept shivering.

"They send another," he said with a thick accent. He turned quickly to look at Merritt and Niku with wide, terrified eyes, searching for confirmation. "Another ship, yes?"

"There are no more," said Niku. "None that can travel the Rip."

Ivan shook his head and looked up. "*Nyet.* They build another."

Merritt peeled off his wet emergency suit and instinctively patted the chest of his coveralls. For one heart-stopping moment, he thought he'd lost the seed pouch. Then he remembered giving it to Gavin.

Without his helmet, water had flooded into his suit at the neck, thoroughly soaking his coveralls. Merritt rolled up the sleeve concealing his wristpad to find the screen cracked and the circuits drowned. He unstrapped it from his arm and dropped it to the sand.

"Look," said Niku, pointing out to sea.

Between the towering, stationary waves floated a hypergel tank. A bald man clung to the side like a shipwrecked sailor, his pale face a mask of terror even at a distance.

"Who is that?" Merritt asked.

"That's Mick," said Niku. "The bar's doorman." He looked over his shoulder, then back out to sea. "We were lucky."

"Something," Ivan said, pointing excitedly at the water. "*Something!*"

Behind the floating escape pod, a wide circular section of the surface flattened out to a smooth pad, contrasting the tumultuous water surrounding it. Bubbles boiled from below.

Ivan screamed in Russian, waving his arms at the stranded passenger, beckoning him ashore.

The water beneath the floating hypergel tank erupted violently, sending it spinning into the air. The passenger's high-pitched screams carried across the wind, to the shore, where they sounded like little more than the calling of gulls.

A massive bulk emerged from the surface, rising like a swelling mountain, its flesh slick and shining. The tank and its former occupant fell against the mass — fell *into* it — and vanished. Thrashing the surface madly, the bulk rolled below the surface and disappeared.

Ivan stumbled backward, farther from the water.

As the surface smoothed out, Merritt's stomach dropped when he saw a line of hypergel tanks floating in the water farther off shore, extending all the way to the horizon.

He turned away from the ocean and promptly threw up on the sand.

Niku stood next to him, surveying the dense forest of bare trees that bordered the shore.

Merritt wiped his mouth and spat. "We need to get to the ship. There are nav beacons that point to the colony."

Niku nodded. "It's a start."

Merritt stood up straight and cracked his back. "Do you have any idea where we are?"

"Galena," replied Niku. He walked up a black dune and stood at the edge of the forest. "Welcome home."

CHAPTER ELEVEN

LEERA

Earth, she thought when she opened her eyes.

She had never seen a more beautiful blue sky, streaked with pure white clouds limned by a beaming sun that warmed her skin.

Leera lay on her back atop a broad, jagged boulder of mineral lead sulfide, every part of her body resting at a slightly different elevation. The remains of her hypergel tank fanned out in a firework of shards around her, stuck in the flattened glob of pink goop.

She squinted at the sun, confused. It was closer than it should be — larger in the sky.

First things first, she thought.

She tried to sit up and screamed as a knife twisted in her lower back.

Panting hard, she forced her muscles to relax as she gently rolled onto her side. Probing her back, she felt a sharp chunk of metal protruding an inch from her lower spine. She grabbed it slowly, clenched her teeth and shut her eyes, then yanked it free.

Her scream carried throughout the forest of strange, light brown trees in which she'd landed. Leera remained on her side, breathing heavily, as she stared at the tall, naked trunks, looming toward every horizon like an army of silent sentinels. They were easily as tall as the massive Redwoods she'd read about in primary school. Atop each were three large, bare limbs of varied size. The limbs grew straight out from the main trunk for several meters, then bent upward at a ninety degree angle, giving the top of the tree the appearance of a clawed hand opening toward the sky.

Leera rubbed her bloody hand against her gel-covered body suit, smearing the black and white fabric with a streak of red.

She sat up slowly, eyes clenched shut with pain from the wound in her back. When she opened them again, she saw that her right leg was broken below the knee, her tibia snapped at a right angle, skewing the bottom third of her leg outward at an unnatural angle.

Leera leaned back, resting the back of her head against the hard rock.

Far above her, as the white clouds in Galena's blue sky parted, the *Halcyon* appeared.

It took a moment for Leera to figure out why it was so much smaller than usual. Once she realized she was seeing it head-on, instead of from the side, she propped herself up on one elbow.

The ship was falling down to Galena.

Fire erupted from the starboard side and vanished. The nose of the ship glowed red-hot.

Pull up, she silently commanded the vessel, willing it to turn and ascend to orbit.

A shield of flame engulfed the front of the ship

as it grew larger in the sky. Distant booms echoed across the landscape.

It looked like it was headed straight for Leera.

"*Pull up!*" she yelled, her body shaking with rage.

The *Halcyon* began to turn. The shield of flame covering its nose morphed into a narrow oval and extended to cover the entire side of the vessel as it banked, angling away from the planet.

Leera laughed and laid back, tears streaming from the corners of her eyes.

One of the engines exploded, emitting a rapidly-expanding Saturnian ring of blue energy.

Leera's joy turned to horror as the ship cracked in half, its front end spinning away from the back, which had been shattered nearly to oblivion by the detonation.

"*No,*" she whispered.

She imagined her husband and son waving to her from a hyperrail platform as she receded into the distance. They grew smaller and smaller, still waving, still smiling, until, at last, they disappeared.

Minutes later, she heard the impact.

Leera had never witnessed a nuclear explosion first-hand, but that was what she pictured when the *Halcyon* slammed into Galena. The ground shook and the towering trees swayed in unison.

A gust of wind blasted Leera as she lay on the rock, then all was silent.

In the distance, beyond the treetops, a mushroom cloud roiled up into the sky, glowing blue and orange at its core.

"Leera!" someone shouted from the forest. A moment later, the call was repeated, this time closer.

She heard the sound of approaching footsteps on soft ground.

"Here," she said weakly. "Walter."

He climbed the boulder and appeared at her side. His body suit was smeared with black, and his short red beard was slick with gel. Blood surrounded a small rip in the fabric over one of his thighs and trickled from a thin cut on his bald head. One lens of his glasses was missing.

"I knew it was you!" he said, his face beaming. "I didn't think—"

He stopped when he noticed her broken leg.

"Oh," he said softly. "What have you done to yourself?" He knelt closer to the fracture. "Not compound, thank goodness." He sat up and looked at her. "I don't suppose any med kits have fallen from the sky while you've been here?"

She shook her head.

"I have to set it," he said. "You understand?"

Leera wiped a sheen of sweat from her face, then nodded.

He turned his back to her, straddling her legs so she couldn't see below her waist.

"Scream if you need to," he said.

It felt like someone ripped her leg off, so she screamed.

Leera awoke to Walter kneeling beside her,

gently shaking her shoulder. She sat up quickly and regretted it, cracking the dried blood that had begun to form over the wound in her back.

"I've nothing to bind it with," Walter said apologetically. "You blacked out, by the way."

Leera noticed he was missing a sleeve.

He had managed to remove it and slip it over her right leg up to her knee, compressing her shin and the large knot that bulged from the bone. She wiggled her toes, but couldn't feel them.

"It will heal straight enough, but you might have a slight limp if I can't get it properly bound soon."

"Thank you, Walter," she said. "And for your next magic trick, how do I get off this rock?"

He scooted to the edge and hopped down to the ground. Leera moved like a three-legged crab, inching her way in painful increments. Walter reached up and grabbed her waist as she slid off the boulder, then supported her weight to set her gently on the ground on one bare foot.

The patched green-and-brown soil was spongy and slightly damp.

"If these trees had branches, I could make you a crutch," said Walter, looking up.

Leera eased down to sit with her back to the boulder, breathing hard from the exertion. She pressed her fingers down into the soft, moist ground. An electric shock snapped her fingertips and she jerked her hand back, inhaling sharply.

"What is it?" Walter asked, hurrying to her side.

"The ground shocked me," she answered, rubbing her fingertips together. "Low-grade current, like a static shock."

Walter stuck his index finger into the soil and yelped in surprise at the shock, but didn't draw back.

"It's constant," he said.

"I would bet the moisture helps with conductivity."

She sank her fingers into the soil again, more slowly, feeling the onset of the shock as a thousand pins dancing over her skin, tingling all the way to her bones.

"Doctor James!" someone shouted from nearby.

Walter stood quickly as Corporal Turner appeared from around the other side of the boulder, wearing a muddy body suit and carrying a slender gray rifle. He was uninjured except for a red scratch on the side of his calf that tore the leg cuff of his skin-tight suit.

He let out a massive sigh of relief when he saw the other two.

"I heard you screaming," he said.

"I'm grateful my howls of pain are so recognizable."

"Doctor Lyden, are you alright?" he asked Walter.

"I'm fine, Corporal. Did you see anybody else?"

Turner shook his head as he looked around the small clearing with wide eyes. Leera thought he seemed a touch manic, wavering between elation and terror.

"Where are we?"

"Not where we're supposed to be," Walter replied.

"So how do we find the colony?" He looked at Walter. "You *can* find it, right?"

"*Hello!*" someone called from the forest.

Turner swung his rifle toward the voice. He quickly lowered it when another passenger from the *Halcyon* came into view. Her short brown hair was slicked back with gel.

"I thought I was alone," she said, looking over the trio by the boulder. "I'm Uda."

"I'm Walter. This is Leera and Corporal Turner."

"Are there no others?"

Walter shook his head. "Not yet."

"We only have a few hours of daylight," she said, glancing skyward. "We need to get to the Halcyon. What's left of it. Each blackbox contains a nav beacon that leads to the colony."

"There's nothing left!" said Turner. "Didn't you see the fireball?"

"Calm down, Corporal," Walter said. "You're supposed to be our escort, remember?"

Turner swallowed hard and wiped his brow. He nodded and gripped his rifle firmly. "Right. Yeah. Okay."

"How'd you get that thing down here, anyway?" asked Walter.

Turner looked at his rifle, confused by the question. "I just...brought it in the tank with me."

"Can you walk?" Uda asked Leera, glancing down at her leg.

She shook her head, strands of wet hair slapping her cheeks. "Not on my own."

"Maybe you should wait here."

"I'll be fine," said Leera.

Turner slung his rifle over his shoulder and bent down to help her up. She groaned when her shin bumped against him. Sweat dripped from her chin as she took her first tentative hop.

"The ship should be easy enough to find, right?" said Uda, walking into the forest in the direction of the mountainous mushroom cloud. "Just follow the fireball."

Turner draped Leera's arm around his neck and acted as her crutch, helping her hop away from the boulder, following after Uda. Walter stayed close behind them, ready to catch her if she fell.

Leera bit her lower lip as pain stabbed her back with each step. They would need to find a med kit soon, or another way to seal her wound. The air of Galena was breathable, but there had been no studies conducted on a microbial level. She shuddered to think of an alien bacterium worming its way into her blood stream and turning it to jelly.

"We can shelter at the Halcyon for the night," said Uda from the head of the line, "if we make it in time."

"How long does night last?" asked Turner.

"Six hours. Slightly longer during the winter."

"Will it be cold?" Walter asked.

"Not so bad this close to the equator," she replied. "Temperature drops below freezing some nights."

"Are you a farmer?" asked Turner.

After a few moments, Uda said, "I am now."

Walter walked next to Leera. "Do you think Niku's alright?" he asked.

"Oh, you know him," she replied. "Like a duck in water wherever he goes" She put her pale hand on Walter's shoulder and squeezed. "I'm sure he's fine."

The trees thinned atop a wide hill, creating a small clearing. The group stopped in the clearing, surveying the tree-covered landscape that sloped away in every direction. Ahead of them in the distance, the wispy remnants of the mushroom cloud snaked across the sky. Below it, the smoking wreckage of the *Halcyon* was strewn for miles, the bulk of it in a heap at the end of a deep, black scar that cut through the forested land.

In the distance to their left, beyond several desolate square miles of nothing but lead-colored rock, stretched a vast, gray ocean, its shore studded with large boulders. Massive peaked waves appeared as tiny pyramids from afar. To their right were mountains with vibrant green peaks that scraped the clouds.

"Is it what you expected?" asked Uda.

No one had an answer.

They set off down the hill, toward the wreckage of the *Halcyon*.

TULLIVER

He was trapped.

Escape pods were equipped with two landing boosters for rapid last-minute course corrections. The main purpose for them was to ensure the pod landed at least somewhat gently on its back, ideally sliding to a gentle stop on flat ground. If such a landing wasn't possible, the pod extended its ground spike and struck the ground like a lawn dart, its passenger compartment filling with impact foam seconds before landing.

Tulliver's escape pod had hit a tall pole as its boosters fired, sending it spinning sideways to smack into another pole. The pod tumbled down to the surface like a flipped coin and cracked against a boulder, denting its hatch inward, further compressing the blue impact foam that filled the passenger compartment.

Without knowing which technique to employ, the pod continued firing its boosters while also extended its ground spike. It hit the ground spike-first at a forty-five degree angle, sinking in up to the base of the pod.

Tulliver could hardly move within the foam. It had done its job and kept him alive during the crash landing, but it was supposed to be ejected as soon as the hatch slid open.

The only parts of his body he could move below his chest were his toes, which he wiggled uselessly within his heavy boots. The porous foam pressed against his face, smothering his breath.

His left arm was pinned at his side, but his right had some room to move. He shrugged his shoulder up and down, bent his elbow, twisted his wrist — the foam would not budge.

Tulliver made a fist and pushed it into the foam. It sank in, molding around his knuckles.

So that's *the trick,* he thought.

He extended his fingers and pushed deeper, working his way slowly toward the dented hatch. One fingertip touched a hard surface. Tulliver tried to grin, but the foam smashed his cheeks down.

It had been so long since he'd needed to exert his full strength that Tulliver was forced to wonder if he still had it in him. Usually he enlisted help for such tasks.

He made a fist once more, and pushed, his entire body shaking from the effort.

The foam around his arm expanded to make room for his flexing muscles. His fist touched the hard surface of the inner hatch. Imagining all his strength flowing to his arm, he yelled with exertion as he forced the hatch away from the foam, inch by inch, until it popped loose with a loud *CRACK* and fell away.

The foam instantly fractured into half a dozen smaller chunks and tumbled out of the pod, scattering across the featureless gray ground.

Tulliver coughed away the oppressive chemical smell of the foam and heaved great breaths of Galena's fresh air. Looking up, he saw the broken top of a towering tree trunk that his pod had impacted. A chunk of its dark inner material had been torn away and now lay strewn across the ground, like tire shreddings.

Tulliver grabbed the sides of the hatch frame and pulled himself up to stand in the pod. He was in a shallow valley. Towering bare tree trunks formed a crown atop the surrounding hills, rising toward the blue sky. The ground was mottled green and brown, covering the entire landscape in every direction, except for a patch around Tulliver's pod that seemed to fill the valley like a lake. Yet the patch wasn't liquid. It was hard, gray, and unnaturally flat — markedly sterile in a vista of earthy colors. The ground beyond the gray patch had a mossy texture and glistened with moisture, while the gray section had a smooth, unbroken surface with slight geometric protuberances, almost like small pyramids, rising several inches from the top layer.

Tulliver climbed down the outside of his pod and extended a boot toward the ground.

The solid gray surface split open to reveal the patchy green and brown soil a short distance below. Tulliver jerked his foot up and nearly lost his balance. He clung to the side of the pod as the split in the gray came together and vanished, leaving no hint of its existence.

He tested the reaction again by lowering his leg a second time. Again, the ground split. This time he stepped against the greenish-brown covering, putting a little of his weight on the spongy surface, then hopped back onto the pod. The gray ground sealed the opening once again.

Tulliver frowned when he looked at the nearest edge of the smooth gray patch. A lead-colored rock mostly buried in the ground had been exposed within the last few moments.

The patch of gray was moving.

"*Ahoy!*" someone shouted at him from afar. "*Hullo there!*"

Tulliver climbed on all fours to the top of his leaning pod. Another pod stood nearly upright on its ground spike thirty meters away, at the edge of a dense stand of looming tree trunks. A short, bone-thin older man with a bright white mustache was inside the open compartment, waving his arms in the air. He wore a dark blue tracksuit and white tennis shoes. The hatch to his escape pod and chunks of impact foam were scattered on the gray ground nearby.

"*Yes, hullo!*" he called when he saw Tulliver. "*You there! Are you hurt?*"

Tulliver thought for a moment, then shouted, "My leg is injured! I can't walk!"

The man looked at the gray ground with trepidation.

"It moves, you know," he said nervously. "The ground moves."

"*Please hurry!*" Tulliver yelled.

The man nodded to himself, then waited, then nodded again and finally climbed down his pod. As he hopped to the ground, the gray surface opened in a circle to admit his white tennis shoes.

After two experimental hops in place, the older man grinned, his mustache curling up in a smile of its own.

"Marvelous!" he cried.

As he walked toward Tulliver's escape pod, espousing the view that they were lucky to be alive, the circular opening in the ground moved with him like a spotlight tracking its subject and sealing again in his wake.

He had crossed half the distance to Tulliver's pod when the hole stopped moving. His ankles bumped against one edge and he looked down in confusion.

"I *say*!" he declared. "I *do* believe I see legs!"

He knelt down to peer in the gap between the gray covering and the softer ground beneath.

"Don't!" said Tulliver loudly.

The gray ground swelled up around the older man like a rising volcano. His terrified face disappeared from view behind a wall of gray as the hill rose higher. The circular opening closed at the peak, then the hill gently lowered back down to the ground, flattening out to its previous unbroken plateau.

The older man was gone, smothered beneath the gray.

Tulliver swallowed thickly and wiped sweat from his eyes with a shaky hand as he turned away. He climbed around to the front of his pod, then settled into the padded compartment and stared up at the blue sky as a distant explosion shook the tree trunks. The trunks swayed against the sky, creaking as if in a strong wind. Tulliver leaned forward to gaze over the edge of the pod. An enormous mushroom cloud billowed into the sky, blue and orange fire glowing from within.

Looking down at the ground, he noticed that the edge of the gray covering had moved again. More lead-colored rocks were visible at its nearby edge. In another few hours, he realized, the edge would move past his escape pod.

It was a simple thing to wait, given the alternative.

Later, when the waning light of day cast long shadows from bare tree trunks, Tulliver stood up in his pod. The edge of the gray patch had receded a meter behind him.

He hopped down to the soft ground and backed away from the gray.

It didn't move toward him. It didn't rise up to cover him.

Cautiously, ready to run in the opposite direction, Tulliver knelt on the moist, springy ground and looked beneath the slowly-moving gray sheet.

Thousands of segmented crab-like legs moved in the narrow space below, churning slowly. Small, barbed spines protruded from the segmented joints.

Looking at the organism from the side, it appeared as a field of smooth gray with small, gray pyramids dotting its surface.

If Tulliver cocked his head just right, he could hear the faintest whisper of movement.

A primal fear bloomed inside him — a fear similar to the one ingrained in the DNA of humanity from a time when they were not the pinnacle of the food chain on Earth. He quickly turned and hurried in the opposite direction, brushing off the sleeves of his jacket as if to be done with the entire ordeal.

The sun was setting, and he wanted shelter. The pods were supposed to have landed near the colony site, but he saw no hint of a settlement.

Climbing a low hill, he came upon another escape pod, this one properly on its back, its ground spike undeployed.

A young boy sat within, knees tucked up to his chest, squeezing a small object in his hands.

Tulliver approached slowly.

"Gavin," he said.

The boy's head snapped up. He shoved the object in his pants pocket as he stood. Tulliver held out his hands in a friendly gesture as he stepped closer to the pod.

"Don't be afraid" he said.

The boy wiped his nose and sniffed. Tears streamed down his cheeks. His small face scrunching up in anger as he touched a thumb to his forehead with his fingers splayed wide.

"I don't understand," said Tulliver, "but you can

understand me, can't you?"

The boy's anger passed as soon as it had appeared, and he sat down with a huff.

Tulliver rested one hand on the edge of the pod and surveyed the horizon. A slight grin passed his lips when he noticed a cluster of pinpoint lights less than a mile away, at the edge of the forest: the colony.

"You're a brave boy," he said, "but you're not safe yet."

Gavin looked at him sharply.

"We need to find the colony before it gets dark," Tulliver added.

Even without knowing sign language, Tulliver could intuit the meaning of the boy's next gesture.

"Because we'll be safe there."

Gavin looked up.

"The ship is gone," said Tulliver. He extended a hand toward the boy. "I can find the colony. I can protect you."

Gavin hesitated, then took the offered hand and allowed Tulliver to help him down from the pod.

"There's a brave boy," said Tulliver.

He patted Gavin as they began walking down the hill, his open hand covering the entire width of his small back. The boy was extremely small for his age, Tulliver realized.

He felt for the locket in his jacket pocket and gave it a tight squeeze as he smiled down at Gavin.

"Your father was brave, too," he said. "Bringing you all this way must not have been easy."

The boy's scuffed the soles of his shoes on the ground as they walked. Soon the noise became daggers in Tulliver's ears, stabbing him with each step.

"Stop that," he growled.

Gavin looked up at him defiantly just as a man carrying a glowing lantern appeared over a hill. He wore the gray uniform of a colony warden and carried a thin stun-baton slung over one shoulder.

"You there! Colonists!" he shouted at them. "This way!"

Gavin ran ahead. He tripped and got his hands out in time to stop his fall, then scrambled to his feet and kept on running without looking back.

Tulliver grunted and followed after, though he took his time. He was breathing hard by the time he reached the top of the small rise.

The warden offered him a hand for his last few steps, and Tulliver feigned gratitude. The young man had a thin blond mustache and a boyish face. A wedding ring dangled from a chain around his neck.

"I thought we'd seen the last of the survivors," he said as he patted Tulliver's back in far too friendly of a manner.

"I was...delayed," said Tulliver, thinking of the moving mass of gray ground cover.

"What about the boy? Is he your son?"

Tulliver chewed on the question a long moment.

"I'm his caretaker."

The warden nodded. "I expect we'll need a lot of caretakers in the weeks to come. Not every passenger is handling the situation well. Some of them weren't supposed to come down to the surface at all."

Tulliver grunted. "Why would they handle it well? And what about you? Colony wardens are on two-year tours, right?"

"That's right." The man looked down at the wedding ring on a chain around his neck, then quickly away. A soft breeze ruffled his mop of light brown hair. "No point in wallowing in despair just yet. We still have a lot of work to do."

"Couldn't have said it better myself," agreed Tulliver.

In the near distance, a human settlement sprawled across a wide clearing inside a ring of towering tree trunks. Strings of lights connected to anemic solar generators formed a drooping canopy over temporary white shelters and circular, hard-shelled tents, bathing the settlement in a warm glow.

Colonists moved about the grounds, carrying supplies, supporting the injured, or staring in resonating shock at the darkening sky, wondering where their ship had gone.

"There's food and water," said the warden, walking ahead, "and clean clothes, if you want them. Orientation is scheduled for the morning. My name is Diego. Find me if you need anything before dawn."

Tulliver nodded when the warden glanced back, then his gaze drifted down to the colony, lit so cheerfully under the strings of lights.

He took a deep breath of the clean air, rubbed the toe of his boot into the soft, welcoming ground.

Yes, he thought with a contented sigh, *a man could be happy here.*

PART THREE

FINDING HOME

CHAPTER TWELVE

MERRITT

The air cooled slightly as Phobis lowered in the sky. The denouement of Galena's twenty hours of daylight offered a brilliant sunset which had lingered for two hours while Merritt, Niku, and Ivan trudged through the forest of bare tree trunks.

They held a course more or less directly in line with where the mushroom cloud had bloomed on the horizon, keeping the sun on their left as they marched away from the gray ocean. A few brief, forced detours had delayed them, the longest of which saw them trailing the edge of a narrow chasm that cut across their path until they could find a safe spot to jump across.

The chasm dropped twenty meters into the ground, then pinched together at the bottom in a wedge. Various debris had lodged at the bottom. Most of it was rock, but there were several odd-shaped pieces Merritt could not identify, and his mind wandered toward the animal life of Galena.

"I heard about your team on the ship," he said to Niku. "There are three of you, right?"

"And one corporal," Niku answered. "Though he was a last-minute addition."

"Military escort?"

"Only gun on the ship, from what I saw."

A smile threatened to pull at Merritt's lips. "Expecting hostile natives?"

"I wasn't expecting *any* of this," said Niku. "When our lab won the government contract, I thought it was a chance to finally do some actual research instead of spending my days trying to cram more vitamins into a single serving of vat-grown soy." He sighed. "We thought we were coming to study the planet's ecology."

"What changed?" asked Merritt.

"Our contact on Earth is a man named Kellan. Just before we left, he burdened us with retrieving a sample that would allow him to secure funding for more trips to Galena."

Merritt frowned. "They're going to stop the service?"

"Cygnus Corporation's contract with the government was set to expire when the Halcyon got back to Earth. The government couldn't afford to renew, so Cygnus planned to cancel voyages through the Rip and stick to dinner cruises over the Twin Cities instead."

The chasm turned at a ninety-degree angle and briefly narrowed. Merritt jumped across easily, followed by Niku.

"What means ecology?" asked Ivan. He kicked a rock into the chasm and watched it fall, then hopped over to join the others.

"The study of how organisms interact with their environment," Niku replied.

"This is your job?"

"Something like that."

"I never met your coworkers," said Merritt, "but I saw you around the ship a few times."

Niku stopped to catch his breath, hands resting on his hips while he looked up at the tree trunks.

"In The Velvet Speakeasy, you mean," he said.

Merritt stopped as well, leaning over the edge of the chasm to look down.

"I didn't want to lay it all out there, but yeah."

"I should have gone into a tank right from the start," Niku admitted. "Would have saved a whole lot of money."

"I wouldn't sweat it."

"Why's that?"

"None of the digital transactions on the ship passed through the Rip. All of your money is still in the Halcyon's data banks, waiting to be relayed from the other side."

Niku grunted thoughtfully. "With every cloud, a silver lining," he said.

The group resumed their trek along the chasm.

"There's still hope," said Merritt. He patted his chest, feeling for the leather pouch he usually carried around his neck, only to remember he'd given it to Gavin. The thought of his missing son tightened his throat and shortened his breath.

"Hope for what?" asked Niku.

"Alcohol on Galena."

Niku laughed suddenly. "I tasted fermented soyflower before I left Earth. It's undrinkable."

They passed a small pool of fresh spring water.

Niku told them that, according to information he received during his briefing on Earth, the water was safe. He cupped a handful of it into his mouth, drank, and didn't die, so Merritt joined him. Ivan waited until after the other two men had their fill, watching them closely, then knelt beside the spring and scooped up fast handfuls, drinking thirstily.

Many more springs boiled up from small pools as they walked through the forest, but native food was nowhere to be found. Merritt's stomach rumbled loudly as he reached the top of yet another small hill. The entire planet seemed to be made of them, rolling endlessly through the forest.

A beat-up hypergel tank rested on the ground just over the hill, at the terminus of a long scar in the soil. Its occupant was still encased in pink gel within the dented outer shell. The plexi window had stopped against a small boulder, shattering it in a white spiderweb pattern.

Merritt hurried down the hill and peered through the cracked window. A man with white hair was suspended in the gel, curled up in a tight ball.

"Help me get the door off," said Merritt.

He tried to roll the tank onto its back, but it wouldn't move. Ivan and Niku stood beside him and shoved, rocking it in place until they eventually managed to tip it over with a loud crunch. Merritt lifted a warped safety panel next to the plexi door and turned the manual override key. The door popped open an inch and stopped.

The three of them grabbed its edge, their fingers sinking into thick pink gel, and pried it open, straining against twisted hinges. They got one of the doors to swing open, but the other wouldn't budge.

Merritt reached down into the gel, sinking his arms up to his biceps, and began to pull out the occupant. He slipped from Merritt's hands when he was halfway out and flopped to the ground like a fish, landing with a slap.

"Henry Tolbard," said Merritt, kneeling down next to him.

"*Haven* Henry Tolbard?" asked Niku.

Merritt nodded.

"What is Haven?" Ivan asked.

"One of the twin cities on the moon," said Niku. "Did you really not know that?"

Ivan shrugged indifferently. "What is moon to man like me?"

Niku ran his hand along the dented shell of the tank, then looked around. "There could be more of them in the forest."

"They'll head for the wreckage, same as us," said Merritt, standing up.

"They might need help finding the colony."

"*We* need help finding the colony. This is already taking too long."

"I don't want to burden you with more bad news," said Niku, "but we might not even be on the same continent as the colony."

Merritt turned to face him. "Be honest. How likely do you think that is?"

Niku sighed and looked away, at the setting sun. "We've only seen one ocean so far. Two oceans border the colony's continent, one north and one south. Narrow seas to the east and west. We're heading north, away from the ocean." He thought in silence a moment, then said, "I was shown a hologram of Galena before leaving Earth. There is a wide river that divides our continent, running between the northern and southern oceans. The colony lies on the eastern half, between the river and the sea."

"So if the beacon sends us east," said Merritt, "and if we hit an ocean before we find the colony..."

Niku nodded. "Then we are on the wrong continent."

Merritt clenched his jaw and turned away.

"But most are connected by land bridges," Niku added. "We can find a way."

"Food!" said Ivan.

He hurried away, a huge grin on his face, and stopped in front of a twisted, spherical bush at the base of a tree. He plucked a softball-sized brown fruit from its sharp branches and took a big bite. Juice spurted from the fruit and splashed over Ivan's hand as he chewed with his mouth open.

"Ivan!" shouted Niku, running over to him.

Ivan stopped chewing, narrowed his eyes thoughtfully, and said, "Hmm."

Then he spat out the fruit with disgust and threw the remainder into the forest.

"Is no good," he said as Niku skidded to a halt next to him. "Is bad. Don't try."

"Don't try *any* of it!" Niku said, throwing up his hands in exasperation. "We haven't tested *any*-thing!"

Ivan slapped his shoulder as he walked past. "Calm down. I have eaten worse."

Henry Tolbard groaned and stretched out on the ground next his hypergel tank. He rolled onto his back and swiped gel from his eyes, then blinked at the orange clouds glowing in the light of the setting sun.

A smile slowly grew on his lips.

"Galena," he whispered.

He spasmed and flipped on his side, then retched gel from his lungs.

"Mouth numb," said Ivan, smacking his lips. "Can't feel tongue."

"That's what you get for biting weird fruit," Niku scolded him.

Merritt knelt next to Henry as he strained to sit up.

"I didn't expect to arrive like this," he said with amusement, staring at his gel-coated hands. He wiped them against his gel-covered body suit. His white hair and beard were tinged pink from the goop.

"We're heading for the wreckage of the Halcyon," said Merritt. "It will be dark soon, and we can't linger."

Henry's smile faded. "Wreckage?"

He stood up shakily, taking Merritt's offered hand for support, and looked to the horizon.

The mushroom cloud had all but dissipated in the sky above the wreckage. All that remained were snaking wisps of blue and orange smoke, trailing up toward the twilit sky.

A mile to the east, five thin, dark streams of smoke rose from the ground, their tops smeared horizontally in a strong wind.

"What are those?" Henry asked.

Niku shielded his eyes against the setting sun. "They weren't there before."

"Hull thrusters," said Merritt. "Five boosters on the port and starboard sides. The ship must have broken apart as it fell. That's where the front of the ship landed."

"What about the mushroom cloud?" asked Niku.

"That's the back of the ship. A detonation that large could only be caused by the antimatter engines. The hull thrusters are standard rockets. That smoke is from their burning fuel."

"So where we go?" asked Ivan.

"To the front," Merritt answered. "Most of the ship's black boxes are up there. We'll have a better chance of finding a nav beacon." He turned to Henry. "Are you ready?"

Excitement glinted in the older man's eyes. "I've been ready for a long time."

Merritt lead the way, Henry following close behind. Niku held up a warning finger as Ivan passed him.

"No more fruit," he warned.

Ivan grinned with swollen lips.

An hour later, the last traces of sunlight huddled near the horizon, smothered by a sky rapidly darkening from purple to black. Six particularly bright stars glimmered in the twilight directly overhead, clustered together in the curved shape of a harp.

"The first six stars they found through the Rip," said Niku, looking up as he walked. "Phobis was the seventh. I wondered what they would look like from the surface."

"The first atmospheric scans of Galena were false," Henry said. "Thrown off by the massive amounts of methane deposits near the southern ice cap. Apparently the probes landed in a field of it and thought the entire planet was toxic. The scientists very nearly wrote it off as uninhabitable."

"Those scientists," said Niku, shaking his head. "Always making mistakes."

Henry chuckled. "And which scientific field do you call your own?"

"Microbiology."

"Ah," said Henry. "I imagine you'll be kept busy for a long time."

"Not without a microscope. My eyesight is good, but not *that* good."

"Perhaps we'll find one on the ship."

Niku looked at him sideways.

"What's the matter?" said Henry.

"You're awfully optimistic."

"Well," said Henry thoughtfully, "someone has

to be, don't you think?"

Merritt stopped abruptly and held out his arm to halt the others. With the sun below the horizon, their progress had significantly slowed in the setting darkness.

"Careful," said Merritt.

The forest ended suddenly at the edge of a two-story cliff. Merritt stood on the precipice, one hand against a tree trunk for support.

Henry leaned forward to look over the edge. "Close one," he said.

"It looks like we can climb down over there," Merritt told them, pointing to the left.

Part of the cliff had collapsed, its rubble forming a ramp that sloped down at a gentler, though still not ideal, angle.

"What's down there?" asked Niku.

The four of them squinted into the growing darkness below, where the land stretched out before them in uniform shadow. No bare tree trunks rose from the plateau, which seemed to extend for miles.

"Flat land, hopefully," said Merritt.

He walked along the edge of the cliff, heading for the dirt ramp.

"Maybe we should camp here for the night," Niku called to him.

"After what we saw in the ocean," said Merritt, "I'd rather sleep under a piece of broken hull than risk meeting something out here."

Ivan hurried after him.

"What did you see in the ocean?" Henry asked with interest.

Niku told him as they walked toward the ramp.

"A land of wonder," said Henry, almost to himself. "And great danger."

Merritt hopped down from the cliff's edge. His boots sank into the loose dirt of the ramp and his feet slipped out from under him. He landed on his back and slid amidst a cloud of dust, rocks tumbling next to him as he dug his hands into the dirt to slow his fall.

His work boots hit something hard at the bottom of the ramp and he pitched forward, slamming to a stop against a tall pillar. He blinked hard, then plopped back down, groaning and rubbing his forehead as he sat in the dirt.

The others called down after him.

"I'm fine," Merritt shouted back irritably. "Just don't jump onto the dirt."

The pillar he ran into protruded from the ground at an angle, rising four meters from a thick base toward the dark sky. One side was razor sharp, and its tip was pointed like a dagger. Its faceted surface glinted dully in the light of Galena's moon, which was a thin smile hovering just above the horizon to the east.

He thought about Gavin and his energy deserted him, weakening his limbs. His breath came in shallow, ragged gasps as his heart swelled with pain, fear, love, and longing. He wanted to rip it from his chest and let it pull him across the world, to his son.

Merritt forced himself to stand. He brushed off his coveralls as the others scrambled down the dirt ramp behind him. Ivan came down on his stomach, coughing as dirt and sand sprayed his face.

"Not flat ground after all," said Merritt.

The pillar he ran into was not alone. It was but one of many that covered the vast plateau that lay before them — square miles of jagged mineral lead sulfide which had erupted from the ground, driven up through the planet's crust to form a labyrinth of towering swords.

Niku looked down at his bare feet and wiggled his toes in the dirt.

"Use the rock to cut off your sleeves," said Henry, already walking toward the nearest pillar. "Slip those over your feet."

In the distance, a sound like the hooting of owls carried across the field of jagged rock.

Niku stopped sawing his sleeve against the razor edge of a pillar and looked around. Merritt stepped past him, studying a narrow alley that weaved through the jagged rocks.

"We should hurry," he said. "Something is out there."

LEERA

After her broken shin went numb, hunger set in.

Leera's head lolled drunkenly against the corporal's shoulder as he struggled to support her weight. Their group had been walking for nearly two hours without rest, and the young soldier had been straining for a while.

The wound in her back pulsed pain with each step, as if an animal had bit into her flesh and clamped down harder every time she put weight on her good leg.

"Need...to stop..." she said weakly. "So hungry."

Corporal Turner splashed through a shallow stream. He stumbled and fell to one knee with a pained grunt.

"We need to rest," he said as he took Leera's arm from around his neck and propped her against a large gray rock. He unshouldered his rifle and stood next to her, catching his breath and surveying their surroundings.

"It will be dark soon," said Uda, glancing at the sky. "We won't make it to the wreckage."

Orange clouds streaked across the darkening blue. Galena's moon appeared behind a cloud — a thin, silver crescent smiling down at the world. It was almost double in apparent size when compared to Earth's own as seen from the surface.

Leera's fingers touched the edge of the stream, and she pulled them away. The clear water rushed over a bed of flat stones. Small tendrils of green algae clung to the stones, dancing in the current.

Walter plopped down next to her, panting. His face was flushed and sweaty, his white-and-black body suit now mostly black from constantly wiping dirt off his hands.

They had been walking up and down rolling hills for the better part of an hour as they pushed deeper into the forest of bare tree trunks. Leera looked up at the tree tops yet again, intrigued by the three thick branches that extended from each one, like the blunted talons of an eagle claw open toward the sky.

Her head swam and knocked against the rock. She leaned sideways and dry-heaved over the spongy ground.

Walter guided her back to a sitting position and she wiped her mouth with her dirty sleeve.

"Look," she said, raising a shaking finger to point past Walter.

He turned around and said, "Well, what do you know?"

A gnarled bush of twisted branches hugged the base of one of the nearby tree trunks, forming a near-perfect sphere as tall as a person. Large brown fruit hung from its branches.

Walter plucked one from a sharp branch and weighed it in his palm.

"It's like a grapefruit," he said, smiling as he displayed it to the others.

"Don't eat it!" Uda warned as she hurried over to him. "It's poisonous."

A look of skepticism replaced Walter's amusement as he studied the fruit more closely.

"How do you know?"

"Even if it isn't, do you want to be the first person to try native food on this planet?"

"We lost all our equipment in the crash," he said. "We have no way to test it."

"There will be equipment at the colony," she replied. "We just need to get there." Then she turned to Leera. "I'm sorry if you're hungry. I am, too. But we can't risk it."

"I know," Leera whispered hoarsely.

Her stomach rumbled in disagreement.

Uda knelt down at the edge of the stream and put one finger into it.

"It should be safe to drink if we're near the source," she said. "That might help with the hunger. I'll have a quick look."

She followed the water's edge upstream.

"We should stick together," Turner called after her.

"Come on, then," she said, not looking back.

The corporal glanced down at Leera uncertainly. She patted his foot and nodded, then leaned her head back against the rock.

"I'll stay with her," said Walter. "Just don't stay away too long. You're the only one with a weapon."

After Uda and Turner were gone from sight, Leera whispered, "Do you really think we need it?"

"The gun?" asked Walter. He thought about it a moment. "No. But knowing he has it makes me feel better. 'No significant life forms', Kellan said. You remember?"

Leera nodded. "But it's a big planet," she whispered.

Walter looked around at the towering trees. "That crossed my mind, too. Speaking of which, does it strike you that Uda knows more than she's telling us?"

Leera's eyebrows went up, and she nodded weakly.

"The Halcyon ran surface sweeps with its scanners on previous visits," said Walter. "And they delivered equipment to the colony site remotely, so maybe they had *some* idea of what to expect down here. I doubt they'd have a way to test plant toxicity without someone being on the surface." Something nearby caught his attention, and he frowned. "Was that there before?"

Leera followed his gaze and saw a circular patch of deep red moss on the ground a couple of meters away.

"I'm not sure."

"We haven't seen that color yet. It's been all green and browns and grays. I was starting to think this was a tri-tone world."

He knelt beside the patch of red and was reaching out to touch it when Corporal Turner burst from the trees.

"We found something," he said, gasping for air.

Walter stood up quickly. "What is it?" he asked, alarmed.

"Best to see it for yourself."

Leera cried out in pain as Turner lifted her up to stand beside him.

Walter walked on the other side, helping to support her weight. The three of them followed the stream up a small incline, into a thicker stand of tree trunks.

In a small clearing, the source of the stream bubbled from the ground — a small, half-moon pool rimmed by vibrant green algae. Water swelled up from below to spill over a flat gray rock and flow into the stream.

"Is it safe?" Walter asked.

"Yes," Turner answered, stopping near the pool.

Walter bent down and cupped a handful of clear water into his mouth. He swished it around, testing it, then swallowed. He tried two more handfuls, then scooped some up and tilted his palm against Leera's lips. The water was ice cold, with a faint taste of earthy minerals.

She coughed and doubled over, her body shaking as she retched.

"She *has* to rest," Walter insisted.

"Only a little farther," said Turner. "Just around those trees."

He draped Leera's arm over his neck and took her full weight, lifting her off the ground and carrying her against his side as he hurried ahead.

Her vision faded in and out, as if the sun were on a dimmer switch.

"Here!" said Turner.

They emerged from the treeline into a wide clearing. Turner gently lowered Leera against a tree trunk and stood up next to Walter.

Leera laughed suddenly as her head rolled on her shoulders. Another patch of thin red moss lay on the ground nearby, and, absurdly, this amused her to no end. She realized she was slipping into delirium.

Walter took a few steps into the clearing, and muttered, "I don't believe it."

Uda stood at the center of the clearing, next to the remains of an old bonfire. Around the edge of the clearing was a ripped canvas medical tent, small hard-shell cabins with broken windows, and an open-air mess pavilion. Every structure was covered with a layer of thick gray dust.

"Another colony," Walter said hoarsely, shuffling numbly toward the middle of the clearing. "I don't believe it."

"The first colony," said Uda.

"But..." said Walter, spinning slowly in place as he surveyed the ruins. "Where are they?"

Uda stood with her hands on her hips as she kicked over a rock near the fire pit.

"Gone," she said.

Leera laughed again. Her head fell back against the tree trunk, and she fainted.

The dreams found her, as they had aboard the

Halcyon.

Dreams of Paul, dreams of Micah.

Each one became a nightmare as she left them behind.

She left her family on a deserted beach, in a crowded market, on Sunrise Station — no matter where they were, she always left her family. She always abandoned them.

Leera woke with a start in a deep, purple twilight. She herself was alone in the ruins of a human settlement, the other survivors nowhere to be seen.

She tried to lean forward but was pinned to the tree trunk. Something moist covered her lower back, attaching her to the tree.

Have I bled that much? she wondered.

Then she looked down at her legs and screamed.

Her injured right leg was covered in a wet, brown moss, heavy as a lead blanket, smothering it from hip to ankle.

"Leera!" Walter shouted off to her left.

He came bounding into the clearing carrying a document binder in one hand and an empty cup in the other. He threw both of them aside as he skidded to a stop in front of her and saw the moss.

"Oh, God," he said.

Leera's hands shook as they hovered over the moss. She was afraid to peel it off — afraid of what she might find underneath.

Walter had no such reservation. He bent down and grabbed a corner. A ragged square broke free, ripping off like a chunk of sod. He sank his fingers into the damp moss and pulled more of it away.

Leera tried to sit up again but couldn't budge. She reached behind her back and clenched a fistful of moss, then yanked it free, grimacing as a thousand tiny moist, fibrous strands within the moss popped loose.

When she and Walter had cleared it all away, Leera wiggled the toes of her right foot. The goose egg that had swollen to the size of a softball over her right shin was gone. The pant leg of her body suit and the makeshift bandage Walter had slipped over her calf were torn open to reveal blotched red skin. Tiny red dots covered her shin like a rash.

She felt the skin of her lower back, probing for the wound she sustained when her escape pod crash-landed.

The wound had healed.

With Walter's help, Leera stood slowly. She put all her weight on her good left leg, then gently tested her right.

"No pain," she whispered.

She stood upright and bent at the knees several times, waiting for the pain to come back. When it didn't, she took a step, faltered, and lost her balance. Walter caught her as she fell and lowered her to a sitting position on the ground.

Leera stared at the pile of torn moss.

"It's the red moss from before," she said.

Walter looked around, searching for the deep red patch that had been nearby when Leera passed out.

"I believe you're right," he told her.

Leera picked up a sod-like chunk and turned it over in her hand.

"It moves," she said, "it heals, then it dies. I'd love to get this under a microscope."

Walter smiled with relief. "Feeling better, then?"

"Loads."

"Then you'll love what we found. I'm sorry we left you like that. I got carried away with searching the ruins."

"What did you find?"

His smile grew broader. "Aliens."

CHAPTER THIRTEEN

MERRITT

The moon dipped below the horizon, leaving only the faint light of a billion distant stars to guide their way through miles of jagged rock. In the wake of the last hint of daylight, a small nebula appeared in the western sky. Bright red, cloudy lines traced a lopsided spiral pattern around a glowing star nursery.

Merritt led the way, seeking out the safest path for Niku and Henry to follow. Even with one of their sleeves cut off and pulled over their feet, they still grunted and cursed when their soles found sharp rock. Ivan followed last, head jerking like a bird's at every sound.

The strange hooting they had heard at the boundary of the pillar field followed them. Niku likened it to the hoot of an owl, but higher-pitched. Each call was identical, with a single emphasis in the middle, as if the owl had been squeezed – *ooo-WAoooo*. It seemed to emanate from the very rock itself, pausing only as they drew near to its source.

Niku tripped on a rock and fell on his hands, letting out a short yelp of pain. He got to his knees, clearly exhausted, strands of his long black hair sticking out of the ponytail he'd secured with a strip of fabric from his sleeve. Fresh blood, black in the starlight, glistened on his palms.

"Quick break," said Merritt, reading the same exhaustion on the faces of Ivan and Henry. None of them said so aloud, but were clearly relieved at the chance to rest.

Merritt walked a few paces ahead, searching for any hint of the *Halcyon* in the darkness ahead. He could see no silhouette on the horizon.

He placed his palm gently against the side of a rock pillar, careful to avoid the side which tapered to a razor-sharp point. Each pillar was the same. The side facing east was dull, with shallow bowls in its surface, as if some of it had been chipped by a rock tool. The western side consisted of two planes converging on one sharp edge.

The only exception to the sameness was a collection of smooth-sided arches a short ways back, rising slightly higher than the pillars to arc gracefully overhead before burrowing into the ground. Ivan had wanted to climb one to get a look at their surroundings, but changed his mind when he saw the others weren't stopping.

The pillars were aligned in a natural grid pattern, which kept Merritt and the others on a straight path through the vast field, heading directly for the wisps of smoke which, he believed, came from the *Halcyon*'s side-hull engines. The five thin lines of smoke had vanished against the night sky, but the group had taken no major turns since losing sight of them.

"There's a hole," said Henry.

He bent over behind a pillar, hands on his knees, gazing into a black hole at its base. The top of the hole reached his knees, and was equally as wide.

"Here, too," said Ivan, pointing at another pillar. "And here." He wandered off, calling out whenever he found another hole.

"What do you suppose it is?" Henry asked, straightening up and cracking his back with a satisfied sigh.

"It's a burrow," said Niku. He wiped his palms on his body suit as he stood, smearing it with blood. "Where do you think the hooting is coming from?"

As if in response to his question, something hooted from within the hole near Henry's feet. He bent down once more to look.

Merritt said, "I wouldn't do—" just as something shrieked from the hole and shot out of it. A brown blur smacked Henry's shoulder as it flew past, sending him spinning to the ground.

Ivan shouted something in Russian and ran back to join the group. They clustered together around Henry, who rocked on the ground on his back, squeezing a gash on his bleeding shoulder and breathing hard through clenched teeth.

"There!" said Niku, pointing at a nearby pillar.

"I don't see anything," said Merritt.

"Halfway up, hugging the rock."

Merritt's eyes strained in the darkness, but all he saw was the chipped pattern on the flat side of the pillar. Then something moved against the pattern, and he discerned the outline of an animal.

Roughly the size of a giant bat, entirely muddy brown, it sprawled against the rock on its flat belly, its four bony legs splayed wide. A crested head bobbed on a thick, corded neck. Its crest was balanced by a beak-like mouth that opened vertically in a silent yawn. A secondary mouth opened horizontally within, stretching the corners of the outer beak. It had no eyes to speak of, instead possessing a matte patch of darker skin above its beak that wrapped halfway around its crested head. Thin membranes connected each forelimb to the one behind it, and seemed to flutter with each rapid breath. In place of a tail, a rigid spike as long as its body protruded from its leathery skin between its two clawed back legs.

With the appearance of this animal, the gentle hooting that had led Merritt and the others deep into the pillar field had ceased altogether. Instead, a chorus of a shrieks echoed out from the base of every pillar.

A susurration of claws on rock whispered around the group as more of the creatures slowly emerged from their dwellings, climbing the pillars.

"There must be hundreds of them," said Merritt nervously.

He stood with his back to Niku and Ivan. Henry grunted as he stood up to join them.

A whisper of clicks drifted through the air as the creatures tapped their claws against the pillars, growing louder and louder, until they all stopped abruptly. Acting in unison, as if they were mirror copies of each other, they shifted against the rock to face the same direction.

"Something is coming," Niku said.

Merritt looked north, the way he and the others were headed. The ground's texture had changed. Instead of narrow lanes of jagged rock between pillars, the lanes were now seemingly paved with large, smooth, hexagonal stones.

One of the stones skittered out of view.

"I don't think they're here for us," said Merritt.

Faster than he could track, the spike-tailed animals on the pillars darted back into their burrows with a swish of air.

"Back to the arches," Merritt said.

"What is it?" asked Ivan, stepping past him.

"The ground is moving."

Ivan's eyebrows went up in surprise as more hexagonal stones skittered into view, crowding the narrow lanes between pillars as they rushed toward the group's position.

He turned quickly and fled in the opposite direction. Merritt jogged behind Henry as he navigated the jagged rocks underfoot, clutching his bleeding shoulder.

"They're moving fast," Niku said from behind.

When Merritt reached the first arch, Ivan was already halfway up one side, talking quietly to himself in Russian as he strained to pull himself higher.

The next arch in line seemed to have more natural foot-holds, so Merritt quickly guided Henry over to it and stood at the wide base while the older man began his ascent.

Niku scrambled up the side of Ivan's arch as one of the hexagonal stones skittered out from behind a pillar, heading straight for Merritt's legs. He jumped up and grabbed hold of the arch, hugging the cool rock as the hexagonal stone bumped into the arch below. It wasn't huge — perhaps only as large as a dinner plate— but that didn't mean Merritt wanted to be on the ground next to it.

Segmented legs swept out from beneath the hexagonal stone, scrabbling at the pillar as the creature tried to climb up. All it managed to do was scratch at the lead-colored mineral, spewing dust and rock slivers in every direction. Up close, Merritt could see small pyramid-shaped protuberances on its back.

With a screech, one of the burrow animals shot out of its hole and crashed into the hexagonal stone, flipping it onto its back. A dozen sharp, segmented legs pumped furiously. The screeching animal leapt onto it tail-first, driving its rigid spike into the hexagonal crab-creature's underbelly with a wet crunch. Moving in rapid fits and starts, the hunter hauled its kill across the ground, toward its burrow. Both animals disappeared into the black pit at the base of a nearby pillar.

Merritt climbed higher as more hex-crabs skittered past, their hard legs scrabbling loudly over loose rocks. He made it to the top, next to Henry, who lay against the mostly-flat upper arch on his stomach, panting from exertion.

Brown blurs shot out from their pillar holes with a screech to snatch the crabs as they ran past.

From Merritt's vantage point, he could see the borders of the pillar field. The ground had changed from the glistening, springy moss-like covering to a solid vista of smooth, gray stone.

"It's a migration," said Henry, his tired voice filled with awe despite his shoulder wound. "Look. There are so many that some are forced to pass through the pillars."

At the northern edge of the pillar field, in the direction from which they seemed to be traveling, the hex-crabs broke against the first line of pillars like waves against a cliff, rising in a boiling mound of churning, segmented legs as they tried to avoid passing the threshold. Most succeeded in joining the mass of creatures that swelled to either side, skirting the pillar field. Others were forced onto the rocky ground and immediately began to scurry through the field to reconnect with the herd on the far side.

These unlucky critters faced a gauntlet of hungry, screeching, pillar-dwelling animals.

"They move a lot faster when they're not with the group," said Niku, looking down from the arch he shared with Ivan.

Theirs flattened out more than Merritt's at the top, providing a less uncomfortable spot to rest.

"They're afraid," said Henry. "It reminds me of wildebeest."

"What-a-beast?" Ivan asked.

"Wildebeest. You wouldn't know them, I imagine. They were part of one of the largest annual land migrations on Earth. *Large* animals. Huge. Each year, they were forced to cross rivers teeming with hungry crocodiles. There was no way around, so thousands of animals never made it to the opposite shore."

"Why they didn't learn?" asked Ivan.

"Crossing the rivers was necessary," Henry answered. "The carcasses of those wildebeest nourished an entire ecosystem. They were simply obeying the natural order."

A group of three hex-crabs darted beneath Merritt's arch. One by one, they were snatched into burrows.

"Looks like we're going to be here a while," he said. "Try not to roll off."

He rested his cheek against the cool stone of the arch, and tried to sleep, but all he could do was think of Gavin.

Hours later, Merritt woke with a start and nearly fell off the pillar. He hugged it tightly as he lay on his stomach, shivering against the stone.

It was still night. Niku, Ivan, and Henry were all passed out, hugging their own piece of arch, their legs dangling loosely to either side.

A lone hex-crab scurried across the ground below, but proceeded unmolested to the far end of the field, where it rejoined its group.

Perhaps the hunters have had their fill, thought Merritt.

Yet, surely with the large number of pillars and the comparatively low number of hex-crabs that were forced to cross the field, the hunters should still be feasting.

Several more crabs skittered past without incident.

An idea tickled the back of Merritt's mind, something that had been floating around, not quite fully formed, tugging at the edge of clarity.

Both the spike-tailed hunters and the hex-crabs spent their days in hiding. The hunters concealed themselves in rock burrows, and the crabs hid in vast numbers, locked together like a moving land mass.

Merritt realized that, from the sky, the field of crabs would look like nothing more than a smooth patch of ground. From what he'd seen by observing them at the edges of the pillar field, they moved so slowly as a group that a quick glance would reveal no movement at all.

Both animal species they had encountered lived in hiding, he thought. *But why?*

A single hunter hooted from its burrow, then all was silent. The few hex-crabs that had been scrambling like mad below Merritt's arch had stopped in place, tucking their legs under their shells to rest on the rocky ground.

In the silence, a rush of wind swelled far above the pillar field. A deep, slow *THWUP* sounded from the sky, like a sail snapping as it caught the wind. Then came another.

Merritt looked up.

Something huge moved across the night sky far above, blotting out the stars. It passed overhead, a black silhouette in the darkness. Giant wings reached out from a wide body.

THWUP.

The wings beat the air as the beast flew past the field, the stars disappearing as it passed and blinking back into view in its wake.

After the sound of its wings had faded, the burrow-dwelling animals resumed their hunt. They darted between pillars as the hex-crabs scurried away, spearing them through their top-shells with spiked tails and dragging them out of sight.

Merritt looked down from the sky, eyes wide with fear, his heart pounding in his chest. He rested his cheek against the cool arch, hugged it tightly, and wished for morning.

TULLIVER

The food options certainly hadn't improved.

Tulliver stared down at the metal plate in his hands. A dented spoon rested in a puddle of soy mush that oozed clear liquid from its wet edges.

Tulliver had walked right to the front of the line after a queue was already formed, and no one said a thing.

Some were too exhausted to make a fuss. Half of them owed him a crop-debt in exchange for services rendered during the voyage. They probably expected him to forget about it if they just kept their mouths shut long enough.

They were wrong.

Let them believe that's the case, said a voice in his head which was not his own. *You could get away with* so *much more.*

It was Ivan's voice, though he spoke very clearly, with only a slight hint of Russian accent.

Tulliver sniffed and left the tent, searching for a place to sit. The voices in his head had started up again after arriving on Galena. They had left him in peace for most of the voyage, but something about this new world had stirred the pot, so to speak.

The line for food extended out of the open-sided mess tent behind him, fifty people long. A few survivors had trickled in over the course of the six-hour night, claiming they had been forced to wait for the gray ground to slide past their escape pods.

Tulliver sat on a mostly-dry patch of ground on the side of the hill overlooking the settlement. He spooned the cold soy mush into his mouth, choking it down in three quick gulps to get it over with, then tossed the empty metal plate aside and belched.

The texture would improve after the first soy-flower harvest. Hopefully someone remembered to pack some spices in the limited supplies that made it to the surface. Tulliver shuddered at the thought of eating the cold, oozing, flavorless, vat-grown mush for another month or more. He plucked out a fibrous brown thread weaving through the topsoil and inspected it absentmindedly. Maybe the chef could start a fire and warm the soy mush for lunch instead of serving it cold. Tulliver wondered who he could talk to in order to make that happen.

He frowned as a revelation teased his mind, dancing just beyond reach. He rolled the soft, fibrous root between his fingers and breathed loudly through his nose, as he always did while concentrating.

The muscles of his face loosened when he figured it out. He did so by working backward from a single question: How was the soy mush brought down to the surface?

According to his sources on the ship, the *Halcyon* had remote-delivered much of the colony's infrastructure while in orbit during previous visits.

Things like rigid tents, build-it-yourself house kits, empty storage silos, and basic farming equipment were consolidated to fit into unmanned surface-delivery systems — cubes of various sizes with rockets on all eight corners. The cubes had only enough fuel to reach the surface, then became, more or less, lawn ornaments.

Yet a tank of liquid food — enough to feed a colony of hungry settlers until the first harvest came in — would be too heavy for the surface-delivery cubes.

It would need to come down in a shuttle, piloted by the wardens.

Tulliver stood, puzzling over the implications of his revelation while the colonists milled about the nascent colony below.

If his suspicions were true, that would mean the shuttle was still on the surface, yet it was nowhere in sight. The wardens had probably landed it a safe distance from camp, fearful that a terrified colonist might try to break orbit.

It would certainly be possible, but, with no *Halcyon* to dock with, the pilot would remain adrift above Galena, unable to return to the surface for lack of fuel.

The urge to relieve himself seized Tulliver with a sudden fierceness.

He walked along the side of the hill, following its broad curve until the colony was out of sight behind him. Entering a stand of the towering bare tree trunks, he hurried to a large bush of sharp, densely-woven, branches — almost like a monstrous tumbleweed — and relieved himself of last night's water. From what he'd heard, latrines would eventually be constructed somewhere nearby, but Tulliver thought it prudent to give back to nature whenever possible.

As he turned back toward the settlement, a pair of dirty work boots on the other side of the bush caught his eye. Moving quietly on the soft ground, Tulliver stepped around the bush to find a dead man lying on the ground on his side, curled up in a fetal position, his skin ghostly white.

The man's bloodshot eyes bulged in their sockets. His tongue protruded from his mouth, black and swollen. He clutched a grapefruit-sized brown fruit in one stiff hand, several large bites taken from its discolored flesh.

Tulliver knelt down and put his thumb on the man's forehead, tilting his face up. It was the *Halcyon*'s equipment foreman. Tulliver had dealt with him often throughout the trip — when the man could be found. He had a knack for avoiding interaction with the rest of the crew. Tulliver suspected he would not be missed.

He poked the brown fruit, then rubbed his fingers together thoughtfully.

Where will they put all the bodies? he wondered.

Three loud bells sounded from the direction of the main camp. Orientation was about to begin.

Like most of the other colonists, Tulliver had spent last night under the stars, nothing between him and the moist ground but a thin blanket. He had slept well enough, but awoke with wet clothes and a stiff neck. There were rumblings amongst the other colonists that the wardens would be putting up more tents until they had a chance to assign the housing kits.

By the time Tulliver made it back to the settlement, most of the survivors had gathered around a makeshift platform next to the mess tent, standing in a loose half-circle around the two wardens running the show. Tulliver maneuvered his way to the front of the crowd. He stood a head taller than everyone else, though as he looked at one of the wardens up on the platform, he wondered if that man wasn't taller yet.

He wore the same tight-fitting gray warden's uniform as the much younger Diego, who stood beside him, yet the material of his clothing bulged over his muscular arms, legs, and chest. Black hair hugged his skull in a strict military cut. He clenched his smooth, square jaw while he concentrated on the screen of his tablet, clutching it like a child's toy in his meaty hand. Like Diego, he had a thin stun-baton slung over one shoulder.

A true giant of a man, thought Tulliver.

An expectant silence fell over the crowd. A cool breeze flapped loose canvas on a nearby tent.

There were a few familiar faces in the crowd, and the rest Tulliver assumed had gone into a stasis pod just after leaving Earth. Everyone who stayed awake had wandered over to The Velvet Speakeasy eventually, even if they didn't become regulars.

Tulliver spotted Gavin standing at the edge of the platform, bags under his eyes. The boy hadn't slept, or hadn't slept well. A thin man with a face like a weasel stood next to him, black-stained fingertips resting on Gavin's shoulders. He made eye contact with Tulliver, then stepped behind Gavin, blocking him from view.

A young boy and girl were the only other children in the crowd. They were roughly the same age as Gavin, and stood hugging their mother's legs. The big warden looked down at them and smiled tightly. Given the way she stood near his side of the platform, facing the crowd more than the wardens, Tulliver guessed they were a couple.

He handed his tablet to Diego and clasped his hands in front of his waist.

"Let's begin," he said in a deep, booming voice. "I'm Warden Cohen. This is Warden Ramirez. Some of you were expecting to go back to Earth. None of you were expecting to be stranded." He looked over the crowd with icy blue eyes, letting his words sink in. "Whether you are farmers, ship stewards, or workmen, I want to make one thing absolutely clear from the beginning. Despite the tragedy of the Halcyon, there is still rule of law. As government representatives, colony wardens are responsible for upholding a predetermined code and enforcing peace. Farmers must still honor their contracts. You are now citizens of Earth's first extrasolar colony. We are alone, yes, but that is no excuse for anarchy."

He glanced at his tablet. "At last count, there are seven unclaimed farming contracts. If they are not claimed within the month, I will open them up for renewal. They will be awarded to those who work hard for the betterment of the colony. Apprenticeship on existing farms will benefit your application."

"What about the boy?" said Tulliver loudly.

Several colonists turned to look at him, then back at the wardens, awaiting a response.

Cohen's gaze briefly flicked down to Gavin.

"The Farming Initiative states that a contract can only be inherited by someone twelve years of age or older."

"The Alder boy did better than the rest of his class," bellowed Tulliver. "Not bad for an eight-year-old. Surely his skill is worth more to the colony than that of one who simply meets the arbitrary age requirement."

Murmurs of assent rippled through the crowd.

"Sounds like a good idea to me," said a man near the platform.

Cohen hesitated, then said, "We will review his contract."

Tulliver caught Gavin peeking out from behind the weasel-faced man. He smiled at the boy.

"What about food?" a woman shouted from the back of the crowd. "Shelter?"

"If you work, you eat," said Cohen. "It's that simple. There are no shortage of jobs, and we've only been here one day. These tents were never meant to be our permanent shelters. The irradiated wreckage of the Halcyon is scattered for miles. Salvage teams wearing hazmat suits will be sent out to collect material for shelter. Certain comforts you were expecting may never arrive. Be prepared to go without. Those of you who paid for housing kits may not get them."

"Now that ain't right," said the weasel-faced man standing behind Gavin.

Cohen fixed him with an icy glare.

"Nor is your situation. You can adapt, or you can give up. It's up to each of you to make the choice." He addressed the crowd once again. "Salvage team schedules and land parcel assignments will be posted later today. That's all for now."

He and Diego hopped down from the platform and disappeared into a small, circular shelter behind it—their makeshift administration headquarters. The weasel-faced man quickly guided Gavin away from the crowd. The rest of the colonists remained by the platform, talking quietly amongst themselves.

Tulliver chewed on his bottom lip, wondering where the wardens had parked their shuttle.

As he made his way toward the admin shelter, shouldering his way through the milling crowd, a short man with a hooked nose and unkempt black beard fell into step beside him. Tulliver recognized him as someone on the *Halcyon* for which he'd done a lot of favors.

"Mr. Tulliver, you have to help me," the man

pleaded, his voice shaking. "I *can't* go back out there." He glanced behind him, into the forest. "Can you keep me out of the salvage group? I-I-I can owe you." He chuckled nervously. "You know, put it on my tab?"

"You already owe too much, Nigel" said Tulliver. "Don't get in over your head."

"But there *must* be something you can—"

Tulliver put his palm flat against the man's chest and shoved, sending him stumbling backward. He tripped and fell, his back smacking the wet ground.

Tulliver pushed aside the canvas door-flap of the admin shelter and stepped inside as if he had every right to be there.

Cohen and Diego sat at a small folding table, several tablets and stacks of binders laid out before them.

Diego glanced up as Tulliver entered, then at Cohen, then back to his tablet screen. A scent of alcohol permeated the small space, emanating from a plastic cup filled with dark brown liquid resting near Cohen's elbow.

"I'm going to miss that smell after the last drop is gone," Tulliver said pleasantly.

"Ah, good. You're here," Cohen replied without looking up. He scribbled a note on his tablet screen with a stylus. "Saves me the trouble of hunting you down."

Tulliver grinned. The man chose his words with care. Cohen set down his stylus and laced his fingers over his stomach as he leaned back in his chair, regarding Tulliver with the same detachment with which one might view a puzzle that didn't need to be solved.

"My reputation precedes me," said Tulliver.

"I know who you are," Cohen continued. "I know how you operated on the ship."

"Then you know how useful I can be."

"Not to this colony," said Cohen. He stood slowly, and Tulliver found himself looking up at someone for the first time since he was a teenager. "You sowed distrust among the crew. You turned several of them against each other. This colony will not suffer your meddling. It will not be divided."

Tulliver spread his hands palm-up in a placating gesture.

"I acquire things for people who need them. I bring people *together*."

"No," Cohen said simply.

"The captain had a different opinion."

"I am not the captain."

Tulliver held his icy glare for a long time, then looked away.

"I can see that," he said with a defeated smile. "Message received, good warden. I won't darken your door again."

He left the shelter quickly, his smile evaporating the moment sunlight hit his face.

A status quo was being established in the colony — a status quo which didn't seem to account for the unique talents possessed by a man like Tulliver.

He had to get ahead of the problem before it was set in stone — before the colonists understood there was no need to honor the debts they had incurred on their journey from Earth.

He found Nigel in the heart of the crowd, speaking with a tall woman with stark white hair.

Tulliver said, "Excuse me," to the woman and grabbed Nigel by the throat.

He hoisted the short man into the air as the crowd stepped back.

"Everyone pays!" Tulliver growled. "No debts are forgiven."

He turned slowly in place, showing Nigel's bulging eyes to the other colonists. The man's legs kicked feebly against Tulliver's side as he choked for air.

He threw Nigel into the tall woman, sending them both falling to the ground. The crowd parted before him as he stomped away.

That felt good, didn't it? said the voice of Roland Day in his head. Tulliver's erstwhile partner-in-crime on Earth had been among the most vocal of his disembodied commentators.

"Shut up," Tulliver hissed as he left the settlement behind and stormed into the forest.

As always, Roland was right.

CHAPTER FOURTEEN

LEERA

The first colony sprawled behind Leera as she sat on a patch of moist, springy ground on a hillside, looking down at a field of unbroken gray rock. Not two hours past, the field before her was mostly brown, streaked with vibrant swaths of green. The far side of the field led into the forest, its floor also blanketed by gray rock.

The edge of the sheet of rock was a few meters from Leera's bare feet. It extended to her left and right, following the gentle rise and fall of hills.

A million segmented legs churned beneath the gray blanket, carrying it ever-so-slowly east, toward the rising sun. Phobis blazed low in the sky, bathing the field and hillside in a warm, orange glow. To the west, she could discern no end to the migrating gray sheet of rock.

A dead animal lay on the wet ground beside her, its pale carapace translucent in the morning sunlight.

Leera picked it up and inspected its flat, hexagonal crab shell, running her hands over three small, pyramidal protrusions. She looked from the dead creature to the moving field of gray rock crawling slowly past the hill. Sunlight glinted off small, dew-covered pyramids that rose from the otherwise smooth field, each one spaced about a hand's width apart.

The shells were locked together so perfectly that their tops created the unbroken field of gray which extended into the distance.

Leera flipped the dead creature over in her lap, resting its hard shell on her thighs. Fourteen segmented, ghost-white legs were folded neatly up against its underbelly, their sharp tips angled toward what Leera assumed was a mouth. The mouth was in the exact center of the creature's underbelly. It was a small, barely-open slit with swollen, fibrous edges, like the mouth of a starfish.

She tried to unfold a leg, but the brittle appendage snapped off in her hand. The sharp tip had a small hole at the end, and a cluster of stiff, brush-like hair protruded from the hole. Leera touched the hair gently, and it crumbled to dust.

Walter had found this particular specimen shortly after her group stumbled across the first colony. It was inside one of the torn canvas tents at the heart of the settlement.

Uda and Colonel Turner had set out before sunrise to map the colony. From what Leera had seen before she passed out last night from exhaustion, there were more structures beyond the ones they'd first discovered. Some had collapsed onto themselves in a heap of rotting canvas, others were damaged yet still standing, and still others were fully intact. Greenish-brown mildew covered them all.

She rubbed her right shin, feeling the small

bump on her tibia where the bone had snapped. All she felt was a dull pain, and she had to press down hard to feel it. The shrapnel wound on her back had completely healed, as well, all thanks to the strange moss that crept over her leg and back after she fainted.

Leera had told Walter to keep a special eye out for any scientific equipment in the first colony. She desperately wanted to get a closer look at that moss.

As if summoned by her thoughts, he emerged from a tent behind her, brushing dirt off a tablet with a shattered screen. He had clipped a black nylon belt around the waist of his skin-tight body suit. A large pocket bulged on one side of the belt, stuffed with odds and ends he'd picked up throughout the settlement.

"I like the new look," said Leera as he plopped onto the wet ground beside her.

Walter looked offended and shook his belt pouch. "Hey, they're making a comeback."

He flipped the tablet over in his hands and studied the back.

"Don't tell me it still has a charge," Leera said.

"It doesn't," Walter admitted. Then he held up a finger. "*But.*"

He rummaged in his pouch and pulled out two cables, along with a small square sheet of black plastic. He connected the cables to the square sheet and to the matching holes on the bottom edge of the tablet.

"Solar," he said as he set everything down on the ground. "Maybe it can tell us something about what happened. Speaking of which, I'm fairly certain Uda knew this colony existed."

"What makes you say that?"

"I came across her standing in a tent last night. She didn't see me, but I watched her for a moment. She picked something up from a shelf inside. It looked like a broken picture frame. I could swear she was crying."

Leera stared down thoughtfully at the migrating hexagon-shelled creatures.

"She trained farmers on our trip from Earth, getting them ready to grow crops on Galena."

Walter nodded. "Maybe she did it before."

"Kellan lied to us," said Leera. "He said no one has been allowed down to the surface until this trip."

"Of course he lied," said Walter. "Do you think he'd be able to convince *anyone* to come back if they found out an entire colony had vanished?"

Leera set the dead creature on the ground beside her.

"You said you found more of these scattered throughout the camp."

"Dead ones. All over the place."

"They all look like this?" she asked, tapping the shell of the dead one by her leg.

"Exactly the same."

"They passed this way before," said Leera. "Without knowing the details of their decomposition cycle, I'd still guess it's been a few years, at least."

"You think they killed the colonists?"

Leera sighed. "I don't see how. It wouldn't be hard to outrun them."

"It could have happened at night, while they slept. Maybe they woke up under a blanket of those...things. Tried to fight their way out."

"Or there's something else on this planet," said Leera. "A virus."

"There are no bodies."

"Dr. James!" called Turner from somewhere behind her.

"Here!"

Turner and Uda appeared at the top of the hill, walking briskly away from the colony. She carried three chromed metal rods in one hand. Each was two meters long, with one spiked end.

"Those crabs are in the camp," said Turner. "Crawling all over it."

"Like someone's pulling a sheet of stone over the entire colony," said Uda.

Leera stood up and walked to the top of the hill.

The foremost edge of another field of the crab-like creatures approached, crawling slowly past the tents at the far end of the clearing.

"What do we do?" asked Turner.

He wiped sweat from his brow and trained his rifle on the approaching sea of creatures.

"Save your bullets," said Walter. "Unless you have a million more."

"What are those?" asked Leera, pointing at the three metal rods in Uda's hand.

She looked down at them as if she'd forgotten what she was carrying.

"I found them on one of the farms," she replied. "I think they're radio spikes."

"They are," said Turner.

"You can't send radio signals through the Rip," said Walter.

"The military uses them to communicate between outposts," Turner told him. "The colonists were probably sending reports to the nav beacon near Aegea. But something's different about these. May I see one?"

"We should really think about leaving," said Walter, eyeing the slowly-approaching crabs.

Uda handed Turner a rod. He inspected the spiked end, then flipped it around and fiddled with a delicate electronics interface at the top.

"This one's been altered," he said. "It can't receive any signals. Someone reprogrammed it to emit a specific frequency."

"Why?" asked Walter.

Turner shrugged.

"They're avoiding the hillside," said Uda, pointing.

The others stood next to her. The approaching wave of crabs were on a direct course to climb the hill, yet they turned aside, sweeping around it like a curving river to pass through the settlement instead.

Leera walked back to the dead creature she had been inspecting on the hillside and knelt beside it. She stuck her fingers into the soft top-layer of the ground, wiggling them deeper, up to her large knuckles.

"No shock," she told the others.

"What are you talking about?" asked Walter.

"I felt a shock before, in the soil. It's gone."

She hurried back up the hill, into the camp.

"Leera!" Walter shouted from behind.

She stood a few meters from the approaching crabs and dug her fingers into the soil. A low-grade shock licked her fingertips and she jerked her hand back.

"Let me see one!" she said to Turner, holding out her hand.

He gave her a metal rod and stepped back, gripping his rifle tightly.

Leera raised the spike over her head and drove its spiked end into the soft ground. She brushed wild strands from her eyes and looked at the crabs.

They were still approaching.

Turner appeared at her side, slinging his rifle over his shoulder. He slid up a small protective cover at the top of the rod and pressed a red button. A sequence of yellow numbers glowed on a tiny screen, and Turner pressed the button again.

The front line of crabs parted instantly, moving to both sides to avoid the path that took them straight into the rod.

"Proof of concept," said Leera with a grin.

She yanked the rod out of the ground and the crabs came back together, sealing the crack in their ranks that had opened to avoid the rod.

"The shock is caused by an electrical current under the top-layer," said Leera, unable to conceal her excitement. "The rods emit a signal that negates the current and cancel it out. That's why the crabs aren't crossing the hill directly. There's no current."

"That's fantastic," said Uda flatly. "How do we get out of here?"

"Back to the hillside," Leera replied, running ahead of the group.

The others joined her on the hill, in the warm morning sunlight. They were stranded on a tiny island in an ocean of alien crabs.

"What's creating the electrical current?" asked Walter.

Leera shielded her eyes as she looked at the tops of the trees looming over the crawling crabs.

"I don't..." she said, breathing hard. "I don't know. Something about the trees. They don't travel beyond the trees." She shook her head. "I don't know."

Something beeped nearby.

"Ah-ha!" said Walter triumphantly.

He picked up his tablet and pulled out the charging cables. Its cracked screen glinted in the sunlight.

"It's working!"

While he swiped and tapped on the screen, Uda took a few steps down the hill and squinted at the horizon.

"They are turning east," she said, nodding toward the sea of crabs. Then she turned to face the others. "What's your best guess for the location of the new colony?"

Leera's mouth went dry. She swallowed thickly, then said, "East."

"Does the new colony have any radio spikes?" asked Turner.

"Even if they did, they wouldn't know how to change the frequency," said Leera. "We have to warn them."

"Maybe there are more spikes in the shuttle," said Walter.

The others slowly turned to look at him. He held up the cracked tablet and showed them the screen.

"One of the last log entries says they parked it nearby. And it still has fuel."

He turned in place, holding up the tablet as he scanned the horizon. A mile to the north, a mountain of mineral lead sulfide rose above the forest.

"There," said Walter. "At the base of that rock."

"The shuttle has a guidance system which should be able to pick up the new colony's nav beacon," said Uda.

"It may even have a working radio," Leera added.

"How do we get there?" asked Turner.

Leera walked down the hillside, toward the sea of crabs. She held the rod out in front of her, but they didn't alter course. Then she drove it into the ground and they scurried away as if she'd just tossed a rock into their midst.

"Leapfrog," she called back to the others.

Uda walked past her, carrying the other two rods. She went right up next to the edge of the migrating crabs and slammed a rod into the ground. Nothing happened.

"The switch," said Turner.

Uda slid open the small protective cover near the top and pressed a red button twice. The crabs jumped away like they'd been shocked, revealing a patch of ground beneath, two meters in diameter. Then she moved quickly to the far edge of the small clearing and repeated the process, opening another two meters of safe ground.

"Stay together," said Leera. "They'll seal the openings after we pass."

The group huddled together as they worked their way slowly north, pulling up the last rod in line and driving it into the soil at the very edge of their small patch of open ground, pushing back the line of crab-like creatures.

"It's a long way to that rock," said Walter. "What if the rods lose their charge?"

"The shuttle will have a charging bay for biolith cells," said Uda. "These spikes probably use biolith."

"Won't do us much good if we die before we get there," Walter added.

"Maybe we can run on top of the crabs," said Turner.

"Until they decide to move out from under us," said Uda. "Then we fall."

Leera drove her spike into the ground. "The charge will hold," she said. "We'll find the shuttle, and we'll reach the colony."

"What if..." said Walter cautiously. "What if there *is* no colony? What if we're the only survivors?"

Leera paused with her hand gripped tightly around the cold metal of her radio spike. After Uda stuck another one in the ground ahead to part the crabs, Leera yanked hers up and swiped hair from her sweaty brow.

"We have to try," she said.

And then what? she thought. *We settle in? Wait for another ship to come? How long will that take, if one ever comes at all?*

She looked up to the cerulean sky, wishing with all her heart to see the *Halcyon* in orbit, waiting to take her back to her family.

The sky was empty except for a single, lonely cloud.

Rage swelled inside her as she looked down from the sky — rage at Kellan, who had lied about the dangers of Galena; rage at the *Halcyon*, for not holding together; rage at herself for leaving her home and her family.

Leera focused on the path ahead, ripping out a spike and driving it back into the ground with purpose, channeling all her pain and anger into each thrust.

Yes, her group of survivors still had a long way to go before they reached the mountainous rock, but she had enough brimming fury to get them there.

TULLIVER

The proposed farm sites had been laid out in a grid pattern south of the colony site. Twenty initial two-hectare sites had been identified from orbit on previous trips to Galena. The patchwork quilt of farms formed a misshapen square over the land, rising with the hills and dipping into broad troughs. The westernmost farms bordered a small river, and had been assigned to red ticket passengers who paid extra for the waterfront land.

Tulliver stood before the land distribution map the wardens had posted outside their tent earlier that afternoon. It had to have been printed aboard the *Halcyon*, where most of the decisions had been made. There were a few hand-drawn alterations to the map, mostly scribbled-out names of farmers known to be missing or deceased.

He traced a finger over the map, starting at the colony and moving south, squinting at the small handwriting squeezed in between wavy elevation lines.

The name *Merritt Alder* had been carefully crossed out. Written next to it in tidy letters was the name *Gavin Alder*.

Tulliver grunted with amusement and tapped the distorted parallelogram of farmland. Most of it was on the eastern slope of a large hill and in the wide trough beneath.

Good for irrigation, he thought. *Good for sunlight. If the soil isn't rotted, the boy's lucky.*

It was not one of the coveted sites bordering the western river, but it was a good deal better than the surrounding farms.

Warden Cohen walked out of the admin tent, focused on the tablet in his hands. He stopped and looked at Tulliver when he noticed him by the map. Tulliver offered him a friendly smile, then turned and whistled as he moseyed away, hands stuck in the pockets of his jacket.

He carried an item in each pocket, items he cupped in his palms and rubbed his thumbs over carefully while his brain worked through the various problems that lay before him.

While his brain puzzled its way through one particular problem named Cohen, Tulliver went to see a man about alcohol.

He took his time as he made his way through camp, impressed by the progress that had been made in such a short amount of time.

Several more temporary structures had been erected that morning to join the few already in the broad clearing at the heart of the new colony. There was now a small medical tent, though the medical supplies with which to stock it had not yet been recovered.

Four hard-shelled bunkhouses squatted beneath trees on the northern edge of the settlement, each one capable of housing eight people.

The camp was a great deal emptier since the farmland assignments had been posted. Most of the farmers were eager to get started, tossing their allotted bags of soyflower seeds over their shoulders and wandering off to find their own piece of the colony.

It would be hard work, Tulliver knew. On Earth, there were probably only a handful of farmers that ever touched their own soil. The rest relied on their machines.

Behind the low-roofed bunkhouses, a young man in a dark gray ship's administrator uniform pulled plastic crates from a large stack and separated them into smaller stacks nearby. After he moved each crate, he would tick a checklist box on his tablet.

Tulliver fixed a slight smile on his lips as he approached.

"The work's just starting, isn't it?" he asked casually.

The supply manager grunted as he set down a heavy crate, his back to Tulliver.

"I've a feeling it will never end," he said in a high, clear voice. He brushed aside a lock of black hair as he stood and turned around. Then he smiled without humor. "Ah. It's you."

"It's me," said Tulliver.

The man went back to work, pulling another heavy crate from the large pile.

"I don't have what I owe you," the supply manager told him. "As you can see, everyone's still getting settled."

He dropped the crate on a small stack with a grunt.

"You can forget the payment, Samar," said Tulliver.

Samar chuckled as he moved another crate. "Oh? Why is that? Did you find religion?"

"I'm thirsty."

Samar wiped his sweaty palms on his uniform shirt and regarded him carefully. He glanced around the settlement before looking back at Tulliver.

"It won't last forever, you know."

"Of course I know," Tulliver agreed. "Until it's gone, whoever has it will be in a very nice position."

"I'd like it to be me."

"I only need a little. Just a few drops, really, and we'll wipe your slate clean."

Samar's eyes narrowed with suspicion. "No more payment?"

Tulliver spread his hands magnanimously, then placed one over his heart. "My word is my bond."

"I'm sure." He looked around the camp again. "How much do you want?"

"Just one little flask. Enough to get me through the night."

Samar hesitated for a long moment, then nodded. He walked around to the back of the large stack of crates and produced an empty plastic flask from a canvas bag. Lifting the lid on one of the crates, he revealed a plastic jug filled with dark brown liquid. He set it atop another crate and held the mouth of the flask to a small metal nozzle.

"The wardens brought this down themselves," he said as he twisted the nozzle handle, filling the flask. He knocked the last drop off the nozzle and screwed the lid back on the flask. "They mean for this to last a few weeks."

"Our little secret," Tulliver assured him.

He handed the flask to Tulliver, who accepted it graciously and tucked it away in his inner jacket pocket.

Tulliver made a goofy face and waved his hand in front of Samar in a mock-religious gesture, saying, "You are free."

Samar laughed and shook his head, then returned to his sorting duties.

Tulliver patted the flask over his jacket as he set off toward the farms.

Leaving the forest of tree trunks behind, he emerged on a low rise overlooking a valley that stretched away to the south and west, toward a snaking river that shimmered in the afternoon sunlight. Beyond the river, two mountains with dark green peaks touched the clouds. In the distance to the east was a narrow sea, enormous gray waves breaking upon its shore.

The owners of the first farm Tulliver passed weren't wasting any time. A stout, older man leaning on a slender shovel and a tall, thin woman a few years his junior had all the pieces of their build-it-yourself home laid out on their property like a giant jigsaw puzzle. They stood near the pieces, arguing over the instructions. A strip of their land had already been hand-tilled, and an open bag of seed lay on the ground beside it.

On the distant hills beyond, Tulliver could see more farmers moving about their property, marking their borders and deciding where to erect their homes.

Those who hadn't purchased a pre-made build kit had rolled out sleeping bags or thin blankets supplied from the meager colony stores. One farmer had dragged the hatch of his escape pod to his farm site and half-buried it sticking out of the ground so he would have something to recline against.

Tulliver crested a small hill and found himself looking down on Gavin Alder's property. The boy worked the ground with a large hand trowel, hacking clumps of soil to pieces. The weasel-faced man Tulliver had seen during orientation was with him, supervising.

The boy's father hadn't purchased a home kit, so the property was empty but for Gavin, his chaperone, and two bags of seed.

Tulliver tromped down the hill, the soles of his large boots sinking into the soft ground.

Gavin saw him approaching and stood up straight. He wiped his sweaty brow with his wrist, adding more smudges to his dirty face.

The weasel-faced man turned to face Tulliver and crossed his arms.

"Not yer property," he said with a thick twang.

"Ain't yours, either," Tulliver replied.

"I'm the boy's friend." He nodded down at Gavin. "What are you?"

Tulliver knelt in the dirt, eye-to-eye with the boy.

"I'm Tulliver."

Gavin looked up at his chaperone uncertainly.

"Look at me," said Tulliver gently. Gavin did, and Tulliver smiled. "I'm not going to hurt you."

He stood to face the other man.

"What's your name?"

"My friend's call me Skip, but you can call me Sir."

"I see no friends," said Tulliver, looking around. "You're alone. Being alone can be dangerous."

"Listen, I didn't make no deal with you, and I don't *want* to make no deal."

Tulliver stepped closer to him.

"How 'bout this deal, Skip?" he said quietly enough so the boy couldn't hear him. "You shuffle away now, and I won't turn you into fertilizer."

Skip swallowed hard as he tilted his head up to contend with Tulliver's dead-eyed stare. He finally looked away and knelt down in front of Gavin, resting a hand on his shoulder.

"I'm over by the river," he told the boy. "If you need anything, just holler at your neighbors and they'll come fetch me."

Gavin nodded reluctantly as Skip stood and jabbed a shaking finger at Tulliver's chest.

"If you hurt him, every soyflower on my property's gonna taste like *you*."

Tulliver watched him stomp away, his bony hands balled into fists.

"Always feels good to have the last word," Tulliver said thoughtfully. "Even if you lose."

He knelt down once more in front of Gavin, then admired the fervor with which he'd been attacking the soil.

"Gonna do this whole field yourself, are you?"

The boy looked down at the ground, and shrugged.

"Tell you what," said Tulliver. "I'll find some folks to help you. They *like* helping. How does that sound?"

Gavin did not lift his gaze from the ground, but he gave a little nod.

Tulliver scratched his nose and looked around the empty field. On a hill to the west, a young boy and girl played a game of tag, laughing as they took turns chasing each other.

Gavin saw them, too.

He watched them for a long moment, then resumed hacking at the soil with his hand trowel.

"It's hard losing someone you love," said Tulliver. "I'll tell you one thing before you find out yourself. It never gets easier. The pain never goes away."

Tears spilled down Gavin's dirty cheeks.

"The sooner you come to terms with that, the stronger you'll be." He grunted as he stood up to look down his nose at the boy. "Don't worry. We'll have this field growing in no time, then you can work off what your daddy owes me. After that, you'll be your own man."

He hesitated, as if he wanted to say something more, but wasn't sure what it was.

"Right then," was all he could manage before turning away, leaving the boy to his tears.

As dusk fell that evening, Tulliver rested against a tree trunk a short ways from the colony. He sat in a nook between two large roots, which were unusual as most of the tree trunks had no visible roots at the base of their trunks.

He had made it his own personal camp until he could acquire something classier. So far, he owned a blanket, a thin pillow, a spare shirt that was too tight, an extra pair of socks, and his red ticket, which was all but worthless down on the surface.

Tulliver could sleep in one of the bunkhouses, but the beds were sure to be too small. He liked it in the open, beneath the stars. They twinkled brilliantly, bestrewn across the purple canvas of the night sky.

Tulliver settled back against the tree, its large roots hugging his shoulders.

The pulpy remains of two native brown fruit were barely visible at the base of a nearby tree. Tulliver stared at them for a long moment, then focused his attention on the stars above.

He had found a good spot between those roots. Yet they were not the only reason he had chosen that particular tree to set up camp.

The noise of a cracking branch drifted through the forest. Tulliver searched the growing shadows for the source.

Fire bloomed in the distant wood, flaring briefly from the ground before calming to a low, contained blaze. Its light flickered on the face of Warden Cohen, who lowered himself to a sitting position next to the small fire. He took a long drink from a flask, then wiped his mouth.

Tulliver pulled his own flask from his inner jacket pocket and twisted its cap absentmindedly as he watched Cohen from afar.

The man was drinking with a purpose. He brought the flask to his lips every few seconds, tilting his head back farther each time. When it was empty, he looked into it, then tossed it aside with disappointment.

Tulliver pushed himself off the tree and worked his way quietly through the forest, toward the fire.

No one should drink alone, he thought.

CHAPTER FIFTEEN

MERRITT

They came across their first piece of the *Halcyon* about a mile from the pillar field.

It was a charred hull plate as tall as a three-story building, standing like a monolith at the center of a ring of broken trees. It had hit the ground at an angle, creating a large impact crater at its base.

Merritt, Niku, Ivan, and Henry skirted the edge of the crater, heading for what they hoped was the primary crash site.

The five slender smoke trails Merritt theorized were rising from the *Halcyon*'s hull thrusters had evaporated during the short night, along with all signs of the hexagonal crab animals and the burrow-dwelling hunters.

It had taken them three hours to delicately navigate their way through the remainder of the field of pillars. Niku's and Henry's makeshift foot coverings were black, red, and shredded by the time they stepped onto soft ground beyond the field.

Even now they limped, groaning occasionally when their feet found anything harder than a wet sponge.

"We better start coming up with names," said Merritt as they walked through an open section of the forest.

"I'm Niku," said Niku.

Henry chuckled.

"You know what I mean," Merritt told him.

Niku grinned. "Yes, I know. What did you have in mind?"

"Well, these things, for starters," said Merritt, gesturing at the tree trunks all around them.

"Trees," Henry said.

"Easy one," Ivan called from the back of the group.

"Okay, then, what about the creatures with hexagonal shells, and the things that were hunting them?"

"Crabs," said Henry. "And crab hunters."

"You're good at this," said Niku with a wry smile.

Henry faked a bow. "I am an explorer, after all. What good would I be if I couldn't find names for new discoveries?"

He winced and flexed his injured shoulder. The wound he sustained from a leaping hunter last night was red and inflamed. It oozed blood from its edges, further staining his body suit.

"And that big animal flying through the air last night?" asked Merritt.

No one offered up an immediate answer. He had told them about what he saw while they slept, as he hugged the arch in terror: a massive silhouette, high in the night sky, passing like a shadow over the stars.

"*Sora-jū*," said Niku gravely.

"What does that mean?"

He looked up at the clouds. "Sky Beast."

"I hope I never see this beast of sky," said Ivan.

They came across two more pieces of wreckage, each the size of a small house, and each one scarring the land where it fell, scraping long, black trenches in the ground.

"Kellan said there was no significant animal life detected on the surface," said Niku as the group walked between the two pieces of debris. "Nothing larger than a teddy bear."

"Then he's either a liar," said Merritt, "or very bad at his job."

"I imagine he told you he got his information from surface scans while the Halcyon was in orbit," Henry said.

"That's right."

Henry smiled knowingly. "The Halcyon held a prograde orbit on each visit to Galena. How can one scan the surface of an entire planet if their ship is following its rotation?"

"He did say to avoid the oceans," Niku admitted.

"With good cause, as it turns out," said Henry. "I'm grateful not to have witnessed that scene on the shore. I'm sorry you all can't say the same."

"Do you smell that?" Merritt asked, sniffing the air.

He stopped near a tree trunk as he looked ahead. The others stood next to him, welcoming a break from their steady march.

"Metal and fire," said Ivan.

"Some kind of chemical," Niku added.

"Fuel?" asked Henry.

"No," Merritt said, taking another few steps. "Coolant. From the engines."

"I thought we were walking toward the front of the ship," said Niku.

"I thought so, too." Merritt walked ahead, moving quickly. "If you see blue liquid on *anything*, don't touch it or you'll lose your hand."

Fire had scorched the back sides of the trees, charring them black. The ones on the outskirts of the primary crash site still had all three large, naked branches at their very tops, bent like elbows to point at the sky.

As Merritt and the others walked through a progressively apocalyptic landscape, the branches were burnt down to small nubs, then the trees themselves shrank in size as the charring intensified.

Soon the group walked through a field of smoking stumps, stopping at the precipice of an impact crater which sank like a canyon into the ground. The broken husk of the front half of the *Halcyon* lay scattered over a mile in each direction within the canyon.

Directly in front of them was the bell-shaped housing of one massive hybrid antimatter engine, lying on its side, half its shell crumpled beneath it, the other half arcing majestically through the air like an industrial amphitheater.

Glistening blue liquid painted its exterior and

the ground all around it, dripping from the vaulted, bell-shaped housing and oozing into a lake within its open mouth.

"One of the engines broke away from the back of the ship," said Merritt. "Don't go near it."

"Can it blow up?" Ivan asked warily.

Merritt began the descent into the crater, half-sliding down a dirt ramp thick with clumped soil and loose rock.

"Probably not," he said. "But I wouldn't light a match."

Behind the engine lay a long section of the ship. Merritt guessed it was equivalent to roughly one-fifth of its entire length, from the torn middle of the vessel moving forward toward the nose. It had broken into wide chunks that leaned against each other at different angles, like a skyscraper that had fallen on its side but managed not to collapse on itself.

"Why did we crash?" Henry asked as he, Niku, and Ivan followed Merritt down into the crater.

"I think a faulty radiation deflector panel protecting the inner hull broke free and damaged the engines," Merritt replied.

"Why wasn't it fixed?" asked Niku.

"Anyone would have died before getting close. Radiation from the Rip flooded the lattice chamber, probably through the hole created by the loose panel."

"Why didn't the captain notice something was wrong?"

"I don't know why. My supervisor tried to tell him."

Merritt felt a pang of regret when he thought of Willef, and of the people he was leading to the officer escape pods at the front of the ship while it was breaking apart.

"But even if there *was* a problem," he continued, "there's no way to perform maintenance on the engines while they're active."

"Hubris and faulty equipment," mused Henry. "Same old story, again and again."

His foot slipped out from under him and he fell on his back. He slid down the dirt ramp, fingers clawing at the loose soil.

Merritt caught his forearm and nearly fell over himself as he stopped the older man's slide.

Henry climbed to his feet slowly, breathing hard.

"Thank you," he said, his voice heavy with exhaustion. He turned to face the sprawling wreckage. "What are we looking for down there?"

"Food," said Ivan quickly.

"For starters," Merritt agreed. "Keep your eyes peeled for an orange box about the size of a large suitcase. The shell is supposed to be blast-proof, but in this case..." He gestured at the ruins of the ship and shrugged.

"The black box is orange?" asked Henry.

"It's a crazy world," said Niku, walking past him, deeper into the crater.

After five minutes of continuous descent, the

bottom of the crater began to level out.

The first piece of debris to greet them at the bottom of the dirt ramp was a broken escape pod, crumpled in on itself like a squashed aluminum can.

Merritt and the others stood beside it, staring at the folds of metal which had once been a smooth exterior.

"It launched too late," he said.

"There are more," Henry told the group, pointing.

What Merritt had thought was a scattering of ship debris was actually a sprawling field of crashed escape pods — pods that had launched from their bays just before the front half of the ship made impact.

"These would be the officer pods at the front of the ship," said Niku.

"Best not to look," Henry said, swallowing hard. "They are still...occupied."

Merritt walked through the field of pods, which stuck up from the ground like tombstones in a graveyard.

"Food!" Ivan said.

He ran past Merritt to a large, half-crushed yellow container that had spilled its contents across the blackened ground. Ivan tore open one of the small silvery bags scattered nearby and emptied the contents into his mouth. He chewed, then spat his mouthful onto the dry ground with a look of disgust. After a moment, he smacked his lips thoughtfully, shrugged, and opened another pack.

"Dry onion," he told the others.

"Hooray," said Niku without excitement as he knelt down next to Ivan and opened a pack. He chewed on it, then said, "Garlic. *Blech*."

"Great," said Merritt, looking around. "We found the spices."

Niku opened another packet. "I knew they were holding out on us. One pack of this would have stopped my stomach from cramping at every meal."

"I wouldn't go that far," Henry offered. "Yet another reason to ride out the voyage in a hypergel tank."

"We should get moving," said Merritt.

"We need to eat," Niku countered, "or we won't have enough energy to keep walking."

"There has to be something more substantial over there," Merritt said, pointing at the biggest section of wreckage.

The others stayed near the spice packets, mixing and matching their contents in their mouths until their cheeks bulged.

"Parsley and beef bouillon," said Henry. "I need water."

Someone moaned in pain nearby. Everyone fell silent and stopped chewing as they looked at each other.

Merritt turned around, looking toward the ship's remains. A lone escape pod lay on the ground twenty meters away, a massive chunk ripped out of its hatch and side. Merritt could just barely make out the ghost-white fingers of a passenger through the jagged hole.

The passenger moaned again.

"They're still alive," said Merritt, and broke into a run, boots pounding the charred ground.

He stumbled to a halt next to the pod.

"I'm here!" he said loudly.

The hatch was cracked down the middle from a previous impact. A portion of one lower corner had been torn away, revealing the bloody legs of its occupant. Merritt pulled the cuffs of his coveralls over his palms and grabbed the broken edge of the hatch. It protested with a loud squeal as he tried to leverage it away from the pod.

Niku appeared at his side. He had slipped his sleeves-turned-shoes over his hands and gripped the jagged hatch, helping to lift.

Metal screamed against metal, and with a loud crunch, the hatch popped free and fell to the burnt ground.

"Willef!" said Merritt.

The foreman lay within his escape pod, bruised and bleeding from a dozen wounds, shaking in his soaked coveralls.

Yet he wasn't shaking from fear, or shock, Merritt noticed. He was crying, his sobs sending deep tremors through his body.

Merritt bent into the pod and grabbed one of Willef's arms. He draped it around his own neck and hoisted the foreman from the pod. Willef howled in pain as Merritt set him on the ground and leaned his back against the battered pod.

The foreman made no attempt to wipe away the tears that flowed down his rough cheeks.

"I—" he said between sobs. "I shouldn't—"

"Time for that later," said Niku, resting his hand on Willef's shoulder.

He moved down to the foreman's legs, checking his wounds. He prodded a particularly deep laceration on his upper left thigh.

"Wiggle your toes and fingers," said Niku.

Willef did.

"Good. You'll have to walk."

The foreman sniffed loudly, then nodded, his jowls quivering.

Merritt walked past the pod, shielding his eyes from the sun to look at the sprawling wreckage of the *Halcyon*.

"We need to look for more survivors, then find a black box," he said.

"I'll check the other pods," said Niku as he walked away.

Willef struggled to glance over his shoulder, but gave up and slumped back against his escape pod. "Tell me what you see," he said.

"Looks like a good chunk of midship to forward," Merritt replied.

"How long is it?"

"I'd say…fifth of a mile?"

"Open at both ends?"

"Yes. Torn to pieces."

Willef nodded. He winced in pain, and said, "You can't…can't go at it from the side. The hull plates soaked up too many rads going through the Rip. They're designed to hold on to it until we negate the absorption, but now...who knows? Even going in from an open side could expose you."

"Fatal?" asked Merritt.

Willef attempted a shrug. "Depends how long you hang around."

"How many black boxes were on the ship?"

"Fifteen. This section would have seven or eight of them. Most were near the bridge."

"Even if there was no radiation," said Merritt, "I doubt any of us could climb up six inner hulls to get to the passenger section."

"Where's he going?" Willef asked weakly, nodding in the direction of the ship.

Merritt turned around, squinting into the sun. Ivan was running toward the wreckage.

"*Ivan!*" he shouted. "Hey, *IVAN!*"

Ivan ignored him, running full-speed toward the remains of the *Halcyon*.

Merritt ran after him. His toe caught a chunk of metal and he fell face-first on the hard ground, scraping his cheek and jaw. He pushed himself up, spat dirt, and ran on.

Ivan was quick. He changed course, angling for the nearest open end of the ship, off to his right. Merritt was already panting from exhaustion by the time Ivan disappeared around the jagged wall of the torn hull.

Merritt gave the wreckage a wider berth, circling around to the open side at a distance of about ten meters. He wasn't sure if that would make a difference, but it felt better in the moment.

Ivan was already a few meters off the ground, scrambling expertly up the wreckage.

The protective inner hulls had pancaked into each other. The outermost hull had vanished into the crater, pushed below the surface under the weight of the bulk above it. The other six hulls were layered on top of it like crumpled striations in a rock cliff.

"No radiation burn!" Ivan shouted down. "Is okay!"

He grabbed a hanging wire, thick as a rope. Merritt's palms started to sweat as Ivan put all his weight on it without testing it first, swinging away from the ship by pushing off with his legs, then quickly climbing up the wire. He hoisted himself into the open passenger section at the core of the wreckage, thirty meters off the ground. Then he turned around to face Merritt, and took a bow.

The floor shifted under his feet and he almost stumbled off the ship, into midair. He caught himself at the last second, all hints of amusement gone from his face.

"What I look for?" he shouted down.

Merritt cupped his hands to his mouth and shouted, "That looks like Deck 4. Look for a wall panel with a big red handle and lots of warning stickers."

"Then what?"

"Orange suitcase with a hard shell."

Ivan nodded nervously, clearly less confident after almost falling out of the ship. He gave Merritt a shaky thumb's up and vanished into the *Halcyon*.

Merritt turned back to look at the others. Willef seemed to be dozing while Niku poked around the nearby wreckage, perhaps searching for medical supplies.

Metal groaned behind Merritt. He whipped around as a slight tremor coursed through the ground beneath his boots. One side of the outer hull sagged noticeably lower before his eyes, dropping several meters.

"*Hurry up, Ivan!*" he yelled.

The entire ground beneath the *Halcyon* shifted as the hull dipped lower. Ivan suddenly appeared above, his head peeking out from the open end of Deck 4.

He smiled and held up a bulky orange suitcase with a hard shell.

Merritt grinned. "I'm coming up to help!" he shouted.

Ivan tossed the suitcase out of the ship. It tumbled through the air and hit the ground on its corner, spinning end over end until it crashed against the side of a large chunk of debris.

Merritt ran over to it while Ivan scaled the open end of the ship, climbing down as quickly as he'd ascended.

Without waiting, Merritt popped the latches and opened the scarred orange lid. Niku walked over, leaving Willef to his nap.

Half of the suitcase's interior was a data screen, the other half a control bank with dials and switches.

The screen was blank. The black box gave no indication of power.

Niku reached past Merritt and pushed a tiny black button at the top of the screen. A small green light flicked on its center.

"We used a similar system to track dig sites at some Egyptian ruins when I was in college," said Niku.

"I thought you were a microbiologist."

Niku shrugged. "I went where the girls took me in those days."

A yellow light glowed to life near the right edge of the screen.

"That's us," said Niku, pointing at the green light. He pointed at the yellow. "That's the colony's nav beacon."

"Is that east?"

"Yes."

Merritt turned to look in that direction, at the two looming mountains in the distance.

"That's where the sun came up."

"More or less," Niku agreed. "If the black box is reading their nav beacon correctly, that means the farmland south of the colony site is beyond those mountains."

"Even if we don't make for the beacon directly," said Merritt, "we'll still find it."

"Exactly."

"What are the rest of these controls?"

Niku fiddled with a dial. "Part of it's a radio."

Merritt looked at him in disbelief. "We could call the colony?"

"If they have their system set up to receive, which they probably do given the circumstances."

"Hey!" Ivan yelled down from the side of the ship. "What's happening?"

"How do we call?" asked Merritt.

Niku flipped a small metal switch and a high-pitch squeal emanated from the box, then faded. He tapped the yellow dot on the display screen, then tapped a few more buttons that popped up with each choice he made.

"Hit that square green button," he said.

Merritt did, and static burst from a small speaker near the screen.

Niku gestured at him to go ahead.

"Come in, colony site," he said uncertainly. "This is, um...we're survivors from the Halcyon. We crashed near the ocean, and...is anyone there?"

He waited a long moment while static popped from the black box.

"There are four of us," Merritt continued. "We're making for a mountain pass to our east, headed your direction. If anyone is listening, one of us is injured and needs medical attention. And if...and if you see my son, Gavin Alder, please tell him his father is alive. Please tell him I'll..." Merritt swallowed hard, his eyes welling with tears. "Please tell him I'll be there soon."

"Hey there, farmer," said a familiar voice on the other end of the line.

"Tull—Tulliver?" Merritt asked, looking at Niku, then back to the black box. "How did you...is my son there?"

"Don't you worry about him," said Tulliver easily. *"He's got old Tully on his side. Can't say the same for you."*

"What?" Merritt asked hopelessly.

"This is a hard enough place for a boy...even without his daddy leavin' him."

"I didn't leave him!" Merritt shouted.

"Well," Tulliver said thoughtfully, *"he's never gonna know that."*

Static popped, and the line went dead.

"What's going on?" asked Merritt.

The colony's yellow nav beacon blipped out of existence.

"No!" Merritt roared. He pounded the screen. "Where did it go?!"

He smashed his fists down into the box, cracking the screen and breaking switches.

He couldn't stop. Blood spattered the broken screen as he hit it again and again.

Niku grabbed his arms and pulled him away forcefully. Merritt struggled to break free. He wanted to rip that box to shreds and stomp the pieces to dust.

Niku tripped and they both fell backward. Merritt jerked out of his reach and lay on the charred ground, his chest heaving with each raging breath.

"We know the colony is to the east," said Niku calmly, wiping dirt from his hands. "We'll find it."

"Is okay?" Ivan called down from the ship. He had paused a few meters off the ground to listen to the radio call.

Merritt stood and brushed off the front of his smeared coveralls.

"We have to leave right now," he said.

Niku lowered his voice and said, "It will be slow going." He nodded toward Willef.

Merritt looked at the injured foreman. "Then the sooner, the better."

The ground rumbled beneath the wreckage, rattling the hull. A piece of debris tumbled from one of the decks and fell, narrowly missing Ivan.

A crack burst open between Merritt and Niku with the sound of a gun shot, sending them both stumbling to the side. Merritt regained his footing and shoved Niku farther from the ship as the crack widened and the ground fell.

He fell with it, plunging into darkness, then landed hard on his shoulder and cried out in pain. Clumps of blackened soil pelted him from above. He rolled onto his back to see the surface five meters above. Niku's head appeared as a silhouette against the bright blue sky.

The ground rumbled and dropped another meter. Merritt wiped dirt from his eyes and saw the bulk of the *Halcyon* opposite Niku.

"*Move!*" Niku shouted.

The *Halcyon* was sliding into the hole.

Ivan stared into the pit with horror, clinging to the open end of the ship as it slid.

Merritt climbed to his feet, took a step into nothing, and fell again.

He pitched forward, falling face-first, and landed in a shallow puddle of liquid, his head cracking against the hard rock beneath it.

Groaning, he rolled onto his back in the puddle. The cool liquid sloshed around his ears, muting the sound of squealing metal as the *Halcyon* loomed in the void above him, obscuring the outline of the sinkhole.

A chunk of the ship teetered on the edge of the hole for a brief moment, and almost seemed as if it would settle back on its hull. Then the edge of the sinkhole exploded in a dirt firework and the ship slipped into the void, gaining momentum as it slid at an angle to crash into the opposite side, blotting out the sun.

Dirt and debris rained down on Merritt from above. He shielded his face and rolled to the side until he bumped against a wall.

All he could do was wait as the shaking ground rattled his bones and the world collapsed around him.

TULLIVER

Tulliver pulled the radio's battery from its cradle, killing the power and ending his conversation with Gavin's father.

He stood in the admin tent, alone. On the table next to the radio, the flashing blue light of the colony's nav beacon splashed intermittently against the interior walls, pulsing from the top of a short metal rod sticking up from a slender aluminum barrel.

A thick black cord ran from the back of the barrel to a power bank beneath the table. Tulliver ripped the plug from the back of the barrel and cast aside the cord. The beacon's blue light flashed, then dimmed, and was extinguished.

Open document binders covered nearly every table surface within the circular admin tent, alongside empty cups and various bits of equipment still packed in padded green wrapping.

Tulliver found an incomplete topographical map pinned to the side of an equipment crate. It showed the area around the colony site to a distance of half a kilometer. A small red circle with an X in the middle had been drawn in to the north, at the base of a hill near a large boulder.

Tulliver tapped the X and whispered, "Gotcha."

The canvas doors flapped loudly as someone ran into the tent. Diego pulled up short, breathing hard as he swept back his mop of brown hair.

"You shouldn't be in here," he said.

"Yet here I am," Tulliver replied.

Diego's gaze flicked to the colony's nav beacon, then down to its disconnected power plug snaking across the ground. He moved forward to grab it, but Tulliver stepped in front of him, blocking his path.

"We need to have a little chat," he said gravely, looking down at the short warden.

"Plug it back in!" said Diego urgently. "We have to broadcast our location for the pods—"

"—which have all landed by now," Tulliver finished.

"Someone might still need it," said Diego as he tried to push past.

Tulliver shoved him. Diego stumbled and fell to the ground, looking up at the bigger man with a mixture of fear and confusion.

"This won't take long," said Tulliver. He slid over an equipment crate and sat on it, then pointed at the topographical map. "That red X is where you parked the shuttle, right?"

Diego appeared briefly dumbfounded, then swallowed as he regained control of his senses. "No, that's just a...an area of interest."

"Mmm," Tulliver said thoughtfully. "So you didn't take a shuttle from the ship. Did you pack all this equipment into an escape pod?"

"It was delivered remotely before we got here.

On previous visits."

"You seemed pretty well set up by the time the colonists arrived."

Diego looked around the tent nervously. A sheen of sweat glistened on his forehead. He seemed to realize he was running out of lies.

"It wouldn't do you any good anyway," he said. "You could get to orbit but there's no *ship*."

Tulliver laughed, his belly shaking. He re-adjusted the crate beneath him. "I don't want to *escape* in it. I want to *live* in it."

"What?"

Tulliver held up his hand and closed one eye. He looked through the arch of his thumb and forefinger, as if imagining it was a viewfinder. "I got a nice spot picked out on the edge of the colony. We'll move your admin tent there, too. Kind of like a...like a city hall, that's what we'll call it."

"You can't *live* in the shuttle," Diego protested.

"Listen," said Tulliver, growing serious. "Our first few weeks here are probably going to be the hardest. The status quo you establish will set like concrete, and chiseling any alternative methods of operation will be...*difficult*."

"What are you *talking* about?" said Diego.

He tried to stand but Tulliver shoved him back down to the ground.

"Sit *down*," he growled. Then he cleared his throat and proceeded more calmly. "I'm talking about how you and I will be working together." He grinned. "For the betterment of the colony."

"I don't want to work with you," said Diego.

Tulliver scratched his chin. "How do you expect to maintain peace amongst nearly sixty people who are angry at their situation? They'll need someone to blame, and you're a government rep."

"Cohen and I can handle it," said Diego. He glanced at the entrance, as if waiting for the big warden to burst through.

"Here's the thing," Tulliver told him, scooting closer to the edge of his crate. "What if you can't?"

"Then we'll figure it out. *We're* the wardens."

"I have a lot to offer the colony. I bring people together. I *connect* them."

"No, you don't," said Diego, shaking his head. "You *take* from them. You put them in debt and you keep them there."

"They come to me of their own free will."

Diego shook his head again. "I know what you are."

Tulliver grunted with amusement. "Oh? And what am I?"

Diego's eyes blazed with anger. "You're everything we tried to leave behind."

Every trace of amusement vanished from Tulliver's face, replaced by a stone mask from which his lightless eyes regarded the pathetic little man on the ground at his feet.

"I'm sorry you feel that way," he said softly, bending down to reach for Diego's neck.

Diego scrambled backward and bumped into a table, spilling a stack of binders to the ground beside him. He picked one up and beat at Tulliver's extending hand. Tulliver swatted it away and grabbed a fistful of Diego's uniform jacket. He picked the short man off the ground and stared into his terrified eyes.

The tent flaps burst apart as Samar, the supply manager, ran into the tent.

"One of the colonists is dead!" he said breathlessly. He suddenly realized he had intruded on an uncomfortable scene between Tulliver and the warden. Samar gestured outside and said, "This way!"

Then he was gone.

Tulliver snarled as he lowered Diego to the ground. The warden pushed away and ran from the tent, the canvas door flapping in his wake.

The bright midday sun beat down on Tulliver's bald head when he emerged from the tent. Two colonists ran past, boots thudding the ground. He followed after them at his own pace, smoothing down the front of his baggy jacket as another colonist hurried past.

A group had formed in an open area beneath the towering trees a short distance from the center of the colony. Tulliver shouldered his way through them to stand next to a cold campfire.

Warden Cohen lay on the ground, curled into a fetal position, skin gray as ash. Stale white foam covered his mouth and neck. His bulging eyes stared past the dead fire, into the distance. Tulliver glanced in that direction and saw two large roots forming a cozy nook at the base of a tree.

Cohen's arm had fallen into the fire before it burned down. It was charred up to his elbow, his hand nothing more than a blackened claw.

Diego knelt down beside Cohen and gently rested a hand on his shoulder. Then he stood and walked to a nearby tree. Bending down, he scooped up two flasks, one metal, one made of red plastic.

Tulliver found Samar in the crowd. The supply manager smirked and nodded ever-so-slightly.

His expression was one Tulliver had seen a hundred times, from a hundred other people who thought they had him pushed into a corner.

Diego sniffed the metal flask and frowned. Then he sniffed the red one and jerked his head away, coughing and wiping his mouth. His suspicious gaze lingered on Tulliver a long moment before he walked back to the campfire.

"Go back to your business," said Diego, addressing the crowd.

"You can't just leave him there," said a colonist.

"I don't plan to," Diego shot back heatedly. He took a quick breath to calm himself down. "Please give me some space, and go back to your business. This is my responsibility."

"You don't have to do it alone," said someone else.

Diego nodded. "I appreciate that." He looked down at Cohen's body. "We'll have a meeting later today. I'll let everyone know the details."

Tulliver grimaced and pushed his way out of the crowd as it began to disperse, walking briskly.

Samar caught up with him and strolled at his side.

"Interesting thing, that red flask," he said.

"Choose your next words carefully," Tulliver warned.

"Now it looks like *you* owe *me*."

"You sure you want to play that game? Because it's one I've been playing for a very long time."

Samar smiled, showing bright white teeth and two particularly sharp cuspids.

"I don't see that you have a choice," he said.

"You were the only one with access to those flasks."

Samar shrugged. "I leave the crates on the ground for all to see. Anyone could have stolen from them. Besides, who do you think people will believe? Our two reputations are very different."

"Is that so?" asked Tulliver. He stopped abruptly and stepped close to Samar, putting the back of his open hand against the supply manager's chest. "And what does mine say about what happens to people who cross me?"

Samar stepped back, smiling and unafraid. "We are linked now. My success is yours, and yours is mine."

He turned and walked back toward the colony. Tulliver spun angrily and stomped away, heading north.

A few minutes alone in the sparse forest was enough to temper his emotions, and soon he was holding his locket as he looked at the treetops, recalling a memory from Earth — a time when he had visited an arboretum with his young daughter, before he'd lost her.

Tulliver eventually emerged from a line of trees into a wide field of brown and green ground cover. A small hill rose before him. On the far side, a massive rock shaped like a skinny pyramid reached for the sky. It leaned slightly to the side, as if the ground beneath had softened.

The shuttle was there, on the ground between the hill and the rock. It was a mono-wing craft in the shape of a triangle, with a bulbous oval cockpit window and flared wing-tips. It rested on three jointed landing arms.

Tulliver grinned as he shuffled down the hill, sweating inside his heavy jacket.

His smile turned to a frown as he stood beneath the shuttle, looking up at its underbelly. Running his hand over the smooth hull, he realized he didn't know how to get inside.

Thought you were smart, Tully, scolded the disembodied voice of Warden Cohen. The big warden, it seemed, had joined the chorus.

Tulliver growled and paced the entire underside of the shuttle, but could find no control panel of any kind. He stopped for a rest, wiping sweat from his brow as he leaned against one of the landing arms. He glanced up at its juncture with the hull, briefly wondering if he could squeeze his bulk into the narrow opening from which it emerged.

"Open up," he said loudly. "Door open," he tried

next.

He walked to the front of the craft and looked up at the shining heat shield hugging its nose. Behind the heat shield was a small, rectangular screen alongside three buttons flush with the hull.

"You gotta be kidding me," Tulliver said in disbelief.

He patted his pockets until he found his red ticket, then pulled it out and looked at it, then up at the screen.

Anyone shorter would have had to find something to stand on, but Tulliver was able to stretch on his tip-toes and swipe his ticket over the panel. The buttons lit up green. He jumped and hit the first one, and nothing happened. He tried the second, and the panel beeped. The hull split in a fine line behind the screen. The line opened wider to reveal the inside of the shuttle as a hatch ramp lowered to the ground.

Tulliver put his ticket back in his pocket and scaled the ramp into the shuttle.

Always so clever, said the voice of Cohen in his mind. *It's going to get you in trouble some day.*

But not today, thought Tulliver.

He took a deep breath of the cool, stale shuttle air, then climbed a short ladder at the top of the ramp. The ladder led to a small, spherical airlock, which was open, and on to the spacious cockpit.

Tulliver sat in one of the two pilot chairs and grabbed the H-shaped flight stick with both hands. He grinned from ear to ear as he turned the stick and leaned to the side.

Behind him, three padded passenger seats formed a small arc below the widest part of the cockpit window, which was an elongated oval starting just over the nose of the triangular craft.

Now for the hard part, thought Tulliver, studying the controls in front of him.

He flipped a couple of switches experimentally, but nothing happened.

Never let a little thing like not knowing how to fly slow you down, no sir, said the internal voice of his old crime partner, Roland Day. *Nothing stops Tull the bulldog, does it? Not when he's got a scent.*

Tulliver shook his head to clear away the ghostly voice and wiped sweat from his eyes.

A rectangular black screen with etched grid lines was set into the control panel just behind the flight stick. Tulliver pushed a small orange button next to it and the lines glowed bright green. A moment later, a white dot pulsed from the center. Then a light blue dot appeared in the upper right corner.

Tulliver smiled like a hungry shark, his fleshy cheeks pushing up to smother his eyes.

Diego had reactivated the colony's nav beacon.

Tulliver tapped the white dot and a small dialogue box popped up on the screen: *SELECT DESTINATION.*

The box faded away, and he tapped the light blue dot. A dotted white line appeared, connecting the two dots. Tulliver settled back into his seat and gripped the flight stick, even though he suspected he wasn't going to have to do anything during the short journey.

The control panel buzzed at him and a red dialogue box popped up on the screen: *WARNING: LANDING ZONE OBSTRUCTED. ABORT?*

Tulliver pushed *NO*.

The shuttles twin engines whined to life at the back of the craft, shaking the hull. Then the two underbelly engines kicked on and Tulliver's vision blurred like a plucked guitar string. He clamped his jaw shut to keep his teeth from rattling as the craft lurched upward, leaving the ground. Almost as an afterthought, he pulled on his safety harness and buckled it over his chest.

Its nose swung around, over the pyramidal rock, and Tulliver could see above the tree tops, toward every horizon. He saw mountains, oceans, and wide open fields decorated with gray rocks of all shapes and sizes — all of it topped by a boundless blue sky studded with the burning yellow jewel of Phobis.

The nose dipped slightly, then leveled out as the shuttle accelerated over the forest, heading for the pulsing, light blue beacon. Tulliver gripped the arms of his chair with sweaty hands, his knuckles white.

After several moments of not crashing in a ball of raging fire, he forced himself to relax, sinking deeper into his cushioned chair.

The shuttle decelerated sharply to hover above the light blue beacon, which pulsed on the center of the screen. The aft engines rotated downward and the craft hovered in place until it stabilized, then slowly descended.

Tulliver leaned forward in his seat, wishing he could see the colony below.

The craft landed with a heavy thud, rocking side to side before settling. Tulliver quickly unbuckled his safety harness and climbed down the short ladder leading through the airlock. He slapped the hatch release at the base of the ladder and waited impatiently as the ramp slowly lowered to the ground.

Its lip crunched down onto the charred remains of the warden's admin tent.

Tulliver descended the ramp casually, thumbs hooked in the belt loops of his pants, a slight grin on his face. He squinted in the bright sunlight as he surveyed the scene before him.

Those colonists who were near the landing site stood huddled in groups of two or three, faces aghast with horror. Several others turned tail and ran back to their farms. Even accounting for the cowards, there were enough there to receive his message.

He walked around the side of the ramp, following the edge of the shallow black crater the shuttle's engines had scorched into the ground.

In the central heap of the charred admin tent, a clawed, bony hand protruded, grasping for the sky. Smoke curled around its twisted fingers.

Tulliver barked laughter, then spun around to

face the crowd.

He spread his arms wide and bellowed, "I humbly accept the burden of administration bestowed upon me by the late Wardens Cohen and Ramirez." He waved a grateful hand toward the blackened limb sticking up from the burnt tent, then placed his open palm over his heart. "And I thank you for your trust in these difficult times. If you need anything, the door to my office is always open."

The stunned colonists gaped at him like fish, and he laughed, shaking his head as he turned to ascend the ramp into the shuttle.

CHAPTER SIXTEEN

LEERA

The nose of the shuttle peeked out from behind the base of a massive mineral lead sulfide boulder. Leera, Walter, Uda, and Corporal Turner progressed toward the shuttle slowly, leap-frogging their radio spikes to create a pathway through the field of gray crabs.

They had been performing their exhausting task for nearly two hours. One person thrust a radio spike into the ground to create a small radius of open ground within the field of crabs while another person walked forward, to the edge of the tiny clearing, and drove another spike into the soil.

As they moved slowly around the boulder, more of the shuttle became visible.

A black starburst of char marks extended back from the nose. A large scar traced a deep line from one edge of the cockpit window to the back of the vessel, where a chunk of the hull had been ripped away.

"We have to fly *that* thing?" asked Walter.

"The last pilot managed to land it safely," said Uda.

"The hatch is open," Turner pointed out.

Between the three landing arms of the shuttle, a ramp extended down from the nose to disappear into the migrating mass of interlocked crabs below.

"Do you think they're inside?" Walter asked.

"Doesn't look like they're interested," said Leera, warily eyeing the ramp. "But that doesn't mean nothing else crawled up there."

They passed the last twenty meters to the shuttle silently, until at last they stood below it, looking up into the darkness at the top of the ramp. Leera took all three spikes and drove them into the soft ground to form a triangle around the ramp, pushing the crabs back beyond the edges of the shuttle's shadow.

Turner unshouldered his rifle and checked its safety, then held it at the ready while he ascended the ramp, his jaw set, his eyes scanning the opening above.

He disappeared into the shadows at the top of the ramp, leaving the other three down below, between the triangle of radio spikes.

Leera watched as thousands of segmented legs beneath the moving gray sheet scrabbled at the ground for purchase. Their passage was almost completely silent but for a steady whisper as their legs continuously stabbed the ground like the needles of countless sewing machines.

The red power switch on one of the radio spikes flickered, and the crabs beyond that spike lurched closer. Leera, Uda, and Walter turned toward it just as the red light blinked out and the line of crabs surged forward, swarming over the dead radio spike. It was pulled beneath the sheet of gray, disappearing without a sound.

The crabs hit the invisible barrier generated by the remaining two radio spikes, peeling up like lifted carpet to avoid passing into it.

"Clear!" Turner shouted from above.

"Go!" said Leera.

She pushed Uda and Walter up the ramp and grabbed the two remaining radio spikes. As soon as she pulled the second one from the ground, the crabs closed in, rushing to fill the empty space.

Leera ran up the ramp and tripped, falling on her elbows with a shout of pain. One of the radio spikes popped from her grip and rolled toward the edge of the ramp. Uda lunged and caught it just as it rolled off. She pulled Leera to her feet and gently took the other radio spike from her shaking hand.

"Thank you," said Leera.

Uda smiled and gestured up the ramp. "You first."

The top of the ramp led to a small cargo hold filled with empty transport crates. Bright green mildew streaked the walls and ceiling, giving off a wet, earthy odor. Leera followed Walter up a short ladder and into the cockpit, where Turner was already sitting strapped into the pilot chair, working the controls.

"Still has power," he said, flipping a switch. A bank of red lights flicked on over his head. "And fuel. Everyone inside?"

Uda entered the cockpit and buckled herself into one of the two seats bolted to the back wall.

"We're all here."

"Closing the hatch," said Turner.

He tapped a command into his console screen and a mechanical whir sounded from beneath the shuttle, followed by a loud metal clunk.

"Barbecued crab for dinner?" he asked, flipping another switch.

The shuttle shook on its landing arms as the engines roared to life, rattling the inner walls. Leera sat next to Uda while Walter crouched down next to her, searching for a way to secure himself to the floor.

"I'm picking up a nav beacon," said Turner over the noise. He pointed at a narrow rectangular screen on his console filled with a faint grid of green lines. "East, beyond a mountain range. Hey, wait a minute." He tapped the screen. "I lost the signal!"

"Did we lose power?" asked Leera.

Turner shook his head. "The signal just blinked out, like someone turned it off at the colony." He swiped the screen to toggle through known nav beacon frequencies. "Luckily, I got a heading before it disappeared. We should be okay. Fuel reserves are…"

He paused as he cycled rapidly through menu screens on his console. Then he turned to look at the others.

"Fuel reserves are at five percent," he told them. "Enough for about ten minutes of flight time."

The buckle of Leera's safety harness rattled as she tightened her straps.

“Then let’s not waste any more fuel,” she said.

Turner nodded and gripped the flight controls. The shuttle lurched upward and the nose dipped, giving them all a good view of the blackened patch of crabs that had been directly under the engine wash. Burnt, segmented legs twitched at the sky from those that had flipped onto their backs. Smoke curled up from the crispy shells of others, and already the dead were being overrun by the living, scrambled over by a fresh sheet of gray, interlocked stone-like carapaces.

Turner pulled back on the controls and the shuttle’s nose pitched skyward. Leera sank back into her seat as the vessel accelerated, heading toward the two green-peaked mountains in the distance.

The shuttle vibrated more harshly as Turner increased speed.

“If we can make it through the pass,” said Uda, her voice quavering, “we’ll find the colony.”

Walter sat next to Leera’s chair, holding tight to a support strut in the wall. She held out her hand and he took it, squeezing it for comfort.

“Fuel reserves at three percent,” said Turner.

Leera sat up in her seat, straining against her harness to look out the cockpit window.

The corporal had wasted no time. The twin mountain peaks loomed over either side of the shuttle, their jagged green peaks sharply outlined against the clear blue sky.

Turner frowned and tapped on his control

screen.

"I'm picking up a signal on the ground," he said loudly.

"A nav beacon?" Uda asked.

He shook his head. "Passengers. Three of them, in the mountain pass."

Leera and Uda shared a quick glance.

"Hang on," said Turner.

He gripped the controls and banked sideways, dropping one side of the ship until he could see the ground through the cockpit window.

"There!" he shouted.

"That's Niku!" said Leera, shaking Walter's shoulder excitedly.

He climbed up the side of her seat to look.

They only saw their fellow team member for a brief moment before the shuttle overtook him, but there was no mistaking Niku's black ponytail, even at that distance. He walked with two other men, one of whom seemed to be gravely injured, as they traversed a narrow valley pass between the two enormous mountains.

"We have to pick them up!" said Walter.

"Not enough fuel to stop!" shouted Turner over the constant rattle in the cockpit. "If we land, we can't take off again." He turned the flight controls, leveling out the shuttle. "Hold on, we gotta get closer to the ground!"

The nose dipped toward the ground just as a shadow shot past, blotting out the sun for a fraction of a second. Turner leaned forward in his chair and looked up, then he looked back at Leera, his eyes wide with terror.

Something slammed into the top of the ship, pushing it down. Metal screeched from above. Loud impacts thudded against the hull, as if the shuttle were being pelted by large rocks.

"We're too heavy!" Turner shouted.

He yelled with exertion as he struggled with the controls. The shuttle dipped lower, its port side dropping steadily.

Walter grabbed on to the base of Leera's chair as the ship turned sideways, flying with its port side aimed at the ground, its starboard toward the sky.

With a metal scream, a chunk of the roof ripped away. Sunlight poured in and wind tore through the cockpit. Leera's hair whipped around her face, stinging her eyes.

Thud, thud, thud, from above.

Something was walking on the roof of the shuttle.

It moved over the hole in the roof, blocking the sunlight. A shadow. Through the hair fluttering over face, Leera saw a single, massive eye, staring down at her.

Turner shouted from the pilot seat just before the shuttle crashed through a tree, snapping the trunk in two. There was an inhuman scream from the hole in the roof as the top half of the tree scraped over the hull, and the shadow was gone.

Leera's stomach flipped over with the ship as it rolled upside-down. Looking up, she saw the ground whipping past — a green and brown blur with the occasional streak of lead-colored rock.

Walter's legs suddenly dropped into view from above as he lost his grip and fell. Leera grabbed for his arms and caught a fistful of body suit. She jerked forward against her harness and screamed when something popped in her shoulder as she took the full weight of his body.

He looked down at the blur of ground below, then up at Leera.

The shuttle bucked as it crashed through another tree. Walter slipped from her grasp and fell through the open hole in the roof. He was gone in an instant, vanishing before she had time to realize what happened.

Leera yelled for him, but her voice was drowned in the roar of the shuttle's engines.

Another tree impact sent the vessel into a sideways spin, slicing over the ground like a circular saw blade.

The shuttle hit the ground.

Leera's safety harness cut into her shoulders as she hung upside-down in her seat while the hull scraped over dirt and rock.

She clenched her eyes shut as debris sprayed into the cockpit, pelting her face.

The front of the craft slammed into a large boulder. The momentum lifted the back off the ground until the shuttle was resting vertically on its nose, teetering between falling against the boulder on its belly or to the ground on its back.

Next to Leera, Uda was breathing like she'd just run a marathon, her sweaty, bloodied face smeared with dirt. She clutched her safety harness with white hands.

Turner worked the controls on his dead console, trying to restore power to the shuttle.

The vessel groaned as it rocked gently on its nose.

"Hang on!" Turner shouted as the shuttle began to tilt.

It fell backward on its roof, sending a burst of fresh dirt into the cockpit. Leera coughed and used a dirty hand to try to rub grit from her eyes.

She fumbled with her safety harness, searching for the release.

"Wait," Uda said weakly.

Leera found the release and pushed it, then fell a meter to the floor, landing on her shoulder with a scream. She flopped onto her back in the dirt, breathing hard, staring up at her chair. Tears streamed down her temples from the corners of her eyes.

Uda unbuckled her own harness and kept a grip on it, flipping over gracefully and jumping down to land on her feet next to Leera. Turner held on to the armrest of his chair and lowered himself down to the roof.

"Well," he said, wiping off his hands. "We're past the mountains." He looked at Leera and Uda. "Where's Walter?"

"He fell," said Uda, nodding down toward the

hole in the hull. She knelt next to Leera and squeezed her shoulder. "We'll go back for him."

Turner stood on the patch of ground where the chunk of roof had been ripped off.

He shook his head. "Moving at that speed..."

Leera groaned as she sat up, holding her throbbing shoulder.

"There was a..." she said, searching for the right word. "There was an *animal* on the ship. Did you see it?"

"No," said Turner, "but I felt it."

"I saw it," Uda said.

"What did it look like?"

Uda hesitated, then said, "It was a monster."

MERRITT

He awoke in darkness, to the sound of coughing.

Merritt sat up slowly, loose dirt spilling from his face and chest. Smothered light crept around the edges of the *Halcyon*'s wreckage above. A chunk of the ship had slid to a stop against a wall of the chasm into which Merritt had fallen.

More coughing in the darkness.

Merritt got to his feet slowly. His head throbbed and his muscles ached, but nothing was broken. He tested his footing and fell forward, landing face-first and getting a mouthful of dirt for his trouble.

He spat it out and croaked, "Ivan?"

Cough, cough.

Merritt crawled through the dim underground cavern, following the noise. In the shadows, a pale hand protruded from the dirt. Merritt grabbed the outstretched hand and pushed aside loose soil to reveal Ivan beneath, white as a ghost. Each cough shook his thin body. Red, swollen blisters covered his face and arms.

His rolling eyes found Merritt's, and he smiled.

"Alive," he whispered.

"Yes, we're alive. You lied about not feeling radiation on the ship."

Ivan tried to shrug. "We needed beacon."

Merritt sighed and looked around the dark cavern.

"For all the good it does us now."

"We climb," said Ivan, straining to sit up.

Merritt pushed him gently back down. "Neither of us can climb that," he said, pointing up. "The soil is too loose and the ship could fall the rest of the way. We need to get clear."

Ivan nodded, and Merritt helped him to his feet.

Ivan spoke softly in Russian. When Merritt didn't respond, he said, "Wash clothes. Radiation."

"First things first," said Merritt.

They stumbled through the darkness, into a low opening in the wall of the cavern. The opening led to a tunnel that disappeared into darkness.

"This cave was already here," said Merritt as he helped Ivan sit against the wall. "If we're lucky, there's a network of them we can follow until it's easier to break surface again."

"There," said Ivan, pointing a shaky finger farther down the tunnel. "You hear it?"

Merritt focused until he heard the faint dripping of water into a puddle.

"Your clothes will be soaked if I wash them," said Merritt.

"Better soaked with water than radiation."

He grimaced as he peeled off his torn jacket and threw it aside. "No, wait," he said suddenly, grasping at the air for the jacket. Merritt pinched a corner of the fabric and tossed it back to him. Ivan's eyes rolled back and his head lolled on his shoulders. A moment later he snapped awake and dug through his jacket pockets. He pulled out a small plastic snap-case and handed it to Merritt.

"What's this?"

Merritt opened the case to find a row of syringe-like needles and a small electronic meter.

"For diabetes," said Ivan. He fumbled for the case and pulled out a two-page instruction booklet from behind the electronic meter. "You know compass?" he asked. "Needle on paper is north."

"Compass?" Merritt said, feeling clueless.

"Rub needle on hair," Ivan told him weakly. "Magnet."

He slouched back on the wall, his eyes closed, breathing deeply.

"Ivan?" said Merritt.

He stood and followed the sound of dripping water deeper into the darkening tunnel. The passage narrowed, forcing him to crawl on a hard rock floor until his hands splashed into a cool puddle of water. A droplet fell from a wet gray rock above his head and *plinked* into the puddle.

Merritt folded up the edges of the two-page instruction guide and gently set it on the surface of the puddle, away from where the droplet had fallen. Next he took one of the small needles from the plastic container and rubbed it flat against the top of his head. He silently counted to thirty, then held his breath as he carefully dropped the needle onto the floating paper.

It spun counterclockwise immediately, then

slowed and spun the other way. The needle pegged back and forth like a metronome, until finally settling into a straight line. The sharper end of the needle pointed deeper into the tunnel. The flat end pointed back toward the ship.

A makeshift compass on Earth would align itself along a north-south axis. Merritt didn't know if the same rules applied on Galena, but he had nothing else to go on. The wreckage of the *Halcyon* was behind him, being mostly to the west when he fell into the underground cavern. If his compass was indeed orientated on a north-south axis, that would mean...

Merritt looked down the dark tunnel, into blackness.

East, he thought. *Toward the mountains.*

He glanced back at Ivan, who still rested against the rocky tunnel wall with his eyes closed, his thin chest rising and falling with shuddering breaths.

Merritt placed the instruction paper and needle back into the plastic snap-case and stuffed it into one pocket of his coveralls as he walked back. He pulled off Ivan's shoes, pants, and shirt. Ivan's eyelids fluttered open briefly but he didn't make a sound.

The puddle was shallow, but deep enough to submerge one piece of clothing at a time. He rubbed each garment on the rocky bottom of the puddle and wrung them out as best he could. For the tattered shoes, he dipped one side at a time and rubbed the outer fabric underwater with a flat rock he found nearby. He laid out the wet clothes on the ground and goose-stepped over the puddle, trying not to soak his own shoes.

The tunnel widened shortly after. It curved gradually to the south, and Merritt realized he would have to stop frequently to use the compass if they made any sort of decent progress underground.

A black void appeared before him, stretching up out of sight.

Merritt had stepped out of the tunnel and into a vast underground chamber. He could see neither walls, floor, or ceiling, but he had the distinct impression the space was enormous. The air was cool, still, and utterly silent save for the occasional echo of single droplets falling into water.

In the distance, perhaps a hundred meters opposite the tunnel opening, a soft blue light glowed in the darkness. It illuminated a patch of wet rock at the base of what looked like crooked trees, but Merritt couldn't be sure at that distance.

He picked up the wet clothes and went back to Ivan, crouching low as he passed back through the narrow tunnel. Ivan watched his approach with bloodshot eyes. A sheen of sweat covered his entire body.

Dark, wet patches covered Ivan's pale chest and thighs. Their discoloration matched the blisters on his face and lips. He tried to speak but coughed, his thin body convulsing.

Merritt helped him put on his loose T-shirt and pants, then struggled to pull on his wet shoes. He hammered the worn heels with his palm to force them into place. Ivan groaned and leaned back against the wall.

"Sorry," Merritt said. "The tunnel opens into a huge cavern up ahead. We'll follow that as far as we can, if you think you can walk."

Ivan nodded slowly. "Not dying down here."

"That's the spirit," said Merritt quietly as he helped him up. "Low ceiling here. Careful."

Ivan crawled through the puddle where Merritt had washed his clothes. Merritt followed him, crouching down as he carefully avoided the water.

"Air feels good," said Ivan as he stood up at the threshold of the pitch-black cavern. He peered at the blue light in the distance.

"Walk slowly," Merritt advised. "There might be cracks in the rock."

He half-walked, half-slid his feet forward across the ground, testing the surface before transferring his full weight. The rock floor was mostly flat, with only slight variation in elevation. The rock was smooth, as if the floor of the cavern had once been the bed of a rushing underground river.

"Compass work?" Ivan asked, his weak voice carrying far in the cavern.

"Like a charm," Merritt replied. "Assuming magnetism works the same here as on Earth."

"Is more for orienting. Assign one end of needle to north, and you always know east."

"Learn that in the Boy Scouts?"

Ivan was silent for a moment. "No Boy Scouts in

Russia. Not much of anything."

A fit of violent coughing shook his body, sending him to the hard ground on his hands and knees. The faint blue light ahead glinted off dark fluid streaming from his mouth.

Merritt walked toward him to help him up but Ivan urgently waved him away.

"*Nyet!*" he hissed, then spat on the ground. He stood up and wavered on shaking legs. "I do this alone."

He began walking toward the blue light, one leg trailing slightly behind in a shuffling limp.

As they approached the oasis of luminescence, the tree-shaped objects resolved themselves into thick, gnarled roots, tangled together as they rose into the darkness of the cavern.

The light was coming from a cluster of fungus-like plants on the rocky floor. Thick stalks emerged from a crack in the rock, rising as high as Merritt's knees. A cluster of fleshy spheres topped each stalk, glowing like small blue suns. Merritt peered into the luminous crack but could not see its end. The stalks had snaked their way up from deep below the cavern.

Ivan touched one of the spheres and there was a *POP* of electric current. He snapped his hand back and wiped it on his wet shirt as a thin wisp of smoke curled up from the glowing sphere. A small black patch where he'd touched the plant slowly vanished, replaced by the uniform blue glow.

Merritt frowned when he noticed the roots

weren't growing from the ground. He tapped one with a knuckle and it swung a few centimeters above the ground like a stiff pendulum.

He looked up, into the darkness above.

"These are growing down from the ceiling."

Ivan coughed, the noise echoing off distant walls.

"Look," he said, pointing. "More up ahead."

Merritt walked out of the small circle of light so his eyes could once again adjust to the shadows. There was another tunnel up ahead, at the far side of the cavern. It appeared no larger than a thumbnail at that distance. Blue light poured through its opening, fighting a losing battle with the darkness of the cavern.

Ivan limped forward, one hand over his stomach, the other hanging lifeless by his side.

Merritt walked into something hard and stepped back, surprised. He put his hands out and caught a swinging root as thick as his own waist. Its bark was wet and gritty. Merritt sniffed his hand and smelled nothing.

The bottom of the dangling root peeled open like a blooming, upside-down flower, casting a blue glow on the rocky ground. Merritt stepped to the side and bumped into another hanging root. The stumpy terminus of the second root barely touched the floor of the cavern. The tip split open into four broad petals that curled up to reveal luminous blue spheres, identical to the ones on the ends of the plant stalks emerging from the crack. Thick, vine-like tendrils retreated up into the thick root when exposed to the cool air of the cavern, tugging the glowing spheres deeper inside their protective sheath.

Merritt backed into Ivan as more roots opened around them, seemingly responding to some invisible stimulus broadcast by the first two he had bumped into.

Like lanterns being lit in the darkness, hundreds of lights swelled into existence near the ground all the way to the bright tunnel on the far side of the cavern, illuminating the massive underground chamber.

Merritt's gaze drifted up, following one of the thick, gnarled roots along its path to the ceiling of the cavern. It connected to a wide, bare tree trunk sticking straight down from the rocky ceiling. A dozen other dangling roots connected to the same tree trunk, forming a splayed bough, the branches of which lost rigidity farther from the trunk and drooped as they descended toward the cavern floor.

He tried to count the number of bare tree trunks embedded in the ceiling, but lost track after thirty.

"These are the trees from above," he said. "They're upside-down. Look there, closer to the ceiling." He pointed at broad, spade-shaped leaves hanging limply halfway up the branches. In the dim blue light far below, they appeared black. "This is the forest canopy."

"Then what is above?" asked Ivan.

"Taproots," Merritt replied.

"Tap what?"

"It's a special root, bigger and stronger than the rest, that goes straight down into the ground. Soyflower stalks have them, too. Only these trees are upside-down, so the taproot grows toward the sky."

"What is the purpose?"

"In this case, it might be a storage organ. Maybe it collects nutrients from the surface atmosphere."

Ivan looked at him. "I thought you work on ship."

"I took a farming class with my son." The thought of Gavin tightened his chest and pushed the air from his lungs. He took a deep breath, and said, "We need to keep moving."

Merritt took a step and the bottom tips of the nearest branches closed, cutting off their internal light sources. The rest of the branches did the same in rapid succession, their petals rolling down to pinch tightly together. The cavern slowly dimmed until it was plunged once more into near-absolute darkness. Soon the only lights were coming from the small crack in the ground behind Merritt and Ivan, and the bright tunnel up ahead.

Ten long minutes later they made it to the tunnel. Merritt had bumped into two more branches, and Ivan stumbled into three, but none of them had opened at the bottom.

They stood before the rock-lined passageway, bathed in blue light, breathing hard in the thin air.

"Wow," said Ivan.

The tunnel extended in a straight line through the rock, roughly the size of a hyperrail tunnel on Earth. It gradually descended, until the far end dipped out of sight. Smaller versions of the hanging branches in the large cavern protruded at crooked angles from the gray rock ceiling. The tip of each one was splayed open to reveal marble-sized blue spheres clustered like grapes in knotted clumps of fibrous white strands.

More spheres grew on thick stalks that sprouted from cracks in the walls and floor.

"Is beautiful," Ivan whispered.

He coughed harshly and doubled over, clenching his stomach. Sweat dripped from his face as he clenched his eyes against the pain. The coughing subsided and he slowly got to his feet.

"Use compass?" he asked, his voice strained.

"It's the only way to go," Merritt replied. "We can check it on the other end of the tunnel." He looked deeper into the long passage, then added, "If there is one."

As they walked down the tunnel, beneath the flowering branches, Merritt paid closer attention to the walls. They weren't jagged, as he would expect from a naturally-formed underground cavern. Like the floor of the massive chamber behind them, the walls were worn smooth, as if by the steady passage of water.

Or something else, he thought. *But if that were true, nothing would be growing. Anything big enough to touch the walls would scrape away all the plant life.*

Ivan coughed again, his hacks punctuating the silence like gunshots. With each cough, the branches in the ceiling twitched.

Merritt stepped forward, approaching a particularly long branch. He clapped his hands right next to it and it shot up into the ceiling, disappearing into a small hole.

"I've just had a disturbing thought," Merritt confided. "Let's pick up the pace."

He looked at Ivan to be sure, and Ivan nodded. Merritt moved at just on the brink of a light jog, glancing back frequently. Ivan half-limped, half-stumbled to follow, but he did so without complaint. His jaw was set, his bloodshot eyes were determined, and he refused any offer for help.

"You think this goes under mountains?" he asked.

Merritt looked up at the dangling branches. "I really hope so."

The glowing branches became sparse as the tunnel widened, eventually opening into a dome-shaped chamber the size of a small house. Several tunnel entrances of varying sizes in the wall led away from the chamber, their interiors occluded by darkness.

A single tree trunk the size of a Sequoia hung suspended from the apex of the dome. Dozens of thick, intertwining branches spread out from its hanging base and gently curved toward the ground, forming an upside-down bowl. The rim of the bowl hovered two meters off the ground. Piercing white light glowed from hairline cracks in the branches and shined off the wet rock walls.

Directly beneath the tree, atop a very slight rise in the floor, was a small, smooth gray boulder. It rested in the middle of a patch of dry green moss, which crawled up its sides, striving to reach the top. Small blue spheres glowed from thin white stalks around its base.

"*Bozhe moi*," whispered Ivan. "This is the place."

He limped past Merritt, climbing the small rise leading to the central stone.

"We can't stop here," said Merritt.

Ivan didn't reply. He limped to the boulder and fell against it as if all his remaining energy had been suddenly yanked away. Merritt hurried to his side as he put his back to the stone and slid down to sit on the ground.

He sighed with great relief and slicked back his wet hair, further accentuating his sharp widow's peak. More blisters had formed on his face and neck. His skin was a pale, sickly green.

"Always thought diabetes would kill me," he said. "Not radiation."

"You're not dead yet."

Ivan suppressed a cough and shook his head. "Listen. The big man on ship, the one you make deal with."

"Tulliver?"

Ivan nodded. "He stole my ticket. He wants in charge. You must stop him." He sighed heavily. "Is very bad man."

"We'll talk about this after we get out of here."

Ivan's hand shot out and gripped Merritt's wrist with surprising strength.

"Don't let him speak." He shook Merritt's wrist for emphasis. "He will ruin everything. You *must* stop him. For your boy."

Ivan coughed and released his grip. He leaned back against the rock and looked up at the glowing branches. A faint smile graced his lips.

"You know," he said weakly, "on Earth, I worth nothing. On ship, I worth nothing." He looked into Merritt's eyes. "Thank you for saving me."

He clutched his stomach and howled in pain, his voice echoing down the tunnels branching off from the chamber. His entire body shook. It bounced against the boulder and the mossy carpeting over the rocky ground.

Merritt gripped his shoulders and tried to steady him. Heat radiated from Ivan's skin through his wet T-shirt. He spasmed once and his body went limp against the stone, his chin resting on his shoulder.

Merritt felt for a pulse, but found none. He gently tilted Ivan's head back so it rested against the boulder, then he stepped back and closed his eyes, searing the visual into his brain. No one else would remember Ivan, and Merritt didn't want to forget.

A low rumble echoed out of one of the tunnels leading away from the dome-shaped chamber.

Merritt opened his eyes, unsure if it was a ground tremor or rushing water he hadn't noticed before. He walked past the boulder and stood before a trio of tunnels roughly the same shape as the one from which he and Ivan had emerged.

The rumbling sound resolved itself into a distinctive noise of smaller rocks grinding against the tunnel walls. The sound was definitely coming from the tunnel on the left. Merritt swallowed hard, realizing that was the tunnel he would have chosen to take — the one that started more or less in a straight line with the one across the chamber.

He took another step toward the dark tunnel. The rumbling sound grew louder, building to a roar as the floor began to shake. An otherworldly shriek echoed out from deep within the dark passageway.

He stumbled backward, his skin crawling as his breath caught in his throat.

Something else besides Merritt was using those tunnels to travel underground — something *big* — and it was headed right for him.

CHAPTER SEVENTEEN

LEERA

Leera touched the small goose egg on her right shin where her fracture had been only hours before.

"Can you walk?" asked Uda.

Leera nodded as she stood on unsteady legs. She wiped an itch on her temple with the back of her wrist and smeared warm blood into her hair.

"I'm bleeding," she said distantly, staring at her wrist.

"Let me see," said Uda, stepping closer. She gingerly prodded Leera's hairline. "A small cut. You'll be fine."

Something behind Leera caught her eye. She bent down and picked up half of a broken radio spike. Shorn wires splayed from one open end like a nest of snakes.

"Here's the other one," said Leera.

She pulled the second spike from a pile of dirt and flipped the power switch.

"Still working," she said, showing the others its tiny, glowing screen.

Corporal Turner searched the cockpit, climbing over warped sections of the shuttle's roof. He found his rifle beneath a small mound of dirt and wiped it off, then cleared the chamber with a loud *CLACK*. A shiny bronze bullet spun through the air and landed softly in the dirt. He retrieved it, brushed it off, and loaded it back into the gun.

"I only have seven rounds," he explained. "We have to climb up to get to the hatch."

"Let's check the hold first," said Uda. "There might be more radio spikes."

They climbed the short ladder at the back of the cockpit, then stepped off onto the ceiling of the small cargo hold near the aft of the shuttle.

Turner leaned back over the ladder shaft and looked up.

"Part of the hatch is missing," he said. "The ramp is twisted. We should be able to crawl out."

"Here!" said Uda.

She waded through a sea of empty storage crates, toward the back of the hold. The rear wall was covered with cargo netting — pockets of varying sizes that pinned equipment in place.

Uda grabbed the corner of one pocket and peeled it down, popping the snaps. Several radio spikes fell free and clattered on the empty storage crates below.

After a quick check, she said, "These four have been modified."

She handed two of them to Leera and tossed the others aside, then peeled off another section of netting. More spikes tumbled to the crates below. Uda picked out the ones that would repel the gray crabs and bound them together using a nylon strap she found nearby. She fastened a carrying strap out of the two loose ends of the nylon, then handed the entire bundle to Turner.

He slung the bundle over his shoulder, and asked, "Ready?"

Uda picked up her three spikes. "All set."

Turner climbed up the ladder leading to the twisted ramp and disappeared through a jagged hole in the hull. Leera climbed up slowly and awkwardly, carrying two of the radio spikes. Turner reached back into the ship and helped pull her up onto the upside-down belly of the craft.

Uda climbed up after her, blinking in the bright sunlight.

The three of them stood on the shuttle, looking past the large boulder near the crumpled nose. Beyond the broken trees and short, black scar where the shuttle had slid to a stop, a thin trail of clear ground extended toward the two mountains to the west. An ocean of gray, interlocked crab shells smothered every other inch of land.

Leera looked to the east, in the direction of the colony. The front line of crabs was less than a hundred meters from the shuttle's crash site, progressing slowly over low hills, like a gray blanket being drawn across the world.

"Do you think they cover the entire planet?" Uda asked.

"Not yet," Leera replied. "We need to get to the colony first. We'll use the radio spikes to leap-frog to the front of the line, then we run."

"I'm going back," said Uda.

Leera turned to look at her, confused. "What?"

"For the people we saw in the mountain pass, and for Walter. I'm going back."

She handed Leera one of her radio spikes, keeping two for herself.

"We have to warn the colony!" said Leera.

"You go," said Uda. "Once those people leave the pass, they won't be able to get through the crabs."

"Uda..."

"I don't want to start my time on this planet by leaving someone to die," she said. "There's an open pathway back to the mountains...for now. I can get there if I hurry."

"Be careful," said Turner.

Reluctantly, Leera added, "We'll be waiting for you at the colony."

Uda scrambled down the side of the shuttle and jumped to the ground. She ran in the direction of the nearby mountains without looking back.

Leera and Corporal Turner spent the next hour leap-frogging two radio spikes to the front line of the crab migration. As soon as they were clear, Turner broke into a fast jog eastward. Leera limped behind him, her shin hurting where it had healed.

He glanced back briefly and she concealed her limp with obvious effort, clenching her jaw and breathing hard through her nose.

Turner slowed his pace.

"Don't," said Leera. "No time."

He nodded reluctantly and jogged faster.

They stopped to drink from a small, clear spring ten minutes later. Leera sipped from her cupped palms in between heavy breaths, but Turner barely seemed winded at all.

"Training," he said simply when she asked how he managed it. "Lots and lots of training."

Leera wiped her brow with the cool water and stood, surveying the eastern horizon. The sun was dipping slowly behind her, and a faint hint of orange was infusing its brilliant yellow light. Leera's gaze swept over the bare tree trunks and the rolling hills.

Simple, she thought, *but beautiful. I miss my family.*

That last thought snuck in at the end, unbidden and unwelcome. She was trying to force herself not to think about Paul and Micah before she could rest —before she could be alone to mourn.

"Do you have anyone back home?" she asked the corporal.

Turner readjusted the bundle of radio spikes on his shoulder and swiped a wet hand over his short hair as he stood. "Couple of girlfriends," he said, grinning sheepishly. "Mom, sister, cousins." He studied Leera's face carefully. "They'll send another ship."

She nodded, even though she didn't believe him. As she looked away, a smear of red on the ground behind a tree caught her eye.

"Is that...?" she asked hesitantly.

"It's not blood," Turner replied.

He gripped his rifle and walked forward slowly, toward the red patch of ground.

"It's the red moss," Leera said as she hurried past

him.

It covered two square meters of the ground past the tree like a thick carpet.

"I think it's moving," said Leera, kneeling next to it and trying to peer beneath the flat, tightly-woven patch of moss.

Turner shouldered his rifle and knelt next to her. "How? I don't see any legs."

"Watch closely," Leera told him, pointing.

A crinkle on the top layer of moss undulated from one end to the other, like a wave rolling toward an ocean shore. A new wave started once the previous one ended, carrying the moss forward, a fraction of a centimeter at a time.

The wave of movement on its top layer stopped when Leera reached out to touch it. Thin tendrils of wet brown root-like material seeped from the moss, flagellating in the air as they slowly extended toward her hand.

Turner grabbed her arm and pulled her back.

"It healed me before," she said.

"And it died," Turner reminded her. "I don't know anything about biology, but that's a big trade-off."

The tendrils retreated back into the moss, and the slow, steady wave of movement on its top layer resumed.

"You're right," said Leera. She smiled at Turner. "Thank you for reminding me. There might only be a few of these creatures on the planet."

"Oh, I don't know about that," said the corporal.

He nodded behind her, and she turned to see another patch of moss on the ground a few meters away. It was at the edge of a natural clearing between a lopsided ring of tree trunks. The trees leaned inward at their tops, their three massive branches nearly touching to create the impression of an open-air dome.

Leera walked into the clearing and stood amongst a dozen patches of red moss. Several were attached to tree trunks, hugging the brown bark.

"Something about this place has drawn them here," she said.

Before Turner could warn her not to do it, she peeled up the corner of a patch of moss. Root-like tendrils popped free of the soil and flagellated wildly, flinging dirt. Leera let go and stepped back, brushing off her hands. Then she knelt down and stuck her finger in the ground until she felt a mild shock.

"I think they feed off the electrical field in the ground," said Leera. "Or maybe the shock stimulates smaller organisms, and that's what they eat with their tendrils. The crabs do it with their legs."

Turner looked up at the inward-leaning trees. "What's so special about this place?"

"There might be a particularly strong current beneath us. Maybe they were born here."

"Born?"

Leera smiled. "Or grown. Spawned. Seeded. Who knows? We have a whole world of questions and no way to answer them."

An image of her son flashed through her mind, and her smile faded.

"But we have plenty of time to find out," she said. "I'm ready to get moving if you are."

The hills grew steeper the farther east they jogged. Leera was expecting to be on the move all day, but a short ten minutes after leaving the clearing full of red moss behind, she and Turner climbed a hill to see a narrow river snaking from north to south, and sprawling farmland stretching eastward beyond.

"We made it," said Leera, only half-believing her eyes.

In the fields below, farmers worked their land, tilling their soil with trowels and shovels when they weren't using small, hand-drawn ploughs.

One of the farmers saw Leera and Turner atop the hill. He pointed and shouted. Another man saw them and dropped his shovel, then ran away, waving his arms and calling out to others as he passed.

Leera walked down the hill, gripping her three radio spikes, with Turner close by her side. They forded the shallow river, its cool, slow-moving waters swirling around their shins.

An aging man and a woman a few years his junior approached them at the edge of the water. He eyed the corporal's gun warily, then looked at Leera.

"Bet you're hungry," he said.

"Welcome," said the woman.

She handed Leera and Turner each a packet of freeze-dried apples.

"Thank you," said Leera graciously. "We didn't know—"

"Shh-sh!" said the man urgently, tugging at the woman's elbow and looking east. "Here he comes!"

The woman said, "Oh!" and hurried in the opposite direction, the man close on her heels.

Leera and Turner shared a confused glance before they realized what the older farmer was talking about.

A man in a long, oversized jacket was approaching them from the east, strolling casually across the neighboring farm, heedless of the carefully tilled soil underfoot. Afternoon sunlight glinted off his sweaty, bald head. Farmers gathered on the hills surrounding the border farm, watching the scene unfold.

The man in the oversized jacket was *big*, Leera saw as he drew nearer — taller than most, and with girth to spare. He spread his arms wide as he approached, and offered a welcoming grin of yellowing teeth.

Warning bells chimed in Leera's brain. Something was off about that man. He struck her as a backward scale on fine snakeskin.

Turner must have shared her sentiment. He set his bundle of radio spikes on the ground and stepped past her, one hand calmly moving toward the grip of his shouldered rifle.

"Welcome!" the large man boomed for all to hear. "Welcome to my colony."

TULLIVER

He was on his way to visit the Alder boy when he heard the shouts. Tulliver paused at the top of a low hill and dabbed sweat from his bald head with a wet rag. He squinted in the bright sunlight, trying to find the cause of the excitement.

Several colonists were running west, toward the river. It was too far to make out the details, but Tulliver thought he could see two people approaching from that direction, wearing the white-and-black body suits of those who had passed some of the voyage from Earth in a hypergel tank.

He grunted and set off down the hill, mildly annoyed to delay his trip to the Alder farm.

Word of his newfound authority had spread quickly. As Tulliver trudged up and down the rolling hills at the border of the colony toward the river, he was pleased to encounter meek farmers who nodded at him deferentially or dropped their gaze and avoided him altogether.

He figured it didn't matter to *them* who was in charge, just so long as they could grow their food in relative peace.

Warden Cohen's wife was another story.

Tulliver thought back to the meeting he had with her only an hour ago. She had come pounding on one of the landing arms of his shuttle, her two whelps at her side, yelling at the top of her lungs for Tulliver to show his face.

He did so wearing a dreadful scowl, but she was unfazed. She demanded an audience. After a brief stare-down, he growled an order that she leave her children outside.

The woman marched up the ramp without so much as a word to her young son and daughter. Once inside the shuttle, she made it clear, in no uncertain terms, that she was no farmer. The big warden's wife hadn't followed him clear across the galaxy to play in the dirt. She and her children were never supposed to go down to the surface in the first place, and she wanted to know what Tulliver was going to do about it.

"No work, no food," Tulliver said simply.

Her shoulders drooped, and she sighed.

"I've just been so lost without my husband," she said quietly.

"Ha!" Tulliver barked, making her jump. "I don't buy it."

The woman stomped her foot in frustration and wiped away a tear.

She's clever, thought Tulliver.

He could use someone like her on his side.

"Tell you what," he said. "You wait a few days for things to settle down, then come back and see me. You might be useful after all."

Tulliver grinned as he recalled the hungry gleam in her eyes. That's what he liked to see. Those were the people he liked to deal with: hungry and ambitious — happy for a slice, but not independent-minded enough to grab for the whole pie.

He came within clear sight of the western river. Two farmers, a man and his wife, were speaking with the two new arrivals, a younger man and a middle-aged woman, who wore torn and stained black-and-white body suits. The younger man carried a bundle of metal rods on his back, lashed together with a thick nylon strap.

As Tulliver approached them, he spread his arms wide and shouted, "Welcome! Welcome to my colony."

He hesitated for the briefest of moments when he saw the rifle slung across the younger man's back, but he bulled through the hesitation and offered the woman his hand. She shook it, and said, "Dr. Leera James," but did not return his wide smile. She carried three metal rods, nearly as tall as her, with one spiked end and a bulging cluster of electronic doodads on the other. They didn't look particularly effective as weapons, so Tulliver disregarded them.

"Corporal Turner," said the younger man, emphasizing the C*orporal*. His handshake was overly firm.

Something to prove, thought Tulliver.

He turned his left shoulder toward the two of them to show off his warden's patch, which he had found on a jump suit in the shuttle and hastily stuck to the sleeve of his own jacket.

"I'm Tulliver Pruitt," he said. "The new government rep for the colony."

"What happened to the wardens?" asked the corporal. "We were supposed to be dealing with them."

"They didn't make it," he said with a requisite amount of sadness and regret.

"So who put you in charge?" asked the woman.

Tulliver turned toward her. "I did." Then he smiled and jabbed a thumb behind him. "The colony is a short walk that way. I'll fill you in."

He turned his back on them and started walking, wondering if they would follow. A moment later, they appeared on his left, walking close together.

"Almost sixty survivors," said Tulliver as he descended a long, sloping hill.

He waved at a farmer in dirty clothing, but the farmer did not wave back.

Need to find those crates of new clothes, thought Tulliver. *Get these people something clean to wear.*

"There are more out there," said Leera. "We saw three survivors walking through a mountain pass, making their way toward the colony. One of our group went back for them after we crashed."

Tulliver glanced at her. "Crashed?"

"In the shuttle," said the corporal.

The woman slapped his shoulder quickly and shook her head. Tulliver smirked and pretended not to notice.

Secrets on secrets, said the ghostly voice of Ivan in his mind. *Just like on Earth. Just like on the ship.*

I told you where to find another ticket, thought Tulliver, swiping his brow with a sweaty hand. *You're faster than me. A better runner.*

And yet there you are, and where am I?

"—like to see what you have set up for the injured," the woman was saying, jogging to keep up with Tulliver's long strides. "I'm sure medical supplies were delivered before the crash."

"What?" said Tulliver irritably.

"I said I want to make sure you're all set up for injured survivors. We...we lost our doctor in the shuttle crash."

"You're a doctor."

"Of systems biology. Not medicine."

Tulliver grunted. "That's unfortunate. We have almost no science equipment. No microscopes, no scanning-whatevers. But we *do* have broken bones. Cuts and bruises. Concussions. We need a *medical* doctor. Someone useful to the colony."

From the corner of his eye, Tulliver saw the corporal rest his hand on the woman's shoulder to get her attention. He nodded in Tulliver's direction and patted the side of his rifle. Tulliver balled his fists and took a deep breath.

The woman shook her head and pushed the front of the corporal's rifle back toward the ground.

"Mr. Pruitt," said the woman tightly. "The colony has bigger problems than dealing with cuts and bruises."

"Oh?"

"There's a mass migration of animals heading

east, right toward us."

He stopped walking and stood in the bright sunlight, chewing his lip and breathing heavily.

"Migration?" he said at last.

"Gray crabs," said the woman. "All moving together. There was another colony before this one."

"That's where we found the shuttle," said the corporal.

"We think…*I* think the crabs killed them."

"I saw them when my pod landed," Tulliver said, repressing a shudder. "It was a small patch, heading away from the colony."

"There are more," she told him. "Enough to cover this continent, and they're headed this way."

"You've seen them?" he asked quietly.

She nodded.

"*Where* are they?"

"If they hold their current pace," she replied, "they'll be at the edge of the farmlands by nightfall."

"Maybe they'll go around," said Tulliver, the words sounding ridiculous even as he spoke them.

"They follow an electrical current in the ground," said Leera. "The current runs near trees, and I'm guessing the colony is right in the middle of a forest. The crabs aren't going to 'go around'."

"What about the river?" asked Tulliver. He stuffed his shaking hands in his jacket pockets to hide them. The warm sweat covering his body turned cold, and he shivered. "Can they swim?"

"I have no idea," the woman said. She held up her three metal rods and pointed at the bundle of identical rods on the corporal's back. "These radio spikes will repel them, but we don't have enough to surround the entire colony. Where's the shuttle the wardens brought to the surface?"

"Why?" he asked, suddenly defensive.

The woman looked surprised. "Because…there might be more of these inside. We need as many as possible to form a perimeter around the colony."

"We'll gather everyone together. Shrink the perimeter."

"We don't know anything about how the crabs affect the soil!" she protested. "They might ingest all the nutrients and deposit organics that will stop our crops from growing. There's no way to know, so we need to find more radio spikes."

He turned on her and jabbed a finger into her shoulder, eliciting a yelp of pain. She stumbled backward and the corporal caught her from falling.

"*No one* goes in my shuttle unless I say so."

The corporal raised his gun and Tulliver took a step toward him. Then the corporal stood up straight and released his weapon as he looked down the hill.

Gavin Alder ran up the hill, staring at the new arrivals. He looked at them, then looked past them, as if searching for someone else. His hands worked quickly, signing words Tulliver didn't understand.

"Your father's not with them," said Tulliver. "I told you he's gone."

The woman looked at Tulliver like he'd just shot her pet.

The boy ignored him, staring instead at the woman. His bottom lip quivered and tears welled in his eyes. He looked once more toward the western horizon, then turned and ran back down the hill.

"Gavin!" Tulliver called after him.

He sighed and flashed a congenial smile, as if he and the corporal hadn't been about to kill each other.

"He misses his father," Tulliver explained. "It's a lot of change in a short amount of time."

He frowned as Gavin ran back toward his farm. Tulliver would need to have a serious discussion with the boy about what he could expect from his future.

"Almost there," he said, leading the way down the hill. "Let's get you all set up at camp, then we can talk about those...those animals." He glanced at the corporal's rifle. "We'll have to put your gun under lock and key. Can't allow someone to grab it from your tent while you're in the latrine."

"They're welcome to try," Turner said casually.

"For a military man, you seem to have a dominant streak of insubordination."

"Depends on who's in charge."

They entered the sparse forest surrounding the core of the colony and passed the blackened circle of burnt ground where Warden Cohen had made his last campfire.

"Some folks like sleeping under the stars," Tulliver explained. "It's a novelty they couldn't enjoy on Earth."

Samar was stacking crates just outside the circle of structures at the heart of the settlement. He stood up straight and grinned at Tulliver, who sneered in response. Samar shook his head, still smiling, and went back to his work as Tulliver led his two charges into the colony proper.

"You've been busy," remarked the woman, looking around.

"Most of the shelters were put up before the Halcyon did her swan dive," said Tulliver. He pointed to an open-air canvas shelter nearby. "Mess tent is there. That little one is the clinic, if you can call it that. Those are the bunk houses. I have some people digging trenches for the septic system beyond those trees, which we'll install as soon as the supply manager can find the pipes. We're in pretty good shape already. Once we find where the Halcyon landed more supplies on her previous visits, we'll be able to get the farmers the homes they paid for and pop some more tents for the ship's crew."

A group of colonists had formed around Tulliver and the two new arrivals while he spoke. The colonists hung back quietly, observing.

"I'll need your red cards before you get settled in," said Tulliver, holding out his hand toward them expectantly. He shrugged. "It's policy."

"You need to send someone out to keep an eye on the migration," said the woman, ignoring him. "We have to get these people to a safe place."

"Is that the warden's shuttle?" asked the corporal, stepping toward it. "There might be more radio spikes inside."

Tulliver blocked his path, glaring down at the shorter man.

"What did I say about going on my shuttle?" he growled quietly.

"What's underneath it?" the woman asked.

She knelt down and looked in the shadows beneath the shuttle. Suddenly she gasped and quickly stood up, looking at Tulliver as if he had suddenly shed his human mask to reveal the monster beneath.

"Yeah," said Tulliver with a sigh. "That's Warden Ramirez. Guess he wasn't quick enough."

But the corporal was.

He dropped his bundle of metal rods and rammed the side of his rifle into Tulliver's stomach, sending him stumbling back. Then he aimed and fired as Tulliver charged him. The first bullet went wide but the second one hit his left shoulder like a hammer-blow.

Tulliver leaped forward, driving his bald head into the corporal's stomach as the third bullet went high. The corporal fell on his back and Tulliver landed on his legs. He scrambled forward and grabbed the rifle with both hands as the corporal raised it to fire again. Tulliver ripped it from his grasp. His eyes were wide and terrible as he leaned his head back, then brought his skull down hard on the corporal's with a loud *CRACK*.

The corporal went limp. Tulliver used the rifle as a crutch to stand, then wiped blood from his forehead as he turned in a circle to glare at the crowd surrounding him. He stopped when he saw the doctor woman and aimed the rifle in her direction.

"No *guns*," he hissed.

Then he pointed the nozzle at the ground and pulled the trigger repeatedly until the chamber clicked empty.

The ground rumbled under his boots. He looked down at it, confused, and took a step back.

The colonists held on to each other for support as the quaking intensified. Tulliver lost his balance and fell to one knee. The corporal was on the ground, shaking as if he were having a seizure, and the woman stood in a wide stance, crouched low with her arms held out for balance.

As the quake subsided, a faint blue glow bloomed in the bullet holes that had punctured the soil. Tulliver slowly reached out for one. A blue sphere emerged from the hole, pushed upward by a thin, luminous plant stalk. He pulled his hand back as an identical plant sprouted from each hole.

The woman touched one with the tip of her forefinger and got a small electric shock for her curiosity.

After several long moments of exposure to the air, the spheres blackened and withered as if held under a torch. They sank into themselves as the stalks to which they were attached curled back into the ground. The blue light faded.

Tulliver grunted as he stood up, then stomped on the withering stalks, grinding them to dust. He tossed the rifle aside and probed the hole in his left shoulder tentatively, wincing as blood seeped from the wound.

"Can you stitch me up?" he asked the doctor woman.

"Did you see that?" she said, gently toeing the edge of a bullet hole in the ground.

"Hey, doc," Tulliver barked, snapping his fingers. "I'm bleeding. Stitch me up."

She dropped the three metal rods she was carrying and hurried to the corporal's side as he groaned. His eyes rolled in their sockets as she helped him sit up. The woman delicately probed the firework of blood on his brow with her thumb, checking the wound beneath.

"I'll take that as a no," said Tulliver.

He picked up one of the metal rods the woman had dropped on the ground and used it for support as he made his way toward the shuttle.

The colonists parted to allow his passage, and he made eye contact with every one of them brave enough to return his stare. There weren't many.

He had expected to leave the shuttle ramp up to keep out the riffraff, but after torching Ramirez upon landing, Tulliver was pleased to discover that the stink of burnt warden was enough to keep most colonists away.

As he mounted the ramp and began the steep, laborious climb, something in the nearby woods caught his eye.

A boy, running.

Tulliver stepped off the ramp and hurried around to the back of the shuttle, blood trickling down his hand as he pressed it against his wounded shoulder.

It was the Alder boy, and he was making for the supply crates. He wore an over-sized backpack that bounced against the back of his legs as he ran. Sweat plastered his brown hair to his forehead. He ran in a wide circle around the settlement, avoiding the cluster of people near the shuttle.

Tulliver took a shortcut through the center of camp, heading straight for the stacks of supply crates. They had been stacked six-high in places, creating a small maze behind the supply tent. Their towers loomed over Tulliver's head as he jogged through the maze.

He came across Samar, who was struggling with great effort to lift a heavy crate and set it atop another. The supply manager smiled and wiped sweat from his brow, then he said, "I knew you couldn't—"

Tulliver put his broad palm over Samar's face and shoved him backward, sending him tumbling over a crate.

Gavin appeared from behind a stack of crates and skidded to a stop in the soil, breathing hard, his frail bird's chest shuddering with each exhalation.

The poor kid is going out to look for his father, Tulliver realized.

The boy's gaze flicked to an open crate of freeze-dried food packets and sachets of lemonade concentrate. Samar stood up from behind the crate he'd tripped over and ran toward the other colonists without looking back.

Tulliver groaned with pain as he took a knee to look at Gavin eye-to-eye.

"Listen to me closely," he said gently. "If you leave the colony, you die. Something is out there that your daddy could not survive. If you go looking for him, it will get you, too."

The boy glared at him, disbelieving every word of it. Part of Tulliver was proud to see that defiance — proud that the kid wasn't just another sheep. Another part of him wanted the boy to obey.

"I'll make a safe place for you here," said Tulliver. "I know it hurts to lose someone. I lost the two people I love most." His hand drifted up to the chain around his neck. He pulled it from the neck of his shirt and opened the small locket to show Gavin the pictures. "I make...mistakes. I always make mistakes." His eyes glazed over as he remembered the day he came back to his apartment to find a note on the kitchen counter — a note, but no family. "They were taken from me," he said. Then he clicked the locket shut and slipped it through the neckline of his shirt.

Don't lie to him, said a woman's voice inside his head — a voice Tulliver hadn't heard in a very long time. She sounded disgusted, as she always had in the final months before he lost her forever. *I left because of the monster you were becoming. And now look at you. You're a thug.*

"I'm more than that," he whispered.

Gavin turned and ran.

Tulliver lunged forward and caught a fistful of backpack. He pulled it hard, picking the boy up off his feet, and flung it behind him, toward the colony. The backpack, and Gavin with it, flew through the air and smacked into the side of a tower of stacked crates, then he fell in a heap on the ground. The tower teetered in place, then toppled over, raining crates down to the ground.

The first one hit on its corner, sinking into the ground next to Gavin's head. It hit so sturdily, without bouncing, that Tulliver realized these were not empty crates.

He reached out for Gavin as another crate landed between them, on Gavin's legs. The boy's eyes shot open and he screamed silently.

More crates fell to the ground with heavy thuds. Gavin strained to push the one from his legs and looked up in horror.

A crate slipped off the tower and fell like a boulder. It landed flat on top of the boy, sinking him into the ground with a sickening crunch of bones, and all was silent.

"No," Tulliver whispered as he climbed over the crates.

A small, bone-white hand stuck out from beneath the fallen crate. It twitched, tapping once against the side of the crate.

Tulliver stepped back, swallowing hard. He turned quickly, looking back at the settlement.

The colonists had returned to their own business. No one had seen what happened.

No one's looking, said the internal youthful voice of Diego, the young warden, as Tulliver walked quickly away from the crates. *It was an accident. No one saw you.*

He bumped into someone with his injured shoulder. He growled but didn't stop as he hurried toward his shuttle. He mounted the ramp and glanced back.

The woman.

The woman looked at him, then at the chaotic scattering of crates on the far side of the clearing.

She walked in that direction.

Tulliver huffed as he climbed the ramp, disappearing into shuttle.

MERRITT

His boots pounded the hard rock floor, echoing down the tunnel.

Aside from the limited glow of blue light from the cluster of luminous plant stalks he clutched in one hand, those echoes were the only way Merritt knew the tunnel wasn't going to dead-end on him.

The sound of loose gravel grinding against stone grew louder behind him as something gained on him. It moved fast — at least as fast as Merritt could run, and probably faster now that the tunnel had leveled out.

He glanced back but saw only darkness.

After he heard the animal shriek from the left tunnel in the dome chamber where Ivan had died, Merritt yanked a fistful of glowing plant stalks from the ground near the central boulder and ran into the middle tunnel.

Something exploded out of the left tunnel shortly after, shrieking wildly. It blocked the light of the dome chamber as it crawled into the middle tunnel to chase after Merritt.

He caught a glimpse of a massive, armored, worm-like carapace as the creature stuffed itself into the tunnel, its tough exterior scraping the walls as it propelled itself closer.

Merritt forced himself to think of Gavin, and the thought gave him a small boost of energy.

The tunnel widened and narrowed, then widened yet again. Merritt risked a look back every time it narrowed, hoping the creature would get stuck. Each time, he was disappointed as it scraped through the pinch, shrieking.

His mind churned with questions as he ran.

Why the shriek? Is it calling its friends? What does it eat down here besides lost humans?

He tripped and almost fell, and the creature came closer. At times it sounded like it was immediately behind him, almost on top of him. Then the tunnel would rise slightly and the grinding echo of its approach would diminish by a fraction.

Merritt focused on putting one foot safely in front of the other in the darkness, pushing the distracting questions from his mind. The one thought he couldn't shake was the fear of stepping over an open pit and plunging to his death.

He kept straining his eyes to look ahead, hoping for a gleam of daylight.

Should have checked the compass when I had the chance, he thought.

There was no way to tell which direction he was going. His pessimistic side told him it was probably north, which would put him on a long track under the mountains. He hadn't bumped into any dangling roots nor seen any other sign that he was beneath a forest. Hopefully, that meant he was already under the mountains, even if he was moving north instead of east, toward the colony.

The sound of grinding rock grew closer behind him, but Merritt couldn't go any faster. He ran with one hand dragging over the rough surface of the tunnel, feeling for a crack, an opening — anything too small for the creature to squeeze into.

Warmth filled the tunnel behind him and something bumped his shoulder. At that same moment, a crack in the wall opened to his right. He leaped into it and slammed against hard rock as the creature rushed past, shrieking when its prey suddenly vanished.

Merritt was in a narrow hollow with no other way out.

He held his meager bouquet of glowing plant stalks in front of him. Wet, gray flesh glistened in the light as the creature squeezed down the tunnel, filling it from wall to wall. Stiff black spikes that had been compressed against its body popped up, flinging moisture on Merritt's chest and face. He spat and turned aside.

The creature stopped.

Merritt tried to hold his breath as the beast slowly retreated back the way it came, its gray flesh undulating in waves as it wiggled toward the dome chamber.

The creature's bulk disappeared from sight, leaving only the darkness of the tunnel outside the crack.

Merritt poked his head out after a long moment and looked up and down the silent tunnel. A sharp odor persisted after the creature's passing, a mixture of unripe fruit and gasoline.

The rock walls shimmered as Merritt stepped out of the crack and held up his light. In the direction of the dome chamber there was only darkness. In the other, a small circle of light hovered in the middle of the tunnel.

Daylight.

Merritt took a step closer to the light.

The creature shrieked behind him — *right* behind him — and exploded forward with a rolling crunch of stone against stone.

Merritt ran for the light. His fistful of glowing plant stalks shredded to pieces as his arms pumped. The circle of light grew larger as he ran, but there was another sound behind him now, a sound like teeth sliding against each other as massive jaws snapped at his heels.

He burst into sunlight on a steep embankment overlooking a mountain pass and stumbled to a stop, shooting a terrified look behind him. The creature did not emerge. With a grinding of stone and one final, forlorn howl, it moved off down the tunnel, deeper into the mountain.

Merritt bent over and put his shaking hands on his knees as he gulped down fresh air. After catching his breath, he wiped his mouth, then held his arm up to shield his eyes against the bright sun.

Merritt took a few hesitant steps as he looked around, trying to gauge his surroundings. He patted the wet pockets of his coveralls, searching for the plastic snap-case containing the makeshift compass.

It was gone.

He had traveled such a great distance underground that he assumed he *must* be on the far side of the two mountains. If the narrow pass between them was aligned mostly on an east-west axis, then he simply needed to follow it toward the colony. Yet, if he was wrong, he would be walking back toward the *Halcyon*. He'd be forced to double back and pick a trail through the pass — a route that would take even *more* time.

Merritt jogged down the side of the mountain, his wet boots slipping over loose rocks. He hit flat ground a few minutes later and kept the mountains behind him as he ran through a sparse forest, over hills and past bubbling freshwater springs. There was no sign of wreckage, but also no sign of the colony.

He ran faster, fueled by the thought of Gavin alone at the colony with no friends and no familiar faces — a child by himself on a strange world with no one watching out for him.

LEERA

She heard the tumble of crates and saw Tulliver Pruitt emerge from the supply stacks. If anyone had ever worn a more blatant look of guilt on their face, Leera hadn't seen it.

He hurried toward his shuttle and collided with another colonist. Then he paused before climbing up the ramp and looked right at her.

A heavy weight settled in her gut — the weight of knowing she shouldn't investigate because she wouldn't like what she found. She looked toward the crates on the far side of the settlement. A silence seemed to pulse out from that spot — a horrible silence in direct contradiction to the brimming life of its surroundings.

She followed that silence to the crates.

They were stacked six-high in some places, creating towers that loomed above her. She stepped around one stack to find a haphazard jumble of them on the ground. A small, bone-white hand protruded from beneath one of them. It wasn't moving.

Leera ran to the crate and heaved, but it wouldn't budge. She screamed for help as she dug her fingers into the tightly-packed soil underneath, trying to lift the crate from the bottom.

Her bare feet dug into the loose, moist ground,

scraping off the top layer to expose mud beneath. She slipped in the mud and cracked her head against the side of the crate. Her fingers brushed the small white hand as she stood. It was cold as ice.

Leera found the crate's latches and popped them open in rapid succession. With a scream of frustration, she picked up the heavy lid and dropped it next to her with a dull thud.

The crate was filled with metal tubes the length of her arm. Each one was packed with as many steel ball bearings as it could hold. The bearings were intended for the enormous grain silo doors that never made it down from the ship.

She hoisted tube after tube from the crate and tossed them aside, working straight down one side to create a hollow.

A wiry man with a weathered face and salted brown beard stubble appeared at her side, chest heaving from running. He looked down at the small white hand in horror.

"Is that Gavin?!" he asked, his smoker's voice thick with fear.

"Help me!" Leera shouted.

The man snapped into action. He grabbed the heavy tubes and threw them behind him without looking. As he worked, Leera dug her fingers under the crate and lifted. It moved.

"Lift!" she screamed.

The man bent down next to her and got his bony hands under the crate. He and Leera yelled in unison as they leveraged the crate up on one side and tipped it over. It fell on its open top with a loud clacking of steel ball bearings.

"Oh, no," whispered Leera as she looked at the boy on the ground.

He was in the middle of a square indentation left by the crate, his head turned slightly to the side, his eyes closed. Blood trickled freely from his nostrils. His flattened backpack was skewed to the side next to him.

Leera knelt down and felt for a pulse on the wrist that had been sticking out from the crate. There was a very clear break in his forearm halfway to his elbow. Given the sunken appearance of the boy's chest, Leera guessed the rest of his bones had suffered a similar fate.

She gasped.

"His heart is beating!" she said.

"What do I do?! What do we do?!" the man asked quickly.

Leera knelt next to the child and scooped him up in her arms. There was almost no rigidity to his body. He seemed to drape over her arms like a thick blanket.

"Maybe you shouldn't move him."

Leera put her lips next to the boy's ear and whispered, "Hang in there."

Then she ran.

She ran away from the colony, through the forest, back toward the mountains. The man who helped her shouted at her back, wanting to know where she was taking the boy.

Leera didn't look back — didn't spare the energy to respond. A sharp knife stabbed her right shin where the bone had healed, but she set her jaw and stared straight ahead, ignoring the pain. She knew exhaustion would get the better of her long before the pain ever could.

She glanced down at the boy's pale face, hoping for a sign of life. The pulse she had felt was so weak she almost missed it — too slow and too weak.

"Where are you going?!" the man who helped her shouted from behind as he tried to keep up. "What are you looking for?!"

"Red!" she yelled back.

"Red?"

Leera looked frantically at the trees as she ran past them, but couldn't tell if she was following the same path as she and Turner took on their way to the colony.

"Any patch of red!" she called out between quick breaths.

"Why?!"

Leera didn't answer. A moment later, she noticed she could no longer hear his footsteps behind her.

The man sounded confused as he shouted, "Merritt?!"

Leera glanced back and saw that he had stopped. Another man wearing torn and dirt-smeared workman's coveralls stood in the forest at the top of a low rise. He was breathing hard and staring intently at Leera as she ran.

No, she thought, *he's staring at the boy.*

Then she saw it up ahead: a red mossy patch, like a misshapen rectangular carpet, in the middle of a clearing. The trees above bowed inward, their tri-branched tips almost touching to form a natural, open-air dome.

She ran into the clearing and dropped to her knees between three more patches of red moss. As carefully as she could, she laid the boy on the ground and stepped back, wiping sweat from her face with the wet sleeve of her filthy body-suit.

At first, nothing happened. She bent down, ready to peel up one of the red patches of moss and lay it over the boy, when the first tentative tendrils snaked out from its flat, spongy body. The faint waves of movement on the creature's back changed direction, and it began to crawl toward the injured boy.

Similar tendrils emerged from the red moss of the other two nearby creatures. The longest tendril touched the boy's bare ankle and curled around it. The boy's leg tugged in that direction as the patch of moss pulled itself closer.

The tendril from another patch coiled around one of his wrists. The boy's arm jerked as the patch of moss slid across the ground with a wet sound.

The man who helped her ran into the clearing a moment later, exclaiming his confusion in the most colorful way possible.

After his expletives tapered off, he asked, "What are they doin', doc?"

"They healed my broken leg," she replied as she watched the patches of moss crawl closer to the boy.

The wiry man swallowed hard. "So this is normal?"

"*Gavin!*" boomed a nearby voice.

"Merritt's not gonna like this..." said the man who helped her.

Merritt burst into the clearing. His gaze quickly swept over Leera and the other man, then he saw the tendril tug-of-war going on with the boy on the ground.

He leaped forward and grabbed the long, rootlike tendril that was wrapped around the boy's ankle with both hands. With a strong yank, he broke it.

Leera shouted, "Stop him!"

The man who helped her jumped on Merritt's back and forced him to the ground. He wrapped his long, sinewy arms around Merritt's waist from behind and got him in a choke-hold. Merritt pounded the man's arms with tight fists as he was dragged backward, away from the boy.

"*Skip, let me go!*" yelled Merritt.

"Easy now!" said Skip as Merritt's boot-heels scraped trenches in the soft ground. "She's helpin' him! These things healed her broken bone, and they're gonna fix your boy."

Merritt made a half-hearted attempt to swipe at Skip's face, and missed. He collapsed in the other man's grasp as he stared helplessly at his son.

"What happened to him?"

"A crate fell," said Leera. "He was crushed."

"Did Tulliver have anything to do with it?"

She glanced at Skip, then at Merritt. "I think so."

Merritt's face twisted in agony as he looked away. He clenched his jaw and seethed.

One of the red patches of moss reached Gavin's foot. It extended a tendril and wrapped it around his thigh, pulling itself up the boy's leg. Another patch of moss covered his left arm like a drawn blanket. When the third patch ruffled the boy's hair as it began to crawl up his scalp, Merritt lurched back to life. He lunged forward and almost grabbed the corner of a moss patch before Skip managed to wrestle him back to the ground.

In unison, a hundred thin tentacles burst from each patch of red moss and covered Gavin like webbing. With a single motion, all three patches pulled toward each other. Their edges intertwined and they became a solid blanket of spongy red material that smothered the boy from head to toe. Leera shuddered at how closely the image resembled a corpse under a sheet.

"Now what?" Merritt whispered.

"Now we wait," Leera replied.

"How long?"

"I'm not sure. I'm sorry."

Merritt looked to the east. "How far to the colony?"

"Just a few minutes, if yer hoofin' it," said Skip.

Merritt's helpless gaze returned to his son.

"I can't leave him like this."

"There's nothing more we can do," said Leera. "I'll stay."

Merritt didn't look up from the red patch on the ground as he said, "I don't know you."

Skip relaxed his choke-hold on Merritt and patted his shoulder.

"But you know me," he said. "I'll stay and watch out for your boy."

Merritt stood up slowly and brushed loose dirt off the front of his coveralls.

"Those things can heal him?" he asked, tears brimming in his eyes.

"They healed me," said Leera. "But I only had a broken leg. Your son's injuries are much more severe."

Merritt took a deep breath, then nodded. "I'm going to the colony. Thank you both."

Leera pointed him in the right direction, and he left at a quick jog, his work boots thudding the soft ground.

"What is he planning to do?" asked Leera.

Skip watched Merritt until he disappeared into the forest.

"All I know is what *I* would do if that was my boy on the ground," he told her. "And it ain't pretty."

MERRITT

Merritt could only imagine what he looked like to the colonists when he ran into the clearing at the heart of the settlement. His previously-blue coveralls were uniformly black from soot, soil, and mud. Strips of his sleeves hung from his elbows like tattered flags. He hadn't looked in a mirror since before the *Halcyon* fell to Galena, but it wasn't a stretch to assume his face was bruised and bleeding.

He had expected to walk in on the middle of a bustling hub of activity — a mini-city in the making. There were tents and a few hard-shelled structures, but the colony was far from bustling. Other than a few people wandering around the clearing without purpose, there was no movement at all. The settlement had just gotten started, and now it seemed like it was already dead.

Several colonists sat on supply crates nearby, facing each other and speaking in hushed tones. They fell silent as Merritt walked past, eyeing him warily. He was certain the scowl he had been unable to get rid of was enough to justify their apprehension.

"Where is he?" Merritt asked them.

A woman with deep lines on her tan face pointed across the clearing, at a shuttle resting over the charred remains of a shelter.

Merritt took a few steps, then paused and looked back.

"Weapons?" he asked.

The woman shook her head.

What would you expect to do with one anyway? he chided himself as he approached the shuttle. He had swung axes, picks, hammers, and fired a nail gun on occasion, but he had no formal weapons training. The most he could hope for was intimidation.

Mist curled up from small holes in the ground at the center of the clearing. The mist snaked lazily between the temporary shelters lining the perimeter.

The shuttle ramp lowered as he approached, stopping Merritt in his tracks. He had been expecting to have to yell and pound on the landing arms until he got a response. The colonists sitting on the crates behind him stood up, and several more emerged from nearby shelters.

A large shadow appeared at the top of the shuttle ramps. Two eyes gleamed in the darkness as they looked down on Merritt.

"The father returns," Tulliver's deep voice rolled out from the shuttle, amplified by its metal walls. "I told the boy you were dead."

Merritt cleared his throat and said, "You were wrong." His voice sounded hopelessly weak in comparison — diminished in the vast open space outside the shuttle.

Tulliver slowly descended the ramp, his heavy boots thudding with each deliberate step. Light swept up his massive body as he emerged from the shadows until he stood at the base of the ramp, thumbs hooked in his belt loops, looking down on Merritt even though the two were meters apart. The left shoulder of his jacket was soaked with blood.

"Where'd you get that?" asked Merritt, nodding toward the warden's patch on the right shoulder of Tulliver's jacket.

The big man glanced down at it and picked off a piece of lint.

"Friend gave it to me."

Merritt glanced under the shuttle, certain he could see the silhouette of a claw-like hand grasping from the ashes.

"You're going to have to give that up."

"Haw!" Tulliver barked, his belly heaving up and dropping like a sack of sand. "To you?"

"To the colony."

"You want it for yourself."

"I want my land, and my son."

Tulliver's amusement faded and his face turned to stone. "What happened to your boy was an accident."

"I don't care. You're going to leave."

Tulliver stepped toward him and planted his boots firmly on the ground in a wide stance.

"Is that right? You think you can handle that all by yourself?" He made a show of looking around the colony. "I don't see anyone with you." His eyes gleamed with suspicion. "You know what I think? I think you're trying to weasel out of the crop-debt you owe me."

"I have no problem paying my debts to honorable people."

"*Honor?*" asked Tulliver in a mocking tone. "You think that matters here?"

"I hope it does," Merritt said quietly.

Tulliver took another step closer, now an arm's length away. "Let me show you what *does* matter."

His hand shot out and caught Merritt in the throat. Merritt grabbed for his own neck as he choked for air, but Tulliver caught his wrists and spread them out wide. He brought his bald head down on Merritt's face with a loud CRACK, hitting his eye socket.

Merritt stumbled back and fell to the ground on his side, clutching at his throat, trying in vain to suck down air. He crawled through the dirt like a worm, wet soil smearing the side of his face as he tried to get away.

Tulliver cracked his neck to both sides and rolled his shoulders, loosening his muscles as he slowly followed after Merritt.

More colonists had appeared at the edges of the clearing. Merritt noticed several farmers with shovels, watching fearfully.

"Go back to your moping!" Tulliver bellowed at them. "This is official colony business." He grunted with amusement, a predatory grin splitting his sweaty face. "Your warden will handle it."

He reached down and grabbed a fistful of the back of Merritt's coveralls and pushed him hard against the ground. Merritt coughed into the wet soil as it mushed around his face.

Tulliver crouched low and spoke into Merritt's ear, his voice a low growl.

"Your boy is mine, and so is this colony."

A glint of gold flashed in Merritt's blurred vision: a small locket dangling from a thin chain around Tulliver's neck. He grabbed it and yanked, snapping the chain. Tulliver howled with rage and grabbed the back of Merritt's coveralls with both hands. With a loud roar of might, he spun and hurled Merritt into the air. He flew several meters across the clearing and hit the ground on his stomach, still clenching the locket.

"Give that back!" Tulliver shouted as he stomped across the clearing.

Merritt got to his knees and wiped mud from his eyes. He threw the locket toward the trees at the edge of the clearing. It glinted as it spun through the air and disappeared into a gnarled bush.

Tulliver stopped and squinted in that direction, then turned his cold gaze on Merritt, who collapsed onto his hands and knees, painfully sucking down air.

The colonists had crept closer during the altercation. They stood in a loose half-circle around the two quarreling men.

Tulliver paid them no attention. He stomped toward Merritt, rage burning in his eyes, and grabbed him by the throat. Merritt's eyes bulged as he found himself unable to breathe once again. He was easily picked up off the ground, lifted up until his feet were dangling and he was looking down on Tulliver.

Tulliver balled his other fist and pulled it back for a punch. His face was twisted by a horrible grimace of anger.

"No," said the woman who had pointed Merritt toward the shuttle, stepping forward.

Tulliver hesitated and glanced in her direction.

"Let him go," said a farmer, tightly gripping his shovel. He stepped forward as well.

Tulliver growled and punched Merritt in the chest, sending him stumbling backward. He tripped and hit the ground on his shoulder with a wet splat, then curled into a ball as he managed to gulp down a lungful of air. He coughed it back out in a painful spasm.

"This man needs to be disciplined," said Tulliver, addressing the crowd. "Without discipline, we're animals. I will tell you one more time. Go back to your business."

"This *is* our business," said a familiar voice.

Merritt lifted his head from the ground as Uda pushed through the crowd of colonists. She held a metal radio spike like a weapon, ready to swing. Niku stepped forward to stand beside her. Behind them, Henry Tolbard supported Willef, who winced and put a hand to his bleeding side.

Despite his own pain, Merritt smiled. He rested his forehead on the soft ground as he got his hands under him, then pushed off with great effort and stood.

Tulliver's gaze drifted over the colonists and he took a hesitant step back.

Merritt wheezed with each laborious breath as he limped past him to join the others. It felt like a boulder was pushing down on his rib cage, crushing his lungs. He stumbled and Niku caught him before he fell, then wrapped one arm over his shoulders and helped him to stand.

"Good timing," Merritt whispered.

"Looks like you had it all under control," Niku replied.

Tulliver growled as he looked around the crowd.

"You need me!" he shouted. "This a dangerous world. How will you survive without someone like me in charge?"

"We'll figure it out," said Uda. She nodded toward the forest. "Go."

Tulliver looked at her in disbelief, then threw back his head and laughed. He wiped a tear from the corner of his eye as he calmed down, then he said, "No."

Uda stepped forward, brandishing her radio spike.

"You think I'm afraid of your little stick?" asked Tulliver, walking toward her. "I'm going to take that away and make you regret picking it up in the first place. *ALL* of you!" he roared, addressing the colonists as he broke into a run, heading straight for Uda. "I'll make you regret EVERYthing!"

Corporal Turner appeared in the crowd as Tulliver charged. A red spot of blood decorated the middle of a white bandage wrapped around his head. He lunged forward as Tulliver grabbed for Uda and brought his closed fist down on Tulliver's neck like a hammer, catching him on the carotid artery.

Tulliver stumbled to a stop and slapped a hand to his neck. He glared blearily at a small spot of blood on his palm as he swayed in place.

"Whass that?" he asked drunkenly, eyes swimming in their sockets as they tried to settle on Turner.

He threw a lazy haymaker over the corporal's head, spun around, and fell on his face in the dirt with a heavy thud.

Merritt kicked Tulliver in the rib cage just to be sure he was unconscious.

"That was some punch," he said to the corporal.

Turner held up his fist and opened his hand to reveal a palm-sized medical injector.

"Animal tranquilizer," he explained. "For the real beasts."

"How long will it last?" asked Uda.

Turner looked at the injector and shrugged. "I don't know. I just told the lady to fill it up."

Merritt extricated himself from Niku's helpful support and winced as he walked away.

"You have some time to figure it out."

"Where are you going?" Niku asked.

Merritt kept one hand over his burning chest. "Back to my son."

He deflected multiple attempts to help him walk to the grove of red moss. The going was slow, but necessary. Merritt needed time to prepare himself for the possibility that Gavin wasn't going to recover from his injuries.

He came into sight of the tree-dome over the grove after cresting a low hill. Wincing with each step, he trudged forward, passing a patch of red moss resting half on the ground and half on a tree.

Skip stood at the edge of the small clearing, nervously chewing his fingernails. He heard Merritt approaching and turned quickly.

"You're not gonna believe this," he said quickly, rushing to Merritt's side.

Merritt allowed Skip to help him down the gentle slope leading to the clearing. Leera knelt down next to Gavin, who lay on his back as if sleeping. Rectangular patches of gray moss covered the ground nearby. One of them had crumbled at the corners, scattering a fine gray dust across the green-streaked soil.

Merritt hobbled forward and collapsed at Gavin's side. He picked up his son's hand and felt warmth. His pale skin flushed a healthy red. It was covered in tiny red dots, like a rash.

Leera smiled and squeezed Merritt's shoulder as he held the back of Gavin's hand to his cheek. Tears streamed down over the boy's fingers.

"Is he going to be okay?" Merritt whispered.

Gavin's eyelids fluttered open and he looked at his father. A faint grin tugged at the corners of his lips as recognition settled in, then his smile faded.

I had a bad dream, he signed with weak hands.

Merritt laughed as he cried. He kissed Gavin on the forehead and told him, “It’s over now.”

TULLIVER

Whispers swam around him as he floated in darkness, whispers of those he had left behind on his journey through life — those whose own journeys Tulliver had cut short.

His eyes popped open and he sucked down air as if he'd been drowning. He lay on his side on the soft, moist ground, the jacket of his right shoulder soaked through to his skin.

The whispers of his dark memories faded, and Tulliver rolled slowly onto his back. The sky had taken on the particular orange tint of late afternoon. A vaporous thought tickled the back of his mind — a warning that wouldn't materialize.

He heard voices nearby.

Tulliver forced himself up on one elbow and groaned with pain. The bullet-wound in his left shoulder burned as if being hollowed-out by a red hot poker. The horizon tilted sickeningly. He was alone in the middle of the clearing at the heart of the colony, but a dozen colonists milled about the perimeter, talking amongst themselves.

None of them had noticed that he was awake.

Then the warning that had been floating around his drugged mind solidified.

The crabs, he thought as a cold fear gripped his

heart. Much as his fear of spiders had nearly paralyzed him as a child with each encounter, the mere thought of the churning, segmented legs of those alien creatures made him shiver.

He blinked hard and looked around the clearing. The radio spikes that the scientist woman said would keep the crabs away from the colony were nowhere to be seen.

Lara? Lora? What was her name?

It didn't matter.

Tulliver rolled onto his stomach, pushed himself up on his hands and knees, and began to crawl.

She thought there might be more spikes in the shuttle. He could put them around the ramp and keep them away while the crab-things swept over the colony like a plague.

But then Tulliver would be alone.

As he crawled across the wet ground, parts of which had turned to mud from the constant foot-traffic of the colony, he realized that might not be such a bad thing after all. Another ship would come, eventually, and he could make up any story he liked as to why he was the only survivor of this ill-fated attempt to tame another world.

But you're never really alone, are you, old Tull? said the distant voice of Roland Day in his mind.

We'll never let you be lonely, added Diego.

Tulliver stopped mid-crawl and harshly rubbed his eyes, trying to clear his vision.

"Hey, he's awake!" one of the colonists shouted.

Tulliver lurched to his feet and took a few unsteady steps sideways before falling back on his side in the mud with a loud squelch. As he looked frantically behind him, a gnarled bush on the edge of the clearing caught his eye: the same bush into which Merritt had thrown his locket.

Tulliver changed course and crawled on all fours, hands and boots squishing in the mud. A look of pure triumph lit up his face as he plucked the locket and its chain from the twisted grip of the gnarled bush.

"Over there!" a colonist shouted.

Tulliver ran toward the shuttle and fell, one fist still closed tightly around his locket.

He crawled through the mud until his open hand slapped down on the cold metal of the shuttle's ramp, then he used one of the ramp pistons to pull himself to his feet.

They were coming for him.

Several of the colonists ran toward the shuttle, calling for help.

Tulliver scrambled up the ramp, breathing like a chased animal. He lunged for the ramp controls at the top and punched a large red button.

The colonists stopped short as the ramp rose quickly. Tulliver panted as he watched it rise to block his view of their knees, their chests, their angry glares.

He closed his eyes and laid back on the cold metal floor as the ramp sealed shut with a satisfying *whumpf*.

Now he could relax. Now he could take his

time.

Unless one of them figures out how to open the ramp with their red ticket, Diego warned. *If you did it, one of them could do it, too.*

Tulliver sighed with exhaustion. The effects of whatever tranquilizer the corporal had injected him with were fading, but slowly.

He performed a woozy search of the shuttle's small cargo hold, but couldn't find any more radio spikes. The others had probably taken the spikes for themselves and holed up somewhere in the forest where they hoped they'd be safe.

No matter. Tulliver had another plan, and it involved putting as much distance between himself and the approaching crabs as possible. He could come back to the colony after they passed. One thing was certain: things would be a whole lot quieter after he returned.

He climbed the ladder up to the cockpit and plopped down in the pilot seat. There was no glowing beacon on the control panel screen for him to tap like there was the first time he'd flown in the shuttle, so he simply tapped a section of the screen to the left of center. Razor-thin green elevation lines on the screen seemed to indicate the selected area was a small plateau on a mountain to the west. Tulliver would land there and wait for the migration to pass him by.

He grinned with sudden satisfaction as the shuttle engines roared to life, shaking him in his seat. He might even be able to roast a few crabs along the way.

The shuttle lifted off the ground and swung about to face west. The nose dipped as the craft rose higher and accelerated passing over the center of the colony. It gave Tulliver even greater satisfaction to see a few people dive out of the way to avoid the heat of his engine wash.

Dizziness swept over him and Tulliver nearly cracked his head on the control panel. He shook the feeling away and buckled into his safety harness.

The control panel beeped at him, and the faint green elevation lines on the screen changed to red as the shuttle's sensors detected movement below.

He was flying over the crab migration.

Tulliver shuddered with disgust and settled deeper into his chair. He briefly entertained the idea of tilting the shuttle so he could get a look at them, then easily dismissed it.

The control panel beeped again. A tiny yellow indicator light blinked off and on near a circular display.

He was almost out of fuel.

Tulliver sat up in his seat and tentatively grabbed the control stick. With the vessel in autopilot, his shaking hands did nothing to affect its course.

Oops, said Ivan in his mind. *Looks like you didn't think of everything.*

"Shut up!" Tulliver yelled frantically.

He tapped the flashing yellow button and got the expected result: it didn't stop flashing.

Find a new place to land, he told himself. *Tap the screen.*

He tapped the screen, and it flicked off. The entire control panel went dark, and the engines cut out.

Tulliver held his breath as he glided in silence. Sweat dripped into his eyes and he hastily rubbed it away.

The shuttle tilted on its nose-tail axis, one wing dipping toward the ground and the other toward the sky. Then the craft rolled over until it was upside-down. The straps of Tulliver's safety harness dug into his shoulders as they strained to keep his bulk in the seat. Blood rushed to his head.

A world of solid gray rushed past the cockpit window above. All Tulliver could do was stare at it as the shuttle rapidly descended.

The craft exploded through a tree with an ear-splitting CRACK. More sharp cracks followed until they came as fast as gunfire, ripping away parts of the hull. Burst trunks scraped over the cockpit as the shuttle rolled onto its side.

The cockpit shattered and broken shards ripped through the cabin. Tulliver screamed as a dozen knives sliced his face, then he jerked forward in his seat as the left side of the shuttle hit the ground.

The vessel pitched forward so the nose hit next, spewing dirt and gray crabs into the air. Tulliver slammed back and forth in his seat as the vessel tumbled nose-to-tail on its side, metal crunching against tree trunks and large boulders as pieces of it flew off into the forest. The tail hit a boulder and the shuttle flipped up into the air, twirling like a tossed coin.

Tulliver went limp in his seat, no longer able to fight the forces that were pulling him in every direction.

The shuttle crashed to the ground on its crumpled side and finally came to a rest.

Steam hissed from somewhere inside the cabin, then stopped. Metal groaned as the broken hull settled.

After all was silent, Tulliver grasped for his safety harness release. He found it and hesitated. He drooped sideways against the harness in his chair, parallel to the wall several meters below him, which had become the floor.

You can catch yourself, Diego assured him. *You're fast enough. You're the fastest.*

Tulliver pressed the harness release and fell. He grabbed for the chair's armrest and missed, then slammed down in a kneeling position against the interior wall of the shuttle with a metal *CLONG*.

He yelled in pain and flopped onto his side, cursing the dead warden as he seethed with rage.

Since the shuttle was missing almost everything besides the central cylinder containing the cockpit, cargo hold, and engine room, the shattered window was nearly on the same level as the ground outside.

Tulliver crawled toward it, over scimitar

shards, his knees throbbing with a pain more intense than the bullet wound in his shoulder. He was sure his kneecaps had each cracked into a hundred pieces.

He wormed his way over the shark-tooth edge of the broken cockpit window and crawled across the spongy ground. There was a large boulder no more than ten meters away. He could get on top of it and wait out the migration.

My locket, he thought suddenly.

He grabbed for the chain around his neck, but it was gone. Tulliver looked behind him quickly, realizing he'd lost it in the crash. Smoke streamed up from the back of the shuttle, black against a clear blue sky.

He tried to stand but screamed when he put pressure on his knees, then collapsed back to the ground and crawled arm over arm toward the boulder.

A clacking sound came from behind.

He looked back as the first of the crabs appeared near what remained of the shuttle. They formed a single line on either side, and that line stretched into the distance as far as he could see.

Tulliver turned away from them and made for the boulder.

Plenty of time, he told himself. *Go, go, go!*

He made it.

The crabs were only seconds behind him when he pulled himself up onto the boulder with shaking hands. He climbed to its blunted peak two meters off the ground and flopped onto his stomach.

He lay there with a serene smile on his face, panting, as the crabs swarmed around the sides of the boulder below.

Gotcha, he thought.

His smile evaporated as a crab tapped the side of the boulder with one of its legs.

Tulliver sat up and crawled to the other side of the boulder. The line of crabs had risen up to cover the bottom of the gray rock, their segmented legs tap-tap-tapping as they were pushed higher by the mass of creatures behind them.

"No!" Tulliver cried out.

He tried to stand and collapsed, so he got to his broken knees as the crabs crawled up all sides of the boulder, closing in on him, coming together to seal the boulder beneath their uniform gray sheath as if it were a wound in the landscape that needed to be smothered.

The lip of the encroaching circle of crabs peeled back from the boulder as it rose above Tulliver's head, revealing the underside of the interlocked crab migration: a churning multitude of sharp, segmented insectoid legs, all reaching out for Tulliver as he quaked in fear against the cold, hard surface of the boulder.

Something glimmered on the rising wall of segmented legs: a small locket dangling from a delicate golden chain.

The edges of the open circle came together overhead, blocking out the sunlight. As the blanket of crabs settled gently on top of him, Tulliver screamed.

LEERA

She drove the last of the radio spikes into the soft ground and twisted it deeper, then pressed the small button at its top to activate its negating signal.

The spike was at one end of a wide half-moon lining the base of a flat hill east of the colony. Leera had chosen that spot for the colonists to wait out the crab migration. The electrical current coursing through the ground near the towering bare tree trunks seemed to stop just below the rise of the hill. Coupled with the radio spikes, Leera hoped the migration would flow around the hill and the people temporarily stranded on its bald plateau.

She had even gone so far as to suggest they move the colony structures to the hill and make it their main settlement. Her predictions for the size and speed of the crab migration indicated it would circumnavigate Galena once every two years, assuming the creatures took a direct route and didn't stop for weather or a seasonal hibernation.

While the crabs represented a threat to the colonists, Leera couldn't help but be fascinated by them. Their anatomy, behavior, how they interacted with their environment — she wanted to know more about all of it.

She wiped a sweaty strand of hair from her forehead and looked up at the orange early evening sky.

I'll have time, she thought sadly.

Even with the warmth of a sunset sky embracing the planet, Leera felt cold inside. Her family was ten-thousand light years away — which meant that unless someone built another vessel capable of traversing the Rip, she would never see them again. It was an impossible distance, and it boggled her mind to comprehend such a vast, empty space between Earth and Galena.

Leera walked up the sharp hill to its plateau, where a little more than sixty colonists waited. Medical supplies from the main settlement had been hauled the short distance to the hill and were being used to sustain two critically injured survivors that had been found that same day. Niku sat on an empty crate near the injured, conversing with the explorer, Henry Tolbard, and the wounded ship foreman, Willef. The foreman leaned back against a crate, an intravenous line pumping fluid into his veins. Corporal Turner slept on a stretcher nearby, a white medical bandage wrapped firmly around his head.

Niku smiled at Leera as she walked past, and she waved. Uda joined his small group a moment later, sitting on the ground next to Niku and handing out strips of soy jerky.

Behind them, in the distance, a thin trail of smoke rose toward the sky. Leera had seen the stolen shuttle take off from the colony and head west. Not long after, it descended into the trees much too quickly to be a controlled landing.

And now, the smoke.

She walked toward the eastern end of the flat-topped hill.

Two out of the three people she'd journeyed with from Earth had survived. The memory of the terrified look on Walter's face as he'd been sucked from the cockpit of their crashing shuttle brought tears to her eyes.

There was a chorus of excitement behind her.

The crabs had emerged from the forest.

Leera didn't look back as she walked to the far side of the hill. She didn't need to see.

Merritt Alder and his son, Gavin, were sitting on the spongy green ground. Gavin was wrapped in a silver heat blanket despite the warm breeze flowing over the hill from the direction of the narrow eastern sea. The breeze ruffled his brown hair. He looked worlds better than he did when she'd brought him to the grove of red moss.

The scientist in her, the one tasked with the preservation of the life-forms she studied, wasn't given a voice in the decision to bring him to the grove. She knew the moss creatures would die if they healed Gavin the way they had healed her broken leg, and it hurt her soul to start her tenure on a new world by bringing death to its inhabitants.

After Skip finished complaining about what the crabs would do to his houses, he had agreed to keep the healing abilities of the red moss to himself.

Leera had asked the others who witnessed the two healing events to keep the secret as well. The small injuries that ailed most of the wounded could be patched with the meager supplies the wardens had brought down to the nascent colony before the destruction of the *Halcyon*. Leera still held out hope more supplies could be found in the wreckage.

Merritt greeted her with a nod as she stood beside him, watching the distant sea. Enormous gray triangular waves rose from the churning waters — rose, but didn't crash down. They hovered in midformation, buffeted by strong winds that streaked white foam across their curved faces. Waves near the shore curled and crashed against black sand beaches, dragging white foam back into the sea.

Something moved under the water, between the risen waves. A massive bulk disturbed the surface, rolling lazily, its wet skin flashing gold in the fading light of day. A darkness spread across the water from the creature, like black ink.

The water exploded upward behind it, and a great winged beast shot out of the sea. Perhaps it was the same creature that had attacked her shuttle. It carried a chunk of flesh bigger than its own massive body in its wide, pyramidal beak. Leathery wings beat the top of the water as it took to the air, rising above the looming waves. It flew west, toward the two mountains Leera had flown over to reach the colony.

A world of danger and wonder, she thought as she watched the slow, graceful flapping of the creature's giant wings. *A lifetime of discoveries waiting to be made.*

Yet would the discoveries be hollow without her family? Could she build a new home for herself on Galena knowing that her family was worrying about her ten-thousand light years away?

Leera closed her eyes and took a deep breath of warm, salty air.

If there was one thing she could do to keep her mind off unwanted thoughts, it was drown it in work — and there would be no shortage of projects in the years to come.

Leera walked back to the ragged band of colonists on the hill, eager to get started.

EPILOGUE

Emily,

It's been a long time since I've written to you, and I'm sorry. I'm also sorry for my terrible handwriting. Some things never change. I haven't held a real pen in so long it's a wonder I even remember how to spell.

The supply manager here at the colony found a crate of paper notepads and ink pens hiding in the scavenged supplies, complete with a golden letterhead bearing the logo of the Halcyon. I think the notepads were for the luxury cabins on the ship because I was never in one and I've never seen the pads before. At any rate, it will be nice writing to you again instead of having to think of what to say as it happens.

Gavin has nearly fully recovered from his accident. I spoke to you about that a few weeks ago. Not sure if you heard me. I'll tell you again soon, but not right now. It's too nice of a day for it. His left leg has a slight limp that I don't think will ever go away. There's also a small scar that looks like a half-moon just under his eye. Other than that, he looks just the same as the last time you saw him. Maybe a little taller.

He's outside right now, playing. Did I ever tell you he had half our fields planted before I ever made it back to the colony? Our first crop is already a head taller than the rest. It's healthier, too. I think I'll leave him in charge and retire early.

The food is treating him poorly, as always. We can't

find any edible native plants, at least on the surface. If I ever get the courage to go back under the mountains, maybe I can find something down there. Until then, every meal is soy.

You wanted to leave Earth so our family could have a better life. I'm working on it. Every day I feel like I'm failing, but then Gavin hugs me, and because of that I'm able to wake up in the morning and start over.

We've started planting your seeds. Most of them don't sprout, and the ones that do aren't producing anything edible. I had high hopes for the corn and the carrots, but the acid in the soil is too much for the seeds. The onions fared better, for a short time. I've planted thirty seeds so far. The pouch is lighter, but there are still many drops of hope left inside. Gavin's even more enthusiastic about it than I am. He's outside constantly, checking the soil and perfecting his irrigation system. If anyone could conjure a sprout just by staring at the soil, it would be Gavin.

We're planning on growing a lot of soy here, and I don't think there will ever be enough of us to eat it. I mentioned the woman that saved Gavin's life, Dr. Leera James. She plotted a population chart for the colony. Without growth tanks or incubation farms from a lab on Earth, the best we could do is a two percent increase every few years. Factor in death rates, and it balances out. More than a few of the farmers might even tip the scales toward the negative within the next decade.

No one would be worried about it if we thought someone else was coming through the Rip. It would take the fastest shipyard in Earth orbit at least six years to make a vessel Rip-capable, longer if they build it from scratch. But no company has the money. Dr. James says the government is too strapped to afford another ship, so there it is, and here we'll sit.

It's not all bleak. We've had three survivors wander in from the wild this week already. I'm sure more are out there. A friend of mine, Henry Tolbard, is leading small teams farther away from the colony, mapping the terrain and searching for others.

Most people who aren't farming have found some way to keep busy. Niku and a few others went back to the first colony and found some usable scientific equipment. I don't think I've ever seen anyone so happy to hold a microscope. He's very interested in the seeds you gave me, and he's doing everything he can to help.

Between all the smart folks working around the clock to learn everything they can about our new home, discoveries are being made every other day. Their excitement is infectious, even though I don't know what they're talking about half the time.

And what a home it is, Em. This planet is truly remarkable. You would love it here because it's everything Earth wasn't: green and blue...and alive. It's the perfect place to raise our son.

But there are dangers.

One colonist died from an infected cut. It was such a simple thing, just a little nick on his wrist that he picked up on a scavenging run. He turned feverish that night and died the next day. Niku thinks it's bacteria from something in the wild, but he doesn't know what. The man who died couldn't speak to tell anyone once he rec-

ognized the infection.

The colony council has added a policy of 'observation only' to its growing list of laws. In other words, they don't want curious colonists touching anything dangerous until we know what's what. (Oh yes, we have laws! You would be so proud of us.)

We haven't seen any crabs since the migration swept past our site after we first arrived. Our best guess is that it will take them the better part of two years to circumnavigate the planet and make it back to this spot, if that's their true migratory pattern. Leera calculated there were about six million of them in a single migration. She called it a moving continent.

I miss you. I feel guilty watching our son live his life all by myself. You'd be doing a lot better job than I am. Some days he won't listen to me, other days he ignores me altogether. Skip says it's 'early onset teenager syndrome'. He would know better than anyone. If another ship ever comes through the Rip, he's expecting his family to be on it.

Some folks here are surprised that others want to stay, even if there's a chance of rescue...even after everything that's happened. I just tell them this is our home now. It was always going to be our home. Most of the colonists are dealing with the situation well. The ones that aren't will come around eventually, I think. As I said, it's a beautiful world.

I hope, wherever you are, that you can read this. Expect many more letters to follow. I don't see our supply of pen and paper running out any time soon.

I'll kiss Gavin for you.

All my love now and forever,
Merritt

MERRITT

He set the pen down and leaned back in his chair. Evening sunlight beamed in through the window he'd cut in the corrugated metal dome house on his farm. The house had once been the rounded top of a tall grain silo, repurposed in the housing initiative that swept the colony in the first few months. The council, of which Merritt was a member, decreed that everyone should have a home.

A few of the farmers got what they paid for before leaving Earth. Small two-bedroom Wilderness Cabins dotted the fields, along with the occasional sprawling Pioneer Lodge. Those farmers who had paid extra for the latter soon found that it took up too much precious crop space on their land.

Skip didn't mind. After it was decided he could receive both of his purchased lodges, he put them next to each other and connected their master bedrooms, trimming his arable land by thirty percent. When Merritt suggested getting rid of one, Skip furrowed his brow, and said, "But then I wouldn't have *two*."

The farmers who hadn't purchased a pre-fabricated cabin and the colonists who were never intending to be colonists in the first place got homes, as well. Some, like Merritt, made their shelters from spare silos that were delivered before the colonists had arrived, as well as salvaged debris.

As Merritt looked out the window of his home, beyond the tall stalks of soyflower bending gently in a light breeze, he saw a smattering of makeshift houses on the neighboring farms.

Uda had claimed the land directly adjacent to Merritt's to the east after the original owner was declared lost in the crash. She had turned a cross-section of a cylindrical silo into her home. It loomed over her property like a watchtower. The flaps of her canvas roof flapped in the breeze, as did a line of drying clothes near the always-open front door.

As Merritt watched the clothes move in the wind, Niku approached the silo tower with a slight grin on his face and disappeared inside.

There was talk of collecting material for more structures from the first colony, but the council had been unable to reach a decision when it came to, as Uda called it, "disturbing the dead".

Leera suggested it would be a bad idea to use the trees for timber after what occurred when Tulliver emptied a few rounds from Turner's rifle into the soil. Most of the colonists agreed with her. They were making do with what they could lash together from the wreckage of the *Halcyon*. The unspoken consensus seemed to be that they would cross that bridge later.

The sound of laughing children drifted across the air outside. Merritt walked to the arched doorway of his home and leaned against the metal frame.

A young boy, the deceased Warden Cohen's son, ran through the soyflower stalks, giggling as the broad leafs slapped his chest and shoulders. His sister chased him, laughing loudly.

Next came Gavin, silent but smiling, crashing through the crop with all the grace of an elephant in a tea room. He tripped and fell, but was back on his feet in a flash, chasing after the other two.

Phobis was just above the horizon, descending quickly, casting long shadows from the stalks of soyflower.

Merritt took a long drink of water from his hip flask and wiped his mouth. He squinted into the brilliant yellow light as he walked the short distance to the edge of the crop field. He rubbed a broad greenish leaf between his thumb and fingers.

Several stars glimmered in the darkening sky. A portion of the six nearest to Phobis were always the first to appear. That night it was Aegea, Cyphus, and Bolon, spread across the sky like gleaming jewels. After the light of Phobis receded below the horizon, a web of distant stars would bloom, followed by the twin nebulae to the west.

And, somewhere north of those, invisible to the naked eye, was the Rip.

Every day, Earth seemed more a passing memory. Merritt tried to hold on to its sights and sounds in his mind, but his experiences on Galena pushed those memories farther away.

He wondered what it was like for Gavin. The boy had spent much of his time cooped up in their apartment on Earth. There had been no parks to explore, no playgrounds safe enough to visit.

On Galena, there was nothing but open space.

Will we tell the children about Earth? Merritt wondered. *Will they tell their children?*

He turned at the sound of approaching footsteps. Gavin ran up to him, breathing hard, a wild look of excitement on his face. He clutched something in his hand, held on to it like he thought it would slip away at any moment.

Merritt knelt down in the cool soil so he was face-to-face with his son.

What did you find? he signed.

Gavin opened his hand to reveal a small yellow potato, perfectly formed. Tendrils of thin, fibrous roots covered its soft flesh.

He looked down on it in wonder.

Merritt rested his hand on his son's shoulder. His eyes welled with tears, and he smiled.

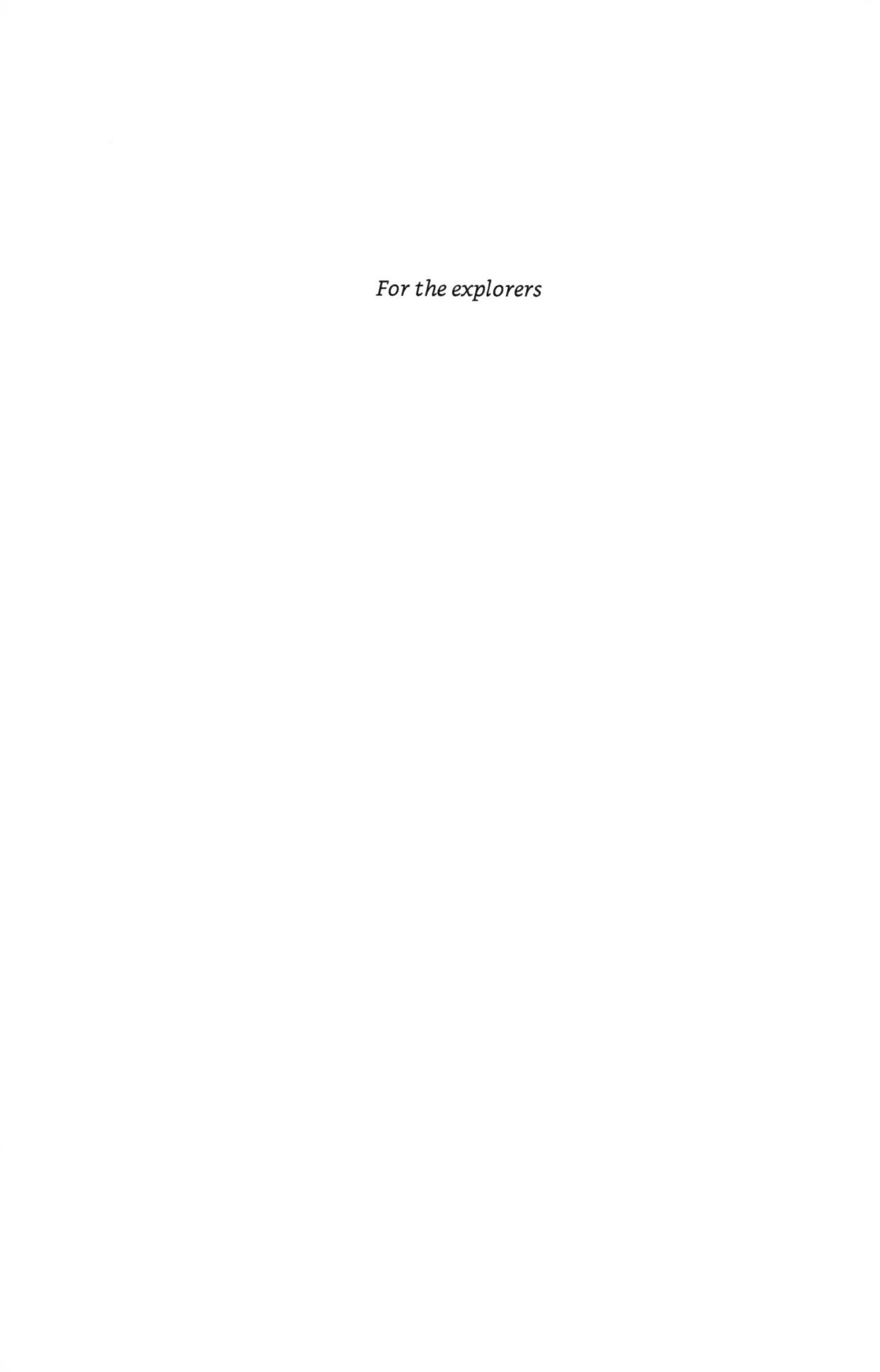

For the explorers

Made in the USA
Las Vegas, NV
08 March 2021